Kat Martin

Creole Fires

A DELL BOOK

Published by
Dell Publishing
a division of
Random House, Inc.

ISBN: 0-440-20803-3

Printed in the United States of America

Published simultaneously in Canada

February 1992

10 9 8 7 6 5

OPM

For my sister, Patti,
who means more to me
than words could ever say.

1

Louisiana, 1837

"*Allons!* Nicki, let's go! We should not have come so far into the swamp."

Michele was right, of course, and Nicole St. Claire didn't miss the uncertainty in her friend's softly spoken French words.

Still, it was a lovely day and the first chance she'd had to get away from the endless procession of friends who had heard of the St. Claires' visit and come to the Christophe plantation to pay their respects.

"You worry too much," Nicki chided. "It isn't good for you." Stretching a bit, she worked the kinks from her back, and filled her lungs with the still-cool Louisiana air.

"*Mon Dieu*, but you are stubborn." Michele glanced over her shoulder. Though she craned her neck and stood on her toes, she couldn't spot the big white plantation house they'd left behind. "I do not like this. There are snakes out here. Besides, I want to get out of these old clothes."

Across the thicket, Nicki just smiled, brightening

her pretty oval face and tilting a pair of vivid aqua eyes.

"Cook says we need two buckets of berries if we want pies for supper," Nicki reminded her. Several inches shorter than Michele, Nicole was petite but not frail, her bosom full and high, her hips shapely, and her waist narrow. "You go ahead. I won't be far behind."

"Your *maman*'s not going to like it." Michele looked again at their surroundings: the meandering inlet that drained the Mississippi River not far away, the heavy carpet of grass at their feet, the towering cypress that seemed to guard this small stretch of uncultivated swampland. She swiped at a gnat that buzzed beside her ear, then jumped as a vine snagged her skirt. "I don't think I should leave you out here alone."

Nicki's copper-haired head popped up from the thicket. "Who would dare to bother us?" *Who indeed?* Nicki thought. The Christophes were one of the wealthiest families in these parts, even if times had gotten tougher. And the St. Claires were widely respected.

Michele still seemed uncertain. "Papa says Alain Lefevre is coming to supper."

If an image of the handsome French boy was meant to lure Nicole away, it failed miserably. "You can have him. I'm not interested."

"Why not?"

"He's far too . . . proper . . . for my tastes, always fawning about and spouting his meaningless poetry. I want someone reckless and dashing. A man who will sweep me off my feet."

"*Mon Dieu*, you are crazy." But Michele knew better than to argue. Nicole St. Claire was as stubborn a young woman as Michele had ever met. Far different from her own quiet nature, Nicki was determined and bold and fearless. It was amazing they could be such good friends.

"You are sure you will be all right?" Michele asked.

"I'll be fine."

Rolling her eyes in vexation, Michele took a last glance in Nicki's direction, but saw only the wriggle of her bottom in the faded blue gingham dress she had borrowed so her own fine yellow muslin would not get soiled.

Michele frowned, wondering again if she should wait, then decided against it. Nicki wouldn't leave until she was well and ready to go, and the lure of a bath and an afternoon nap were far too strong.

Lifting her worn brown slightly too-short skirts up out of the way, Michele headed back toward home, eager to be rid of her dowdy clothing and once again dressed in expensive silks and satins.

Nicki watched her friend cross the rise and disappear out of sight. She wished she could see Michele more often, but with Cote Verde, the Christophe plantation, here in La Ronde on the Mississippi, and Meadowood, the St. Claire plantation, near Napoleonville on Bayou Lafourche, they visited just a few times a year.

Michele Christophe was a good and loyal friend. Still, as Nicki bent to her task, filling the wooden bucket to overflowing with the plump and juicy blackberries, she was glad for these few minutes alone in the warm spring sunshine.

With a contented sigh, she lifted her tattered, borrowed skirts up out of the way and started a little farther into the thicket. She hadn't gone more than several paces when she heard a twig snap in the underbrush, then the sound of men's laughter, harsh and grating, echoed somewhere behind her.

Nicki froze. In a spot behind some bushes just a few feet away, two men in shabby clothing stood grinning at her clumsy movements in the too-large dress, their eyes fastened on the portion of calf she exposed above the top of her sturdy brown shoe.

Letting the dress fall back into place, Nicki fixed them with one of her usually disconcerting aqua-eyed stares. "What is it you men want?" She asked them in French. When they answered with only a scowl, she repeated the question in English.

The taller man arched a bushy brow, apparently surprised she spoke his language without an accent. "We's just bein' neighborly."

When he stepped closer, Nicki caught the odor of whiskey and stale tobacco. His shirt and trousers, shabby and unwashed, hung on his too-thin frame. Running a rough hand along her cheek, he smiled, exposing crooked yellow teeth, and Nicki felt the first faint tremors of alarm.

"You're not from around here," she said, backing away from him.

The shorter man, a stocky fellow with graying hair, canvas breeches, and a red-checked shirt moved closer. "Saw you and yer Frenchy friend pickin' berries. Thought we oughta stop by and say hello."

"This land belongs to the Christophe family. You men are trespassing."

The tall man chuckled softly. "What business is that of yers? You ain't no Christophe, that's fer damn sure." His eyes moved over her tattered blue gingham dress, which hung on her like a well-used potato sack.

"She's sure a perty 'un, Chester."

Don't go off half-cocked, she told herself, beginning to think in English, the language she usually spoke. It was one of her mother's favorite expressions. "If you gentlemen will excuse me, I've got to be getting back." She tried to brush past, but the man named Chester caught her arm.

"You ain't going no place—leastwise, not yet." In a single, quick motion, he grabbed the ruffled neckline of her dress, twisted his fingers in the frayed blue fabric, and ripped the material away.

"Damn you!" Slamming her foot into the man's bony shin, Nicki tried to jerk free, but Chester only tightened his hold. With a muttered oath and a grin of anticipation, he forced her up against his chest while his hard arm wrapped around her waist.

"You got spirit, that's fer sure. I like a little spirit in a woman."

She shuddered as the cool air touched her bare skin and the man's clammy hand slid up her arm. "Let me go!" Nicki struggled harder, but the tall man just laughed. Tightening his hold on her waist, he dragged her toward a grassy depression protected by a growth of vines and weeds.

"You can squirm all ya like," he said, shoving her down on the ground. "Ain't gonna make a fiddler's damn. Me and Billy gonna take ya just the same. You can make it easy on yourself or hard. Either way, we're bound to take our pleasure."

When she tried to scream again, he clamped a hand over her mouth, ripped away the balance of her faded blue dress, and dispensed with her single drooping petticoat.

This can't be happening! But it was. Fear clutched at her insides, a feeling she had rarely known. With a long, thin leg, Chester pinned her thighs while Billy stretched her arms above her head. They were watching her breasts now, the rise and fall of the soft white flesh above the line of her corset.

Nicki's heart thundered in a cadence of panic and despair. Why hadn't she listened to Michele? What in God's name was she going to do?

It took her a moment to realize the men were looking at her oddly, their eyes carefully assessing her lacy pantalets, snowy white corset, and expensive embroidered chemise—quite a contrast to her ragged borrowed clothing.

"Ain't no sharecropper's daughter wearin' dainties the likes of these," Billy said.

Chester swore beneath his breath. For a moment he seemed uncertain, and Nicki's hopes soared. She tried to threaten him with her father's wealth and power, but her words were muffled behind his hand.

"Don't make a damn now," he finally decided. "We've gone too far to stop. 'Sides"—he grinned, flashing his yellow teeth—"my privates is hurtin' so bad I gotta do somethin' to relieve 'em."

With that they jerked her to her feet and began to tug at the laces at the back of her corset. "Gimme your pigsticker, Billy."

The stocky man chuckled and pulled his big Arkansas toothpick from the leather sheath he wore at his side. Nicki had seen men at the docks in New Orleans carrying knives like that. A glint of sunlight on the heavy silver blade brought a moment of panic, a second shot of fear, then the courage to act.

Catching them off guard, she jerked free, twisted, and slammed her knee into the tall man's groin. A loud *oof!* and moan as he doubled over and slumped to the ground was her reward. Nicki didn't wait for the stocky man's reaction. She bolted, racing toward the men's horses she'd spotted tied in a clearing not far away.

Please, God, she prayed, knowing it would take a miracle for her to reach the animals, untie one, and climb into the saddle before the stocky man caught up with her.

In the Louisiana swamplands, her miracle appeared in the form of a hidden vine. She heard her pursuer's heavy footsteps, heard his uneven breathing, then a string of oaths as he stumbled and crashed to the ground. She'd say a dozen Hail Marys later, she vowed, and kept on running.

She was shaking by the time she reached the horses. If only she could untie the second one and scare it away, but the stocky man had regained his feet and wasn't far behind. Instead she freed the smaller of the two, a little sorrel mare who looked like she could run, and climbed into the saddle. It was the first time Nicki had ridden astride and the sensation felt awkward and uncomfortable. Lacking other alternatives, she leaned over the mare, dug her heels into the horse's flanks, and they bolted from the clearing.

A glance behind confirmed that the man named Chester blocked her way to the house. She'd make for the road into town instead—*surely the other one wouldn't follow!* But the hoofbeats bearing down on her said he intended to do just that.

Nicki tightened her knees, gripping the flat leather saddle the best she knew how. Her feet didn't reach the metal stirrups, and her position astride felt so unfamiliar she wasn't sure she could stay aboard. But as the animal's speed settled into a steady, ground-eating gallop, her confidence grew. She cleared the swamp and increased her speed. If she could make the stone wall at the end of the open field and still stay mounted, she'd be home free.

At least that was what she thought until she sailed over the wall and her pursuer did the same.

Dear God, what now? Clutching the horse's reins tighter, leaning over its neck, she urged the mare faster. There was help in La Ronde, someone who could stop these madmen from their assault.

The little mare was lathered and breathing hard by the time Nicki galloped full tilt down the main street of La Ronde, just a tiny parish town where nearby planters picked up supplies. In her heaven-or-hell ride to safety, she was glancing over her shoulder, trying to see if her pursuer still followed, when a wagon laden with hogshead barrels pulled into her path. The mare saw the impending disaster before Nicki did, rearing on its hind legs in a desperate attempt to wheel away from the heavy dray before it was too late.

Nicki felt the animal's back tilt crazily, felt herself falling, saw the world spinning by, and closed her eyes to the painful landing she was about to make.

Instead she felt her body jolted against something hard, yet yielding, felt the brush of fabric against her skin, and opened her eyes to find herself cradled in a man's embrace. With memories of the one who followed still fresh in her mind, she began to struggle. It was the man's deep voice, his words spoken softly in French, that stilled her movements.

"You are all right, *chérie*. I won't let you fall."

Nicki swallowed hard, fighting for control, finding it difficult to speak. She glanced behind her.

"There's a man following me," she told him in the same soft language. "There were two of them. They tried to . . . they wanted to . . ." She glanced down at her lacy chemise, torn in several places and covered with dirt and twigs. Her hair had come loose from its pins and tumbled in a copper mass around her shoulders. Above the line of her corset, her breasts rose and fell with every ragged breath.

The Frenchman's smile faded and his voice turned hard. "You have nothing to fear, *chérie*."

Nicki felt the soft material of his dark blue tailcoat pressing against her skin as his hold tightened protectively. The determined set of his jaw confirmed his pledge, and Nicki believed him.

"My clothes . . ." she whispered, willing him to understand. But she needn't have spoken.

Dodging the now-halted wagon, the driver who walked toward them wearing a look of concern, and the crowd beginning to build, he carried her out of the narrow dirt street and onto the wooden boardwalk.

Breathing in the scent of his spicy cologne, Nicki wrapped her arms around his thick neck to steady herself. He was a big man, she realized, feeling his powerful chest and arms. Handsome, too, with smooth skin tanned by the sun, and wavy dark-brown hair that glinted with amber highlights. She could

easily remember the deep grooves etched beside his
mouth when he'd smiled at her, though they'd been
replaced by a worried scowl. His eyes were a warm
shade of brown.

She glanced up at him as he strode the wooden
walk, carrying her effortlessly. There was nothing
warm about those eyes now, she discovered as he
ducked into Gaudin's General Mercantile. They were
dark and forbidding. His mouth, once full and sensuous, had thinned to a narrow line, and a muscle
bunched in his jaw.

"Madame Gaudin," he said to the plump little
shopkeeper, "it appears *la petite mademoiselle* is in
need of something to wear." The command in his
voice was unmistakable. Carrying her through a curtain that closed off the back of the store, he set Nicki
on her feet and flashed her a reassuring smile. "You'll
be safe here until I return."

He watched her a moment, assessing her, it
seemed. His finger traveled lightly across her cheek,
sending a ripple down her spine, then he turned
away. His smile no longer in place, he whispered a
few brief words to the shopkeeper, glanced once
more in Nicki's direction, and strode back toward the
street. She noticed the width of his shoulders, out-
lined by the fit of the navy-blue tailcoat that tapered
dramatically over his narrow hips. Encased in the
tailored gray pants he wore, taut muscle defined his
powerful thighs as he moved.

The curtain fell behind him, and the rotund little
shopkeeper approached, pulling Nicki's thoughts in a
different direction.

"I have been instructed to take very good care of

you, mademoiselle." Madame Gaudin tucked a strand of graying hair back in place and smiled.

Glancing toward the curtain, which still fluttered from the tall man's departure, then down at her torn and dirty clothes, Nicki swallowed hard. Her face still felt bloodless, her mouth dry, her fingers cold and numb.

"Do not worry, mademoiselle," the woman said, sensing her distress. "I will find you something to wear and none will be the wiser."

"The whole town will be the wiser," Nicki told her, finding her voice at last. *"Mon Dieu*, what a spectacle I made." She sighed in despair. Why did she always manage to get herself into trouble? Her father would be furious and her mother, usually a little more sympathetic to her exploits, would certainly not be pleased.

"Quite a lovely spectacle," the woman replied, eyeing Nicki's full bosom and nipped-in waist. Madame Gaudin smiled and touched her cheek in the same spot the Frenchman had, though her fingers felt not nearly so warm. "M'sieur du Villier seems more than a little bit taken with you."

"Who?" Nicki asked, praying her ears had deceived her.

"Alexandre du Villier. Surely you know of him? His family is the richest in these parts. They own the great sugar plantation, Belle Chêne."

"That was . . . that was Alexandre du Villier?" Nicki's face paled. "But I thought the du Villiers were visiting their estates in France."

"Le duc has gone. I have heard he is ill. Alexandre is leaving today to join him. His brother, François, will remain to manage Belle Chêne."

"Oh, no," Nicki said, feeling even more despondent. "My father will be furious."

"Your father and the du Villiers are friends?"

"Yes. Since the war."

"I have not seen you before. You are not from here?"

"No." She extended one small hand. "I'm Nicole St. Claire. From Meadowood on Bayou Lafourche. We're here visiting the Christophes."

"You are the daughter of Etienne St. Claire?"

"Yes."

The plump little woman's voice took on an aura of reverance. "Many know of your father. He was a great hero in the war against the British. It is an honor to meet his daughter."

"Thank you. I'm happy to meet you too."

Madame Gaudin smiled, but her eyes whisked over Nicki's torn and dirty clothing. For the first time, it dawned on her that Madame Gaudin might think Alexandre du Villier had something to do with her missing clothes.

Oh, Lord, what next? "About my dress, madame . . ." As Nicki hurriedly explained about the men who had attacked her, her half-naked ride through the streets, and Monsieur du Villier's timely rescue, a relieved Madame Gaudin pulled her behind a second curtain that closed off the fitting rooms from the rest of the shop.

She was a seamstress as well as the wife of the storekeeper, she explained when she returned with a pale pink muslin day dress embroidered with tiny darker pink flowers, the sleeves set low on each shoulder.

"It may be a bit too long, but it will be easy to shorten."

"It'll be fine just as it is," Nicki told her. "I've got to get back before dark."

"I am certain M'sieur du Villier would be happy to escort you, even if his journey must be postponed."

"*Ah, non!*" Nicki rolled her eyes. "That is the last thing I need."

Madame Gaudin clucked at her. "You are right, of course. You are much too young for that wild stallion. But who knows . . . ?" She shrugged her plump shoulders. "Maybe in a few years, when he returns from the Continent . . . ?"

Nicki grinned with the sudden realization that the idea wasn't at all unappealing. Hadn't she said she wanted a man who would sweep her off her feet?

"Most likely he will have forgotten me," she said, wondering if indeed he would. "He'll probably be married to some dowdy aristocrat."

Madame Gaudin's eyes twinkled with mischief. "Maybe . . . maybe not. I think he will not soon forget *la petite mademoiselle* with eyes the color of a Caribbean sea who rode the streets of La Ronde in her corset and chemise."

Nicki groaned at the reminder and finished getting dressed. "I don't suppose I could impose upon your kindness a little more and ask you not to tell him who I am?" Maybe her father wouldn't find out after all.

The plump woman grinned mischievously. "He will ask—but I suppose for Etienne St. Claire's daughter, I could forget who you are—at least for the next few years."

"Thank you, madame. I'll be forever in your debt. Oh, and if you'll send the amount due for the dress to

Meadowood . . ." She hated to spend the money.
Times had been hard of late. She and her mother had
been careful with every penny.

"M'sieur du Villier has already taken care of it."

"He has?" Nicki said in English, falling back into
the language she spoke at home, though her father
was French, and at the Salem Academy, the school
she attended.

"*Pardon, mademoiselle?*"

"*Excusez-moi*. Tell M'sieur du Villier I am grateful
for his kind assistance." Her father wouldn't like the
idea, but maybe he wouldn't have to know. And the
du Villiers could certainly afford it more than her
family could right now. Just this once, she decided,
she would ignore her damnable pride and be practical.

As long as she didn't have to face him.

Determined to be gone before her handsome res-
cuer returned, Nicki finished brushing the dirt and
leaves from her underthings, and pulled the pretty
pink muslin dress on over her head.

"Where is she?"

"*La petite mademoiselle?*" Madame Gaudin asked,
amused by the handsome Frenchman's obvious interest.

"Who else?" he grumbled. "How many half-naked
young women do you have in your fitting rooms?"

Madame Gaudin pursed her lips and shrugged her
pudgy shoulders. "Gone, m'sieur. She was afraid her
parents would worry. Henri took her home in the
wagon."

Henri was Madame Gaudin's scarecrowlike husband. Sending the lovely mademoiselle home with no

one to protect her but Henri Gaudin only increased Alexandre's worry.

"He also took a pistol," she said in answer to his deepening scowl. "You did not find the men who attacked her?"

"Not a trace. But with the swamp and the river to hide them, there was little chance."

"*Sacrebleu!* What kind of men would harm such an innocent?"

Alex's jaw tightened. "Who was she? Does she live near here?"

"*Non*, she is just here visiting friends." Madame Gaudin smiled at his look of disappointment. "You should be grateful you are leaving. *La petite mademoiselle* is far too young for you—only fifteen, she said."

Alex's brow shot up. "Fifteen?" he repeated, incredulous.

"If you had been paying attention to her face and not her ripe little body you would have noticed."

Alex chuckled softly. Being twelve years her senior, he should have been more observant, but he rarely found himself attracted to one so young. "I suppose you're right."

"What a beauty, *n'est-ce pas?* Like an angel."

Alex smiled. "An angel with copper hair and aqua eyes and a body ripe for a man's touch. . . . As you say, I'm fortunate to be leaving such dangerous temptations to somebody else."

But all the way to the docks, and later as he watched the cane fields along the Mississippi disappear and the lights of New Orleans approach, he couldn't help envying the man who would finally bed her.

By the time he reached the shores of France, he had all but forgotten her. Only once, when he caught sight of a woman with eyes not nearly so vivid, did he wonder who that fortunate man might be.

2

New Orleans, 1840

Nicole St. Claire huddled in the corner of her damp and musty cell in the police prison of the Second Municipality on Baronne Street.

On a rough-hewn plank table a single white candle flickered against the damp rock walls, casting eerie, ominous shadows. Several uniformed watchmen stood outside the door, but they paid Nicole no heed. Instead, their attention focused on the activity in another small cell where two other women had been brought in several hours earlier.

"I can't stand to hear them screaming," Nicki whispered, pressing her hands against her ears. *The women's anguished cries, and the rats.* These were the things she hated most about the dismal prison. And missing the warmth of the sun. She had been cold since the day she'd arrived two weeks ago, cold and desolate, and afraid clear to her bones.

"It'll be over soon," said Lorna Mackintosh, the buxom, dark-haired girl who shared her cell.

"I wish there was something we could do." There was laughter now, deep and mocking, and the sound of rending fabric. The woman cursed the men but fell silent after a series of ringing blows that echoed against the walls of the cell and sent shivers of dread up Nicki's spine. Unconsciously she twisted the folds of the dreary brown wool dress that dragged the earthen floor at her feet.

"The only thing ye kin do," Lorna told her, "is keep quiet and pray it dinna' happen to ye." Lorna still carried the bruises of her own assault, though the guards had been careful to put them where they didn't show.

So far Nicki had been lucky.

"I'll never forget what you've done for me," she told Lorna. "No matter what happens."

Nicole had met her Scottish friend when she'd first been brought to the prison two weeks ago, in a state of near hysteria. Lorna, a runaway bond servant, had been wary at first, but Nicki's heart-wrenching sobs had finally moved her to action.

"Hush now," Lorna had whispered, coming to a place on the dirty straw pallet beside her. "Ye dinna want them to notice ye. Stay quiet and maybe they'll forget ye for a while."

"I—I don't belong here," Nicki stammered brokenly. "This is all a terrible mistake."

"Aye, lassie. No human bein' belongs in a scourge of hell the likes o' this. But ye've got to get hold o' yerself. This won't be for long. Ye'll come up for sale in a fortnight, just like the rest o' us. Then ye'll be outta here."

"I don't care if I never get out. I don't care anymore if I live or die. I've got no place to go, no one left who gives a whit about me."

Lorna studied Nicki's pale face in the flickering

candlelight, noting the bruises on her cheek, dark and purple against her smooth skin, the delicate strands of copper hair that hung down from her worn brown bonnet. "Ye speak like an educated lass. Ye musta had someone who cared. Someone who saw to ye schoolin' and all."

Nicki closed her eyes. In just three years her life had been turned upside down. "My parents," she whispered, but it seemed so long ago she could scarcely remember. Almost another lifetime. "Before the depression, we owned a plantation on Bayou Lafourche."

"Aye. 'Tis a lovely spot. I been there once myself."

Nicki smiled at that, a soft sad smile of remembrance. "Our house stood two stories tall. With graceful white columns out front and tiny dormer windows. It was made of pink brick from clay along the Teche. In the evening, the sun turned it the most lovely shade of rose you've ever seen."

Nicki swallowed the lump that swelled in her throat. She never used to cry, now it seemed she'd been crying for years.

"So ye lost ye home in the Panic?"

Nicki nodded. It felt good to tell someone the things she'd been holding inside so long. "I knew Papa had been having money problems. . . . I used to help him with his ledgers. . . . I just didn't know how bad it was until after he died. He was so worried, you see. His heart . . . he just couldn't stand the thought of losing Meadowood . . . of hurting Mama and me." Tears washed her cheeks and she turned away.

"Go on," Lorna prodded. " 'Tis time ye finished wi' it so ye kin get on wi' ye life."

"I don't have a life!" Nicki snapped, suddenly angry for all she had lost. "I never will again." She cried then, harder than she'd ever cried before. Lorna put an arm around her shoulder, but didn't try to stop her. Eventually the tears were replaced by quiet sobs that eventually ceased altogether.

They talked until late in the evening. Lorna spoke of her home in Scotland and of the family she had lost. "I thought coming to America would be the answer to my prayers." She scoffed, glancing around the dirty cell. "Well, there's nothin' for it now but to try to make the best o' things."

"That's what Mama said after Papa died, but she couldn't seem to find the will." Nicole released a weary breath. "I tried to keep things going, but it was just too late. Our friends were all gone—most had lost their homes and fortunes the same way Papa had. The day the men from the bank came to foreclose, Mama met them on the porch with a musket. When they tried to reason with her, she collapsed. Some sort of stroke, the doctor said."

"So ye indentured yerself," Lorna put in when Nicki didn't go on.

"I couldn't think what else to do. There was no one left who would take me in—the only one I could have turned to was a man named du Villier, my father's best friend, but he died in France that same year. His younger son, François, was managing the family plantation outside New Orleans, but he and Papa . . . didn't get along."

"We've all had our misfortunes, lassie," Lorna said, "but it seems they hurt more when ye've been sheltered from them for so long."

"The Turners—the people who bought my indenture—were really very nice, and the contract was supposed to end on my eighteenth birthday. It wouldn't have been so bad, except for the others. . . ." She shivered just thinking about Armand Laurent and his cruelty, then that deceitful bitch, Adrian Paxton, whose lies had landed her in prison. "I never thought it would turn out like this."

But it had, Nicki thought, pulling herself to the present as the moans across the hall began to fade, replaced by the woman's bitter sobs.

"Ye've got to look on the bright side, lass." Lorna drew her to her feet. "Tomorrow ye'll be leavin' this godforsaken place. Where'er ye end up will be no worse than here. In a few years yer indenture'll be paid and ye'll be free to do as ye please."

"Seven years is hardly a few years," Nicki said bitterly. Her three-year indenture had turned into ten. It sounded like an eternity. She closed her eyes against a wave of despair. "I don't know if I can survive it."

"Ye've made it this far, haven't ye?"

"I wouldn't have if it hadn't been for you."

On that day two weeks ago when the watchmen had begun their nightly assaults on the women, Lorna, who was nine years older, had read the terror on Nicki's face.

"Ye've not been wi' a man, have ye, girl?"

"No," Nicki whispered, wishing she could move away from the cell door but unable to stop watching as one of the guards forced a woman's legs apart, groped for the opening at the front of his breeches, and shoved his stiff male member inside her. The woman's pleas for mercy and her thrashing movements only seemed to excite him more.

Lorna's fingers bit into Nicki's shoulders, pulling

her away from the grisly scene and into a corner. While Nicki watched the door in terror, expecting the guards to burst in at any moment, Lorna took charge.

"We'll hide ye right under their noses," Lorna said with a spark of determination.

"What?"

With swift, sure movements, she braided Nicki's hair, looped a thick copper plait beside each ear, then replaced her soiled brown bonnet.

"We need to flatten ye breasts," Lorna told her, and the light of understanding finally dawned. Tearing strips of material from her stained and dirty petticoats, Nicki bound them around her, and Lorna tightened them until she could barely breathe.

"Remember, lassie, keep ye head down," Lorna warned. "Ne'er look 'em in the eye. With ye hair pulled back and nothin' ta fill out ye bodice, ye dinna look more'n twelve or thirteen. Old enough to interest some o' 'em, but most'll take a woman o'er a girl, if they've a choice."

And that was exactly what they did.

Lorna hadn't fought them, and Nicki had been too terrified to do more than stare in horror at their brutal violation. They had come again two nights later. By that time, some of Nicki's courage had returned, and over Lorna's protests, she'd been ready for them. Hiding behind the door, a wooden stool gripped in her hands, Nicki knocked the first guard unconscious. The second, a young man new to the watch, had hastily taken his leave, retrieving his fallen comrade on his way out the door. As luck would have it, a new group of women prisoners were brought in that same night, providing fresh sport for the watchmen. Since then, Lorna and Nicole had been left alone.

"Maybe someone decent'll buy ye this time," Lorna said. Tomorrow would mark the fourth time Nicki had been sold in the last three years, but the first time she'd ever been publicly auctioned.

"Not very likely. I'm not just a bond servant anymore—now they think I'm a thief."

"Aye, but a bairn can be forgiven a few indiscretions. Pray they dinna notice the age on ye papers."

"It doesn't really matter. I can't go around dressed like a child forever. Eventually they'll find out I'm a woman. God only knows what will happen then."

Lorna found it difficult to argue with the truth. Her friend was a fine, educated lady, but misfortune had a way of setting its sights on a body and there was no way of explaining why. Nicki should have had a fine life, married some decent young man who would love her as she deserved.

There'd be no husband now. Most likely, just a fatherless bastard or two. There were laws to protect indentured servants, but the men who could pay the price for them could also pay the law to look the other way. With Nicki's criminal record—and the face and figure she hid beneath her dingy clothes—she had almost no protection at all. Lorna sighed. Life was never easy.

Worried about the day to come, Nicki slept fitfully on her pallet of straw on the cold dirt floor, then paced the cell all morning. Without the sun for guidance, it was difficult to tell how many hours they'd been waiting before they heard the sound of shuffling feet outside their door, but it was probably late afternoon.

"It'll be our turn next," Nicki said, hearing the opposite cell door clank open, then the sound of women's voices as the guards began to herd them down the hall. She could almost see herself standing on the auction block, men calling out prices as if she were no longer human, just some object up for purchase—which, in fact, she was.

Shame and dread washed over her. *What would you say, Papa, if you were here?* But in her heart she knew.

"No one can shame you, *ma fille*. You can only shame yourself." She remembered his words so well, it was almost as if he had spoken.

"Stay close to me," Lorna was saying. "I know most o' the wealthy lads about town. The miserable ol' goat who owned my contract was a newspaper man. There werna' much about anyone ol' man Forsythe dinna know. When we get outside, I'll let ye know which o' the bidders to encourage, which to discourage."

"And just how am I supposed to do that?"

"Yer a smart lass. Ye'll figure it out when the time comes."

Nicki's shoulders sagged. She'd figure it out—at least she would try. She would do the best she could, just as she had been doing for the past three years. So far she hadn't done a very good job.

The sound of a key grating in the lock sent a tremor of fear up her spine. She'd never been afraid before, not the way she was now. Neither had she known such uncertainty, such humiliation. She was thankful she had indentured herself under her mother's maiden name. No one would believe that Nicki Stockton, the dirty, emaciated waif who watched them with haunted eyes, was Nicole St. Claire, Etienne St. Claire's daughter.

"Hoist your skirts," the guard instructed, meaning to chain the women's legs together for the trip to the auctioneer's platform.

As the heavy iron band clamped around her slender ankle, its cold, hard edge biting into her tender flesh, Nicki turned to the woman who had earned a special place in her heart.

"I'll never forget you, Lorna." A hard ache swelled in her throat. "I wish there were some way to repay you for the kindness you've shown. If there's ever anything—anything I can do. . . ."

"Yer a good friend, Nicki, lass. I'll be prayin' for ye."

Clutching each other for support, they walked toward the door and the uncertain future that awaited them.

"I don't know about you, but this damnable weather is getting me down. I could use a drink." Alexandre du Villier clapped his best friend, Thomas Demming, on the back.

Though it wasn't really cold, it was overcast and windy. Unusual, with summer approaching. Always an optimist, Alex figured at least he wasn't hot and uncomfortable in his double-breasted forest-green tailcoat. His white cravat and pleated white shirt looked as fresh as they had when he'd put them on this morning.

"I hear they just got in a shipment of Napoleon brandy over at the St. Louis Hotel," Thomas said, the breeze whipping his gray broadcloth frock coat and shiny blond hair.

"Perfect," Alex agreed in his near-flawless English. Since his return to Belle Chêne last year, Alex had chosen to use English as much as possible. He was an American by birth, though one of French ancestry—French Creole. Although he'd spent a great deal of his life in France, been educated at the Université de Paris, La Sorbonne, and spent a year at L'Ecole Polytechnique, it was Louisiana—and Belle Chêne—he called home.

"What do you think about the price of sugar this year?" Thomas asked him as they crossed dusty Royale Street, heading toward the end of Exchange Place, where the hotel was located.

Alex didn't answer. His attention was fixed instead on the group of people gathered near the hotel rotunda. "What's going on over there?"

The answer became apparent as the men drew closer. "Slave auction," said Thomas, but the color of the skin was wrong.

"Indentured servants," Alex corrected, his steps beginning to slow. "From the prison. Runaways and thieves, mostly." He disliked human bondage. Too many years of living in France, where all men were free, and since the liberation, treated for the most part as equals.

"Yes." Thomas's distaste was equally apparent. "Let's head around back and go in from the rear."

Alex nodded. But catching a glimpse of the small figure standing on the platform, his steps once more began to slow. Instead of turning away, he found himself moving closer. Thomas, a bit confused but rarely surprised by anything Alex did, followed along behind.

"How much am I bid for this sturdy little bit of

baggage?" the auctioneer intoned, proceeding with his singsong money chant. "She's young yet, as you can see. But she's comely, bound to be a ripe 'un when she matures."

Unlike the others, Alex noticed, whose shoulders sagged in defeat, the girl stood ramrod straight, shoulders square, chin held high, looking neither right nor left. There was something about her. . . . *What was it?* Alex moved a little closer, threading his way through the crowd.

"Three hundred dollars," a gangly man in a stove-pipe hat called out. The girl glanced in the man's direction, then over to a dark-haired woman who stood against the wall. The buxom woman nodded and the young girl smiled at the man, a pleasant smile, tentative, but not insincere.

"Five hundred." It was Valcour Fortier, a black-haired half-Spaniard, half-Frenchman Alex had known since childhood. Fortier was one of the wealthiest men in New Orleans—he was also the cruelest, most ruthless bastard Alex had ever had the misfortune to meet.

The woman near the wall seemed to agree. She was shaking her head vigorously, trying to warn the girl on the platform, whose face had turned an even paler shade than it was before. Alex could barely make out her features for the worn brown, coal-scuttle bonnet she wore, but her hair, though dirty and matted, appeared to be a warm shade of copper.

Her demeanor a little less regal, she glanced at Fortier, who gestured to the auctioneer. With a lewd smile of understanding, the skinny little man lifted the young girl's skirts, exposing her slender bare feet, a portion of her calf, and a glimpse of her thin white cotton drawers, just above the knee.

"Stop that!" she shrieked, jerking her skirts from the auctioneer's hands. Her defiance brought a ringing slap that echoed above the crowd, but still she held her ground.

"She's young, boys. Needs a man's hand to teach her her place, is all." The auctioneer smiled at the bidders, easing the tension.

"Six hundred," the gangly bidder said, and again the girl smiled, turning to face him more squarely.

It was then Alex saw them—a pair of aqua eyes so vivid they took his breath away. It was her eyes he'd noticed before, he realized, her eyes that had drawn him into the crowd. He had been sure he had only imagined them.

"One thousand," Fortier said with finality.

Cursing his bad luck and shaking his head, the gangly bidder walked away.

"Is there none here who can see the potential of this young girl?" the auctioneer asked, hoping to gouge Fortier for a few dollars more. He raised her arm and drew back her sleeve. "She's got good, strong muscle. Seven years left on her contract. Surely you can imagine the delights she could bring . . . with just a little patience." He grinned and patted her bottom, sending a wash of color to the girl's pale face. She closed her eyes a moment, fighting to bring her embarrassment under control, but she continued to look straight ahead.

"She's a thief," Fortier called out. "None will pay more."

"I'm not a thief!" the girl threw back at him. "I'm not!" That brought a second stinging blow.

"Hold your tongue," the auctioneer warned, cruelly gripping her arm. "Give Mr. Fortier a smile."

When he released her arm, the girl proudly drew herself up. She watched Fortier a moment, correctly assessing his determination to own her, looked to her friend who was still vigorously shaking her head, then dropped into a sweeping curtsy. She smiled at Fortier so sweetly it seemed someone had turned on the sun.

"Mr. Fortier," she said, her voice soft and dripping with honey. "I'm honored that you should find a pitiful creature such as myself worthy of your attentions."

Alex didn't miss her faultless speech, nor the hidden venom with which she spoke. He didn't miss the disdain for Valcour Fortier that her honeyed words belied.

But he almost missed her tears.

When she moved her head, they glistened on her smooth cheeks like raindrops, a sorrowful contrast to the smile that lit her face.

"Twelve hundred," Alex called out, and could scarcely believe he'd said the words.

"Fourteen," came Fortier's bid. After a contemptuous glance in Alex's direction, he looked back at the girl with undisguised hunger, confirming Alex's fear that he wanted her in his bed. It was well known in the *Vieux Carré*, the French Quarter, that Fortier had a penchant for young, untried women—the younger the better. This one would more than whet his appetite.

"Two thousand," Alex said, and the crowd fell silent. Only the rattle of a prisoner's chains marred the stillness.

Fortier laughed softly, but his laughter sounded forced. "I wasn't aware your tastes ran to those so young. Had I but known. . . ." He shrugged his shoulders in a gesture of nonchalance, but his dark eyes screamed his fury.

"Have her brought to my carriage in an hour," Alex instructed the auctioneer, ignoring Fortier's lewd remarks. "You'll find it at one twenty-one Royale Street. I'll have a draft there waiting for you." The auctioneer nodded, and a fat guard led the girl away.

Before she had disappeared from sight, Alex was regretting his actions.

"What was that all about?" Thomas asked with a touch of amusement that only increased Alex's self-directed ire.

"I haven't the remotest idea. Sometimes I even amaze myself."

Thomas knew better than to comment any further.

The men moved up the stone steps and into the hotel's elegant interior. The St. Louis was a landmark in New Orleans; its imposing dome, rising above the city, could be seen from blocks away.

"I think we'd better get you that drink," Thomas said. "You look as though you could use it."

Alex shoved open the paneled cypress doors to the gentlemen's bar with a little more effort than necessary, and moved toward one of the tables. Quiet conversation and the sound of men's heavy laughter rose up around them. Some played cards, others stood at the long, carved mahogany bar.

Alex barely noticed them. He had acted rashly, for reasons even he couldn't quite fathom. Now he was paying the price.

"I promised Lisette I would take her to dinner.

How do you suppose she'd enjoy an evening with Belle Chêne's newest dependent instead?"

"I wouldn't try it if I were you. She's already in a temper over your soon-to-be-announced engagement."

"That was settled with a few new ball gowns and a trip up the river on the *Natchez Queen*." Few women could resist the luxury of the *Queen*, the most luxurious steamboat on the Mississippi. "This is business. The girl's a two-thousand-dollar investment. I may have been fool enough to buy her, but I'll damned well guarantee she'll earn back every penny and then some."

"Why don't you just leave her at the prison for the night?"

Alex felt a tightening in his chest just to think of it. He could almost feel the stinging blows the girl had been dealt on the platform—he could well imagine the brutality she had suffered in her rat-infested cell.

"She's Belle Chêne property now. I want her ready and able to carry her share of the load."

Thomas just smiled. Alex might talk tough, but he was a man who went out of his way to treat his workers fairly. Each family on the plantation had its own cabin, garden, and chickens. They attended church, observed Christian holidays, were married by a priest, and families were never separated. On Belle Chêne, slaves earned a living much as sharecroppers did, including bonuses for extra effort in the cane fields.

Many of the planters resented Alex's progressive tactics, but the du Villier family represented power and social status, and had for years. Few were willing to voice that resentment aloud.

Valcour Fortier was among those few.

"You certainly got Fortier's temper up," Thomas said with a grin as the two men sipped their fine Napoleon brandy.

Alex swirled the amber liquid in his glass. "He doesn't like to lose."

"Why do you suppose he backed off?"

It went unsaid that Feliciana, Fortier's plantation, was in far better financial condition than Belle Chêne. The depression of 1837, and his brother François's mismanagement, had seen to that.

"Probably because it just isn't good business to pay that much money for a thief, no matter how young and tender she might be. Money means everything to Valcour. No woman-child, especially one who can't be trusted, is worth making a bad investment."

Just saying the words, which were damned well true, reheated Alex's temper. "Now, if you don't mind, let's talk about something else. I've got less than an hour before I'll be forced to acknowledge my folly. It's not an evening I look forward to."

Nicki sat forlornly on the damp straw pallet in her dark and musty cell, her legs drawn up beneath her chin, her arms wrapped protectively around them as she waited for the hour of her departure.

She shivered, though it wasn't really cold, and prayed she would see Lorna again. Since her friend had been led onto the opposite end of the platform just as Nicki had walked away, they'd had no chance to speak, no chance even for that brief communication that would have warned her about the man who had bought her contract.

Nicki had been certain the black-haired man with the dark eyes and Spanish features would win, though at Lorna's horrified expression, she prayed he would not. The way he had looked at her had made her skin crawl, but he'd seemed so confident of his purchase, so determined, she'd finally given in to an urge to show him her disdain. Then the other man in the crowd had materialized out of nowhere—saving her from some dreadful fate she could only imagine, or immersing her in something worse.

She had tried to see his face beneath the stylish gray narrow-brimmed high hat he wore, but everything happened so quickly that he was gone before she got the chance. All she had noticed was his height, which was several inches taller than the men around him, and that his shoulders were broad.

He appeared to be a large man—and big meant powerful. Nicki shuddered. Powerful enough to hold her immobile against her fiercest struggles. Powerful enough to do the ugly things the watchmen had done to Lorna and the other women prisoners.

Nicki closed her eyes, fighting down her fears. She had always been so fearless, so confident. Now it seemed, at the most inopportune time, she would remember the beatings she had received from Armand Laurent for her defiance, the suppers she'd missed because of her arrogant nature and too-haughty ways. It had taken some doing, but she'd finally learned to suffer in silence, to keep her bitter retorts to herself. Her reward had been imprisonment for a crime she didn't commit.

Outside her cell, Nicole heard the watchmen's weighty footfalls, their ribald laughter as they headed down the hall. *Wherever I go has got to be better than this*, she told herself firmly. But as the heavy iron door swung wide and she was led away, she wasn't really so sure.

3

Nervously wringing her hands, Nicole St. Claire stood beside the gleaming black barouche that waited on Royale Street in front of a sign reading: Thomas P. Demming, Attorney-at-Law.

A gray-haired watchman stood on one side of her while an equally graying black man, dressed in fashionable red and gold livery, stood on the other.

The guard pulled a timepiece from his pocket and flipped open the lid. "We're a few minutes early."

"He be here," the old Negro said. "He be here right on time."

And he was.

Nicole had just glanced toward the corner when the tall broad-shouldered man she had glimpsed at the auction came around it, striding in their direction. Nicki blinked, blinked again, then swayed against the carriage wheel, gripping the spokes for support. *It couldn't be!*

But it was. Alexandre du Villier. She would know that handsome face anywhere. During her hard days of indenture, as she had huddled on her narrow cot trying to get warm, or scrubbed the hard wooden floors, or washed a mountain of dirty laundry, she'd thought about him, wondered what had happened to him. Wondered if, back in her other lifetime, he might have come to call on her as she had once wished.

She glanced up at him as he drew near, accepting the papers the guard handed over but perusing them only briefly. When he looked down at her, her heart began to pound. *Would he recognize her too?* Dear God, she prayed he wouldn't.

She couldn't bear to face him in her filthy rags and matted hair. But then maybe that was why he'd bought her. He had remembered her and was here to rescue her again. Her heart increased its pounding, and the rags that bound her breasts felt so tight she couldn't breathe.

He was handing the guard a draft now, just as he had promised, while the driver returned to his seat at the front of the carriage. Nicki fought a moment of panic as a pair of hard brown eyes locked on her face, and his big hand lifted her chin. He assessed her a moment, his dark look traveling over her bruised and dirt-smudged face, then down the front of her soiled brown wool dress, where the bodice hung loose and to all appearances, empty.

A glimmer of something moved across his face, and she wondered if it might have been a flash of disappointment.

"There'll be no thievery at Belle Chêne," he said as if an edict had been spoken. "Now get in the carriage."

With those harsh words, Nicki's hopes crumbled. She was property, nothing more. He hadn't remembered her at all.

She swallowed past the lump in her throat and blinked against the tears so close to the surface. She'd been a fool to think he would care if he did know who she was—and she wasn't about to remind him. Her father had gone to Belle Chêne for help with his failing plantation and got nothing but a slap in the face. Nicole had been standing outside the door to his study when he had returned.

"François was just as I remembered him," her father told her mother. "Selfish and uncaring. He said his father may have been an easy mark, but François du Villier was a businessman. He had his own problems to worry about and his brother felt the same." She would never forget the look of despair on her father's handsome face or the tears in her mother's eyes.

Steeling herself against the bitter memories, Nicki took a seat opposite the imposing man in the expensive dark-green tailcoat. She was careful to keep her eyes cast down, as she had learned in prison, but couldn't resist a single surreptitious glance. She found him watching her with as much curiosity as she watched him. She knew she should glance away, but for the life of her she could not.

He looked as handsome as she remembered, maybe more so. There was an air of maturity about him now that hadn't been there before. His jaw looked stronger, his features a little harder. The sensuous grooves beside his mouth were gone, and there were tiny lines beside his dark-brown eyes. He looked older, as if the responsibilities he now carried had taken the last of his youth.

He seemed almost angry, she suddenly realized, and wondered if she could possibly be the cause.

When he said nothing more, just kept staring at her as if he wished she would disappear, she felt her own temper beginning to build.

"I'm not a thief," she finally told him, certain the words were hovering in his thoughts. She had done nothing to deserve the things that had happened to her in the last three years. Nothing at all!

"That's not what your papers say." He propped one long, muscular leg on the front of her seat. "They say you were caught with your employer's emerald brooch hidden in a pair of your drawers."

Nicki flushed crimson. How could he refer so casually to something so personal? "My employer found the missing brooch, which is not surprising, since she is the one who put it there."

"And just why would she do that?" he asked with a mocking note he did not try to hide. He leaned back against the seat, his shoulders so broad they took up most of the tufted red leather.

"W-why?" she repeated, hating the accusation in his eyes. She wanted to fling the truth at him, but God in heaven, she couldn't tell him it was because the woman was jealous. He'd never believe a wife would be jealous of a twelve-year-old girl! "I don't know," she lied, wishing she could sink lower in her seat, but drawing herself up instead.

The Frenchman's eyes turned harder than they already were. "Well, you can be certain that I won't be stashing any jewelry in your drawers, so you had better not turn up with any."

Nicki bit her tongue so hard it hurt. Who the devil did he think he was? "Must you constantly make reference to my underwear?" Her jaw clenched so tight she practically hissed.

"You mean you own some?"

Her eyes went wide. "You are . . . you are . . . *not* a gentleman."

Alexandre grinned at that. The dimples were back. "I'm happy to see they haven't broken your spirit completely. Tell me . . . how is it a little gutter rat like you speaks such educated English?"

Gutter rat! And to think his father had once been called "friend." "If I'm such a despicable person, why did you buy me?"

Alexandre's smile faded. His eyes swept over her ragged dirty clothes and the stringy matted hair she tried to cover with her bonnet.

"I needed a little amusement."

With those final hard words, they rode along in silence, the carriage filled only with the sound of spinning wheels and the clip-clop of horses' hooves on the cobblestone streets. Nicki's heart pounded harder than the hoofbeats. He needed a little *amusement.* Etienne St. Claire's daughter, ragged and filthy, was an amusement. A thing to be laughed at, a thing to be scorned.

What did a man like Alexandre du Villier find amusing about someone as pitiful as she? she wondered. And how long would she have to wait with her insides churning to find out?

As if in answer, the carriage wheels stopped, the driver jumped down, and the door swung wide.

"We here, Mista Alex."

Alex climbed to the street, and the driver helped Nicki climb down.

Alex motioned toward the inside of the carriage. "Give that seat a good scrubbing, Ukiah. She's probably got lice."

Nicole St. Claire, once her father's pride and joy and a much-sought-after belle, could have died right there on the spot. And worst of all, it was true.

She swallowed hard and glanced away. She wouldn't let the Frenchman know how much his words had hurt her. She might look wretched on the outside, but inside, St. Claire blood flowed through her veins.

"Where are we going?" she asked, fighting the urge to weep.

"To get you a bath." He was scowling at her, his words meant to sting. Even the joy of being clean couldn't allay her misery. She just prayed it didn't show.

Heading toward a high wrought-iron gate, they entered a small, well-kept courtyard. Inside, jasmine, wisteria, honeysuckle, and clematis bloomed in profusion, and a small marble fountain made a shower for the birds. At the opposite end of the garden sat a two-story pale-pink structure, much the color of her home at Meadowood, with tiny white shutters and a wrought-iron balcony off one of the rooms upstairs. Alexandre opened the heavy carved cypress door, and they walked into the entry where a uniformed butler waited stoically for Alex's hat and gloves.

"Whose house is this?" Nicki asked, admiring the lovely parquet floors and molded ceilings. Expensive Aubusson carpets warmed the salon, and delicate porcelain vases sat atop Queen Anne tables.

"Mine."

"But I thought you . . ." *But I thought you lived at Belle Chêne, or were still living in France.*

"But you thought what?" he snapped.

Why was he so angry? "Nothing."

"Any more questions, mademoiselle," he mocked, "or might we go upstairs and attend your bath?"

His sarcasm sent a surge of fury through her veins. Why hadn't she remembered him as the caustic, mean-spirited man he was? Instead she'd remembered his handsome face, the way he had come to her rescue in the dusty streets of La Ronde. He was still just as handsome, but she'd learned these past few years that a person's looks meant nothing. What mattered was what was in one's heart.

Lifting her dirty skirts up out of the way, and with as much aplomb as she could muster, Nicki headed upstairs.

A thin-faced woman in a mobcap and apron stepped into the hall in front of them. *"Bonjour,* your grace," she greeted him in French, and Nicki sucked in a breath.

Good Lord, now that Charles du Villier was dead, Alexandre was a duke! *Le duc de Brisonne.* How could she have forgotten?

"I told you not to call me that," Alex said harshly.

"Pardon, m'sieur."

"I also asked you to speak English. Both you and your mistress could well use the practice."

"Yes, m'sieur," she answered dutifully.

"I take it she has not returned."

"No, m'sieur. She was in quite a temper when she left. She said she was not about to spend the night with a common criminal, even with you here to take her mind off it."

Alex almost smiled. As Thomas had predicted, Lisette had been furious. When he'd told her about the bond servant he would be bringing from the prison, she had stormed out of the house. If he couldn't start giving her more attention, she'd raged, she would leave him for good. Of course, they both knew she wouldn't.

Lisette had a violent temper, which Alex tolerated only because she showed that same hot passion in bed, but she would never jeopardize her comfortable position as his mistress.

"I have readied the water as you instructed," the maid said.

He swung his gaze to the girl, who swallowed hard and nervously licked her lips. "What's your name?" he asked.

"Nic—Nicki Stockton."

He studied her more carefully, trying to see past the soiled brown bonnet and the dirt on her face. "You don't have any relatives near here . . . a half sister, maybe, or a cousin?"

"No."

"I once met someone who looked a little like you. Same hair color, same eyes. But she was older, and she was French." He hadn't thought of the girl in La Ronde for years. That he remembered her at all surprised him, considering she'd been little more than a child.

"She certainly didn't smell like you," he added cruelly, still resentful he had somehow been duped into taking on one more responsibility he could ill afford. "That one smelled of violets. You smell as if you've been living in the bottom of a chicken coop."

The girl's face turned ashen. Shoulders that had been proud and straight even as she'd stood on the platform now sagged in weary defeat. Her bottom lip trembled and she fixed her eyes on the floor.

"I know," she said, the sound of the words so soft and plaintive it tore at his heart.

Alex felt like an ass. What the hell was the matter with him? He had been goading the girl since the moment he'd met her, punishing her for his own stupidity. But she'd done nothing to deserve his harsh words. It wasn't her fault he'd acted so rashly.

Alex tipped her chin with his fingers. Tears welled in her eyes and slipped down her cheeks. "I'm sorry, *ma petite*," he said softly. "None of this is your fault."

With his thumb and forefinger, he wiped the wetness away, leaving traces of her pale complexion where the dirt had been. He flashed an apologetic smile. "The past is behind you. You are safe now, and as long as you uphold your end of this bargain you will be. Marie's going to help you bathe and dress, then tomorrow I'll take you home to Belle Chêne."

Home. How long had it been since she'd lived in a place she thought of that way? Afraid Alex would read her wistful thoughts, Nicki tried not to look at him, but found it impossible. As difficult as ignoring the warmth of the fingers he had rested beneath her chin, the sound of his voice when he'd spoken to her with gentleness, the way he had before. The anger was gone from his voice now, his expression one of concern.

He turned to the chambermaid. "See she's well taken care of."

The woman nodded, guided her into one of the upstairs chambers, and closed the door behind them.

Nicole felt the woman's hands on the buttons at her back. "If you don't mind," Nicki said, as soon as they were unfastened, "I would rather do the rest myself." She couldn't risk discovery just yet. She needed time to find out the truth about the du Villiers. Were they friend or foe? Did their families' long-standing relationship really mean nothing, or would Alexandre du Villier help her?

The woman nodded, accepting her desire for privacy. "You will find one of my daughter's old uniforms on the bed. It is worn, but it is clean. It will fit you, I think."

As soon as Marie left the room, Nicole peeled off the rest of her grimy clothes and the rags that flattened her breasts. They ached a little from the uncomfortable bonds, but it was a small enough price to pay. It dawned on her suddenly, she would have to find something to replace the dirty lengths of petticoat—she couldn't stand the thought of putting them on again.

Glancing around the chamber, she noticed it opened into a bigger room and peeked inside to find a larger chamber gaudy with frills and cloying with the smell of sweet perfume.

Wondering whose room it could possibly be, she quietly backed away and returned to the task at hand. A search of the carved antique chest of drawers turned up nothing, but in the bottom of the rosewood armoir she found an old muslin sheet which she hastily tore into strips and stashed beneath the clean black uniform on the bed. Then she headed toward the big copper bathing tub that sat in the corner.

The water in the tub had cooled to just the right temperature by the time Nicki stepped in and slid beneath the surface. The scent of rose drifted up from the water.

She used to love violet, she remembered, the memory coming from somewhere far away. Then another thought occured: Alexandre du Villier, Duc de Brisonne, had remembered her. At least a little. For the first time in years, her other lifetime seemed not so far away.

Enjoying her bath, Nicki scrubbed herself all over. A bottle of harsh-smelling liquid had been set out for use on her hair. When she had finished using it, she started scrubbing herself again. Marie came in before she'd finished, so she slid lower in the soapy water.

"There is no need to hurry." She flashed Nicole a smile. Marie stood a few inches taller than Nicki, with mouse-brown hair and a plain but unlined face. "What did you say your name was?"

"Nicki. Nicki Stockton."

"Nicki," she repeated, her voice warm and friendly —until she noticed the slight disturbance Nicki's search of the room had caused. Her warm smile narrowed to a disapproving line.

"It isn't what you think," Nicole said quickly, but Marie ignored her words. Stiff-backed, the chambermaid headed out the door.

Why did everything she tried to do turn out wrong? Nicki despaired as she finished her bath and hurriedly toweled herself dry. Worried Marie might return before she was finished, she quickly rebound her breasts and pulled on a cotton chemise. Clean and smelling of soap, the thin, worn fabric felt the height of luxury, the simple black uniform with its crisp white apron more precious than a Paris gown.

Using the silver-handled brush on the dressing table, Nicki combed her hair, then braided it and circled each braid beside her ear. The white starched mobcap went on next, covering most of her once-again shiny copper hair. When she glanced in the mirror, she noticed the dress rose several inches above the floor, displaying a bit of white-stockinged ankle and a length of petticoat, the style fashionable for a younger girl.

She did look young. She had always had a look of innocence. But her woman's body had allayed any doubts about her age. Now that her figure was disguised, she didn't doubt her ability to deceive the most discerning. It would serve her purpose for a while.

Awaiting Marie's return, Nicole sat down on the tapestry stool in front of the dressing table and looked out the window at the garden below. She was enjoying the riot of color, the yellows, lavenders, and pinks, when the door slammed open with a rush of air and Alexandre du Villier strode into the room.

His thunderous expression told her all she needed to know.

"I thought you understood," he said, his voice again hard. "I'll not tolerate your thievery—" Alex stopped in mid-sentence. For an instant he thought he had entered the wrong room. The girl who stared back at him bore little resemblance to the waif he had purchased at the auction.

"Thank God Fortier never got a good look at you. He'd damned well have paid the two thousand."

"Two thousand?" she squeaked, coming to her feet. "That's what you paid for me?"

"Yes, though you may rest assured I already regret it." God, did he. The girl was little more than a child, yet he felt a tightening in his groin just to look at her. Hair the color of newly minted pennies, eyes like aquamarines. Her lips were full and the loveliest shade of pink. *Nom de Dieu*, he had never been attracted to such a young girl.

"This is your last warning," he told her. "Unless you wish to wind up back on the auction block, you'll learn to behave yourself."

"Please . . . it wasn't the way you think." Just the thought of being sold again made her feel sick. "I was just . . . looking around . . . at . . . at all the pretty things you have." Women's things, she realized, the truth finally dawning. Frilly lace and heavy perfume. Alex was married! "I—I just couldn't help myself."

Alex was watching her face, and it was clear he knew she was lying. She wanted to die.

"Those pretty things belong to somebody else. You'll do well to remember that."

"M'sieur du Villier," she said softly, repeating his name as the maid had, careful to say it with a trace of an English accent. "I appreciate what you've done." *So far.* She hadn't forgotten his ominous threat about her being an *amusement*. "I won't steal from you. I give you my word."

"And just how much is a thief's word worth?" His look said not one franc.

"I'm not a thief. I know you don't believe me, but it's the truth. I didn't do the things they say. I've never stolen anything. As far as my word is concerned, I value it above all things. It's all I have left."

Alex regarded her closely, the straightforward way she met his eyes, the proud tilt to her chin. This time she was telling the truth. He was sure of it. There were hundreds of people living on Belle Chêne. Hundreds of people who were his responsibility. He had learned quickly how to judge a man or a woman, and he was rarely wrong.

"All right, Nicki. I'll accept your word."

"You will?" She looked so surprised, he almost smiled.

"That's what I said." He extended his hand, but the girl just stared at it, reminding him of some untamed wary animal. He held his hand immobile, allowing her to test his intentions until tentatively she reached for it. Her fingers felt small and warm in his, but it was her smile that touched his heart. It was only the second time he had seen it and instantly his regret in buying her began to fade.

"I don't imagine you've had a lot to eat lately."

She wet her lips at the mention of food. "No."

"Why don't you go downstairs and see what Cook can find for you? I told her you'd be down."

"Thank you," she said, but didn't move.

"Go on," he prompted.

With another quick smile she was gone, leaving a certain dimness in the room. For the first time Alex realized it was getting dark outside.

Nicki had been just a child when last she had seen Belle Chêne.

Too little to remember the magnificence of the great white plantation house rising two stories, with an attic above the half story that lifted it off the damp black earth near the river. Dozens of columns ten feet apart surrounded each level, creating wide galleries that kept the rooms cool in summer. A massive hip roof, enhanced by tiny dormer windows, separated tall brick chimneys at each end of the house.

But even as the carriage rumbled up the oak-lined

drive beneath draping gray-green moss, Nicole remembered the beautiful black mantels of rare Belgian marble she would find in the receiving rooms downstairs, the pink Baccarat crystal chandelier with its hand-blown chains of small individual links that lighted the entry. As luxurious as Meadowood had been, none compared to Belle Chêne.

The grinding of the carriage wheels against the oyster-shell drive in front of the house marked their arrival. Alex helped her down, and they walked inside.

"I've brought you some help," he told the housekeeper. "Nicki, this is Mrs. Leander. She'll get you settled in."

Mrs. Leander, a buxom, graying woman at least half a head taller than Nicki, took her firmly in hand and led her to a tiny attic room on the third floor of the house.

"We can always use a good worker," Mrs. Leander said pointedly.

"I'll do my best," Nicki promised.

That night she slept fitfully, tossing and turning in her unfamiliar surroundings. She shivered, though the room felt warm, and dreamed of Armand Laurent. Dark, disturbing dreams of lashing fists that battered her body, and broken bones that tore through her tender flesh. Of blood that turned her world red and oozing, and tears that would not end.

Then the haunting laughter of the guards rose up, the anguished cries of the women.

Nicki bolted upright. Her nightshirt, damp with sweat, clung wetly to her body, and her heartbeat hammered in her ears. It took a moment for her to realize there was no threat of danger, but eventually the warmth in the room seeped into her awareness, dissolving the cobwebs of fear; and the cheery quilt that covered her comfortable bed eased her mind.

Pulling the gay little pink squares beneath her chin, touching it almost reverently, she finally drifted to sleep.

That had been nearly two weeks ago. She'd seen Alex only a few times since, but she *had* made some discoveries. She found out his household was well run and her work schedule not too strenuous. Her duties, mostly working in the kitchen outside the main house, ended right after supper, often before it got dark. She had Saturday afternoons and Sundays off, just as the sugarcane workers did.

A simple parish church, constructed for the workers, held Catholic services every week. Nicki attended, though she still kept much to herself. For the most part, she was allowed the run of the plantation, more freedom than she had known in the last three years.

About Alex himself, according to Mrs. Leander and some of the other women on the staff, he could probably part the Red Sea. They fussed over him endlessly, worried that he worked too hard, worried that he didn't eat properly, worried that he worried too much. Nicki found herself more and more intrigued.

"Why does his wife live in the city, while he spends most of his time out here?" she asked, careful to keep her interest nonchalant.

"M'sieur Alex is not married," Danielle Le Goff, the upstairs maid replied, tittering behind her hand. She was a short, plump, giggly girl with wistful gray eyes. Pretty, in a robust sort of way, with thick dark-brown hair that glistened in the sunlight slanting in through the open window. "But he is not lonely. He has his lady friends."

"You mean he has a . . . mistress?"

"Oh, yes. Mademoiselle Lisette has been . . . entertaining him of late, but—"

Mrs. Leander's heavy footfalls stopped Danielle in mid-sentence.

"She's too young to be knowing about such things," the housekeeper said. "Once she's grown and married, she'll find out for herself." She thrust the broom Danielle had laid aside in the dark-haired girl's direction. "Get on back to work."

She turned a kinder eye on Nicki. "As for you, young lady, if you've finished with the floors, there's a trunkload of silver needs polishin'."

Nicki followed her into the dining room, thinking how much she liked the kind-hearted older woman. But her mind was not on the silver caddies that awaited.

It was on Alex and his mistress. *Lisette.* The woman who lived in his town house on Toulouse Street. She had known such women existed, of course, but she'd never really seen one. It was said that Richard Paxton, the man who had last owned her contract, was having an affair with a married woman, but that wasn't quite the same. A mistress was supposed to be beautiful, witty, and exciting. She was certain Alexandre's mistress would be all those things and more —and for reasons she wouldn't examine, the thought put a damper on the balance of her day.

Nicki had just finished her second week at Belle Chêne when François du Villier arrived—and with him the first hint of trouble.

4

Since one of the older servants was ill, Nicole was helping serve supper in the dining room.

It was a sumptuous room, with a Hepplewhite table seating twenty, carved high-backed rosewood chairs, and a gilt-and-crystal chandelier. Peach silk draperies hung at the windows, which overlooked vast manicured gardens and a small man-made lake.

Carrying a cut-crystal water pitcher, Nicki pushed open the heavy swinging door that separated the warming pantry from the dining area. For an instant she thought the man who glanced in her direction was Alex, but the only real similarity between the two men was their dark-brown hair and eyes. François was more slender and several inches shorter. He was handsome, but his features were finer, almost feminine, while Alex had a far more masculine appeal.

"I wondered when you'd find your way home," Alex said to him, speaking in French, which he seldom did, his tone far from kind. "I take it you ran out of money."

"I'm back on the dole, *mon frère*." François's

mouth turned up in a cynical smile. "What's the matter, not glad to see me?"

"I used to be. Before you discovered your main ambition in life—to do as little as possible and spend as much as you possibly can."

François's face turned red. "Easy for you to say. You're the one with the title and lands. All I have to my name is what your *generosity* provides."

Nicole busied herself with the water goblets, but she didn't miss the muscle that bunched in Alex's jaw.

"Belle Chêne was all yours, François. I'd have stayed in France if you could have made it work. You were the one who put everything at risk."

"There was a depression, for God's sake—a panic. I was lucky to keep the place running at all!"

"Lucky?" Alex repeated. "I'll grant you, times were tough, but luck has nothing to do with the success of a place like Belle Chêne—it's hard work that counts! Something you, younger brother, know very little about."

François shoved back his rosewood chair and stood up, slamming down his napkin in the process. "I won't be talked to this way. I'm going back into town."

He started toward the door, but stopped at the sound of Alex's voice, whose tone had changed to one of regret. "François . . . why must we always quarrel like this? We never used to."

His brother didn't answer.

"What's happened is past," Alex added. "What's important is Belle Chêne. I could use your help."

"I'm no good at running a place like this—as you so clearly pointed out. You'll figure out something.

You always do. In the meantime, I've taken a suite at the St. Louis Hotel. That's what I came here to tell you. If you need me, which I doubt, you'll find me there." Without a backward glance, he stalked out of the room. A few moments later, the front door slammed behind him.

Alex shoved his nearly untouched plate away and leaned back in his chair. Nicole stood at her post beside the door.

"Ah, *ma petite*," he said in French, assuming she wouldn't understand, "why must life be so complicated?" He looked defeated, as she had never seen him before.

"You should eat, m'sieur," she said in English, pushing the plate back in front of him, the mountain of buttered squash still steaming beside the delicate, wine-basted chicken.

He smiled at her concern. "If you will sit with me a moment," he answered, surprising her, and maybe even himself.

"I have duties . . . things I should—"

"So do I, *ma chère*, so do I."

She sat with him, beginning to see why the others watched after him so. Alexandre du Villier was an island. A man with grave responsibilities, and no one with whom he could share them.

"It must be difficult," Nicki said, "having so many people to watch out for and no one to help you."

For a moment he looked at her oddly, wondering, it seemed, if she might have understood what he had said, then brushing the notion away. "It was a simple task when we were a family—my father, François, and I—but all that has changed."

"What about your mother?" Nicki asked.

He shrugged his powerful shoulders. "I didn't see her much. My father raised us. The three of us were very close." Some of the tension in his body seemed to ease. He dug into a golden-brown crab cake, then started on the chicken. "Are you hungry? I could have them bring you a plate, if you like."

Nicki smiled, wondering how many men as wealthy as Alexandre du Villier would invite a servant to dinner. "I already ate. You were telling me about your mother."

"My mother and father were never close. My father wanted heirs; his children meant everything to him. My mother was rarely around—it was an arranged marriage, you see. Beneficial to all concerned, but allowing the maximum amount of freedom to each of them."

"I suppose that's the way it's done among the aristocracy." Nicki thought the whole thing sounded dreadful.

"So you know about that."

"I'm not stupid, m'sieur."

"Far from it," he countered with amusement. "But I don't care much for titles. I prefer to think of myself as an American. There are no dukes in America."

It pleased her that he should feel this way. Made him seem more human, not so unreachable. "At least you're free to marry someone you love."

Alex scoffed. "Love. I don't believe in it. A man marries a woman for the benefits that union will bring to the families—and of course, to produce heirs."

"But what about feelings? Surely you wouldn't marry a woman you cared nothing about?"

Alex chuckled softly. "Don't look so disappointed.

There are ways for a man to . . . exercise his more
. . . sensual nature. Places other than the marriage
bed."

"You mean with a mistress," she said flatly, and
Alex grinned, flashing his dimples.

"You continue to amaze me."

"I heard the servants talking. Besides, I was in her
house, remember?"

"The house is mine. Lisette will live there as long
as she pleases me. After that, I'll find her a small
place in the country, or maybe some other city, if that
is what she prefers."

"Good heavens, you sound like you're putting her
out to pasture. My father worshipped my mother. He
would have done anything to make her happy, and
my mother felt the same about him." A lump swelled
in her throat just to think of them.

Alex took a drink of his wine. "Maybe that's the
way it appeared to you, but personally I've yet to see
it."

"Does Lisette know how you feel?"

"Lisette is a practical sort. She'll do whatever's
most profitable for Lisette."

Nicki gaped at him in wonder. "A mistress who
loves you for money, and a wife who loves you not at
all." She shoved back her chair and stood up. "I may
be younger than you, m'sieur, but in some ways I'm
wiser." Shoulders squared, she walked toward the
door.

It occurred to her briefly that Alex might be angry.
Instead she heard his rumble of laughter as the door
swung closed.

How could a man not believe in love? she wondered when the dishes were finished and she headed

upstairs to her small attic room. Surely there was
some woman somewhere who could show Alexandre
du Villier the meaning of love. For the first time, she
began to think about telling Alex the truth.

Alex pondered his unusual dinner conversation as
he stood at the rail of the steamboat, *Belle Creole*, on
his way downriver to New Orleans. His fight with
François had put him out of sorts until Nicki had
come in, fussing over him, convincing him to eat the
food he'd been sure he couldn't swallow.

He chuckled to himself. She was a charmer all
right. He wondered where she had learned to speak
such educated English. He would find out, he decided, the next time they talked. Surprisingly, he
found himself looking forward to it. Nicki spoke to
him as if she were his equal, a trait he found fascinat-
ing in one so young. She had a quick mind and a
good wit, yet she seemed sensitive and caring. He
wasn't usually so open with people. Maybe it was her
youth, her freshness that appealed to him.

It pleased him that the others liked her too. Mrs.
Leander called her "a joy to work with, never com-
plaining, always willing to do more than her share."

Danielle told him about the kittens Nicki had
found. Their mother had been killed, so Nicki fed
them with a rag dipped in milk, one drop at a time.
She had been up half the night tending the starving
little creatures, then gone to work at dawn without
complaint.

Patrick, the fifteen-year-old stable boy who lived in
the barn, had asked Alex her name the first time he'd
seen her, but Alex had ignored him. He wasn't about
to have that young pup chasing after her. She was far

too young. Besides, she had too much to offer a man. When the time was right, Alex meant to see she had the chance to better herself.

The loud hoot of the whistle drew his attention as the big white steamboat reversed her powerful stern wheels and churned up the water beside the dock. Tonight he would see Lisette, take off the edginess he'd been feeling of late. She wasn't much of a conversationalist, but then, what he had in mind took very few words.

As he walked along the wharf, crossed Decatur, and headed up Toulouse Street toward his town house, he couldn't help remembering what Nicki had said about love. She was young and in many ways still naive. Let her cling to her illusions for as long as she could. She'd already discovered some of the harsh realities of life. Later she would find out another hard fact—just as with fairies and gnomes, there was no such thing as love.

Since Alexandre was working late in the fields and wouldn't be in for dinner, Nicole had finished her kitchen duties early. The sun was still bright, so she headed toward the stables, a habit she had developed of late.

As she walked along the brick path a flight of sandhill cranes winged by overhead, and small black children played beside the garden. The smell of bayberry scented the air from the candles being made not far away.

So much like home, Nicki thought, realizing how much she was coming to love the big plantation.

Entering the cool interior of the barn, she climbed up on the bottom rung of a stall and leaned over the gate. With just a few softly spoken words, a big blooded bay stallion named Napoleon trotted over, and Nicki petted his velvety nose.

"So, *ma petite*, are you as passionate about horses as you are about people?"

At the sound of Alex's voice, Nicki whirled to face him. He stood right behind her, close enough so their bodies almost touched. He was dressed in tight beige riding breeches and a full-sleeved white linen shirt, open a few buttons down. Clothes she had seen him in when he worked around the plantation, though tonight his white, flat-brimmed planter's hat was gone.

"I like horses very much." She swallowed past a sudden dryness in her throat. Her heart had increased its tempo, and a warm, hollow sensation tickled the pit of her stomach.

"Do you ride?" The muscles in his thighs bunched as he propped a black knee-high boot on one of the slats of the gate. Dark-brown chest hair curled at the front of his shirt, pulling her mind off his question. When she didn't answer fast enough, he assumed she did not. "How would you like to learn?"

A voice inside her warned, *say no*, but she rarely listened, and she wasn't listening now. "I'd love to."

"Then I'll teach you."

She felt his hands at her waist, big hands, warm and strong, lifting her down from the stall.

"Patrick!" he called out, and the lanky stable boy she had seen several times before appeared from his room at the end of the barn. "Saddle Orange Blossom."

"Now?"

"I'd prefer you do it sometime between now and tomorrow morning," Alex remarked dryly.

The tall boy glanced at Nicki, sizing her up as he'd done the first time she had seen him, then left to do his master's bidding.

"A lady rides sidesaddle," Alex told her, as if her bottom couldn't possibly fit the horse any other way. "Come over here, and I'll show you." His voice rumbled seductively, while a ray of late-evening sunlight turned his tanned skin a rosy shade of gold. He was smiling down at her, his teeth strong and white, dimples etched appealingly into his face. It was all she could do to look away.

Alex seemed not to notice. Effortlessly hefting a weighty sidesaddle onto a bale of straw, he helped her climb up on the tapestry seat.

"Hook your leg up over the horn."

She did as she was told, beginning to warm to the game. "Like this?"

"Not exactly. Straighten your spine a little."

He positioned one hand on her calf, fitting it more carefully, while the other maneuvered her hip into proper position. Nicki felt the warmth all the way to her toes.

"That's better," he said softly, but there was tightness in his voice that hadn't been there before.

"Orange Blossom's ready," Patrick called out, and Alex seemed almost grateful. They moved into the corral, where Patrick waited with the dun-colored mare.

"She's twenty years old," Alex told Nicki. "Wouldn't harm a fly."

She had no time to comment before his hands circled her waist, and he lifted her up on the mare. With controlled, businesslike movements, he looped one leg over the saddle horn while positioning her other leg in the stirrup. No matter that the horse was so old it could barely stand, it felt wonderful just to be riding again.

"Use the reins to guide her," Alex instructed, showing her the proper way. "Keep your back straight and your balance centered over the saddle."

Nicki did as she was told, restraining an urge to charge out the gate and off through the cane fields. By the time it was dark, Alex had taken her through the walk, trot, and canter.

"You've got a natural ability for this," he said, and she felt a little guilty for her deception. "If you like, we can work together in the evenings until you get good enough to go out of the corral."

Nicki grinned. "That would be marvelous."

He looked at her oddly. "How old did you say you were?"

Oh God, what had she done to set him off? It was hard to play the role of a child when she'd done everything in her power to forget her childhood. "How old?" she repeated, stalling for time.

"*Exactly* how old?"

Twelve seemed out of the question. "Thirteen," she said, and was grateful for the darkness. "I'll be fourteen in October." October twenty-fourth was her natal day, at least that much was true.

"You seem older."

"I was forced to grow up in a hurry."

He nodded, apparently satisfied. Patrick returned for Orange Blossom, who nickered softly as she was led away. Alex made no attempt to leave, but joined Nicki where she stood by the fence.

"How did it happen?" he finally asked. "How did

you come to be indentured? You're obviously educated. How in God's name did you end up in jail?''

Nicki propped her arms on the rail and looked out among the towering oak trees that loomed like great gray shadows in the distance. The last of the light had fled, leaving the corral illuminated by the stars overhead and the round sphere of a moon. She had wondered if he would ask about her past. It didn't seem likely, yet she had both feared and hoped he would.

"We lost our home in the depression. My father died rather unexpectedly, and my mother and I were left alone. That same year my mother died. They said it was a stroke, but she missed my father so much, I think she died of a broken heart."

"Surely there was someone you could turn to, someone who would help."

Your father! her mind accused. *Your family. We came to you, but you wouldn't help us.*

"Most of our friends were in worse trouble than we were. In the end, I thought the best idea was for me to indenture myself for a few years, learn a trade so I could fend for myself." Alex watched her closely, his interest encouraging her to go on.

"The Ramseys indentured me as a favor, since my family had known them for years. Unfortunately, it wasn't long before they also ran into hard times. They sold me to a man in New Orleans who seemed very upstanding on the surface. . . ." Nicki shuddered as the memory swept over her. Whenever she thought of Laurent, a cold, dark fear settled inside her.

"Every time he got drunk, he beat me. I carried his bruises all over my body. Once he broke my arm. . . ." Nicki stared off in the distance, fighting the ugly memories. "I was glad when he sold me. I didn't care who bought me, I only wanted to get away."

"Mista Alex?" It was Lemuel, Alex's valet. "Mista Thomas here to see you."

Alex glanced down at Nicki, hating the painful memories that darkened her pretty face. It sickened him to think of the cruelty she had suffered. He was glad he didn't know the bastard's name who had treated her so badly.

Unconsciously, Alex clenched his fist. He glanced from Nicki to Lemuel, waiting for him patiently, several yards away.

He ran a finger along her cheek, wishing there was something he could say, but unable to find the words. "I'd better go."

He had almost forgotten his meeting with Thomas Demming. They had the new shipping contracts to go over, so Thomas had volunteered to come out to the house. In truth, Alex knew Thomas enjoyed his brief forays into the country, his overnight stays at Belle Chêne. And Alex enjoyed the conversation. It was rare he got a chance to really relax.

Nicki put out her hand. "Thank you for the lesson. It was very kind of you. I'd almost forgotten how it felt to be treated as a human being."

Alex's expression turned grim. He looked as though he wanted to say something, but didn't. "Don't stay out here too long," he finally said, then turned and walked away.

Nicki headed back through the barn on her way to the house. Whale-oil lanterns lit the interior, and the place smelled of horses and new mown hay. The stable boy stopped her before she reached the door.

"Say, lass, you made a good show o' it, for your

first time out." Thumbs hooked in the top of his blue canvas pants, he grinned down at her. He was a pleasant-looking boy, tall and fair, with light-brown hair and hazel eyes, though she couldn't quite see them in the lamplight.

"Thank you." There were dozens of Irish working on the plantation. Fleeing a famine in their own country, they'd immigrated into the area by the scores.

"Name's Patrick O'Flannery. What's yours?"

"Nicki Stockton."

"Pleased to make your acquaintance, Nicki." He smiled again; a pleasant, honest smile, it seemed. "Sidesaddle's all right, I guess, but if you really want t' ride, you've got t' sit astride like a man. I could teach you, if you want."

"M'sieur du Villier is teaching me." She still couldn't believe it. But he'd said he would, and Alex did what he said.

"Yeah, well, you can ride with him as you like, but if you ride with me, I'll show you how to have some fun."

Nicki's eyes lit up. Patrick O'Flannery had the look of the blarney, but one never knew for sure. "How do you mean?"

"I mean, you keep practicin', then we'll wait until dark one night, and take a couple o' the duke's good 'uns out for a run."

"Steal them?"

"Nothin' like that. Just give 'em a little exercise."

It sounded like heaven. "I'd love to ride Napoleon," she said, just itching to feel the big blooded stallion beneath her.

"Not 'im. The duke would be mad as all get-out if

he found out we took Napoleon. But any of the others . . .''

Some of the finest horses in the world graced Belle Chêne's stables. To ride them would be a joy she hadn't known in years. "What'll they do to us if we get caught?" Weighing the consequences of her actions was something Nicole had rarely done. But now that she knew what it was to be caned, her face battered and bruised, she gave it some thought.

"Might give us a few extra chores. Never got a lickin', so you don't have t' worry on that score."

Nicki grinned. Extra work she could handle. Riding free again, feeling the wind against her face, would be worth the risk.

"I'll be gone for a coupla weeks," Patrick said, "takin' some o' the horses up to Plaquemine to the races. You keep practicin' and when I get back we'll make a night o' it."

"All right, Patrick—you've got a deal."

Alex headed upstairs to bathe before his meeting with Thomas Demming.

Lemuel, the aging black man who served as his valet, had readied the copper tub and laid out his clothes, a dark gray frock coat, burgundy waistcoat, and darker burgundy breeches. A tray of cold meat, cheese, bread, and fruit sat on a mahogany tilt-top table beside his favorite overstuffed chair, along with a bottle of wine and a stemmed crystal goblet.

He smiled at the old man's efficiency. There'd be late supper for him and Thomas, served to them in the study, but this would do nicely until then.

Lemuel always looked after him. Alex made a

mental note to check on the old man's rheumatism, make sure he wasn't working too hard.

After a hurried bath, Alex toweled himself dry and started getting dressed. He should be thinking about the contracts Thomas was here to review, but found his mind on his little copper-haired bond servant instead. He was glad he had bought her, he admitted, remembering the stories she had told. He couldn't stand the thought of her mistreatment—and he liked her. He had discovered that again tonight as he had before. She was open and honest. Guileless, as he wouldn't have expected from one who had led such a difficult life.

What he didn't like was the physical attraction he felt whenever he was in her presence.

Nom de Dieu, the girl was still a child. Well, not quite a child, but certainly not old enough for his conscience to allow him any real interest in her. She seemed older than her years, to be sure. But her body was far from ready. Where were the lush curves he'd always found attractive, the swell of bosom his hands should be eager to hold?

It was insane, and he knew it. But a problem just the same. He'd been thinking about it all evening as he watched her on the old dun horse. And he thought he'd found a solution.

In three more years, four at most, Nicki would be grown. If she matured anywhere near her potential, she would be a beautiful woman. She liked him; that much was obvious. And she certainly had no one to provide for her. What better candidate for a mistress?

Alex was a patient man, he could wait if he had to. His instincts told him the girl would be worth it. In the meantime, he could surely control himself. After all, he had Lisette to warm his bed, and soon he'd have a wife as well. With a smile of satisfaction, Alex combed his dark-brown hair, straightened the cuffs on his ruffle-fronted white shirt, and headed downstairs.

"Thomas," he said, striding into the elegant receiving salon and extending his hand, "it's good to see you."

Smiling, the slim blond man in navy-blue tailcoat and fitted gray breeches came to his feet, accepting the handshake heartily. "It's good to see you too."

"Thomas isn't the only one who's come to call. I hope you don't mind, darling."

Alex turned at the sound of a female voice approaching from behind him. "Clarissa . . ." He captured her slender, white-gloved fingers. "I wasn't expecting you back for another two weeks." Leaning over, careful not to muss her elegant silver-blue, satin-trimmed skirts, he kissed her cheek.

"Fortunately, Maxwell's improvement was more rapid than we'd anticipated." Maxwell Thornton was Clarissa Endicott's brother-in-law. He had fallen ill two months ago, so Clarissa had been staying with her sister, Margaret, in New York to await his recovery.

"Besides," she finished, rolling her pale-blue eyes, "Margaret can be such a trial." Tendrils of pale blond hair that escaped from smooth, carefully coiffed coils on each side of her face floated with the shake of her head. "I couldn't wait to get home."

"It's good to have you back," Alex said dutifully, and Clarissa smiled. She was a tall woman, fine-boned and sparsely built. She was pretty, in a straightforward sort of way.

Though she was English by birth, her family had arrived in Louisiana when she was a child. The Endicotts owned Elmtree, one of the larger neighboring sugar plantations. But they had made the majority of their fortune in the engraving business. Endicott and Company printed individual currency for most of the southern states, each with its own monetary value and differing rates of exchange.

Clarissa stepped back to look at Alex, noting the lines of fatigue beside his eyes, the tiredness no amount of pretense could hide.

"Still working late, I see." Her words rang with concern, but also a note of approval. The Endicotts believed in hard work. They'd built a dynasty over the years; Clarissa intended to see it grow and prosper.

"I meant to get in a little earlier, but with Fortier's note coming due, we're under a great deal of pressure." He never minced words with her. As the woman he would marry, she expected the truth and gave nothing less herself. It was part of their arrangement.

A servant appeared carrying two crystal snifters of brandy and a stemmed glass of sherry on a silver tray. Each of them picked up a glass, and they seated themselves in front of the marble-manteled fireplace, which with summer coming on was brightened by a spray of purple wisteria instead of a fire.

"It doesn't really seem fair," Thomas said. "François let the place run down so badly you've got to work fourteen hours a day just to get it back in shape."

Alex sighed and leaned back in his chair. "It really wasn't his fault. My father knew my brother's capabilities. François has never been interested in the family businesses. Father expected too much of him."

"As I understand it," Clarissa said in that no-nonsense way of hers, "your father needed you to manage his affairs in France, which left him very little choice."

"Yes," Alex agreed, "I suppose that's true."

"François is a self-indulgent, spoiled little boy," she said. "You're better off without him."

Alex forced back a denial. Though what she said was true, it was not her place to say so. Compassion wasn't one of Clarissa's virtues. "He's having some problems right now. He'll settle down."

"He'd better," she said. "After we're married, Belle Chêne and Elmtree will be one. I certainly don't expect him to be squandering Elmtree money the way he does yours."

A muscle bunched in Alex's jaw. Marriage to Clarissa wasn't going to be easy. But the advantages, at least as far as Belle Chêne and the du Villiers were concerned, far outweighed the obstacles.

"François is my responsibility, Clarissa, not yours." As his wife, Clarissa would have her say in family matters, that much was only fair, but the final decisions would be his. He had made that clear before they'd decided to marry. He was certain it wouldn't be the last time he would have to make his point.

Clarissa seemed to be weighing her next words. "You're right, darling, of course. And speaking of responsibilities, that's one of the things I wanted to discuss. Thomas, I'm glad you're here. I want all of this spelled out in detail; everything's to be completely legal.''

Alex arched a brow, but didn't speak. Clarissa was an intelligent woman. Whatever she had in mind would probably benefit both of them.

5

While Nicole waited impatiently for Patrick O'Flannery's return and their promised outing, she met Alex out at the stables four nights each week after supper. Though he never mentioned it, the other three nights he caught the steamboat into the city. Nicki didn't have to ask the reason.

Lisette. It galled her, though she tried to tell herself it shouldn't.

Alexandre du Villier had provided the first real home she'd known in years. What more could she ask? But each night after they finished with the horses and she returned her room, she knew. She wanted him to look at her as a woman. Wanted the friendship he had given her to grow into something more.

It was a fantasy, a dream that could never be. A duke would never involve himself with an indentured servant no matter what her family heritage had been.

Closing the door behind her, Nicki removed her mobcap, unbraided her hair and brushed it out, then removed the child's-length black-and-white uniform she had been given upon her arrival. Off went her petticoats, chemise, then the uncomfortable strips that bound her breasts. Thank God, she occupied the room alone. At least her secret remained safe.

But how much longer did she want it to? She was coming to trust Alexandre du Villier, coming to believe he might help her, maybe even release her from her contract. But where would she go? What would she do?

She'd been raised on a plantation, groomed to be a planter's wife. It was the woman's job to help with the family business, to make a home for her husband and children, and to look after the workers, the hundreds of people it took to make the miniature city run smoothly.

It was a hard job, but a rewarding one. She would have been good at it. Her mother had been an essential part of Meadowood, and she'd taught Nicole everything she knew.

Then, thanks to some tariff that had been passed, the bottom had fallen out of the sugar market, her parents had died, and Meadowood was gone. She was eighteen now and worse off than she'd been three years ago, when she'd first indentured herself. At least back then she'd had a goal, a plan to set her life back in order.

The Ramseys had promised to teach her accounting, a skill she had dabbled in on occasion and seemed to have a knack for. There were few women in the profession, but Nicole thought that with the small amount of money she would have coming at the end of her indenture, if she learned well enough, eventually she would find employment.

"God in heaven!"

Nicki whirled at the sound of the voice. Mrs. Leander stood in the open doorway, staring at Nicole's bare breasts, making the sign of the cross as if to ward off evil demons. She stepped inside and staunchly closed the door.

Nicki swallowed hard. "I—I didn't hear you knock."

A hurrumph was her reply. "All right, little missy, just what the devil is going on?"

Nicki pulled a soft cotton nightgown over her head, but without her bindings, it couldn't disguise the ample bulge of her breasts. "Please, Mrs. Leander. I was only trying to protect myself."

"Protect yourself? By deceiving us all? Pretending to be something you aren't?"

"I didn't set out to. It just sort of happened." Praying for the housekeeper's understanding, Nicki went on to explain about Lorna and her narrow escape from the guards at the prison. "Then it was time for the auction and Lorna thought I might be . . . well . . . spared ill treatment if I kept on pretending."

The older woman crossed herself again. "Lord have mercy. We do have a problem."

"Maybe it's just as well," Nicki countered. "M'sieur du Villier will have to find out the truth, sooner or later. It might as well be now."

"Are you daft?" The housekeeper's snowy brows shot up. "Miss Clarissa would never stand for you being here."

"Who's she?" *Not another of his mistresses!*

Mrs. Leander looked surprised. "Surely you're not so old you're hard a hearin'? Seems to me the servants are always talkin' about her, spoutin' off as to what a cold sort she is and how poor Master Alex is settin' himself up for a lifetime of grief."

"I guess I haven't been paying much attention lately."

"Miss Clarissa's the master's intended. She'll be runnin' Belle Chêne by the first of the year."

"What?"

"Soon as the hot weather is past, she's plannin' an outlandish affair to announce their engagement and the official date of the weddin'. Probably right after the harvest. Party's gonna cost a fortune, but since she's payin', I guess it doesn't hardly matter."

"He—he's getting married?" she repeated dumbly, still unable to believe it.

"That's what I said. And there's no way Miss Clarissa's gonna put up with the likes a you under Master Alex's roof." The housekeeper eyed her from the top of her copper hair to the small bare feet that peeped from the bottom of her nightshirt.

Nicole sank down on the bed. "If he sells me again, I'll just die." She twisted the folds of her nightshirt and stared at the hands she rested in her lap. "Belle Chêne is the only home I've had in years. I can't bear the thought of leaving—I just can't." Salty tears rolled down her cheeks.

Mrs. Leander sat down beside her. "Here, here, now. Master Alex wouldn't sell you to somebody cruel." Nicki only cried harder. Mrs. Leader cradled her head against one plump breast.

"It's all right, dearie, don't fret yourself so." She patted the top of Nicki's head. "If you're that set on stayin', we just won't let on for a while. Once the master and Clarissa are married and she's settled in, she'll probably let you stay. She's a practical sort. Master Alex paid handsomely for you. She'll want to earn back every cent."

That wasn't the most comforting thought, but at least she would be able to stay at Belle Chêne.

"Then you won't give me away?"

"Wouldn't dream of it. Wouldn't want to give Miss Clarissa the satisfaction of steppin' in. I'll deny I ever said it, but I think the master's makin' a bad mistake. He's a fine man. He deserves someone who'll love him, not just a woman who's marrying him to increase her holdin's and improve her social position."

"Alex doesn't believe in love."

"So it's Alex, is it?"

"I don't call him that. I just think of him that way."

"For your own sake, dear, you'd best not let your mind wander in that direction."

Nicki took a steadying breath and forced a smile she didn't feel. "You're right, of course." Mrs. Leander stood up and so did Nicole. "I won't forget your kindness."

Mrs. Leander frowned. "I hope it's a kindness I'll be doin'."

Nicki wondered what she meant.

The following day Patrick returned to Belle Chêne, pulling her thoughts away from Alex's coming marriage. A little adventure was what she needed to put things in perspective. How long had it been since she'd ridden free, done exactly what she wanted?

Eyes bright with anticipation, she met Patrick out at the stables just before midnight.

"I'm riding Napoleon," she announced without preamble.

"Are you daft? No one rides him but the duke."

"You said we wouldn't get caught. If we're going to do this, then I'm riding Napoleon."

Patrick scratched his head and looked uncertain. Then he grinned. "Ye've the spirit of the Irish, me girl," he said, exaggerating his accent. "Just don't say I didn't warn ye."

They saddled the horses, Nicki insisting on a sidesaddle, though Patrick seemed determined she should ride astride. "You'll break your damned fool neck in that contraption."

"I ride better this way," she said, not bothering to tell him she had ridden this way for years.

They led the horses into the trees behind the stable before they mounted, Patrick giving her a knee up, then swinging up himself. Napoleon, edgy and fighting the bit, danced and snorted, and it occurred to her he'd probably never been ridden this way before. She spoke to him softly and soon had him gentled and ready to go.

"Ye've got a way with 'im, lass." With a smile of approval, Patrick dug his heels into the tall black gelding he rode, and they were away, hooves thundering over the hard-packed earth.

Nicki couldn't remember a better night. With the stars above and the huge bay stallion responding to her every command, she felt more free than she had in years. After several hours of riding beside the cane fields, they stopped at a stream to give the horses a drink, dismounted, and dangled their bare feet in the water.

"You're a pretty one, lass," Patrick said to her. "You'll make a fine-lookin' woman one day."

"Thank you, Patrick."

"Make a fine wife, too, I'll wager, with your fancy talk and educated ways." He flashed her an approving glance and started to say something more, but

Napoleon whinnied, reminding them that the hour was late, and they decided it was time to head home.

Nicki was grateful. Patrick was at least two years younger than she, though he thought it was the other way around. He was a nice boy, someone she wanted to keep as a friend. She hoped he would be understanding when he found out she had been lying to him.

Fleetingly, it crossed her mind that Alex might not take her deception any better.

"I'll race you to the top of the rise," Patrick called after her once they were mounted and ready, and the horses thundered away. Running neck and neck through the first leg of the race, Napoleon, at Nicki's urging, took a downed fence and began to pull ahead. As they crossed a fallow field, he led by two lengths, running flat out, his ears laid back against his head, his neck stretched into the wind. The big bay stallion was enjoying the race as much as she was.

Laughing with the rush of victory, Nicki slowed him just before they reached the rise that overlooked the house and stables below.

"That felt wonderful!" she said. Reining the horses to a halt, they dismounted beneath an oak tree, giving the animals a chance to blow.

"You're really somethin', lass." Patrick looked at her with nothing short of awe.

"She's something, all right," said Alex, stepping from behind the tree. "A foolish little bit of baggage who's bound and determined to get herself killed."

Patrick swallowed so hard Nicki could hear it. "She—she's a fine rider, your grace. You taught her well."

"Take the horses back to the barn," Alex commanded him. "Sullivan wants a word with you." It was obvious the stable manager had more in mind than conversation.

"Yes, your grace."

"And don't call me that."

"No, your grace . . . I mean, no, sir."

Alex waited until Patrick led the horses away, then turned a hard look on Nicki, whose heart hammered so hard she could barely breathe.

"As for you, *ma petite* . . ." He gripped the top of her arms and pulled her up on her toes. "What in the name of God did you think you were doing? Napoleon is a very valuable animal. On top of that, he's dangerous. It's a wonder you didn't get yourself killed." He shook her—hard. "I ought to turn you over my knee and give you the thrashing you deserve. In fact . . ." He tightened his hold and glanced toward a fallen log, looking as if he meant to do just that.

Nicki's eyes went wide. His expression looked murderous. She could feel the power in his hands where they gripped her arms, read the anger in the set of his jaw. Suddenly she was back in the Laurent house, fending off her owner's heavy blows, fighting to ignore the pain, desperate not to show her fear. She whimpered and went limp in Alex's arms.

"Please don't hurt me," she pleaded, her voice filled with terror. "Please . . ."

Alex's hold gentled. He couldn't have touched her for the life of him. Her pretty aqua eyes had grown so huge they engulfed her pale face, and she was trembling all over. "Ah, *ma petite*. So brave one moment, so fearful the next. What in God's name have they done to you?"

She started to cry then, soft little sobs that pulled at his heart. He drew her into his arms and let her cry against his chest until the wetness touched his skin through the fabric of his shirt.

"It's all right," he soothed, brushing strands of copper hair from her tear-damp cheeks.

"I can't tell you I'm sorry. It felt wonderful to be free again, even for a night."

Alex pulled away. "Belle Chêne isn't a prison," he said gruffly. "And asking you not to steal my most valuable stallion is hardly asking too much."

"Don't say that—" She glanced up at him, meeting his hard look squarely. "I didn't steal him. I was only exercising him for you."

"You most certainly did that."

"If it displeases you so much, I'll promise not to do it again."

Alex felt the pull of a smile, but kept his voice stern. "You won't do it again because next time I'll carry out my threat. In the meantime, you'll work two extra hours a day for the next two weeks. And if you've done anything to Napoleon, you may still get that thrashing."

Nicki watched him from beneath her thick, dark lashes. He was mad all right, furious in fact. But his expression showed concern. Had Alex been worried about her?

"Now get back to the house," he finished.

Alex watched her run down the hill. *What was it about her?* He'd been furious when, unable to sleep, he'd wandered out to the stables and found Napoleon gone. He hadn't believed for an instant the horse had been stolen, but he never would have guessed who was riding him.

When he'd seen her racing the stable boy over the hill toward the rise, he couldn't quite believe his eyes. She had learned well, better than he could possibly have imagined. Still, Napoleon was not a horse to be trifled with. That the animal had accepted the strange new saddle at all surprised him. Then to be controlled by someone her size . . . well, she'd been lucky this time, but she might not be so lucky the next.

He probably should have given her the licking she deserved. The next time she got the urge to go riding off in the middle of the night, she would have something to remind her not to!

Alex scoffed at himself. Since when had he begun to discipline the servants? He must be losing his mind. The girl was getting to him—making him feel protective in a way he hadn't before.

Alex shook his head. That Nicki was special he had no doubt. For the most part, he was glad he had bought her contract after all. She deserved a chance in life, a chance to better herself. If it weren't for the growing attraction he felt for her, he wouldn't give her employment at Belle Chêne a second thought.

As it was, however, every time he looked at her, he felt a little like Valcour Fortier. He kept wondering how her body would look once she filled out, how her shiny copper hair would look unbraided and draped around her shoulders.

Three years, he told himself. In three years you can make her your mistress. With the problems Belle Chêne was facing, his upcoming marriage, the tension between him and his brother, which they seemed unable to resolve, and the hard work it took just to run the plantation, he'd be so busy that three years wouldn't be so long.

Nicole didn't see much of Alex for the next two weeks. He worked long, tiring hours in the cane fields, and thanks to her midnight foray, she had extra duties as well. Once, when she'd seen him out on the veranda where she was sweeping, she had purposely avoided him.

It wasn't that she was sorry for what she'd done—her wild night of freedom had been worth it. What bothered her was the way she'd behaved in front of him.

How could I have let him see me that way? She should have taken whatever punishment Alex handed out and never said a word. Whatever he would have done to her would have been finished there and then, and her self-respect would have remained intact. Instead she'd behaved like a coward.

It wouldn't have happened if she hadn't picked that particular moment to remember Armand Laurent, the cloth merchant who had bought her contract from the Ramseys. Laurent had taught her the meaning of fear. His drunken episodes had left her battered and bruised, with cracked ribs and broken bones, and constantly in terror of when it would happen again.

Then had come Adrian Paxton. The beautiful dark-haired woman had never physically abused Nicole, but in lying about the stolen brooch and sending her to prison, had demonstrated just as clearly the power one human being could wield against another.

That was then and this is now, Nicki told herself firmly. You're Etienne St. Claire's daughter. You're not in prison anymore, and even if you were, it's time you remember just exactly who you are. She prayed she'd be able to live up to her convictions, but even if she failed, she felt better having made the commitment.

By the following Monday, she was back to her normal work schedule. Out behind the stables, where she sat beneath an oak tree to lunch on some meat and cheese, she spotted Alex striding toward her.

"I thought I might find you here," he said, surprising her.

"You were looking for me?"

"I've missed you," he teased. He looked as handsome as ever in his tight beige riding breeches and snowy linen shirt. His flat-brimmed planter's hat shaded his dark-brown eyes from the sun.

Nicki's cheeks felt warm and her heartbeat had speeded up the moment she had seen him walking toward her. She wanted to tell him she'd missed him, too, but didn't.

"I've got to ride out to the sugar mill in about an hour. I thought you might like to go along. You'd get a chance to ride again, and I think you'd find it interesting."

It sounded wonderful. She couldn't tell him she'd spent hours in her family's mill at Meadowood. Her favorite night of the year had been the harvest celebration—the sugarhouse ball—where all the workers and their families drank rum or syllabub, a mixture of white wine and whipped cream, and danced until dawn amidst the vats of drying sugar.

She wanted desperately to say yes, but shook her head instead. "Today's Monday. I've got floors to sweep and beds to change—"

"I told them I needed your help for a couple of hours."

Nicki smiled. "In that case, I'd love to go."

With a sweeping glance that made her suddenly short of breath, Alex's dark eyes raked her from head to foot. She would have given two more years of servitude to be wearing a beautiful gown instead of her dowdy black uniform.

"Why don't you go in and change?"

Into what? she thought, suddenly angry. He knew she had nothing else to wear. "I'm afraid this will have to do." She lifted her chin. "If I'm going to embarrass you, maybe I shouldn't go."

Alex smiled indulgently. "I asked Mrs. Leander to have a few things made for you. She told me this morning they were finished. You'll find them upstairs in your room."

Her expression must have been priceless. "You're giving me new clothes?"

"They're waiting for you upstairs."

Nicki felt an ache in her throat. Alex had been thinking about her, concerned for her. She smiled at him, hoping it would tell him more than her words. "Thank you. That was very thoughtful."

"You'd better hurry."

Nicki nodded and headed toward the house, grateful he'd asked the one person who knew her secret. She would love the childish outfits, even if they did look silly, and Mrs. Leander would see they were loose enough in the bodice to hide her curves.

She reached her room to discover the dresses were even worse than she'd imagined. There was a soft-yellow muslin and a pale-pink bastiste, each with matching wide-brimmed bonnets. The dresses would have been lovely, except for the excess of ruffles on the bertha, which covered the front, and the too-short skirts, the youthful length emphasized by an underskirt of frilly white lace. Beside them on the bed, a pair of long white pantalets, trimmed with ruffles at the bottom would show beneath the hem.

Nicki grimaced at the thought. How she yearned to dress like a woman again, to feel like a woman. Her bindings seemed tighter and more uncomfortable than ever. Then she noticed the simple navy-blue riding habit at the opposite end of the bed. The bodice was loose, but only narrow rows of tiny self-tucks decorated the front. It was short, but no ruffled underskirt emphasized the fact. And there was a small, matching narrow-brimmed navy-blue hat to complete the outfit.

Nicki held it up to her and twirled in front of the small wood-framed mirror above the simple oak dresser. These were the first new clothes she'd had in years. Alex had been thoughtful enough to buy them.

Hurriedly, she put on the riding habit, the jaunty little hat, and headed down the back stairs. Alex had the horses saddled and ready. Hers was a tall chestnut gelding.

"I thought you might find Maximillian more to your taste than Orange Blossom."

"He's beautiful," she said, stroking the horse's sleek dark neck.

Alex cleared his throat. *She's too young for what you're thinking*, he reminded himself, discovering the horse wasn't the only thing of beauty he could see. He almost wished he hadn't ordered the dresses. This one set off Nicki's smooth complexion, the shiny copper color of her hair. She looked young, and then again she didn't. He shouldn't have asked her to go along, he realized, deciding he wouldn't again make that mistake.

But she was smiling at him with such anticipation that he couldn't back out now.

"Thank you for the dresses," she said as she climbed atop the big stone mounting block and situated herself in the sidesaddle as if she'd done it a thousand times. "They're the first new clothes I've had in years."

"You're welcome." Alex swung up on Napoleon's back. They moved off toward a road that skirted the swamp behind the big plantation house.

"Belle Chêne means 'beautiful oak,'" Alex said. "My father named it for that huge tree near the entrance."

"It's a lovely name. Perfect, I think."

Alex seemed pleased. "Most plantations front a river or bayou," he explained as they rode along. "The refined sugar is transported from here by boat into the docks at New Orleans. The price is negotiated by a man called a *factor*. He gets the best possible price and manages all the money."

"Sort of an accountant."

Alex smiled. "Yes, but with a lot more responsibility."

Nicki nodded her understanding. The *whir* of birds winging up from the swamp drew their attention to a great white egret, his graceful neck and beak extended, his wings flapping in slow precision as they carried him aloft.

"The swamp is as necessary to the sugar business as the river," Alex went on. "It's where we get the wood we need for the fires that burn beneath the sugar vats. We also use it to drain the excess water from the fields."

Nicki smiled at him encouragingly. She hated to pretend she didn't know these things, but Alex seemed to be enjoying her interest so much she didn't want to stop him. "How do they go about planting?"

"It's done in the springtime. The workers plow rows about six feet apart. Stalks of seed cane are laid in six-inch-deep furrows. New cane comes up from each joint of the cane."

"When do they harvest?"

"Not until fall. Between October and December, depending upon when the sugar content is right. But if you wait too long, the frost can be ruinous."

She loved the sound of his voice—low and resonant, and touched by a trace of the French he had been raised with. It was a masculine voice, one that made her warm inside just to hear it.

They rode along the dirt road between the four-foot-high rows of cane. As far as she could see up the road, cane stalks waved like an emerald sea, a curtain of green that shut out all who did not belong. Black-skinned workers toiled alongside Irish immigrants who were paid a dollar a day for their back-breaking labor.

"The road doubles back between the fields and winds up down by the river," Alex told her. "The mill is built close to the water so that the sugar barrels are easy to load onto the steamboats." They broke into an easy canter, Alex allowing her to practice her riding skills, and soon came upon the sugarhouse.

It was a great barnlike structure, bigger than the one at Meadowood, and a cluster of heavy machinery like nothing she'd seen stood off to one side. Half a dozen workers swarmed around the machinery, while others hammered and nailed from inside the building.

"We're doing some reconstruction," Alex explained. "Modernizing the mill." He dismounted and helped her down, his big hands circling her waist. Nicki tried not to notice how warm and strong they felt.

"By the time the cane is harvested, it's over six feet tall. It's quite impressive to watch the workers using their big billhook machetes—one stroke to cut the blades from the stalk, a sweep across the top, then one across the bottom. Afterward, the cane is loaded onto two-wheeled carts and brought to the sugarhouse, where it's dumped into the crushing press. Up until now, mules provided the power to turn the heavy stones used to squeeze the juice from the bagasse—that's the fibrous material that's left over. We're installing a steam engine to take over the job. It should be a lot more efficient."

"What happens after the juice is crushed out?"

"It's drained into a series of vats where the water is boiled away and the impurities drained off. We're planning some improvements there as well."

Nicki smiled. "I'm quite impressed, m'sieur. Where did you get all these modern ideas?"

Alexandre smiled back. "Why don't you call me Alex? At least when we are alone."

"All right. Alex."

He seemed to approve of the way she said it. "I spent a year at L'Ecole Polytechnique in Paris. That's where I met Norbert Rillieux. He's been working here at Belle Chêne, helping to oversee the changes."

"Such as . . . ?" By now Nicki was truly curious.

Her father had mentioned reading about experiments using charcoal to refine the sugar to a whiter color than they were currently able to produce, which would bring an increase in price. He'd also told her about the increasing use of chemicals—acids and bases—to more accurately predict when the sugar content was highest.

"M'sieur Rillieux has invented something called a 'vacuum system,'" Alex explained. "It's still in the experimental stages, but he believes—and so do I— that it'll make our whole operation more efficient, and therefore more profitable."

"There would seem to be a certain risk involved in something still unproven," Nicki said.

Alex smiled. "You have a good mind, *ma petite.* There is a risk, of course. But I'm convinced the plan will work." *Nom de Dieu,* it had better. If the new equipment failed to increase production and the quality of the sugar itself, thereby bringing in more money, the du Villier family would lose Belle Chêne as well as their estates in France. Even François didn't know how close they were to financial ruin.

"I hope I'm not interrupting." The voice behind them, cold and reserved, belonged to Valcour Fortier. "I heard about the work you were doing here. Very innovative. Thought I'd drop by and take a look for myself."

His eyes took in the two of them and a knowing expression crept over his hawklike features. "I compliment your . . . judgment, Alexandre. She was worth the money after all."

"Back off, Valcour. It isn't what you're thinking." *At least, not yet.* Alex felt a moment of guilt at his intentions, even if they were some years away.

"Whatever you say, *mon ami.*" Fortier chuckled softly, but his hard, dark eyes raked Nicki from head to toe.

There was no mistaking his thoughts. Unconsciously, Nicki stepped a little closer. It was all Alex could do to keep from putting his arm around her in a gesture of protection.

"Have a look, Fortier," Alex told him, pointing toward the heavy equipment. "You might learn something useful."

Fortier did not seem amused.

Guiding Nicki back toward the horses, Alex lifted her up on the sidesaddle, then swung up on Napoleon. Fortier headed toward the heavy equipment being installed as the two of them rode away.

"I don't like him," Nicki said when they reached the stables.

"Stay away from him," Alex warned. "He'd like nothing better than to carry you off with him. He's an unscrupulous bastard."

"Surely he wouldn't . . ." But the expression on Alex's face said that's exactly what he would do.

"His plantation, Feliciana, borders ours. He rides the boundaries quite often. Just be careful if you happen to be out there alone."

"I don't have a horse. How could I possibly—"

Alex pinned her with a glance. "That didn't stop you before."

Nicki didn't answer. He was too damnable perceptive. She would ride again, and they both knew it. But next time she wouldn't ride Napoleon—and she wouldn't get caught.

"I'd better be getting back to work," she told him after Patrick led the horses away.

Alex nodded, and she wondered at his thoughts. He headed off toward the house. Nicki took a different path leading in the same direction. When she rounded the corner toward the servants' entrance, she glanced toward the wide front porch and stopped dead-still in her tracks.

Across the way, smiling up at Alex, the blond-haired woman in the modish green day dress had to be Clarissa.

6

Nicole stood transfixed at the side of the house. She knew she should keep on walking; it was dangerous for Clarissa to catch the slightest glimpse of her. Still, her feet refused to move.

Alex bent over Clarissa's gloved hand, touching it briefly to his lips in gentlemanly accord. His posture was exactly correct. Gone was the easy grace, the almost arrogant nonchalance that had been his manner just a short while before.

Clarissa, a blond-haired, slender, proper-looking woman, laughed at something Alex said, then accepted the arm he extended, and they walked across the oyster-shell drive toward the veranda, where Danielle was busily sweeping. Engrossed in her task, the plump little maid didn't notice the pair until her broom swept into the full silk skirts of Clarissa's pale-green day dress.

"What do you think you're doing?" Clarissa demanded.

"Pardonnez-moi, mademoiselle," Danielle squeaked, breaking out of her trance.

"Speak English, you fool."

Alex bristled, though he often made the same request. "She said she was sorry. She just didn't see us."

"Why don't you watch what you're doing?" Clarissa railed at Danielle, ignoring the sharpness in Alex's voice. "You may as well learn to pay attention now. In a few more months you'll be taking orders from me. I won't allow such slovenly behavior."

"Clarissa," Alex warned, his voice even harder. "Danielle said she was sorry. What more do you want?"

"Danielle?" she repeated, incredulous. "Just how well do you know this girl?"

"Her mother worked here for some years before she died," Alex explained, though he seemed loath to do so. "Danielle's engaged to one of the grooms at Feliciana. As soon as they marry, Valcour will make a place for her there."

Clarissa appraised Danielle from top to bottom, taking in her overripe figure, the rosy hue of her pretty but slightly moon-shaped face, far less delicate than her own. Danielle's fingers still clutched the broom, her knuckles white with tension. Careful to keep her eyes fixed on the ground, she dropped into a curtsy.

"I am a very hard worker, Mademoiselle Endicott. I will not be any trouble."

"You'd better not be." With a last warning glance at Danielle, Clarissa turned back to Alex, who looked none too pleased. "She just needs a little supervision," Clarissa told him with a smile that said the subject was closed. Resuming her hold on his arm, she let him guide her into the house.

Nicki sagged against the corner of the building.

How in God's name could Alex saddle himself with a woman like that? If he meant to bring Clarissa Endicott to heel, he certainly had his work cut out. Why, the lady was one of the most obnoxious, overbearing females she had ever seen!

One more thought occurred—Mrs. Leander was obviously correct. If Clarissa Endicott found out Nicole was a mature, unattached female, she'd be sold again. Nicki shuddered at the thought. Still, as she headed off toward the kitchen, she wondered just how meek and mannerly she could be when dealing with Alex's wife.

And just how well she would handle the fact when Alex was a married man.

For the next few weeks the days heated up and the humidity increased. Still, Nicki was used to the long, hot summers, and the big plantation house had been designed to capture the cool river breeze.

Clarissa stopped by occasionally to begin the early stages of her coming engagement ball. She had decided to hold the soiree in late September, since the fever season would be at an end and those planters who had left for the summer would have returned to their homes. Dedicated to Elmtree as much as Alex was to Belle Chêne, Clarissa was spending the hot summer months running her plantation.

"She's picked Belle Chêne for the party," Mrs. Leander told Nicki, "'cause she wants to impress the high society folks. The ballroom's a whole lot bigger and far grander than her own."

Though she came to the house several times, Clarissa rarely saw Alexandre, since he was busy with his extensive work on the sugar mill. Once or twice

Nicole had crossed paths with her, but Clarissa, who rarely spoke to the servants directly, had barely noticed. Usually she just instructed Mrs. Leander in the tasks she wanted done and went on as though the rest of them didn't exist.

It broke Nicki's heart to think of Alex married to a woman like that. After all, she rationalized, she and Alex had become friends of a sort; she just wanted to see him happy. The unfamiliar feelings that twisted her stomach into knots whenever she saw the pair together was nothing more than dislike, an instinct that the two were ill-suited.

She wished she could come right out and tell Alex he was making a mistake, but it was hardly her place. And since their ride to the sugar mill, he always seemed to be leaving about the time she arrived, or too busy to spare a moment for conversation.

She hadn't seen him for two weeks when she received a summons to the kitchen and was informed she would be helping to serve the evening meal. She was also cautioned that Clarissa would be in attendance, as well as François, and Thomas Demming.

So far, the day had been cooler than most, the night breeze fresh and pleasant. Maybe she would take a walk along the river when she finished, she thought, shoving open the door to the dining room.

"How is the work on the mill progressing?" François asked Alex as Nicki helped serve the first dish, a delicious-looking mock turtle soup.

"As well as can be expected." Alex glanced up at her just before she placed the gilded porcelain soup bowl in front of him. She could feel his eyes on her, his expression warm with greeting though no words were spoken. "It's a major task, but we've got the best men possible for the job."

"I'm sure everything will be ready on schedule," Clarissa put in. "Alex never disappoints."

"You can always count on Alex," François added with a sarcasm impossible to ignore.

"Why must you constantly act like a spoiled little boy?" Clarissa chided. "Surely you have better things to do than make snide remarks to the brother who has done nothing but try to help you."

François's face turned red. "Oh, he helps me all right. Helps me to be a sniveling dependent."

"François . . ." Alex began.

"Don't humor him, Alex. You're far too lenient as it is. If he were my brother, I should simply cut his purse strings. It's amazing how quickly one's 'sniveling dependents' fall back in line."

"This isn't the place, Clarissa," Thomas Demming softly warned.

François cleared his throat. "Thomas is right," he agreed in the first show of maturity Nicki had seen. "Please accept my apology, Alex." A look of contrition replaced the hostility in François's boyishly handsome face—as well as another emotion Nicole assessed as despair.

When François glanced at Alex, his features were schooled once more into indifference, but Nicki believed Alex had sensed his brother's turbulent emotions even as François had tried to hide them. What was going on between the two? Did Alex understand his brother's feelings, or was he just as baffled as Nicki was?

The conversation continued somewhat stiltedly through the main courses of the meal, a baked fillet of fish, sweetbreads glazed with French peas, and a roast quail larded with jelly. As each sumptuous dish was served and cleared away by the servants, Nicole kept the water goblets filled. She had just reached Clarissa when the squat, middle-aged black man who was removing her plate overturned a half-full goblet of white wine, spilling several drops on Clarissa's apricot satin skirt.

"You clumsy oaf—what is your name?" She dabbed furiously at the few damp spots with her white linen napkin.

"Joshua, ma'am. I's awful sorry."

"I daresay, Alex, your servants are much in need of discipline."

"Need I remind you—"

"Joshua, you'll work a full day on Saturday," Clarissa interrupted. "Next time you'll be more careful."

"Saturday's my little boy's birf'day," Josh pleaded. "I promised him—"

"It's all right, Josh," Alex told him.

"It isn't all right," Clarissa cut in. "Your servants must learn proper behavior—and the sooner the better."

For the love of God, who does she think she is? Nicki could barely keep the words from sliding off her tongue. When Clarissa started ranting her displeasure again, it was more than Nicole could stand. With a grim smile of satisfaction, she lifted the water pitcher and dumped the contents in Clarissa Endicott's lap.

The room fell silent.

"What . . . what . . . ?" Clarissa leapt to her feet, the high-backed chair crashing to the floor behind her. "Who is this . . . this . . . ill-mannered child?"

The expression on Alex's face was priceless. He seemed torn between laughter and fury. François and Thomas Demming both looked ready to explode.

"My name is Nicki Stockton." How she'd love to tell the spiteful woman the truth.

"Your parents must have been ill-bred, ignorant boors." Clarissa mopped furiously at her skirts. "You will apologize this minute."

A moment ago Nicki would have. It seemed little price to pay for such a triumph. Now, with the slur against her family, that was impossible. "No" was all she said.

"What?"

Nicole glanced across at Alex, whose stunned expression now looked grim.

"Apologize, Nicki," he warned, "then go to your room."

"I won't apologize. This odious woman has slandered my family. But I'll be more than happy to leave." With a swish of her too-short, childish-looking skirts, she headed toward the door.

Alex shoved back his chair and came to his feet. "Nicki!" he called after her.

"I'm not leaving without an apology," Clarissa stated flatly.

"And you shall have it—that much I promise you!" With those parting words he followed Nicki into the pantry, catching up to her before she could reach the back stairs. Wordlessly, he gripped her arm and tugged her down the hall toward his study. Once inside, he resolutely closed the door.

"Need I remind you that you are a servant in this house?" Alex said harshly.

"I know, Alex. I just couldn't stand to see that woman—"

Alex cursed. "From now on you will address me as M'sieur du Villier."

"Yes, m'sieur." He was madder than she'd thought.

"I won't go so far as to say Clarissa didn't deserve exactly what she got." He almost smiled. "But it's hardly your place to decide. Clarissa Endicott will soon be my wife. You'll have to learn to get along with her sooner or later."

"As will you, m'sieur," she reminded him.

"Exactly." But he certainly didn't look happy about it. "Now, you'll go back in there and apologize and that will be the end of it."

"I can't do that."

Alex's eyes turned dark. "And just why the hell not?" His mouth had thinned to a narrow line, and a muscle bunched in his jaw. The old, familiar fear began to curl in Nicki's stomach.

"Because she has insulted my family. Aside from that, she doesn't deserve it. I have no intention of apologizing to that horrible woman—not now, not ever."

Alex grabbed her arms and dragged her against his chest. He glowered down at her until her knees felt weak. "You are my responsibility. I have given my word that you'll apologize and that's exactly what you will do."

Nicole shook her head. "I won't and there's nothing you can do to make me. You may beat me if you like, it won't change a thing."

Alex looked ready to murder her. "Beat you? That's the best idea you've had since I met you." He tightened his hold on her arm and dragged her toward the tufted leather sofa in front of the fireplace. This time when her face paled, and she looked ready to faint, he didn't weaken.

"I should have done this before," he said, draping her across his knees and pinning her against his muscular thighs.

This time she refused to beg for mercy. She felt her skirts being raised, then the room darkened as they billowed around her head, cutting off the lamp light. Nicki closed her eyes, torn between embarrassment and determination. At least she hadn't cowered in fear as before.

Barely able to contain his fury, Alex tightened his hold on Nicki's tiny waist, raised his hand—then stopped its descent in midair. One glance at the figure across his knees and Alex saw not the narrow, bony hips of a little girl, but the full, lush curves of a woman. Even the thin white cotton drawers couldn't disguise her tantalizing bottom. Her narrow waist he'd noticed before, but the roundness of the tight little derriere that had been hidden beneath her skirts he hadn't even imagined. Now that he knew, it was almost more than he could stand.

Nicki wasn't a woman—and yet she was. It was infuriating—maddening! Alex felt a rush of blood to his loins—which only enraged him more.

With an anger directed more at himself than at her, he jerked Nicki's skirts back down and hauled her to her feet. Her face was flushed with embarrassment, but she seemed no less determined than before.

"You're going to apologize one way or another," he

commanded, tugging her to the door. "Mrs. Leander," he bellowed, "see that she doesn't leave her room until she's ready to apologize to Mademoiselle Endicott."

Her expression said she'd be in there till·spring.

"She's to have nothing but bread and water," he added, deciding lack of food ought to bring her around if nothing else would.

To Nicki he said, "You don't run this house, I do. I know she deserved it, but that doesn't alleviate the problem. Sooner or later you'll have to face her. I want it to be sooner." With that he stormed toward the dining room, only to find Clarissa had taken her leave.

"She says she won't return until you've put your servants in their proper place," Thomas told him.

"Damn," Alex muttered.

François chuckled softly. "I'd have paid a thousand francs to see Clarissa get her comeuppance. Thank God you invited me tonight."

"Don't push it," Alex warned.

"Since our dinner seems to have lost its appeal," Thomas put in smoothly, "what do you two say to a trip into the Quarter? We can still make the nine o'clock boat if we hurry."

Alex latched on to the idea like a prisoner reprieved from the guillotine. He'd spend the next few days with Lisette. He didn't want to see Nicki suffer, nor make her embarrassment more acute. When he returned in a few days, the apology would have been rendered, the entire incident would be behind them, and things would be back to normal.

After a few brief instructions to Mrs. Leander, including orders for Nicki to be taken to Elmtree as soon as she had seen reason, the men were on their way.

"You seem distracted, *mon chéri.*" Lisette ran a long-nailed finger down his spine.

They lay naked and sated on the big four-poster bed that had once belonged to his father. Except for the bed, which Alex had insisted upon, the chamber they shared in his town house, a room he'd allowed Lisette to furnish, was overdecorated and gaudy. Ruffles seemed to fill every nook and cranny. Sometimes he felt as if he might choke on them.

"It's time I went home," he told her. "There's always so much to do." In truth he'd discovered that three days with Lisette was far too long. They'd made love again and again, though each time he felt less satisfied than before. By the time he'd eased out of her this morning, he'd begun to wonder why he bothered. Maybe it was time he found someone new.

Alex brushed the notion aside. It would be expensive and time-consuming to farm out his current mistress and set up another. Besides, there was no one at present who intrigued him—except a child-woman he could not have.

At least he'd come to a decision about Nicki. His grandmother would be arriving from France in a couple of weeks to spend some time and attend the engagement ball. Together they could choose a proper boarding school for Nicki. When she returned to Belle Chêne in a few years time, if he still felt so inclined, he could make her his mistress.

"I wish you would stay a little longer," Lisette said, throwing him what she believed was a devastating pout.

He doubted she meant the words. He'd ridden her long and hard this time. Demanded more and been less considerate than usual. She looked well-used and was probably a little bit sore.

"I think you're not so sorry to see me go," he said, allowing himself a smile.

"You do not need to gloat. It is unbecoming."

Alex finished dressing, and Lisette followed him downstairs. She kissed him passionately, as if to insure his return. It was the furthest thing from Alex's mind.

Making his way along the still-quiet cobblestone streets, the first rays of dawn beginning to heat the damp summer air, he reached the docks well before the first boat headed upriver. A short time later, he arrived at Belle Chêne.

Though the hour was still early, the grounds stirred with early morning activity as workers began their morning chores. After checking with Mrs. Leander, he'd have time for a full day's work in the fields, then be able to spend the evening catching up on the paperwork in his study.

Already dressed in riding breeches and a clean white shirt, clothes he kept at his town house, Alex pulled open the carved mahogany door and strode into the entry of the big white plantation house.

The butler, a tall black man named Frederick who was always cheerful, accepted his white flat-brimmed hat with little more than a nod. Hanging it on the gilded rack beside the door, he quietly walked away.

Danielle scurried past with her eyes cast down and not so much as a smile.

Lemuel, his aging valet, greeted him briefly at the foot of the stairs but seemed unusually concerned with a scuff on the toe of one shiny black shoe. When Alex dismissed him, he merely shuffled away.

"Mrs. Leander!" Alex shouted, bringing the buxom woman on the run. "What the hell's going on around here?"

"Well . . ."

"If something's happened, why wasn't I notified? It wasn't as if you didn't know where I was."

"That's just it, sir. Nothing's happened."

"If nothing's happened, why is everyone looking so glum?"

Mrs. Leander wrung her hands, a gesture of worry Alex had rarely seen. "It's the little miss, sir. She's been in her room for nigh on three days."

"She's what?"

"At first we did as you asked. I mean, we took her nothin' but bread and water. By yesterday she looked so pitiful, I . . . well, I took her up a tray of supper." Mrs. Leander squared her shoulders as if she dared him to disapprove.

"Go on."

"She wouldn't eat it. Says it's a matter of honor, sir. Says you bein' a man of honor yourself, you ought to understand."

Alex swore a string of oaths beneath his breath, then took the stairs up to Nicki's third-floor room two at a time. He knocked only briefly before he opened the door to find her propped in the window seat, reading a book of Shakespeare's sonnets. It surprised him she should be so well educated, though it probably shouldn't have.

"M'sieur du Villier," she said, "how good of you to drop by."

"You look terrible." Alex strode toward her. Though her eyes still shone with their incredible aqua lights, her skin looked waxy, and she'd definitely lost some weight. Alex felt rotten. He hadn't meant for this to happen, had been sure she'd give in just as soon as she knew he was gone.

"You've got to start eating," he said with careful control, fighting an urge to comfort her. He wished he could say he was sorry.

"Is that an order?"

"*Merde.* You damned well better believe it's an order." Picking up the tray of untouched food Mrs. Leander had left the night before, he carried it over to the bed. From beneath the white linen cloth, he tore off a chunk of bread and spread a slab of soft yellow cheese across it.

"Eat this," he commanded.

Nicki felt her throat begin to close. "Anything but bread," she said softly.

Alex felt another stab of guilt. "How about this?" He handed her an apple.

Nicki smiled and nodded. Accepting the bright red fruit, she bit down hard, savoring the sweet juices. Alex went to the door and called for Danielle to bring up a breakfast tray.

"You're a stubborn bit of baggage," he said, returning to her side.

"I knew you'd understand," Nicki told him, "sooner or later. There are some things a person just can't compromise."

Alex's smile faded. "That's where you're wrong— there are times a person *must* compromise."

Nicki looked up at him but didn't speak.

"I want you to eat a good solid meal. Afterward, there'll be a carriage waiting to take you to Elmtree."

Nicki set the apple aside, unable to swallow the bite that had suddenly lodged in her throat. Alex hadn't understood at all; he had merely changed tactics. "I can't do that," she whispered.

Alex said something she didn't quite catch, then his expression changed to one of appeal. "Not even for me?" With a soft half smile, he ran a finger along her cheek.

His words, and the rush of warmth that raced down her spine, were almost her undoing. Almost, but not quite. She was a St. Claire. She'd been protecting a friend and giving just deserts to a woman long overdue. And Clarissa Endicott had slandered her parents. She wouldn't back down no matter the price.

She shook her head. "Not even for you."

Alex's features turned hard. "I've given my word. You'll apologize just as I've instructed or—"

"Or?"

"Or tomorrow I shall sell you to Valcour Fortier."

Nicki felt as if the world had stopped spinning, and she had careened off the edge. "You wouldn't do that."

He looked at her hard. "I'm afraid I would."

She didn't believe him, couldn't believe him—and yet. . . . She had trusted and been hurt too many times to rely on her instincts. She couldn't afford to take the chance. Tears filled her eyes but she refused to let them fall.

"I shall do as you wish," she said softly. A tear rolled down her cheek, but she wiped it away with the back of her hand. Moving past Alex as if he weren't there, she ignored Danielle, with her heavily laden breakfast tray, ignored the smell of porridge and bacon that made her stomach rumble mercilessly, and walked to the stairs.

Though Alex had hoped she'd eat something first, he didn't stop her. Instead he ordered a carriage brought around, and in minutes, Ukiah, who had returned to Belle Chêne from the town house, had the horses whipped up and rolling down the hot, dusty lane out of sight.

As he watched them disappear along the River Road beneath the hot summer sun, Alex pondered his decision. Maybe he should have told her the truth— that it appeared more likely each day that the very survival of Belle Chêne depended on this marriage. He had hoped he wouldn't have to accept the financial proposition that Clarissa had laid out, but the new equipment was taking longer than expected to install, and the exceptionally dry summer weather had hindered the crops. Maybe if Nicki understood . . .

Nom de Dieu, what in God's name was the matter with him? He didn't have to answer to a servant! The girl was a handful. More than a handful. He'd be glad to see her go. Maybe the school she'd be attending would get rid of her stubbornness and teach her to be submissive. He pictured her that way, meek and pliable, and didn't like the image.

You had no choice, he reminded himself. But he'd never forget her look of disillusionment, the betrayal she'd felt when he'd threatened to sell her to Fortier. He hadn't meant it, of course, but he'd run out of options.

At least the matter was ended. In an hour Nicki would be home and their argument eventually forgotten.

Only, Nicki didn't come home.

7

Alex spent the day in the fields, returning just before dusk. He was hot and tired and brooding. All he'd thought about was Nicki and the way she had stood up to him. He was proud of her, he realized, regretting more than ever that he hadn't just told her the truth.

Then again, maybe the truth wouldn't have swayed her. Belle Chêne was his home. It meant everything to him and the sons he would one day entrust it to. Why should a young girl understand how important it was to him? Why should she bend to his wishes? Yet instinctively he knew if he had made his reasons clear she would have.

"Where is she?" he asked the moment he arrived at the house, barreling through the front door so hard the crystal beads on the chandelier did a dance above his head.

Mrs. Leander looked concerned but resigned. "She isn't back yet. Neither is the carriage."

"What?"

"Don't get all fired up. You know Miss Clarissa.

She probably set the girl some task as a punishment for her behavior. I doubt it'll do her much harm."

It sounded so like Clarissa that Alex knew the housekeeper was right. *"Nom de Dieu*, that woman will be the death of me yet." He moved toward his study, thinking to pour himself a drink, Mrs. Leander trailing behind. "I should have gone with her." He lifted the crystal stopper from a decanter of brandy and poured himself a liberal dose. "If she isn't back before dark, I'm going after her." He downed the brandy in a single swallow.

Mrs. Leander nodded her understanding. "I'll let you know the minute I spot the carriage."

Nicole wearily opened the door of the stylish black phaeton that Ukiah had driven around to the service entrance. Before her foot touched the first rung, he was there to help her down. A worried frown lined his face, but his grip felt steady and strong.

She thanked God for it—it was all she could do to stand up. Her clothes were soaked with perspiration and clinging to her body. Her stomach had stopped grumbling and started to roll uneasily. Strands of her hair had come loose and were plastered to the back of her neck. The strips that bound her breasts, soaked clear through, had chaffed her skin red and raw.

"Mista Alex ain't goin' like dis, no sir."

"I don't want him to know." Nicki fought her trembling hands and the pain that throbbed unbearably every time she moved them. "Promise me you won't tell him."

Ukiah looked away.

"Promise me."

"If dat's what you want, I won't say nothin'. But dat don' mean I think it's right."

"Thank you, Ukiah."

The black man helped her into the warming pantry, which, thank the Lord, was empty, and she headed toward the servants' stairs at the back of the room. The door that led to the main part of the house flew open, stopping her on the second stair.

For a moment Alex just stood there, as if he couldn't quite believe his eyes. "What in God's name has happened to you?" He strode across the room, his long legs carrying him to her side in the time it took to reply.

"Please, m'sieur, I'm afraid I'm not feeling very well." She wet her parched lips. "If you wouldn't mind, could we continue this conversation a little later?"

"Tell me what happened."

"Nothing, m'sieur. Please, I must go. . . ."

Alex caught her just as her knees buckled beneath her. Swearing in both French and English, he scooped her into his arms and strode up the stairs. "Mrs. Leander!" he bellowed.

Nicki wrapped her arms around his thick neck and clung to him. It was hard not to remember the time he had held her this way before.

"I'll ruin your clothes," she said softly as he reached the landing, worried about her soggy garments.

"To hell with my clothes."

When he turned down the hall instead of heading up the third-floor stairs, she looked at him oddly. "Where are you taking me?"

"I want the doctor to have a look at you. I want you properly taken care of."

"No!" Nicki shrieked.

Alex ignored her. Using a booted foot, he shoved open the chamber door and headed for the high, carved four-poster bed with its satin-and-lace counterpane. Mrs. Leander rushed in just in time to pull back the mosquito netting and turn back the covers.

"Please," Nicki whispered. "I'm all right now, really I am."

"Have a bath brought up," Alex commanded the housekeeper, "and bring her fresh clothing." Mrs. Leander left to do his bidding.

"Tell me what happened," Alex said.

"It's over and done with. Can't we just leave it alone?"

"What did Clarissa do to you?" Alex repeated as if she hadn't spoken.

Though she wished he would let things be, she couldn't help enjoying his concern. She smiled up at him as he sat on the edge of the bed beside her, his heavy weight making the wooden slats creak beneath the deep feather mattress. It was then that he noticed her hands.

"Good God! How the hell . . . ?" They were red and swollen, both back and front. Huge, clear blisters had already begun to fill with water.

Alex tilted her chin, forcing her to look at him. "Tell me."

As usual, he left her little choice. "Clarissa was furious. So mad she could hardly speak. Even my apology didn't help—she said it was insincere." Nicki fought a smile. "Actually, it was."

"Go on."

"She said an apology wasn't enough. That I hadn't learned my lesson. She had one of the servants bring her a ruler." She winced as Alex cradled her small hands in his large ones to examine them more closely. "I could have stopped her sooner," Nicki admitted, "if I'd been a little less stubborn."

Alex's expression turned murderous. "Then what happened?"

"When she finished, she had me locked in the tool shed."

Alex's stomach rolled. If the temperature outside was unbearable, the heat in that shed must have been stifling.

"I wouldn't have minded so much, except for the bugs and the spiders." Nicki shuddered involuntarily, and Alex's throat went dry.

"I hope that's all, because if I hear one more word, I just may murder Clarissa." When Nicki didn't answer, just stared at him as though she believed he might, Alex came to his feet.

"I never meant for this to happen, *ma petite*. I said you'd be safe at Belle Chêne, but you weren't." Wishing there was something more he could do, he reached down and swept back a damp strand of silky copper hair. "I still want the doctor to see you."

Mrs. Leander's arrival with the servants carrying water for her bath interrupted Nicole's refusal.

"I want you to eat something and get some sleep," Alex gently instructed. "I'll take care of Clarissa."

"Please, Alex," she said, forgetting not to use his given name. "I don't want any more trouble."

"This is my house—not Clarissa's. You belong to Belle Chêne. That makes you my responsibility, not hers. I won't stand for her interference—not one moment more." With that, he stalked out of the room.

"I won't have it, Clarissa," Alex raged. "I won't allow you ever to mistreat one of my people again!" He paced the length of the thick Persian carpet, casting huge, dark shadows beneath the crystal chandelier.

He had decided against waiting until morning. He wouldn't be able to sleep until the episode was settled —one way or another. "How could you do such a thing?" he pressed, fighting the urge to strangle her. Every time he thought of Nicki's endless hours in the blistering tool shed, it almost made him sick.

"In truth," she replied, apparently not intimidated, though she stood well out of his reach, "I forgot the little twit was out there. I had so much work to do and—"

"I don't want to hear it." Alex raked a hand through his wavy brown hair and forced himself under control. "If you're to be my wife, there'll be no more physical violence against my people. That is the understanding we must reach, right here and now. If you can't abide by that rule, this marriage will not take place."

"Alex, darling. I can't believe you're so upset." At the hard look in his eyes, Clarissa pulled her heavy gingham wrapper a little closer. She had been readying herself for bed when Alex stormed into the entry demanding to see her.

"But Miz Clarissa done retired," the butler had told him.

"I don't give a damn. Tell her she's to come down here now, or I shall go up and fetch her down."

From the look of him now, he had meant every word. She had never seen him so angry. "I was only trying to teach the girl the value of self-discipline," she told him. "If she's to be of any use to us, she must certainly learn—"

"I'm warning you, Clarissa. This is not open for discussion. Make your decision. Now."

Clarissa swallowed hard. For the first time since she'd entered into their marriage agreement, she had doubts about her decision. She'd known Alex was a man to be reckoned with; she just hadn't known the extent to which he intended to impose his authority.

"Am I to have no say at all in the way our household is run?"

"Of course you will. I look forward to your assumption of duties as my wife." He released a weary breath. "In truth, I could use your help. My concern is with the people you'll be responsible for. I want them treated with courtesy and respect. I'll accept no less."

On this issue he seemed determined. But there would be years ahead of them, years for her to assert herself and her authority. "And the Elmtree household would remain under my supervision, just as it is now?"

"It would be my hope that this more gentle approach might eventually expand to encompass your people as well, but that is up to you."

"Then I shall do as you ask, and I'm sorry for any inconvenience you feel I may have caused." *Sorry.* Such a simple word, and yet Alexandre's little bond servant had nearly choked on it. The very way she said it seemed as though she meant the opposite. No matter what Alex said, sooner or later the girl would bend to Clarissa's will or her contract would be sold.

"Then I consider the matter at an end," Alex told her. "We'll speak of it no more."

"Would you care to stay for some tea?" Clarissa asked, grateful the subject was closed. "Or maybe some brandy?" She tucked a strand of pale blond hair up into her nightcap.

"I've got a long day tomorrow. I'd better be getting back."

Alex was a very hard worker. She liked that about him. It was one of the reasons she'd approached him with the idea of marriage in the first place.

"Then I'll see you sometime next week," she said. "There's much I still have to do before the soiree."

Alex nodded. He bowed formally over her hand and took his leave. Through the heavy lace curtains at the window, she watched him swing into the saddle of his big blooded bay stallion. He was a handsome man. Powerfully built with strong hands and masculine features. She knew his reputation with the ladies, knew he kept a mistress in town, and assumed he intended to continue that arrangement even after their marriage.

It made little difference to Clarissa. She would do her wifely duty, bear him sons, breed children for the state and the country, but the idea of sharing his bed held little appeal.

She wasn't a virgin, hadn't been since she'd slept with one of the engravers from her father's factory when she was seventeen. She had wanted to understand this strange attraction between male and female, especially since she hadn't known when, if ever, she would marry.

Her night with William Lackey had been sorely disappointing. What a man got out of the sweaty, uncouth rubbing of bodies she couldn't imagine. As for Clarissa, she'd been celibate ever since.

She hadn't lied to Alex about her virginity. She had told him the story, and though he'd been surprised at first, he hadn't doubted the truth of her years of chastity. It seemed fathering male progeny from his own loins was Alex's only concern.

After her confession, when she had presented her proposal—her plan for uniting the two great plantations through marriage, the meshing of her family's wealth with that of the du Villiers—Alex had recognized the advantages immediately. The following day he'd agreed, and their plans had been set in motion.

At the age of twenty-four, Clarissa had accomplished all that she could as an unmarried woman living on her own. What she needed now was a man. As the wife of Alexandre du Villier, she would have power and wealth beyond anything she had dreamed.

She worried she would also have a lot more man than she could handle.

The following week Nicole returned to her small attic room. Mrs. Leander had soothed Alex's concerns about her health, and by the following week her hands had completely healed, allowing her to resume her full load of duties. She was sweeping the entry, immersed in her work, when a commotion outside the front door drew her attention.

Frederick answered the determined knock and a tiny gray-haired woman dressed in elegant black silk mourning clothes swept into the foyer.

"*Bonjour*, Frederick," she said. "Where is my grandson?"

Frederick smiled delightedly. "I'm afraid he's away on business, madame. You weren't expected until next week."

"Well then, I shall have a chance to relax a bit before his return." She swung her glance to Nicole, whose brows arched in recognition at exactly the same instant.

The gray-haired woman smiled. "Nicole St. Claire," she said in the French she was most comfortable speaking. "What on earth are you doing here?"

The broom fell with a clatter to the floor. Nicki just stood there, speechless and staring, until the old woman crossed the few paces between them and embraced her. It was a warm embrace, kind and caring. The kind of hug her mother used to give her when Nicki needed it most. Nicole's throat began to close, the sadness of the past three years rising up like a suffocating wave.

With a whimper that became a sob, Nicki wrapped her arms around the little Frenchwoman's shoulders. Tears welled and slipped down her cheeks. Her body trembled, and her crying turned to full-blown weeping.

Astonished, Rachael du Villier just held her, rocking her tenderly back and forth and crooning gentle, comforting words in French.

"*Grand-mère* is here," she soothed. "Everything is going to be all right."

"Oh, *Grand-mère*," Nicki sobbed.

"There, there, *minette*. You must trust me to take care of you."

Nicki just nodded. For the first time in the past three years, she no longer felt alone.

Since the foyer was hardly the place for discussion, and Nicki's crying had finally ceased, they made their way, arm in arm, up the stairs to the room the older woman always occupied during her visits. It was a bright sunny room that dissolved the balance of Nicki's sorrow.

Rachael led her to the embroidered silk settee in front of the pink-marble hearth. "Now. You will tell me why you are dressed as a servant, and sweeping the entry of my grandson's home."

It all tumbled out, in a jumble of words and occasional tears. The whole ugly story. When Nicole had finished, she leaned back against the sofa, too drained to say much more.

"I knew nothing of this. Nothing of your father's troubles at Meadowood. Alexandre wrote me of Etienne's death, but made no mention of his family. We assumed you and your mother had returned to England."

"She had no one left there."

"Why did you not come to us for help?"

"Your son was already dead by the time things got really bad. Papa went to see François, but he wouldn't help. He said Alexandre felt the same."

"François," she scoffed. With a wave of her hands, she made her feelings for her younger grandson clear. "François is not Alexandre. Surely you did not believe Alex would turn you away once you told him who you were?"

"At first I wasn't certain. Later, after I came to trust him, it was my pride—a du Villier discovering

St. Claire's daughter was a bond servant and a criminal. In the end, once I'd learned of Clarissa and Alexandre's coming marriage, I couldn't face the idea of leaving the only home I'd known in years."

"If only you had come to me, *ma fille.*"

"I wasn't even sure you still lived. I didn't know where to find you." Fresh tears welled and slipped down her cheeks. "Everything seemed so mixed up, I just didn't know what to do."

Rachael dabbed at Nicki's tears with a lace-trimmed handkerchief. "It does not matter. From now on, you will leave everything to me." With soldierlike movements that swished the full black skirts of her mourning clothes, worn for the son who'd been dead nearly two years, the old woman marched to the door and began giving orders.

Nicole's few possessions were to be moved to the room next to Rachael's. A bath was ordered, and the best dressmaker in New Orleans was to be brought to the house no later than the following morning.

Nicole could scarcely believe the activity around her. "But what about Alex? What will he say when he finds out?"

"Frederick tells me Alexandre is away on business until next week."

"He's probably with Lisette," she said without thinking, then wished she could call back the words.

"His mistress?" Rachael shook her head, eliciting a look of surprise from Nicole. "*Non.* Frederick says he has gone to Mobile to discuss a shipment of sugar. He will be back on Wednesday. There is to be a small dinner party in my honor. We shall see that the daughter of an old family friend is also in attendance."

Nicki's eyes went wide. "You mean, you aren't going to tell him?"

"He should have been smart enough to have seen for himself. Besides"—she smiled mischievously—"this should be so much more entertaining."

Entertaining? "Oh, God," she whispered in English.

"Leave Alexandre to me," Rachael told her, speaking with the assurance of the grand old duchess she was. But the confidence in the old woman's words did little to allay Nicki's fears.

"*Grand-mère!*" Alex called out, spotting the old woman on the stairs. When she reached the foyer, he swept her up in a warm bear hug and soundly kissed her weathered cheek. "You're looking as fit as ever."

"And you, *mon fils*, look tired. You work too hard, Alexandre." They embraced again.

"Now that you've arrived, I've an excuse for a few days off. When did you get in?"

"My ship docked several days early," Rachael told him. "I arrived last week."

"I hope you haven't been bored."

"Actually, I have been blessed by a visit from an old family friend. Etienne St. Claire's daughter. I insisted she attend our dinner party."

"Is she here?"

"Yes."

"With her mother?"

"I am afraid her mother has passed away."

"I'm sorry to hear that. I hope you've extended our condolences and offered any assistance she might need."

"As a matter of fact, I have." She smiled at him warmly.

"I look forward to meeting her. She was just a child when last I saw her. I really don't remember her much."

"She is quite grown-up now." Rachael hid an almost wicked smile by bending her head and brushing a piece of lint from the folds of her black bombazine day dress. "As you shall see for yourself at supper."

Alex nodded. "Until then, why don't you and I catch up on what's been going on."

"An excellent idea, Alexandre. I should like very much to hear exactly what has been going on."

Nicole took more care with her toilette than she ever had in her life. The bustle of activity below had signaled Alex's arrival several hours earlier. Time and time again she had been tempted to go him. Tell him the truth herself, instead of waiting, as *grand-mère* had instructed. She hadn't because the old woman seemed so sure of herself, and of her influence with Alex.

Nicki prayed the duchess was right.

Danielle came in just as Nicki finished her bath and pulled on her chemise. "I have come to assist you, mademoiselle," Danielle said stiffly, "as Madame du Villier requested. From now on I'm to be your lady's maid."

Nicki laid a hand on the plump girl's arm. "I'm the same person I was last week, Danielle. We were friends then, I hope we still are."

"Of course, mademoiselle."

"Then why don't you just call me Nicki, as you did before."

"*Ah, non,* I could not possibly."

"It would please me if you would."

Danielle looked uncertain. "What would *le duc* say?"

Indeed. What would Alex say? "That is for me to worry about, not you." Nicki smiled warmly and extended a hand. "Friends?"

Danielle grinned, accepting the handshake and falling back into her usual relaxed manner. "So, if we are still friends, I can tell you about my latest meeting with René." René Bouteiller was her fiancé.

"You had better. I want to hear every juicy detail."

Danielle giggled. In her own lush way, she looked feminine and attractive. More than one man had asked for her hand, but René had won her heart. "I will tell you while you get dressed."

With their relationship back on an even keel, Nicki allowed Danielle to assist with the pretty embroidered undergarments she now wore and to tighten the laces on her corset. Seated on a pale-blue tapestry stool in front of the gilded mirror above the dresser, Nicki fidgeted nervously while Danielle coiffed her hair into a cluster of long copper ringlets that fell below her shoulders on each side of her face.

Once she dressed, her bosom swelled promisingly above the low-cut bodice of her aqua watered-silk gown. *Grand-mère* had selected the fabric to match the color of her eyes. It was cut in the latest fashion, with a deep V at the waist both front and back, which emphasized the swell of her hips and breasts in relation to her tiny middle.

Nicole lovingly smoothed the fabric. It had been years since she'd dressed in silks and satins, years since she'd felt feminine and desirable. Though she feared the scene Alex might cause, she relished the chance to show him she was a woman. She knew she shouldn't, but couldn't stop praying it would somehow make a difference.

"They've all gone into dinner." It was Mrs. Leander. "Madame du Villier says you may come down whenever you're ready."

They had planned it this way—for Nicole to be late in making an appearance, hoping to put Alex in a position that would demand his acceptance of her as his guest.

"Are you sure I look all right?" she asked, though the image in the mirror said she had never looked more beautiful.

"You look lovely." Mrs. Leander flashed a reassuring smile. "You just let Madame take care of things. She knows Master Alex better than anyone on earth."

Nicki started to leave, took a few uncertain steps, then impulsively turned back and hugged the buxom housekeeper. "Thank you for everything."

Mrs. Leander patted her cheek. "Go on with ya now. Keep your chin up."

Nicole just nodded and headed down the stairs. It took every ounce of her courage to slide open the dining room doors.

"I believe our last guest has arrived," Rachael said with a smug look that traveled from Nicole to her grandson.

Alex was seated at the head of the table, engrossed in conversation with Thomas Demming, who sat beside Clarissa on his right. Rachael sat to his left, beside an empty seat reserved for Nicki. On the other side of the empty chair, François leaned indolently against the carved back of his seat. Alex was reaching for his wine when he spotted her standing in the open doorway. His hand paused midway to the glass.

"May I present my grandson, Alexandre," Rachael said with a smile that could only be regarded as triumphant.

"How do you do?" Nicki replied woodenly.

Grand-mère turned to the woman on Alex's right. "This is Clarissa Endicott, Alexandre's fiancée."

"I believe we may have met." Nicki couldn't quite resist. Clarissa just gaped at her.

"M'sieur Thomas Demming, my grandson's attorney and very close friend," Rachael continued.

"M'sieur Demming," she said.

"And my other grandson, François."

"A pleasure to meet you, I'm sure."

Alex came to his feet. His brown eyes swept over her, taking in her elegant copper curls, the swell of her bosom that rose and fell with each nervous breath. He sized her up from head to foot, then his eyes returned to her face, his dark look pinning her to the spot. The icy glimmer of rage was unmistakable, his fury evident in the hard line of his jaw. Nicki swallowed hard.

"It is impolite to stare, Alexandre." Rachael's voice cut through the stillness. "Why don't you seat Mademoiselle St. Claire?"

Both François and Thomas shoved back their chairs at exactly the same instant and came to their feet.

"It's all right, my friends," Alex assured them smoothly, though there was no mistaking the underlying venom in his voice. "I shall properly assist Mademoiselle . . . St. Claire—just as soon as we've had a moment alone."

Nicole looked at Rachael beseechingly. The old woman just smiled.

Alex gripped Nicki's arm until she winced. "Excuse us," he said, and hauled her out of the room. Wordlessly he guided her down the hall to his study. Nicole recalled the last time he'd dragged her into the very masculine cypress-paneled room, and her cheeks grew warm.

She glanced up to find Alex staring down at her, his eyes hard while his mouth tilted into the least-amused smile she'd ever seen.

"Who are you?" he asked.

"Your grandmother told you who I am."

His eyes raked her, appraising her, assessing her as if he still couldn't believe the girl in the aqua silk skirts was the same scruffy urchin he had rescued from the prison.

"I don't believe it."

That was one possibility she hadn't counted on. She straightened her spine. "Etienne St. Claire was my father. Margaret Stockton St. Claire was my mother. Over the years, your grandmother and I have visited often."

"Nicki Stockton," he repeated, beginning to realize what she had done. "Nicole St. Claire."

"Yes."

"You were the girl in La Ronde."

It was hard to resist a smile. "You bought me a dress."

Alex looked at the elegant aqua gown, at the eyes it so perfectly matched, at her narrow waist and luscious breasts. Her skin looked clear and smooth above the low-cut bodice; her neck rose gracefully atop her delicate shoulders. She was all he'd imagined—and more. "It appears I have bought you several."

Nicki glanced away. "I wanted to tell you the truth. I didn't because . . ."

"Because of your damnable pride," he countered when she didn't finish. "Isn't that it? You'd rather suffer in silence, work as a common servant than ask for my help. And there was also the added benefit of allowing me to make a fool of myself."

Nicole's head came up. "I don't know what you mean."

"Oh, don't you?" He looked angry again. "You're half French. You speak the language fluently. You've understood every word I've said since the moment you met me."

"I usually speak English. You just assumed I couldn't speak French."

His anger seemed to swell with her every word. "How you must have laughed when I taught you to ride. You'd been riding for years, hadn't you?"

She took a step backward. "Yes, but—"

"You let me lecture you about the sugar business. But Etienne's daughter would have known all about it." He looked angry enough to strike her. For a moment she thought he might, and the old fear moved over her.

"It wasn't that way," she said softly. "I enjoyed your company. You were the first person who had shown me kindness in years."

"How you must have enjoyed yourself—Alexandre du Villier attending the instruction of a bond servant."

She backed toward the door, but he only drew closer, until her back touched the hard wood paneling, and his breath fanned her cheek. She could smell the wine he'd been drinking and the spicy scent of his cologne.

"It wasn't like that," she repeated, genuinely afraid now. "I couldn't tell you. I wasn't sure what you would do."

Alex grabbed her arms and pulled her even closer, glowering down at her with such contempt she fought not to look away. When he jerked his arm upward in an angry movement, she squeezed her eyes shut and flinched against the blow she was sure would come. Tears stung her eyes and one rolled down her cheek. When Alex's hold gentled, she opened them to find him staring at her with astonishment.

"Surely by now you know I would not hurt you." His voice held a gentleness that hadn't been there before. "I would never hurt you."

"You would have sold me to Fortier," she accused, embarrassed that he'd once more seen her weakness. It shouldn't have happened. Would not happen again. "How could I trust you?"

"You're Etienne St. Claire's daughter, for God's sake. I would have helped you."

"You don't understand. I was fighting for survival. I would have done anything, said anything. You can't know what it's like to be treated as an animal, to be debased and humiliated. If I had it to do again, I would do the very same—whether you liked it or not!"

She was crying now, but in anger, not fear. "You can't know the horrors of a place like that. The rats and the filth. The things they did to the women. . . ." Her voice trailed off as the bitter memory washed

over her. "Just being there made me hurt inside."
Unconsciously her hand crept to the place above her
heart. "Sometimes I still hurt. . . ."

The last of Alex's anger drained away. "Don't cry,
chérie." Drawing her into his arms, he held her
against his chest. "There is no more need for tears."
Her breasts, full and high, pushed invitingly against
his black evening jacket. How cleverly she had disguised them.

Across his hand, silky strands of copper hair glistened in the lamplight. He wanted to free it from the
pins that held it in place and bury his fingers in the
long, gleaming strands. He wanted to press his
mouth against the smooth white skin at the nape of
her neck.

It dawned on him that his body had been responding to the woman she had been all along, was responding now in a way he hadn't let it before. It took
a mountain of willpower not to kiss her, but instead
bring his desire for her under control.

"I never would have sold you to Fortier," he said
softly. "Never. And believe it or not, I do understand."

He knew what she meant about survival, because
he had spent six months of his life in an Algerian
prison. He'd been twenty at the time. Certain
France's war was a glorious thing. His father had
disapproved, of course, but been understanding. It
was something his son just had to do.

Alex had returned a different man. Harder. More
cynical. He'd learned to survive in that prison. Been
forced to go against the very things he believed in just
to find his next meal. He knew exactly what Nicole

St. Claire had suffered—knew how the women in those terrible places were treated.

He tightened his hold. "Those days are past," he said, tilting her face up to look at him. "You're back where you belong and this is where you will stay."

Nicki pulled back to look at him. "I love it here. I have since the moment I arrived."

Mon Dieu, she was lovely. Far more beautiful than his wildest imaginings. He hated the mistreatment she had suffered, the violation. But the fact that she was no longer a virgin only made things easier for the two of them.

Recalling her trusting expression and the attachment she felt for Belle Chêne, Alex felt a little guilty. But his town house in the city would make a proper home—just as soon as he moved Lisette to the country and got Nicki settled in. His loins swelled at the thought.

"It's time we returned to the others," he said, his voice a little husky.

Nicole brushed the last of the tears from her cheeks. "I must look awful."

"You look beautiful." They were the most precious words she had ever heard. "But if you'd like to make certain, it will give me a chance to smooth the way for you a little."

That snapped her back to reality. Clarissa hadn't been fooled—not even for a moment. By now, both François and Thomas Demming knew exactly who she was.

"I'm really not very hungry. If you don't mind, I think I'll just skip dinner tonight."

Alex smiled indulgently. "You've come this far, *ma chère*, it's time you finished. You're Etienne St.

Claire's daughter. Whenever you feel uncertain, just keep that in mind."

Nicole pondered his words and returned his smile, hers a bit more tremulous. "Thank you, m'sieur."

"You may as well call me Alex. You never really stopped anyway."

Nicki's cheeks grew warm. "I didn't think you noticed."

"There is very little you have done, *chère*, that has gone unnoticed."

Nicki wasn't sure what he meant, but she liked the look he gave her when he said it. It made her insides flutter and her cheeks grow warmer still.

Alex extended his arm, and Nicole accepted it. He led her to the foot of the stairs, and she started her ascent, meaning to freshen up for a moment while Alex spoke to his guests.

"I'll expect to see you in there momentarily," he told her with a look that brooked no argument.

"As you wish, Alexandre." With another soft smile, she headed upstairs.

Alex watched the gentle sway of her hips. A burden had been lifted from his conscience this night. His little bond servant had been replaced by a voluptuous woman who would soon warm his bed.

He wouldn't rush her. She had suffered too much; she was bound to be wary and apprehensive. He would take his time, woo her into accepting him. It never crossed his mind that she would refuse him. As she had said herself—what other choice did she have?

8

The remainder of Nicki's evening went far better than she had expected.

With Alexandre and his grandmother—a duke and a duchess whether they used their titles or not—staunchly behind her, Nicki's position as friend of the family had been firmly established. That she was Alexandre's bond servant was a subject that had been settled before Nicki came back into the room.

Alex had explained that his father and Etienne St. Claire had been best of friends. The two had been officers in the American army, enlisting for a short period when the United States had gone to war against England. At the battle of Borgne, just outside New Orleans, Etienne had risked his life to save a wounded Charles Alexandre, who lay unconscious and bleeding in the muddy battlefield that had once been the McCarly plantation.

"It's a debt the du Villiers have not forgotten," Alex said, and François glanced away. Rachael didn't miss the guilty gesture. The younger man looked pale and more than a little bit shaken.

"We have much to discuss, François," Rachael

said pointedly. But she wouldn't bring the subject up in front of Alexandre. François had displeased his brother enough these past few years. Discovering François had turned the St. Claires away in their time of need would only make things worse between them.

Clarissa's burst of temper had lasted only a moment. "You can't actually mean to allow this . . . this . . . *servant* to sit at your table."

"She is a friend," Rachael had said, silencing her with a single warning glance—at least for as long as the duchess remained at Belle Chêne to act as chaperone.

Thomas Demming had surprised her. He looked at Nicki the way the young men used to who came to call at Meadowood. Before the evening ended, he asked her into the city to attend a production of *La Fitte, the Pirate of the Gulf*, which was playing at the St. Charles Theatre.

When she glanced at Alex, she found him glaring at Thomas with obvious disapproval. For an instant she fumed—and almost said yes. Then saner thoughts returned, along with the hurt in knowing Alex thought her unfit company for his friend.

With a few quiet words, she declined the invitation.

"Well, my dear," Clarissa intoned at the end of the evening, drawing herself up and curling her lips in what pretended to be a smile, "enjoy your stay at Belle Chêne." Her tone implied it would be brief. "It is unfortunate, under the circumstances, we got off to such an inauspicious beginning. But those things happen."

It wasn't an apology and they both knew it.

"Alex, darling, I'd be grateful if you would see me home."

Alex inclined his head in agreement, and the party dispersed, Thomas and François returning to the city, Rachael and Nicole to their rooms upstairs.

"I told you things would work out," Rachael said smugly.

As far as Nicki was concerned, that remained to be seen. "Good night, *Grand-mère.*" Wearily, she opened the door to her room.

The very next day, while Alex worked in the fields, Frederick announced a visitor. Nicki was surprised to find François waiting in the receiving salon.

"Good morning, m'sieur," she greeted him formally. "Have you come to see *Grand-mère?*"

"I've come to see you. Might we speak a moment in private?" Immaculately dressed in dark-gray breeches and a light-gray tailcoat, he seemed a softer version of Alex, only younger, and much less self-assured.

"Of course," she agreed rather stiffly. She hadn't forgotten the way he had treated her father, and the fate she had indirectly suffered because of his refusal to help.

François pulled the salon doors closed while Nicki took a place on the cream brocade sofa. François seated himself beside her. Arranging the skirts of her pale-blue dimity day dress gave her a little time to watch him.

"I know what you must think of me," he said. The lines of his face looked taut, his eyes a little uncertain.

"I know my father came to you for help and you refused."

The air seemed to hiss from François's lungs. *"Dieu du ciel,* a hundred times I have berated myself for that meeting. I want you to know I never dreamed things would turn out the way they did. I was younger. Foolish. Overwhelmed with responsibilities. By the time your father came to Belle Chêne, the place was in terrible financial condition. I'd borrowed money to keep it running, and already spent most of that. There was really nothing left to give him, but rather than tell him the truth, I made it appear we were unwilling—unkind instead of unable."

Nicole was surprised at the depth of François's regret, but not at his troubles. Alexandre had made reference to the difficulties he had been facing since his return. "Is Belle Chêne still having problems?" she asked, worried about the added burden she might be.

"Alex has worked things out. He always does." His voice held a note of resentment.

"Different people are gifted with different talents," Nicki told him. "Alex has a talent for solving problems, managing a plantation. Your talents lay elsewhere."

François's dark head snapped up. "You know about my painting?"

That did surprise her. "No. But if that's your gift, you needn't be ashamed of it. Nor should you begrudge your brother his."

"I know you're right, but . . ."

"But what?" It felt good to know François was not the ogre she had once thought him. Merely a young man involved in a situation over his head.

"But it's difficult always coming in second best. I

disappointed my father. Now I'm disappointing Alex."

"I don't think you give your brother enough credit. He loves you. I can see it in his eyes whenever you're here."

"We used to be close." François looked wistful.

"You can be again. I know Alex would like that. It seems you want it too." She smiled at him. "Now, tell me about your painting."

François's youthful face lit up. They talked for the rest of the hour, the younger du Villier relaxed and open with her in a way he hadn't been before. It seemed another obstacle lay behind her, that she was climbing toward the light from the darkness in which she had lived these past three years. She wondered at the dissention between the two brothers, but hoped that sometime in the future it might be resolved.

Nicki saw Alexandre a great deal over the next few weeks. She expected he might be resentful of her deceit. Instead, he acted attentive, solicitous, and completely the gentleman.

Insisting that she accompany them, he took Rachael on a carriage ride around the plantation, intent on showing his grandmother the improvements he was making, though they still had not been completed.

"Every three hundred acres yields about two hundred hogshead of sugar, *Grand-mère*. Each brings roughly a thousand dollars per barrel. With our increased yield and finer quality, we should far exceed that projection."

"Assuming the weather stays right," Nicki put in,

knowing that the unpredictability of the weather was always a factor in any sugar crop.

"I stand corrected." He flashed her a cheek-dimpling grin.

That night he escorted her upstairs to her room.

"I had a wonderful day," she told him.

"So did I, *chérie*."

"You're being awfully kind about this, Alex. I know it's been a shock for you, but—"

He silenced her with a finger to her lips. "I told you, what's past is past." Bending down he brushed her cheek with a kiss. Though he barely made contact, tiny goose bumps feathered up her spine and a hollow sensation rippled in the pit of her stomach.

"Good night," she whispered.

When he discovered she could play the pianoforte, he insisted on a concert, then lauded her performance. "Talent as well as beauty," he said.

"Mostly determination," she told him, but warmed at the compliment. "My mother insisted. She said it was a woman's duty to provide solace in the household."

"There are many ways a woman can provide solace." His warm brown eyes turned dark.

He was different around her now. Less distant than he'd been before. He was still as casually arrogant and self-assured; the change in him was subtle, hard to describe. It seemed there was a boldness in his eyes, a disturbing quality that hadn't been there when he'd looked at her before. There was something about that look that made her heart beat faster, her insides feel liquid and warm.

When he walked her upstairs that night, his kiss on her cheek was far less brotherly. He stood closer and held her hands, tracing a pattern with his finger on her palm until she trembled and moved away.

She found herself looking forward to their moments of conversation, the meals they shared with Rachael in the evenings. Whenever Alexandre was near, Nicole felt womanly, feminine in a way she hadn't in years. She knew she was attracted to him. More every day.

Alex belongs to somebody else, she told herself firmly, but a voice inside said, *He doesn't love Clarissa. He isn't engaged to her yet.*

You're a bond servant, she argued. *His bond servant. You have a criminal record.* She thought of the displeasure on Alex's face when Thomas Demming had asked her out. Alex felt he owed the St. Claires a debt and was trying to repay it. He bought her beautiful clothes, and she no longer scrubbed floors in his house, but the fact was he *owned* her. He had said nothing to change that; she wasn't sure he would.

On top of that, she was no longer his equal in society, would never be again. It was a fact of life she had known all along, yet still had trouble accepting.

That evening after supper they went for a walk in the gardens. Nicki had been surprised by Alex's suggestion, as well as *Grand-mère's* approving smile.

"You children enjoy yourselves," Rachael said. After a dutiful kiss on the cheek from each of them, she took her leave and went upstairs.

Alex chuckled softly. "You've won her over completely."

Nicki smiled. "I love your grandmother. She's one of the kindest women I've ever known."

"And you're one of the loveliest."

Nicole felt the heat in her cheeks. She did look

pretty tonight. More than pretty. The dress she wore, a lavender silk with delicate puffs at the shoulders, swept low in front, exposing a sizeable portion of her breasts. She had worn her hair in soft curls beside her face with a lovely white magnolia above one ear. Alex wore a silver brocade waistcoat beneath perfectly tailored black evening clothes.

Moonlight shone on his satin lapels as they walked along the manicured rows of boxhedges to the tiny lake Charles du Villier had had built and stocked with swans. A cool breeze swept in off the river, keeping the insects at bay, and the temperature was finally dropping a bit.

"You're just as I imagined you'd be," Alex said.

Nicki arched a brow in surprise. "You thought about what I'd look like when I got older?"

"Often. Actually, you've exceeded my fondest expectations."

She smiled at that. They talked about the weather. About his grandmother, about the crops. She didn't mention her meeting with François or his painting, since he had asked her not to. They didn't discuss the papers of indenture he still owned. They just discussed lighthearted, frivolous topics. The kind she might discuss with a suitor. But Alex wasn't courting her—or was he?

Almost as if in answer, when they walked beneath the drooping branches of a willow, he turned her into his arms. He looked down at her and though his expression remained gentle the darkness had returned to his eyes. She found them mesmerizing to the point that she couldn't look away.

It seemed so natural when he kissed her, so right somehow. It was a gentle kiss, undemanding. She could taste the brandy he had drunk after supper, smell the spicy scent of his cologne. It occurred to her that she had wanted Alex to kiss her since that day in La Ronde. Wanted it every moment since she had been at Belle Chêne. Alex ended the kiss long before Nicki wanted him to.

And he knew it.

"We'd better be getting back," she said, embarrassed he could read her so clearly. In her other life, it wouldn't have been so. She had been sure of herself then, always in control.

"Tomorrow night we'll take the steamboat up the river a ways."

"The three of us?" she couldn't help asking, certain *Grand-mère* would chaperone.

He shook his head and smiled indulgently. "The two of us."

What about Clarissa? she wanted to say, but didn't.

Nicole awoke feeling a little out of sorts. Pondering the scene with Alex in the garden, she hadn't slept well. She hated the tenuousness of her future, had worried all night about her unsettling emotions toward Alex and the disturbing doubts that nagged at her and would not go away.

With the details of the engagement party complete, Clarissa hadn't been to Belle Chêne in weeks, but that didn't stop Nicki from thinking about her. She wondered if Alex thought about her too.

Rising earlier than usual, Nicki dressed in a rust-colored riding habit—another of the garments *Grand-mère* had insisted upon—and headed out the door. The sky seemed bluer than normal, and a light breeze blew puffy clouds along the horizon. The perfect day for a ride and the chance to spend some time alone.

"So it's true." Patrick stood in the open barn door. The sun had just risen, yellow rays that skimmed through the cracks lighting dust devils that swirled where he pitched hay.

"I'm afraid so."

Patrick had been away on a breeding trip with one of the stallions. Today was the first time Nicki had seen him since her status had changed. She kept walking in his direction, drawn by the musty smell of the barn, of new-mown hay, horses, and well-aged leather. Smells she had always loved. "I hoped we might still be friends."

Patrick surprised her by grinning. He propped his pitchfork against a stall door and crossed one worn boot atop the other. "Guess it really doesn't matter. You never had eyes for naught but him, anyway."

Nicki stopped dead in her tracks. "Why, Patrick, that just isn't so!"

He laughed softly. Reaching down, he picked up a golden stem of straw and clamped it between his teeth. "Have it your way. To my recollection, you will anyhow."

Nicki smiled at that. She was about to order Maximillian saddled when Alex strode into the barn.

"I thought I'd find you here." As he moved beneath the open window, amber lights danced in his dark-brown hair. He looked handsome in his riding breeches and snowy cotton shirt. They were the clothes that suited him best, Nicki decided, noting the well-defined muscles in his thighs, the width of his chest and shoulders.

"There's a breeze blowing in off the river," she told

him, trying to ignore the memory of being held in his arms. She hadn't forgotten the muscles that had bunched beneath her fingers, or the gentle way he had kissed her. "The air's a little cooler this morning. I thought I'd take a ride."

"Good idea. I'll go with you."

So much for her time alone.

The horses were readied, and Alex lifted her onto the sidesaddle, holding her longer than he should have. The heat of his hands stirred a warm sensation that slid through her limbs like warm molasses.

"Thank you," she said, but her mouth had gone dry and she had difficulty forming the words.

Alex climbed up on Napoleon, who pranced and whinnied and fought the bit harder than usual. "There's a mare on the wind," Alex said, looking at her pointedly.

Nicki's cheeks went warm. Alex chuckled softly and lightly set his heels to Napoleon's sides, urging the stallion down the road. Nicki rode beside him, thinking again what an imposing figure he made astride his big bay horse.

"My grandmother has excellent taste in clothes," he said, appraising her riding habit, just a shade darker than her copper-colored hair. "Or did you choose it?"

"We both did." They were riding toward the river, beside the cane fields, which had grown even taller. "I want you to know I appreciate all you've done for me." A bit self-conscious, she touched the imported Belgian lace on her cuff. "I know these things were expensive. I wish there was some way I could repay you."

Alex reined up beneath a moss-draped oak that

fronted the wide Mississippi, flowing past with barely a ripple. "Your father saved my father's life. They were friends. That makes us friends. I thought you understood that."

He helped her dismount, and they tied the horses so they could drink and splash in the water. As they walked back under the oak, Nicki almost asked him if that meant he would release her from her contract, but her position was still too new, too tenuous. And she wasn't sure she wanted to know.

"I liked your friend Thomas," she said instead, opting for the first fresh subject that came to mind.

Alex's expression turned hard. "If you liked him so much, why didn't you accept his invitation to the theater?"

The anger in his tone surprised her, but she didn't let it show. With studied nonchalance, she pulled a leaf from an overhead branch and twirled it between her fingers. "Because you obviously didn't want your friend's reputation sullied by someone like me."

Alex looked thunderstruck. "Is that what you thought?"

Nicki lifted her chin. "What was I supposed to think? You obviously disapproved." *And you own me.*

Alex moved closer, inching her step by step against the trunk of the oak. The gentleness she had seen in him these last few weeks was gone. "I didn't want you seeing him because I didn't want . . . complications."

"Complications? What's that supposed to mean?"

"It means . . ." He seemed to be weighing his words. A wide hand raked back his hair, but his eyes remained fixed on her face. When she tried to glance away, he turned her chin with his hand, forcing her to look at him. "I didn't want you seeing him, because I wanted you for myself. The truth is, I may have been fooled by your little charade, but my body wasn't. I've wanted you almost from the start."

His words were a tonic that soothed, yet stirred. Alex desired her. He was pursuing her as a woman. The knowledge made her head spin. Her heart, already beating in staccato, pounded even harder. She felt more of her old power returning, the feminine instincts that had once come so naturally back in the life she'd led before.

"You desire one woman, yet you are pledged to another."

"Clarissa isn't important," Alex said with finality, making her confidence swell. "What matters is that I'm a man and you're a woman. A full-grown woman. What I feel for you is no longer forbidden."

He ran a finger along her jaw, then cradled her cheeks between his palms. His hands felt warm and strong, imparting his feelings as if he had spoken. His mouth came down in a slow, deliberate kiss that held none of the restraint of the night before. It was a searing kiss, a demanding kiss that took her breath away.

With expert determination, he coaxed her mouth open, exploring the inside until her own tongue began the same sensuous movements. His hands slid around her waist, and Nicki swayed against him, letting him pull her close. She could feel the rough texture of his shirt, the muscles that moved as his hands played over her back. The heat of his body seeped into her limbs, making her weak and shaky, but she didn't pull away.

When he trailed hot kisses along her cheek to nibble her ear, Nicki whispered his name and slid her arms around his neck. His hair felt soft against her fingers, the muscles of his shoulders bunched, and a liquid warmth touched the place between her legs.

He was kissing her again now, plunging his tongue inside her mouth. Nicki dug her fingers into his shoulders, and Alex groaned. His hands moved down her body, over her bottom where he cupped the fullness to settle her more firmly against him. Nicki's senses reeled.

Alex felt the blood pounding at his temple, and the fire in his loins burned hotter. Nicki's warm, full breasts pressed against him, her nipples hard with desire. Even through the folds of her skirt, her bottom felt lush and perfectly curved to fill his hands. His arousal, already hot and pulsing, stiffened even more, thrusting itself against her, determined to make itself known.

Moving his palm along her bodice, he unfastened the tiny covered buttons that closed up the front of her dress and slid his hand inside. The heavy weight of her breast, the smoothness of her skin, and the pebble-hard peak he teased with his fingers increased his passions, and white hot desire surged through his veins.

Trembling all over, Nicki whimpered softly and leaned into his hand.

"Let me make love to you," he whispered, his fingers still working their magic.

Nicki jerked away as if he had slapped her. Clutching the open bodice of her dress, she stared at the bulge in his breeches that no amount of will could disguise. Though she hadn't moved or spoken, the flush was gone from her cheeks, replaced by a sudden pallor. Alex felt sure she was recalling what had happened at the prison.

"It's all right, *chérie*," he soothed. "I'm not going to do anything you don't want."

If anything she looked paler.

"I didn't mean to rush you. I'm sorry."

She shook her head as if to deny his words, but still she did not speak.

"I know what you're thinking. I know what you've been through, but it doesn't have to be like that. What happens between a man and a woman can be beautiful, *chérie*. I promise you."

"You don't understand."

"I should have gone slower, given you more time—"

"It wasn't your fault," Nicki said, surprising him. "It was mine. I could have stopped you, but I didn't. I don't know what came over me. I wanted you to kiss me—I enjoyed it—but I didn't know that I would want you to . . . to . . ."

He tilted her chin with his hand. "You didn't know you would want me to what, *chérie?* To hold you? To touch you in places that once seemed forbidden?"

She looked up at him and could not lie. "Yes."

Alex drew her into his arms. Nicki could feel his relief in the tension that drained from his body.

"We'll just take things slowly. Everything is going to be all right."

The last of Nicki's apprehension fled. Alex would take care of things. He always had, hadn't he? She realized suddenly how much she had come to trust him. How much she depended on him. She nodded her understanding, and Alex grazed her lips with a feather-soft kiss. Wordlessly, they gathered the horses and started back to the house.

They rode in silence for a while, but even with what had happened, she wasn't uncomfortable with him. "You said something back there," she said as they rode along, "something about knowing what I'd been through."

He nodded. "When I was younger, I spent some time locked up myself."

"You did?"

"Yes."

"Where?"

"Algeria. I was serving in the French army. Some of us were captured. The prison was a hellhole."

"How long were you in there?"

"Six very long months. Fortunately I made a friend who helped me through it. A big Turk named Ram. He's worked for me off and on ever since. Unfortunately, the sea keeps luring him away."

"My friend was named Lorna." She felt a tightness in her throat. "I'll never forget her."

"Tell me how you came to be in such a place," Alex coaxed softly.

Nicki told him about Richard Paxton, the man who had bought her contract from Laurent. She talked of Paxton's unwanted attentions and his wife, Adrian's, jealousy. "She planted the brooch, declared it stolen, then found it in front of Richard and sent for the authorities. You know the rest."

"What happened is past, *chérie*. For both of us." Alex smiled at her, but his vision was drawn across the fields to the knoll that rose above the western boundary where a lone rider watched them. Alex shaded his eyes against the sun, but he knew who it was.

"Fortier," he said, glancing down at Nicki. "Promise me you won't ride alone."

"But surely he won't bother me once he knows I'm under your protection."

"To him you will always be the little thief you were at the prison. He wants you. Fortier takes what he wants."

A shiver touched her spine. "What would you do?"

"I'd kill him . . . or he'd kill me."

9

The heavy rap of the silver lion's head on the massive front door stopped Nicole at the top of the staircase.

On her way to the dining room to breakfast with *Grand-mère*, she watched with curiosity as Frederick pulled open the door and a crisp breeze blew in, along with a dark-haired woman just a few inches taller than Nicki. Olive-skinned and lovely in her burgundy silk day dress piped in black, the same onyx hue as her eyes, the woman smiled at Frederick and asked to see Alexandre.

"Who is she?" Nicki whispered to Danielle, who had walked up beside her.

Danielle pulled her a discreet distance away, where they could watch without being seen. "That is Mademoiselle Aimee, M'sieur du Villier's mistress."

"Lisette?" she repeated, incredulous. She couldn't help noticing the woman's seductive beauty, the full red lips that curved in a bit of a pout.

"Oui."

Unconsciously, Nicki's fingers dug into her palms and a cold knot formed in the pit of her stomach.

Within minutes, Alex strode into the foyer. "I asked

you not to come here," he said by way of greeting. That he was upset was apparent by the scowl that lined his face.

"Why 'ave you not come to see me?" Her accent thick but charming, Lisette seemed equally annoyed. "You 'ave been away too long."

"I'm hardly at your beck and call, Lisette. I'll be there when I'm damned good and ready."

Lisette's pout became more pronounced. "What 'ave I done to displease you? You do not desire Lisette anymore?" Her look said she didn't believe it for a moment.

And neither did Nicole.

When Alex didn't answer soon enough, she twirled away from him, displaying her elegant clothes. "I look beautiful, no?" Her face seemed softer, her expression less contrived. Her black eyes sparkled with an almost childish delight.

Alex's anger faded. "You look lovely." Lisette beamed at the compliment, once more certain of her allure. "As a matter of fact," Alex told her, "I was planning to see you tonight." Taking her arm, he led her toward the door. "Why don't we go for a walk in the gardens where we can speak in private?"

As soon as they'd stepped through the doorway, Lisette turned into his arms and kissed him. Nicki didn't miss her look of triumph—or the possessive way she clutched his neck.

"How dare he!" In a swirl of bright yellow skirts, she turned and raced back to her room. If she didn't get out of the house in the next few moments, she would probably kill them both! She had never been so angry in her life. Yesterday Alex had been professing his feelings for her. Kissing her and touching her in a way no man had. Tonight he would go to Lisette!

Rage enveloped her. She wanted to race down the stairs and pull out every single strand of the woman's glossy black hair. She wanted to slap Alexandre's too-handsome face and call him the bastard he was.

Danielle helped her pull on her riding habit. "You are angry? No?"

"I am angry—yes! How dare he consort with that . . . that . . . woman! For heaven's sake, his grandmother is sitting in the dining room. He is certainly not a gentleman, and I intend to tell him so."

Danielle caught her arm. "I do not think that is such a good idea."

"And just why not?"

"Because if you do, *le duc* might think you are jealous."

"Jealous! Of that . . . that . . . loose woman!" But even as she said the words, she knew that was exactly what Alex would think, arrogant rogue that he was. What's more, it was true. She was jealous of Lisette and furious at Alex. And the fact that she was only made her madder.

Pulling on her soft leather riding gloves with short, determined tugs, she marched past the main staircase and down the hall to the servants' stairs that led into the butler's pantry. Once outside, she took in great gulps of air to calm herself and marched off toward the stables.

She would ride Napoleon—alone—whether Alex liked it or not! As long as she stayed away from Fortier's boundary she would be safe.

Patrick had the good sense not to argue. He'd never seen her in such a state, but he recognized her determination in the stiff set of her shoulders, the way she tapped her riding crop in measured beats against her boot.

"Be careful," he warned. "Weather appears to be changin'. Could be a storm brewin'. You never know when a bad un'll blow in off the gulf."

"I won't be gone long." She'd be gone just as long as she liked! To hell with all of them. Alex owned her contract, but not her soul. She was no longer treated as a servant, but as a pampered guest. Until Alex put a stop to it, she would do as she pleased whenever she got the chance.

Leading Napoleon over to the mounting block, she settled herself in the sidesaddle. The stallion seemed quieter today and it occurred to her why. Alex had turned him in with the mare. The thought sent her temper careening over the edge. Men! She dug her small, booted feet into the stallion's sides. Was there nothing else they thought about?

"Have you seen Nicki?" Alex asked Rachael, who sat by herself in the dining room. Her breakfast plate was all but scraped clean, except for a lonely piece of corncake she couldn't quite finish.

"She was supposed to join me, but she never came down. Maybe she is reading."

And maybe she'd seen Lisette. An occurrence he had hoped to avoid. Cursing softly, he set off to find Danielle. He'd already checked Nicki's room and found her gone. Maybe Danielle would know where she went. He found the rotund maid out in back, airing some quilts to use in her mistress's room when the weather turned cold.

"Have you seen Nicki?" he asked.

"*Oui, m'sieur.*"

"Well, where the hell is she?"

"She went riding. You know how she loves to ride."

"Who went with her?"

She only shrugged her shoulders. A stiff breeze ruffled her black cotton skirts. Alex glanced up to find the sky had turned cloudy, a flat gray mass that warned of a coming storm.

"She'd damned well better not have gone alone," he swore, heading off toward the barn. When he found Napoleon gone and Nicki's sidesaddle missing, he had his answer, but wished to God he didn't.

"She went off by herself, didn't she?"

Patrick didn't waver beneath his hard look. "There's no stoppin' the lass once she has her mind set. But I wouldn't worry too much. I told her to watch the weather."

"And you believe she has enough sense to come in out of the rain?"

Patrick knew better than to answer. "Which one will ya be wantin'?"

"Voltaire is probably the fastest."

Patrick led the big gray horse from its stall and hurriedly brushed his back in readiness for the saddle. As soon as he had finished, Alex set the lightweight leather in place, pulled the cinch tight, and swung aboard.

He'd find her, he vowed—and when he did, he would wring her pretty little neck.

Nicki took a trail that bordered one of the cane fields, riding Napoleon at a gallop. She'd been pushing him hard, but the stallion seemed tireless. The wind had picked up and the clouds had grown thicker, but Nicki didn't falter. She wouldn't go back until her anger was depleted, and she could face Alexandre as if she didn't care.

By now she realized how foolish she would be to confront him. She was living by his generosity, nothing more. He could sell her at a whim, rid himself of his burden in a heartbeat. She didn't think he would do it, but after what she had witnessed in the foyer, she couldn't be sure.

Thunder rolled in the distance, but she saw no lightning. Surely the storm was still some distance away. She slowed Napoleon and dismounted, walking him beside a small tributary stream that drained into the not-too-distant swamp. She still felt so furious, it amazed her. How could she be jealous of a man like him? Why had she been foolish enough to trust him in the first place? She knew what men were like, didn't she? Firsthand, she had seen what they could do.

Nicki plucked a sprig of tall grass that grew at her feet where Napoleon was grazing. When she glanced up, she saw a rider coming toward her. She didn't recognize the tall gray horse at first, but the man who sat atop him, riding with such grim determination, she knew in an instant. Damn him! Damn him to hell!

Alex reined up and dismounted just as the first few drops of rain began to fall. "What the devil do you think you're doing out here? You promised you wouldn't ride alone."

"You only assumed I wouldn't. I never gave you my word."

"I thought you understood how dangerous it was."

"I didn't go near Fortier," she said.

"I don't care. I don't want you taking any chances. From now on, you'll ride with me or someone else— or not at all."

"Go to hell."

Alexandre's eyes turned dark. "Say that again."

"Go to hell."

He grabbed her arms and hauled her against him. "Why, you stubborn little baggage. You'll do exactly what I tell you."

"Or you'll what? Lock me in my room? Starve me again?"

Alex let go of her. "I just don't want to see you get hurt."

"Why not? You've always got Lisette to keep you amused."

"Lisette?" he repeated. Alex took in Nicki's battle stance, the fiery gleam in her pretty aqua eyes. "So that's what this is about." He chuckled softly. "You're jealous."

"Jealous! Of you and that . . . that woman? You must be out of your mind."

Alex grabbed her waist and pulled her against his chest. Fighting a grin of satisfaction, he nuzzled the place beside her ear. Nicki tried to push him away, but he held her easily, enjoying the feel of her, the warmth of her breasts as she struggled against him.

"Get away from me!" she warned, her voice charged with fury. "You're nothing but an arrogant— womanizing—bastard!"

He thought her temper more seductive than ominous. "I'm glad you're jealous. *Mon Dieu,* I've never seen you with so much fire."

Nicki jerked away. Before she could stop herself, she drew back and slapped him hard across the face, the resounding crack like the sound of the thunder in the distance. "Oh, God," she whispered, feeling a jolt of the old, familiar fear.

Alex only smiled and rubbed a hand across his cheek. "You pack quite a punch for someone so small."

"I—I'm sorry. I didn't really mean to . . . I just . . . you just made me so angry."

Alex reached for her but she stepped away, still uncertain what he meant to do.

This time he grinned, exposing the sensuous grooves beside his mouth. "I take it you saw us in the foyer."

"Yes," she said softly, wishing she could disguise the hurt.

"I was going to see her tonight because I wanted to tell her we were finished."

"What?"

"Since she came to the house instead, I told her today."

"You—you told her you wouldn't be seeing her?"

"That's right."

"Because of your feelings for me?"

"Exactly."

"But you told her she looked lovely. You kissed her."

"She did look lovely. But I didn't kiss her—she kissed me. There's quite a difference. One I'll be happy to demonstrate if you'll give me the chance."

He was telling the truth. She could tell by his arrogant smile, his self-satisfied expression. "Oh, Alex."

Nicki launched herself into his arms, clutching his neck as he caught her up and swung her off her feet. His mouth covered hers, and she tasted the mascu-

line warmth of his breath. She opened to him, letting
his tongue inside, then teasing it with her own. It was
a sweet kiss, meant to tell him how wrong she had
been, how sorry she was to have doubted him.

"Forgive me?" she asked.

"Almost anything," he told her and kissed her
again, molding his body against her until she felt
weak. Only the raindrops, heavier now and beginning to soak through their clothes, brought them
back to reality.

"It's a long way home," she told him with a soft
smile, "we'd better get started."

"We aren't going home. There isn't time. This
storm looks worse than I thought. We'll head up to
the lodge. It isn't that far away."

"All right." She let him guide her to the horses, the
rain now falling steadily. He helped her up on Napoleon, mounted Voltaire, and they started off.

Along the path, the cane fields stretched beside
them, waving their dark-green leaves like an eerie,
undulating sea. The workers had long gone back to
their shelters. On the opposite side of the road, the
tall cypress trees that guarded the swamp whistled
and moaned. Dry branches cracked and popped,
leaves swirled and eddied and blew away.

"We're really getting some wind," he shouted over
the howl of the storm. "We need to get inside before
this gets worse." With that he nudged the big gray
faster, and Nicki did the same to the bay. A bolt of
lightning split the sky, and the clouds opened up in a
downpour. They rode hard until Alex turned off the
main road and onto a smaller, now muddy path that
led into the swamp. Branches whipped above their
heads, and Nicki wondered at the wisdom of going

into such wild terrain. Then she spotted the top of a redbrick chimney above a two-story log house just coming into view.

Alex dismounted in front of the low, overhanging front porch and helped her down. Her rust-colored riding clothes, drenched and clinging to her body, were now a soggy mud-brown mess. Her copper hair was soaked, and most of the pins holding it in place had fallen out.

Alex turned the heavy brass doorknob and swung the door wide. "Go on in. I'll take care of the horses and be right with you."

Nicki nodded and Alex led the animals off toward a fenced corral with a lean-to at one end. Nicki closed the door against the storm and turned to survey the interior of the lodge.

Is was more like an oversized cabin. A huge brick fireplace made of bayou clay dominated the high-ceilinged room. A staircase led to the floor above. Most of the furniture, including the brown leather sofa in front of the hearth, was roughhewn, made from cypress logs. There were braided rugs on the wide plank floors and simple white curtains at the windows. It was more quaint than elegant, but everything looked clean and tidy.

The door swung open, and Alex walked in amidst a stirring of leaves. For the first time she noticed that his clothes were as wet as her own.

"I guess I should have turned back sooner," she said, feeling a little bit guilty.

Alex tried to scowl, but a smile played on his lips. "I guess you should have."

The wind outside blew a branch past the window. Nicki shivered. In two long strides, Alex reached her side. "It's still early in the year for a fire, but tonight I think we could use one."

As he set to work at the hearth, snapping twigs and setting logs on the grate, Nicole glanced around again. "Does someone live here?"

"No. We use it for hunting. Mostly deer, but sometimes bear. Some of the men like to hunt raccoon. Nora James, the overseer's wife, sees to keeping it clean." He finished with the fire and returned to her side. "We'd better get out of these clothes."

For the first time, Nicki felt uncertain. "We're alone here, Alex. It wouldn't be proper for me to undress."

Alex smiled indulgently. "It wouldn't be proper for you to catch pneumonia, either."

His long legs carried him across the room to the wooden staircase, which he climbed to the rooms above. He returned with two soft woolen blankets.

"You can wrap up in this." Handing her a blanket, he turned her back to him so he could unfasten her buttons. Though she didn't like the idea, it was hard to argue with his logic. She certainly didn't want to get sick.

"We can dry them in front of the fire," he added as he peeled down her soggy bodice.

"Alex!" Nicki shrieked, pulling away from him. "What are you doing?"

"Playing lady's maid," he answered with a grin. "Now, will you stand still?"

Nicki's cheeks flamed, but she did as she was told. Alex helped her out of her skirts and petticoats, then unlaced her corsets, leaving her in chemise and pantalets. The wetness had penetrated even those, turning them almost transparent. She knew because when she glanced up at Alex, his eyes were no longer on her face. Instead, he was staring at the dark-pink circles peeking through the fabric, her nipples hard and puckered against the cold.

Watching his expression, the darkness that had gathered in his eyes, Nicki suddenly couldn't breathe. She just stood there, mesmerized by the way his eyes moved down her body, pausing for a moment to measure her tiny waist, then examining the curve of her hips. They settled on the dark red curls at the juncture of her legs.

"Beautiful," he whispered softly.

With trembling fingers and a pounding heart, Nicki drew the blanket around her.

Alex only smiled. He was thinking how innocent she looked. But then, in a way she was. From the venom with which she had spoken of her past, it was obvious the men she'd been with had taken what they wanted, used her to satisfy their needs with no concern for hers.

Tonight all that would change.

Tonight he would show her the joys of love, pleasure her in the countless ways he had imagined. He couldn't have planned it better if he'd tried.

10

Clutching the blanket around her, Nicki watched as Alex unfastened the cuffs on his shirt, worked the buttons down the front, tugged it free of his pants, and stripped it away.

Naked to the waist, his breeches clung wetly to the muscles of his legs and the taut, round flesh of his buttocks. She sucked in a breath at the sight of his aroused manhood, pressing determinedly against the front of his pants.

Cheeks bright with color, she turned toward the fireplace, but she didn't miss Alex's soft chuckle of amusement. She could hear the sound of his tall black boots hitting the floor, then the rustle of fabric. It occurred to her that, as arrogant as he was, he might just be immodest enough to remove *all* of his clothing.

"Take off the rest," he commanded, and she knew without doubt that was exactly what he had done.

"Not on your life."

"Need I remind you I'm more than twice your size?" he said from behind her.

"No. And I haven't forgotten what an overbearing tyrant you can be, either."

When Alex chuckled again, Nicki whirled to face him. "You're enjoying this!"

He stood just inches away, the blanket wrapped casually around his waist, his muscular arms folded across his wide chest. Deep grooves lined each side of his mouth.

"Exactly."

In her wildest dreams she couldn't have imagined the way Alexandre du Villier would look standing half-naked in the firelight. His hair looked more golden than brown, his eyes almost tawny. The hair on his chest curled seductively, and his skin was so smooth and tanned she ached to touch it.

"Well?" he pressed, interrupting her thoughts, for which she was grateful. "I'm waiting."

Nicki made a frustrated sound in her throat. She would lose this argument and she knew it. The thought of him removing her clothes by force flooded her with embarrassment—and something warm and liquid that seeped through her veins. "Turn around."

"What if I promise to close my eyes?"

"Damn you, this isn't funny. Now turn around."

Alex made a grand show of turning his back to her, the blanket, worn arrogantly low, clinging to his long, powerful legs.

Hurriedly, Nicole stripped off the last of her soggy garments, tossing them with a plop over one of his wide, bare shoulders.

He didn't even flinch. "That's better," he said.

Striding toward the fire, he pulled two wooden ladder-backed chairs to one side, constructed a makeshift clothesline using the handle of a broom, and draped their wet clothes over it. Then he joined her on the leather sofa, where she sat with her knees drawn up beneath the folds of the blanket.

With more practice than she cared to acknowledge, Alex pulled the last of the pins from her hair, letting the heavy mass tumble down her back in a riot of damp copper curls. He separated the silky strands with his fingers.

"I've dreamed of doing this." With a look of appreciation, he twirled a single soft curl around his hand, bunching the muscles in his arms with the movement.

Nicki slid away from him, moving as far toward the end of the sofa as she could get. "I think it would be wiser if you sat on the opposite end."

He smiled. "Not on your life." Easing himself along the sofa until he reached the place beside her, he slid an arm around her waist and pulled her close. His mouth over hers silenced her protest.

Nicki pressed her palms against his chest, trying to dissuade him, but the feel of his skin, the curly brown chest hair teasing her fingers, made her clutch at him instead. When Alex coaxed her lips apart and slid his tongue inside, Nicki whimpered softly. Alex's hold tightened, and he deepened the kiss. His breath felt warm and tasted masculine, stirring the heat that swirled in her stomach until it spread through her limbs.

Alex used his mouth and hands to relax her. He knew the exact moment when Nicki's guard came down, knew the very instant she began to surrender. Still, he didn't press her. He didn't want her compliance—something she had given unwillingly to the men who went before. Alex wanted her response. He wanted her clinging to him in passion, calling his name and begging him for more.

He moved his palms across the blanket at her back, wound his hand into her damp copper hair, and cradled the nape of her neck. His other hand eased upward from her waist. He could feel the rapid flutter of her heartbeat, hear her shallow intake of breath. Easing the blanket apart, he slid his hand inside to cup her breast.

Nicki pulled away. "Alex?" she whispered, uncertain.

"It's all right, *chérie.*"

His fingers skimmed across her flesh, and Nicki felt goose bumps race down her spine. His hand caressed her breast, cupping it, lifting the heavy weight, then teasing her nipple until it hardened, no longer from the cold but from his touch. She moaned softly. Nothing she'd experienced had felt like this. Nothing she had imagined.

Alex's mouth moved from her lips to her cheek, tugged on the lobe of her ear, then his tongue traced a fiery path inside the rim. She couldn't think straight —and didn't want to. With a will of their own, her hands began to knead the muscles of his chest and shoulders.

Alex pulled her down on the sofa and parted the front of her blanket. His face looked dark and hungry. "Alex?" she said again, knowing she should stop him, but no longer willing to.

"I promise I won't hurt you."

Alex would never hurt her. Had never hurt her, though he had every legal right, and she'd sometimes given him cause. No matter what happened, she was safe with Alex. The knowledge drained the last of her control. When his lips moved along her shoulders, over her breast to fasten on her nipple, Nicki whispered his name in a way she hadn't before. "Please . . ." she added softly, not certain exactly why.

It seemed the word he'd been seeking. She felt his hand move lower, to part her legs and stroke the inside of her thighs. She tensed for a moment, but the feeling was so incredible, so heady and mysterious, she began to relax and let him have his way.

"That's better, *ma chère*. Just let me take care of everything." His finger skimmed through the tight copper curls that sheltered her sex, then slid inside. Ripples of sensation washed over her. Instinctively, she arched against his palm. Why was she so wet? she wondered fleetingly, then lost the thought to the excitement coursing through her. His finger moved easily in and out, setting up a rhythm that made her writhe and moan. Something was swirling inside her. Something hot and pulsing and elusive.

"Please, Alex," she pleaded.

Alex loomed above her, positioning himself between her thighs. "Trust me."

And she did.

When she felt his stiff member pressing against her, demanding entrance to her body, she thought of Lorna and the guards for only an instant. Then it was Alex. The man she trusted above all others. The man she had come to love.

It seemed an odd time to discover the truth—and then again it didn't. For a woman, this was the ultimate gift. She would give it to no other.

Alex eased himself inside until he could go no farther. A little confused, he slid out and then in again. Still he found the passage blocked.

"It's all right, Alex," Nicki told him. "I'm not afraid."

It dawned on him like the bolt of lightning that flashed outside. The breath he'd been holding rushed from his lungs. "*Mon Dieu*, you're a virgin."

She looked confused. "Did you think I was not?"

"But the beatings you took? The guards at the prison—"

Alex seemed so upset, Nicki decided to resolve the matter herself. Tightening her hold on his shoulders, she pressed her body against him, forcing him farther inside. Flesh ground against flesh and Nicki bit her lip to keep from crying out.

"Damn." Though the heat of her narrow passage engulfed him, Alex stilled his movements and held himself back. "The worst is past," he soothed, pushing his guilt away with his words and hoping her pain had begun to ease. "It only hurts the first time."

Nicki smiled bravely and nodded her understanding. Even that gentle movement ate at his control. He had wanted to please her, wanted to give her pleasure like nothing she'd dreamed. Now he wasn't sure he could wait that long. Kissing her until she relaxed, he began to move inside her.

At first Nicki tensed with Alex's efforts, but with each passing moment the pain receded a little more. Alex's tongue teased her mouth while his hands caressed her breasts, making her forget the pain. Unconsciously, she lifted her hips against each slow penetration, and Alex groaned. He began to move faster, deeper, filling her in a strange, compelling way. He was driving harder now, his body pounding against hers until she felt something elusive begin to build.

Though she didn't know what it was, she dug her fingers into his shoulders and arched her hips, praying he would give it to her. Instead his body began to shudder, his muscles tensed, and he called out her name.

Eventually he grew still. His breathing returned to normal, but he didn't move away. Propped on his elbows, he drew a heavy breath and slid down her body to look into her face.

"Are you all right?"

"Yes."

"Why didn't you tell me?"

"I thought you knew."

He wouldn't have taken her if he'd known. *Or would he?* He'd been with dozens of women, in countries all over the world. But he'd never wanted a woman the way he did this one. There was something about her—he had sensed it from the start. He'd have taken her sooner or later—he had to.

Besides, he rationalized, she belonged to him. He had paid good money for her—and she had desired him. In the long run, it would make things easier for both of them.

"You're not displeased?" she asked.

Hardly. In fact, now that he thought about it, there was something endearing about the way she had given herself to him. Most of the women he'd known had slept with him to satisfy their own needs, done it for money, or for something else he could give them. With Nicki, it seemed almost a gift.

"I couldn't be happier," he said, and she smiled. A

soft, tentative smile that touched him in places he thought himself immune.

"I was certain I wouldn't like it."

Alex smiled. "But you did."

"It was wonderful—all but the part that hurt."

"That part is over." He noticed one of her small hands toying with the folds of the blanket on the floor. She was squeezing it absently. The other hand drew quick little circles on his shoulder.

"Nervous?"

"Not exactly. Just a little edgy. Like I've an itch I can't quite scratch."

Alex chuckled, a soft, deep rumble in his chest. "I think I know what will help." Cupping her chin with his hand, he dipped his head and kissed her. She felt his growing passion, hard and throbbing, before she realized his intentions. Then he was sliding inside her, burying himself to the fullest, and sending a ripple of pleasure down her spine. Alex seemed bigger than ever, hot and hard and wonderful. She clutched his neck and kissed him back, using her tongue just as he had, letting her hands roam over his body.

For the first time she let herself explore him, running her fingers along each new sinew and plane. She touched one flat copper nipple, circled it with her finger, and Alex groaned.

"Keep that up," he whispered, "and I won't be able to relieve your itch."

Nicki wasn't certain what he meant, but as he began to move, more slowly this time and with more determination, an ache began to build between her legs. Alex cupped a breast and sucked it into his mouth, his tongue working the hard bud until she tingled all over. The ache grew more intense.

Alex's hips moved in and out in a sensuous rhythm she found herself matching, stroke for stroke. He was moving faster now, each of his thrusts so deep and hard she began to feel them not as separate movements but as a series of stabbing, white-hot waves that rolled over her until she seemed to drown in them.

She laced her fingers in his hair, arched her back, and moaned. Alex silenced her with a kiss, his tongue thrusting deep into her mouth with the same hot rhythm as his body.

The tight coil of heat throbbing in her loins seemed as if it might consume her. Her body stiffened, arched, then her passions hurled over the edge. She thought she cried out Alex's name, but the mindless swirls of pleasure, white-hot and bright behind her eyes, were so intense she couldn't be sure. She gave herself up to them, reveled in their sweetness, and felt Alex shudder and stiffen in response.

Eventually, he rolled to his side, carrying her with him, and the last of the tension in her body drained away. For the first time, she realized her cheeks were wet with tears.

Alex tilted her chin with his fingers. "I didn't hurt you?"

Nicki smiled up at him. "No. It was the most beautiful thing that's ever happened to me. It was as if a part of you reached inside and touched my soul."

Strangely enough, Alex knew exactly what she meant. He had never experienced a feeling so powerful. It was beyond his sexual experience. Beyond anything he had felt with anyone else. It disturbed him that she could reach parts of him that no one had, make him feel things he didn't want to feel.

"It isn't always that way," he said, wanting her to know what had happened between them was special, but not quite certain why it should be so important. "I mean, with someone else, it might have been different."

"I wouldn't have done it with anyone else."

Why did those words mean so much to him? He glanced toward the fire. The blaze had simmered to coals. Outside, the wind still blew and lightning flashed, but the roll of thunder had moved some distance away. "We can make a pallet here on the floor or go upstairs. Unfortunately, the beds up there aren't much wider than the sofa."

"Let's stay here by the fire." She wanted to see him. To lie next to him and watch him sleep.

"All right." He settled her on the sofa with a kiss, pulled the blanket over her, and went back upstairs.

In minutes, he returned with an old blue quilt and several more blankets. After making a place for them on the floor, he scooped her into his arms and carried her onto the pallet. She went with him willingly. It seemed those few minutes without him had been far too long.

"Don't move," Alex instructed, inching away from where she sat cross-legged on the blankets. "I want to look at you."

Her nipples grew hard at his words. She drew herself up proudly, letting him assess her, wondering at her lack of embarrassment.

"If I'd had to wait three years," he said, "you would have been worth it." His voice sounded low and seductive. Even in the glow of the fire, his eyes were dark.

Nicki thought how beautiful he looked, but didn't

say so. Alex wouldn't have understood her choice of words. How could a man as powerfully built as he, a man who could send his enemies fleeing with one hard scowl, understand that he could be beautiful as well as masculine?

"*Dieu du ciel*, he said softly. "God in heaven, I want you again already." He pulled her down on the blankets. "If you're not feeling up to it. . . ." He looked at her with concern.

"I want you too."

He kissed her, and she could almost taste his passion. In minutes, she was hot all over, tingling with desire, and Alex was deeply inside her. It seemed just where he belonged.

They made love two more times that night, the most incredible night of Nicki's life.

She awoke to find the room bathed in sunlight and Alex heating water for a bath.

"I think I shall take Danielle's place permanently," he said with a smile as she stepped into the steaming copper tub.

"I think I should like that." She bathed and washed her hair, dried it in front of the fire, then braided it and let it trail down her back. Alex bathed but had no razor with which to shave. She thought his night's growth of beard only made him look more handsome.

He helped her do up the buttons at the back of her riding dress, then gave her a thorough kiss that stirred another round of heat between them. When Alex stepped back, she noticed the hard arousal that pressed against the front of his riding breeches. Blushing, she glanced away.

Alex chuckled softly. "I can't seem to get enough of

you. If I weren't afraid *Grand-mère* would have half the workers combing the fields for us, I'd stay right here and make love to you for the next two weeks."

The mention of Rachael's name brought the first rush of sanity Nicole had known in the last two days. "What will you tell her?"

"The truth." At her stricken look, Alex added, "most of it, anyway. We were caught in the storm and forced to spend the night at the lodge."

"Since I have no reputation left to ruin, I suppose it doesn't really matter."

"If memory serves, you were the little minx who took off in the middle of a thunderstorm."

She smiled at that. "When will you tell Clarissa?"

"She may not hear about it at all. If she does, I'll tell her the same thing."

"I mean about us."

Alex smiled indulgently. "It's true Clarissa has little interest in being my bedmate, but she's only understanding to a point."

Nicki felt a tremor of unease. "She'll have to know sometime. Don't you think it would be kinder if you told her right away?"

Alex didn't answer. He seemed to be judging her words. The smile had gone from his face, his expression, no longer warm, seemed wary and uncertain. "And just what is it I'm supposed to tell her, *ma petite*?"

Nicki swallowed hard. Why was he making this so difficult? "About your feelings for me," she said softly.

Alex felt a building knot of dread. He prayed he was wrong. Moving closer, he took her hands between his and noticed how cold they had grown.

"There is no need to tell her about us. As long as we remain discreet, Clarissa will not be a problem."

Nicki licked her lips. Her mouth felt so dry she could barely speak. "Tell me you don't still plan to marry her."

Alex didn't answer.

"Say it, Alex. Tell me it isn't so."

Alex's expression turned grim. He tightened his hold on her hands and pulled her closer. "I thought you understood. We talked about this before. A man marries for the benefits the union can bring. For the advantages to his family. Clarissa means nothing to me. She never has."

Nicki moved her head from side to side, trying to deny his words. Her stomach had knotted and a hard lump closed her throat. "Oh, God," she whispered, struggling to break free of his hold.

Alex looked at her pale face and fought to keep his voice calm. "Listen to me, *ma chère*. Clarissa is unimportant. She means nothing."

Nicole jerked free. It was all she could do to stay on her feet. The room was spinning around her, airless, and suddenly too warm. "She means nothing? Nothing? The woman will be your wife. If she is nothing, what am I? Less than nothing. Not fit to wipe your shoes."

She whirled toward the door, but Alex caught up to her in three long strides, his hard arm going around her waist. "Stop it. That isn't the way it is and you know it."

"Isn't it?" Tears flooded her cheeks, but she didn't wipe them away. "You're tired of Lisette. You wanted someone new to fill your bed. How could I have been such a fool?"

"This has nothing to do with Lisette or anyone else. What happened between us was what we both wanted. It was beautiful. You said so yourself."

"It was beautiful because I thought you cared for me."

"I do care."

She only shook her head. "Let me go." She tried to pry his arm away.

"Not until you understand."

"I'll never understand, Alex. Never." Shoving him so hard that he tripped and fell backward, she raced to the door. She was crying freely now, the tears so thick they blinded her. Outside, the ground was muddy, the path she ran down overgrown with grass and branches that had fallen in the storm. She didn't know where she was going; she didn't care. She only knew she had to get away from Alex, had to run from the awful grief she felt inside.

Branches tore at her skirts and cut her cheeks, and still she raced on. She could hear Alex behind her, begging her to stop. The swamp seemed to enclose her, the ghostly gray moss that swayed eerily from the overhanging branches seemed to beckon her on. There was water on both sides of her now, dark and dank and forbidding. The whispering wind seemed to call out her name.

She realized it wasn't the wind but Alex, just moments before he tumbled her to the ground, rolling her into a pile of leaves and twigs as he landed on top of her.

Sobbing hysterically, she fought him. She pounded his chest, tried to scratch and claw. "Leave me alone!"

Alex held her immobile, pinning her wrists and her

thrashing body, but careful not to hurt her. When the last of her strength had ebbed, he gathered her into his arms.

"I thought I loved you," she sobbed. "How could I have been so wrong?"

Alex closed his eyes. His chest felt leaden, and so tight he could barely breathe. He had known she would object to becoming his mistress. At least at first, just for a while. He hadn't counted on this. Hadn't dreamed she'd expect marriage. Cradling the back of her head with his hand, he rocked her gently back and forth.

"I thought you'd understand," he said. "I never meant to hurt you."

She only cried harder, her small body shaking with the force of her tears. It tortured him to see her like this, to know that he had been the cause.

"I thought you were a man of honor. Someone I could trust."

Her words cut like a sword. *A man of honor.* She had once thought him that. Now she did not. "Please, *chérie.*" Why did it matter so much? She was a servant, for God's sake. A thief. He clenched his jaw against the lie.

She was a lady. His lady.

"I can't stand to see you this way." He couldn't bear the anguish in her voice, couldn't stand to think of the harm he had done. "Try to understand."

At the pain in his voice, she glanced up at him. His eyes looked bleak, his face a mask of despair. "It is you who does not understand." Nicki closed her eyes against a fresh wave of pain, but her anger had fled, leaving her empty and alone. "It doesn't matter," she whispered. "It was a silly, foolish dream to think you would want someone like me."

Alex tightened his hold. "I want you, dammit," he said hoarsely. "I still want you."

"Just like the others," she said softly. "They wanted me too."

Alex gripped her arm. "Not like the others—you've got to believe that."

"Why should I?"

"Because it's the truth." She laughed at that, a grating sound that chilled him to the bone.

"The truth?" she repeated. "For me the truth is different each day. With each man who owns me. Your truth is not much different from Fortier's."

Alex's heart constricted. No words would come to defend him.

Nicki brushed the tears from her cheeks with the backs of her hands. "I think we'd better be getting back," she said with a calmness that only made him feel worse. "I wouldn't want the others to worry."

"Nicki, please. Let me try to explain."

She came to her feet, brushing off the dirt and twigs and smoothing her hair. "There is no need, m'sieur. I understand only too well." Turning her back to him, she walked off toward the lodge.

Alex didn't try to stop her. He felt sick inside. Sick and empty.

One thought loomed above all others: *What in God's name had he done?*

11

Nicole waited in the lodge while Alex saddled the horses. Her face felt pale and bloodless, and her hands trembled. But she'd shed her last tear.

Whatever she and Alex had shared on their pallet in front of the fire was over and done. Locked away in her heart until she was strong enough to remember it without weeping. She was his bond servant, by law little more than a slave. Though he had seduced her with his care of her, with expensive clothes, and suppers at his lavish table, she'd been a fool to believe that Alexandre du Villier, le Duc de Brisonne, could ever have loved her.

She wondered what her father would have said if he had known. Surely he would have been disappointed in her. Yet when she pictured his face, he seemed incredulous. She realized he would have been fooled as easily as she.

"You are a St. Claire," he would have said. "How could any man do better?"

Oh, Papa, such pride you have given me. The burden was heavy. Too heavy. She wasn't sure how much more she could bear.

They returned to the house in silence. Nicole was grateful for the time to school her emotions and put them away. She had done it before, hadn't she? Learned to control herself, suffered whatever she was dealt while she kept her feelings locked inside.

"Thank heavens you are both all right." *Grand-mère* met them at the door.

"It was quite a storm," Nicki said with a smile that felted pasted on, yet she knew looked sincere. "I was lucky Alexandre came along when he did."

Alex said nothing.

Nicki dismounted on her own before Alex could help her. She didn't want him to touch her, wasn't sure of the limit of her control.

"Well, you both look tired," Rachael said, linking an arm through Nicole's. "What you need is rest and something to eat."

"I want to check the horses," Alex said. Without a glance in Nicki's direction, he picked up Napoleon's reins and led both animals away.

Once inside, Nicki pleaded a headache. It wasn't a lie. "I just need a little rest," she said.

"I will have a bath sent up." Rachael looked at her with concern. "And some food. I am sure you will feel better after you get some sleep."

Nicki nodded. Upstairs Danielle helped her undress, then left her alone. It wasn't until later that she noticed the rash around her throat, the small nips Alex had made with his teeth and his mouth—tiny marks that branded her.

She laughed at that, a grating sound that came out harsh and unfriendly. Alex had branded her skin just as he had her heart. He couldn't have seared her more deeply if he'd used a white-hot iron.

After her bath, she slept. It was a deep sleep, but hardly peaceful. More the drugged sleep of exhaustion. She declined supper, and *Grand-mère* was understanding. After all, she'd weathered a terrible storm.

And so she had. The storm of her desire. The storm of her passions and feelings of love for a man to whom she meant nothing.

Nicki slept fitfully, but by morning she felt better. Until she opened the carved armoire door in search of something to wear. Up until now, she had accepted the clothes as a deed of kindness, a result of the friendship her father and Alex's had shared. Etienne St. Claire would have done no less for Charles's son, if he had been in need.

Now, looking at the clothes, it hit her like the rainstorm she had just weathered.

Bought and paid for—just like Lisette.

Her stomach knotted and the bile rose in her throat. Had he planned it this way from the start? Meant to lure her into his bed with elegant gowns and words of endearment? Well, she wasn't tempted by fripperies and meaningless flattery. She wasn't Lisette—and the sooner Alex found that out the better.

Careful to choose her simplest muslin day dress, Nicki headed downstairs in search of him. She wanted this matter settled. Wanted him to know she had no intention of sharing his bed again. But most of all, she wanted to know what he would do with her once he had discovered she wouldn't bend to his will.

In the foyer, just as she feared, Frederick told her Alex had already gone. With an unhappy sigh, she turned toward the dining room—and ran straight into Clarissa.

"Good morning," Nicki said, unconsciously squaring her shoulders and lifting her chin.

"Indeed," Clarissa said. "Feeling better?"

"Much better, thank you." She watched the woman for signs of derision but found none.

"I don't suppose you'd be able to help me?" Clarissa asked. "Our engagement ball is only two weeks away, and I've a list of unfinished details a yard long."

Nicole's stomach tightened. "Just tell me what needs doing."

They made their way into the drawing room, where Clarissa had spread out her lists. Nicole was to help organize the servants. Most appropriate, she thought, and almost smiled.

By week's end every detail had been handled. Alex had been called away on business, or at least that was what he had claimed. He would be returning the night of the party. Nicole's ball gown arrived the day before, *Grand-mère* having insisted on the dress some weeks ago.

"Try it on," the old woman gently commanded, smiling broadly, obviously pleased by the finished creation, a sheer white organdy shot with gold. The bodice dipped low in front, while the skirt, outrageously full, was gathered in swirls above an underskirt of gold brocade. It was the loveliest gown Nicole had ever seen.

And it sickened her to wear it.

"It's beautiful," she told Rachael, who sat rocking before the chamber window, where sunlight stole in to light the room.

"You make it beautiful," Rachael said.

Nicki tried to smile, but her bottom lip trembled.

"They're all going to know about my past," she said softly.

Grand-mère sighed and shook her head. "There is no way to keep the servants from talking. They will know, but it does not matter. You are a St. Claire and under our protection. They will know that too."

On impulse, Nicole reached over and caught the old woman's hand. "There's something I've been wanting to ask you. But first I want you to know how much I appreciate everything you've done."

Rachael waved away her words with an impatient hand. "I have done little worth mentioning. What is it you wish?"

"When will you be leaving Belle Chêne?"

"Sooner than I planned, I fear. A friend has fallen ill. I received word just this morning. It appears she will survive her sickness, but her recovery will be long and difficult. I will be leaving for France a week from today."

"Take me with you."

Grand-mère arched a thin gray brow, but didn't seem put off by the notion. She sat rocking quietly while Nicki waited, holding her breath.

"I think that is a fine idea. I cannot imagine why I did not think of it myself."

"Oh, *Grand-mère!*" Nicole threw her arms around the old woman's narrow shoulders and hugged her until she worried Rachael's fragile bones might break. "You won't be sorry. There's much I can do to help out. Anything you need. Anything."

"Hush, now. Do not talk nonsense. You will come with me, and I will introduce you into society. Your past will be unknown there. Somehow we will manage to keep it that way. We will find you a husband."

That wiped the smile from Nicki's face, but she said nothing to *Grand-mère*. One problem at a time, she thought. First she must leave Belle Chêne, her indenture, and Alexandre du Villier a continent behind.

Alex leaned over the rail of the *Saratoga*, a small, sleek sailing vessel that carried passengers to the towns along the coast. He was on his way home from Mobile, on his way back from his second voyage to that city in the last few months. But unlike the first, which involved Belle Chêne business, this trip was personal.

He had come to seek the help of Bayram Sit, the friend he had run into on his first journey. Ram had been working the docks, healing from a leg injury he had suffered at sea. Fortunately, by now the leg wound had healed, but Ram had not yet signed aboard another ship.

"It is good to be at sea again," Ram said, running a hand across his smooth, clean-shaven skull, "if only for a few short days." The big Turk splayed his legs against the roll and sway of the ship, his muscular arms clasped behind him. He wasn't a tall man, but few were more powerfully built.

"You're sure you won't mind spending some time in the *Vieux Carré?*"

Ram just laughed, a hearty rumbling sound that moved his drooping black mustache. "I'll enjoy the chance to live high on the hog for a while."

Too easily, the Turk had agreed to return with him to New Orleans. Alex wondered if his friend had read the look of desperation that haunted him from the mirror.

"About the girl," Ram said, seizing his attention once again. "Maybe you should tell her the rest."

Alex released a weary sigh. "She's got enough to worry about. Hopefully, she'll never have to know."

Ram nodded. They stood by the rail in silence, each lost in thoughts of his own. "Think I will go below," Ram finally said, "join the men in a game of chance."

As his friend disappeared through the low wooden hatch, Alex watched him absently. He glanced across the waves, his thoughts still in shadow. Only a sliver of moon reflected on the water, while a soft breeze fluttered the sails above his head. In the distance, tiny yellow dots of light beckoned from the far away shore. The vague outline of houses reminded him of hearth and home, and that brought fresh thoughts of Nicole.

I thought I loved you. How could I have been so wrong? Her words had plagued him for days. Nicki was young and naive, foolish enough to believe in love. He only wished he hadn't been the one to destroy her girlish dreams.

Alex rarely doubted himself or his actions, but this time he regretted bitterly what he had done. He should have been clearer in his intentions. Nicole was an intelligent woman. Surely she would have seen the wisdom of his plans. When she calmed down, he told himself, he would speak to her again, *make* her understand.

But even as he said the words he wondered what wisdom there had been in taking a young girl's virtue? In convincing her to trust him and then destroying that trust?

Alex pulled his collar up against the bite of the wind. He had to stop thinking about Nicole, start worrying about his family. It was almost certain now that without Clarissa's help, he wouldn't be able to repay the money François had borrowed from Fortier. They'd lose everything.

He had his grandmother to consider, his brother, the children he would one day raise. He owed them something. He owed his father. He couldn't loose Belle Chêne.

Alex's hold tightened on the rail. It occurred to him then that without Nicole he had nothing of value to lose.

The music of the orchestra drifted in from the ballroom, located in the far right wing of the house. They were playing a Viennese waltz, a lovely song that reminded Nicole of the balls she had attended back home. Those had been gay times, wonderful times filled with fanciful visions of the future.

The merriment tonight only saddened her. As if the gods who pulled her strings were up there somewhere laughing at her.

With a heavy sigh, she checked her appearance in the mirror, noting with distant satisfaction that she had never looked better. Fixing a smile in place, she headed out the door.

It took all her courage to walk down the wide staircase. She should have gone down earlier, joined a group of party-goers and slipped in unnoticed. Instead she had waited until the last possible moment.

From the foot of the stairs the music sounded louder, and she smelled the fragrance of gardenias. Huge bouquets of flowers filled the entry and lined the halls. Frederick stood beside the open doorway in a crisp white shirt and satin-lapeled black tailcoat, ramrod straight. He grinned at her and winked.

It was a small bit of encouragement, but one she needed. She smiled back at him and headed toward the ballroom. Few people noticed her entrance into the huge, flower-filled room until the orchestra finished the waltz. After a light round of applause, a dozen couples swung their attention in her direction. Several more people noticed her, then several more. Was it her imagination, or was the room a little too quiet? It seemed scores of eyes were fixed on her, and not one smiling face.

The sound of a chair scraping against the black-and-white marble floor drew her attention to a tall man who came to his feet beneath the crystal chandeliers and began striding toward her. Another approached with equal haste. François du Villier reached her side an instant before Thomas Demming. His smile of understanding was the greatest gift she had ever received.

"Mademoiselle St. Claire," he said, bowing over her hand. "You are without doubt the most beautiful woman in the room."

"I'll second that," said Thomas. His smile, too, looked warm. "Since it appears François has claimed the first dance, I should be honored if you would allow me the second."

"I'd like that very much."

As the orchestra began another song, François looped her arm through his. He turned to the crowd with an air of subtle warning.

"I see you have found an escort," *Grand-mère* said with an approving smile as she walked up beside them. "François will be the envy of every man in the room."

"Thomas is already jealous," François said.

Nicole felt a rush of warmth at his words. "It is I who am fortunate," she said, and meant it. She was coming to like François, to read in him a gentleness she hadn't seen before.

François led her onto the dance floor and by his actions forced the others to accept her presence. He was a wonderful dancer, the most graceful she had ever known. His touch was gentle at the small of her back; the hand holding hers felt slender but strong. His soft smile and light conversation distracted her from the unpleasant scene of her arrival, and eventually helped her relax. She didn't realize she was searching for someone until she heard the amusement in François's voice.

"He's out on the terrace," he told her, bringing a shot of color to her cheeks.

How could she be looking for Alex? "I wasn't sure he'd gotten home," she said lamely.

"He made it, but none too early. We had to send a carriage for Clarissa. She was fuming by the time he got downstairs."

She couldn't help smiling at that. "A marriage made in heaven."

François laughed aloud, a boyish, rippling sound. The dance came to a close, and Thomas arrived to claim the next. He had just pulled her into his arms when Alex appeared in the doorway, Clarissa close beside him. The smile Alex had been wearing faded, replaced by a hardness Nicole knew only too well.

He doesn't like me dancing with Thomas, she realized with a jolt of satisfaction. Thomas was wealthy, handsome, and unattached. Alex respected his long-time friend's intelligence and sense of fair play. In short, Thomas Demming was tough competition for any man. Well, almost any man.

She glanced again at Alex. In the past she would have withered at a look as black as that. Tonight she was Nicole St. Claire. She bowed to no man.

Smiling up at Thomas, she said something that made him laugh, and they waltzed off among the crowd. The mirrored walls reflected a swirl of organdy and gold, a handsome blond gentleman in black, and a scowling Alexandre du Villier.

For the first time in days, Nicki's spirits lifted. Alex wasn't one bit happy about her choice of partners. And if Alex wasn't happy—Nicki was. She laughed at Thomas's repartee, flirted outrageously, and smiled even more brightly. When the music ended, Thomas whirled her up to where Alex and Clarissa stood.

"Enjoying yourself?" Alex said to Thomas a bit stiffly.

Thomas grinned. "More every minute." He smiled at Nicole, who had the good sense not to smile back too warmly.

"I see you finally made it," Alex said to her. "I wasn't sure you were up to it." She didn't miss the note of challenge.

"We all have our crosses to bear." She glanced pointedly at Clarissa, who was busily discussing the sugar harvest with a gentleman beside her.

Alex looked handsome in his tailored black evening clothes, perfectly fit to the width of his shoulders. In just one week, she had forgotten how tall he was, how tanned and smooth his skin. It made her ache inside just to look at him—which piqued her temper even more.

"Congratulations to you both," Thomas put in, kissing Clarissa's cheek.

"I believe this dance is mine," Alex said to Nicole, his eyes still baiting her.

Thomas answered for her. "Only if Miss Endicott has one left for me." At Clarissa's nod of agreement, Thomas placed her hand in his and the two of them waltzed away.

Alex extended an arm to Nicole.

"I'm sorry, m'sieur," she said with an air of satisfaction, "it seems my card is already full." With a triumphant smile, she turned to leave, but Alex caught her arm, his grip insistent.

"You'll dance with me here," he warned, "or I'll drag you out on the terrace and you'll dance with me there."

Nicki set her jaw, her aqua eyes snapping fire. "This is your engagement ball. Since you, m'sieur, are the host, I suggest you pay attention to someone who enjoys your company."

"And I suggest you dance with me before I make a scene."

She knew he would do it. There was very little Alex would not dare. Holding her tongue against another biting retort, she let him draw her stiffly into his arms.

"We need to talk," he said without preamble.

"If the discussion involves becoming your mistress, there is nothing left to say."

His hand tightened on her waist, and he pulled her indecently close. "Sooner or later you're going to hear me out, if I have to tie you up and gag you. Now, you can make this hard on yourself or easy. But I suggest you agree to listen. Because if you don't, everyone in this room is going to know there's something going on between us."

"Nothing is going on between us. Not now. Not ever."

He smiled, his eyes dark and mocking. "That's where you're wrong," he said softly. But he shifted his position until they were once more dancing as proper etiquette deemed.

"Tomorrow afternoon," he said, knowing the party would last through most of the night. "Two o'clock, in my study."

"*Oui, m'sieur*," she agreed in perfect imitation of Danielle. "After all, what am I but a lowly servant?"

Alex's eyes grew so dark, they looked black. A muscle bunched in his cheek. He said nothing more, just danced with her in silence. But when the dance was over, it was to François, not Thomas, he returned her. In spite of herself, Nicole felt pleased.

Though he tried to keep his attention on Clarissa, Alex found himself watching Nicole through dance after irritating dance. She looked beautiful in her shimmering white-and-gold gown, her copper hair swept into long, silky curls that cascaded onto each shoulder. Her soft, white breasts swelled invitingly, stirring a memory of how tantalizing they had felt in his hands. Every time he looked at her his body hardened and he had to glance away.

"I'll expect you to be discreet," Clarissa said, surprising him. She glanced at Nicole, but made no further comment.

"I'll keep that in mind," he answered dryly. That

she cared so little bothered him for the very first time. *A mistress who loves you for money, and a wife who loves you not at all.* Nicki's words. The words of a naive young girl.

Or the wisdom of a beautiful woman?

Just before supper, Valcour Fortier arrived. Alex knew he had been invited. Valcour was a member of the elite planter society, and though the two of them didn't get along, Fortier had never openly done anything that Alex could object to. That privately he was cruel and sadistic, especially in his dealings with women, was a subject carefully glossed over.

"Congratulations," Fortier said to Alex, brushing a light kiss on Clarissa's cheek.

"Thank you," Alex replied formally, accepting Fortier's handshake.

He had to admit, Valcour was a handsome man. With his dark good looks and brooding black eyes, women usually found him attractive. Only Clarissa seemed immune. She smiled at Fortier's flattery and accepted his invitation to dance, but was obviously not interested. Alex found himself almost wishing she were. He wondered with a bit of cynicism how Valcour Fortier would hold up beneath an onslaught of Clarissa's dubious charms.

It wasn't until sometime later that he spotted the Spaniard, as Valcour preferred to think of himself, dancing with Nicole. Even from a distance he could read Nicki's nervousness. Just watching the way Valcour's hand caressed her tiny waist made Alex's stomach tighten.

* * *

"So, Mademoiselle Stockton is really Mademoiselle St. Claire." Fortier was the first person who'd had the courage to speak the words.

"Do you find that distasteful, m'sieur?" Nicki asked.

"I find it amusing."

Nicki stiffened. She had agreed to the dance because the man had backed her into a corner. He seemed to be good at that. "I'm afraid I don't."

Fortier smiled indulgently. "It's warm in here. Why don't we go out on the terrace?"

"No," she said, a little too quickly. Fortier's laughter was soft, too soft, an unnatural sound that made her shiver inside. If she lived to be a hundred, she would never forget the way he had looked at her that day at the auction.

"Still afraid, little flower? You shouldn't be. Had I bought your contract, you would not be here, but warming my bed. With me you would find pleasure like nothing you've dreamed."

Nicole felt the blood drain from her face. She was grateful the music ended before Fortier had time to say anything more. Nicki thanked him for the dance, though it galled her to do so, and took her leave. When she was sure he wasn't looking, she made her way out onto the terrace.

It felt good to be away from the strained conversation, the warning glances that Alex seemed to cast her way with each new man who partnered her. To his obvious chagrin, she merely smiled and kept on dancing.

The air felt cool on the terrace, but there were several couples nearby, and she wanted to be alone. Heading down the wide marble steps, she walked

among the rows of boxhedges along the path that led
to the lake. Small oil lanterns trimmed with bright
yellow ribbons lit the way.

Seating herself on a gray stone bench, she looked
out across the moonlit lake toward the overhanging
oaks in the distance. The evening breeze washed over
her, soothing her ragged nerves. She found herself
enjoying the solitude, content to be away from her
problems, if only for a while.

She wasn't there long before footsteps crunching
on the oyster-shell path drew her attention, and a
shadowy figure approached. Valcour Fortier sat
down on the bench beside her.

"Mind if I join you?"

Nervously, she wet her lips. "I was just about to go
in." She started to rise, but Valcour pulled her back
down.

"There is no need to hurry. It's a beautiful spot, is it
not?"

"Yes. Lovely."

Valcour touched her cheek, turning it with his
hand to study her profile. "Not nearly so lovely as
you."

Nicki turned away and started to rise, but Fortier's
grip on her arm forced her back down.

"You should have been mine," he said.

Before she could stop him, his arms went around
her and his mouth closed over hers. Nicki pressed
her hands against his chest and tried to break free.
She felt the first small stirrings of fear. Remotely she
noticed he tasted faintly of tobacco, and his lips felt
dry, but not unpleasant. When his tongue probed her
mouth seeking entrance, she renewed her struggles,

but felt him jerked away so abruptly she almost toppled over.

"I believe Mademoiselle St. Claire was just leaving." Alex voice held the hard edge of steel, and his eyes were so dark they looked as black as Fortier's. He released his hold on Valcour's shirt.

"So she said," Fortier agreed, smoothing the wrinkles from his clothes. The skin over his high cheekbones looked taut, but his voice sounded even and controlled. "It seems your bargain was far shrewder than even you imagined," he said to Alex. Then to Nicole, "Another time, mademoiselle." With a slight, mocking bow, he turned and strode away.

Nicki sat down on the bench in silence, her heart hammering as if fighting to escape her chest.

"What are you doing out here?" Alex's voice cut through her numbness. She looked up to find him scowling down at her.

"Spending a moment by the lake," she told him, gathering the remnants of her composure. "Is that something else of which you don't approve?"

"I've warned you about him. I thought you'd have enough sense to keep out of danger."

Nicole set her jaw; her small hands balled into fists against her sides. "Forgive me, your grace. I shouldn't have encouraged him, but after all, I find him so attractive."

"Stop it."

"Next time I'll work harder to control my passions."

"Stop it, damn you!" Jerking her roughly into his arms, Alex's hard kiss silenced her. Nicki pressed her hands against his chest and tried to twist away, but he held her easily, forcing her mouth open and plunging his tongue inside.

Nicki felt the heat of it, the swift jolt of desire, just before she tore herself free. Her breath came fast and hard as she fought for control. "You warn me away from him, but you are no better!"

Alex stood there, his wide chest heaving in and out. Finally his grim look softened. "I'm sorry," he said, raking a hand through his wavy dark-brown hair. "You did nothing to deserve what I said."

"Or what you did?"

Alex almost smiled. "It's difficult to regret kissing you, *chérie*, when I've thought of little else these long days past."

She felt the pleasure of his words like a blossom opening inside her. It only strengthened her resolve. "Well, you had better *stop* thinking about it." With that she turned in a swirl of sheer white organdy and started back down the path.

"Two o'clock," he called after her, reminding her of their afternoon meeting.

Just the sound of his voice piqued her fury, but she didn't let it show. In truth, she was looking forward to their meeting. She had been wanting to get things settled. Tomorrow would be the perfect time to spring her little surprise.

12

Alex sat behind his carved mahogany desk working on a green, leather-bound ledger, but his mind lingered on Nicole. For the tenth time in the past few minutes he glanced at the walnut clock above the mantle. Five minutes till two.

If she wasn't there by two-fifteen—and he wasn't sure she would be—he would go up to her room and get her.

At one minute till, a polite knock sounded at the door and Alex breathed a sigh of relief. Rounding the desk, he turned the silver doorknob to find Nicole in a sunny yellow day dress, *Grand-mère* standing at her side. One look at his grandmother's serene expression said that whatever Rachael was doing there had nothing to do with what had happened between him and Nicole that night at the lodge.

"Good afternoon, *Grand-mère*," Alex said dutifully, with a kiss on her wrinkled cheek.

"*Bonjour*, Alexandre. You look as though you have recovered from the party."

He had dressed casually in dark-brown trousers and a light cotton shirt. He wanted to set an informal tone for his meeting with Nicole. He wanted her to feel at ease with him, the way she had before.

"And you, *Grand-mère?* Did you enjoy yourself?"

"As a matter of fact, I did. So much so, I have decided to come out of mourning for your father. It's been quite long enough."

For the first time, he noticed her pale-blue day dress. She had worn nothing but black since the day of her arrival. "Father would have approved."

"Perhaps. In many ways I never really knew him. My husband—your grandfather—insisted on playing the larger role in our son's upbringing, and I was young and foolish enough to let him."

"I'm glad you and I were more fortunate," Alex said, meaning it.

"Your mother made the same mistake," she continued, "by letting Charles singlehandedly raise you." Clucking her disapproval, she affectionately touched Alex's cheek. "It seems none of the du Villier men has learned the value of a good woman."

"Oh, I don't know"—Alex smiled warmly at Nicki —"I believe we know enough to recognize a treasure when we find one." His eyes roamed over her. "You should wear yellow more often, *chérie.* It more than agrees with you." But then, she looked beautiful in just about anything—or nothing at all.

"I'm glad you approve," she said lightly. Too lightly. Where was the temper he had left her with the night before?

He gave her a chaste kiss, too, though it was hardly what he wanted. The smell of violets drifted up, and he fought a sudden hardening in his loins. He liked the way her dress showed off her tiny waist, the way she wore her hair, in soft copper curls beside her

cheeks. But he didn't like the way she smiled at him
—as if she knew something he didn't.

"Is there something you wished to see me about,
Grand-mère?" he asked, intent on getting to the business at hand.

"It can wait." She seated herself beside Nicole on
the tufted leather sofa.

Alex cleared his throat. The little minx wasn't getting off this easily. "I asked to see Nicole because
there are some things we need to discuss." He sat
down in the winged-back chair across from them.

"Go right ahead," *Grand-mère* said.

"In private," Alex added. He had never known his
grandmother to be so dense.

"*D'accord,*" she finally conceded with a sigh. "I
only stopped by to ask you to make arrangements for
our passage. I have already checked with your friend
Thomas. He says there is a ship departing for France
next Saturday."

"But surely you won't be leaving so soon?" Alex
arched a brow in surprise.

"I am afraid I have no choice." Rachael explained
about her friend's ongoing illness and ended by saying, "At least I shall not be making the voyage with
only a lady's maid for companion."

Alex frowned as an inkling of suspicion crossed his
mind. "And just who will be traveling with you?"

"Why, Nicole, of course. We discussed the idea at
length while you were away. It is the perfect solution,
n'est-ce pas?"

Alex clamped his jaw to keep from swearing. He
fixed Nicole with a gaze meant to wither, but she only
shrugged her shoulders. "It's the perfect solution,"
he agreed. "Except for one minor problem."

"And what is that?" Rachael asked.

"She isn't going."

"What!" Nicki came to her feet. "But why not? Surely you wouldn't deny your grandmother a traveling companion. It's a very difficult journey."

"I said, you aren't going."

"But—but I can't stay here . . . not after you're married. Clarissa wouldn't stand for it."

"You won't have to. You're moving into the town house."

Nicole's face paled. She started to speak, but the words seemed lodged in her throat. *Toulouse Street. The place he kept his mistress.* Clutching the folds of her skirt, she sank back down on the sofa, her chest so tight she could barely breathe. "Please, Alex," she said softly, "let me go with *Grand-mère.*"

"No."

"Alexandre," Rachael said, moving toward him, an odd expression on her face. "Are you certain you know what you are doing?"

For a moment he didn't answer. "I own her contract—or rather, Belle Chêne does. She isn't leaving. The subject is closed."

Rachael watched him a moment more, then instead of getting angry, which he expected, she graced him with a smile. "Whatever you say, Alexandre." She walked over to Nicole, who looked incredulous, and patted her trembling hand. "Alexandre knows what is best," she said.

"But *Grand-mère—*"

"I shall miss you, *ma fille.*" Turning, she flashed Alex a brief smile and left the room, closing the door behind her.

Nicole just sat there, staring at him but not really

seeing. Tears shimmered in her eyes, but she blinked them away. "I never thought you could be this cruel."

Alex sat down beside her, clasping her cold hands between his warm ones. "I don't want to hurt you. I've never wanted that."

"Then let me go."

He glanced out the window toward the gardens. Swans floated on the surface of the lake and a soft breeze fluttered the moss in the overhanging oaks. "You agreed to listen. I'll expect no less."

Nicole didn't answer, but she didn't look away.

Alex took a deep, calming breath, and willed his words to come out right. "In the beginning—once I knew the truth about who you were—I believed keeping you as my mistress was your best chance for happiness. I knew you cared for me—and I wanted you. Badly." He paused, but still she didn't speak. "I knew you had been abused. I thought you were no longer a virgin. Since there was no way of keeping your past a secret, no way to find you a proper husband, I felt sure you'd be better off with me."

"I could have gone away. You could have helped me make a start somewhere else."

Alex scoffed at the notion. "And just who would take care of you?"

Nicki squared her small shoulders and lifted her chin. "The same person who was doing it before you came along—me."

"You?" he repeated, wondering if he could possibly have heard her correctly. "Need I remind you what a botched-up mess you made of it?" That shut her up. "In these times, a woman alone in the world has little chance for survival, let alone happiness."

"I won't be your mistress, Alex. I don't care what your reasons are."

"You let me make love to you. You wanted me as much as I wanted you."

"I thought I loved you. I was wrong."

"So now I'm to believe you care nothing for me at all?"

"It happens to be true. What I felt was gratitude, nothing more."

"Gratitude? You let me make love to you out of gratitude?"

"That's right."

Alex pinned her with his eyes. "You're a liar." Pulling her down on the sofa, he kissed her, an insistent kiss that demanded she respond.

Nicki fought against it, pushing him away and forcing herself to ignore the heat that seared her body, the wicked warmth that moved through her, stealing her will. When Alex coaxed her lips apart and slid his tongue inside, Nicki felt a jolt of desire like nothing she'd known. It was all she could do to resist it. All she could do to keep from sliding her arms around his neck and moaning his name. Though her hands were pinned between them, she remembered the strength of the muscles beneath his shirt, the silky touch of his curly brown chest hair.

She could feel his arousal, hot and hard against her thigh; his hand caressing her breast, kneading it softly through the soft linen fabric of her dress. Against her will, her nipple hardened and ached against his palm.

One moment of weakness, one tentative touch of her tongue against his, and then she twisted away.

"Stop it! Can't you understand I don't want you anymore?"

Alex mocked her with a soft rumbling laugh. "What I understand, *chérie*, is that gratitude has nothing to do with what is going on between us." His voice, still husky with passion, swept over her like a caress. "I want you and you want me. It's just as simple as that."

Nicole rearranged her dress with trembling fingers. "You're wrong. But even if you were right, it wouldn't matter. I won't be your mistress—I won't be your whore."

Alex released a weary breath. "I've got to marry Clarissa. François borrowed money against Belle Chêne and the du Villier estates in France. I've been racing against time, trying to repay the debt, but time has run out. Problems have come up in France. Even with the improvements we've made, the crop won't bring in enough. The only way I can pay off the loan is to borrow the money from Clarissa. She suggested it some time ago. The documents have already been signed. The money will be mine on the day of our marriage."

He looked so bleak, Nicki couldn't help feeling sorry for him. It was all she could do not to touch him. "I'm sorry, Alex. I didn't know."

"No one does, and that's the way I'd like to keep it."

"Can't you get the money somewhere else?"

"*Mon Dieu*, I've tried. I can get some, but not enough. The only reason François got so much from Fortier is because Valcour wants Belle Chêne. He knew we'd never be able to repay it. He was counting on that. And I can't let it happen."

Nicole knew what it was like to love one's home and family. She knew what it was like to lose them. "I'm sorry," she said again, and meant it.

"The marriage is only a financial arrangement. I tried to tell you that before."

Nicki's brow arched up in surprise. "But surely Clarissa will want children?"

Alex looked away. "There's the matter of heirs, of course."

"Of course," she said stiffly.

"I wish things could be different, but they can't. At least this way we can be together."

"No," she said simply.

"Yes, damn it!"

Nicki surged to her feet. "I refuse to discuss this any longer. I won't be your mistress, Alexandre. There is nothing you can say that will make me change my mind. And since that is the case, I'll ask you again to let me leave with *Grand-mère*."

Alex's expression turned thunderous. "You belong to me. You're mine and we both know it! You'll stay right here with me."

"Damn you! Damn you to hell!" With that she stormed from the room. She wouldn't waste words on either of them again. As soon as Rachael left for France, Nicole was leaving too. She would make it on her own this time.

She had to.

"I'm going to miss you." Nicki hugged the tiny woman who stood beside her on the docks at New Orleans.

Around them, gulls screeched and wailed, and ships' rigging clattered and clanked in the stiff afternoon breeze. Sailors of various shapes and sizes, some dressed in duck pants and striped shirts, some in military uniform, prowled the wharf around them.

Along with Alex and *Grand-mère*, Nicki had left Belle Chêne aboard the first downriver steamboat, her first trip into the city since she had left the prison.

"I will miss you too, *ma fille*," Rachael agreed.

Tears washed Nicki's cheek, and she clutched the old woman tighter. Several times after the confrontation in Alex's study, Nicki had gone to *Grand-mère* and asked the old woman to intercede on her behalf.

"My grandson has never shown such care for a woman," she had said, "and a fine woman you are, my child. Alex must see how right you are for each other—if he does not, I believe he soon will. You will see." She patted Nicki's hand. "You will see I am right."

Nicki couldn't tell her that even if he did care, he had to marry Clarissa. Instead, she had smiled and let the subject drop.

She looked at the old woman now.

"I will return next fall," Rachael told her. "Or Alexandre can bring you with him when he comes to inspect the estates." It was as if *Grand-mère* had forgotten her grandson's coming marriage. That life at Belle Chêne would go on just as before.

If only that were so.

"You'll write often?" Nicki pressed, but as soon as the words were out, she realized she wouldn't be there to read any letters.

"Of course I will. And you make certain Alexander writes too."

"I will," she softly agreed. She and Alex had maintained a stiff air of cordiality for his grandmother's sake, but Nicki didn't believe Rachael had missed the subtle hostility. They had spent the day shopping for the last-minute items *Grand-mère* had wanted to take home to France, lunched at Chez Louis, the finest restaurant in the *Vieux Carré*, and still had plenty of time to situate Rachael and her lady's maid aboard their first-class cabin on the ship.

"You must not be sad," Rachael told her, dabbing the moisture from Nicki's cheek with a white-lace handkerchief. "Alexandre will take good care of you."

Nicki knew a moment of despair. "I'm sure he will." But she wasn't going to give him the chance. She and Alex would be returning to Belle Chêne before nightfall. Three days later she would be back in the city. Permanently. Or—if Alex had his way—at least until he tired of her as he had Lisette. On Tuesday she would be moving into his town house. What he didn't know was that by Monday she would be gone.

"I love you, *Grand-mère*," Nicki told her.

The old woman repeated the words in French, wiped her own teary eyes, kissed her grandson good-bye a second time, and accepted the arm of the tall, dark-blond sea captain who had come down from his ship, *Sea Gypsy*, to escort her aboard.

"She's in good hands, my friend," Captain Trask said to Alex, with a pleasant smile that contrasted the chiseled angles of his face and the darkness of his suntanned skin.

"There's no one I'd trust more." Alex had known Morgan Trask for the better part of ten years. Trask had made a sizeable fortune in the cotton industry as well as the shipping trade. He was solid and knowledgeable—and one of the toughest men Alex had ever known.

Rachael gave Nicki a last brief hug, then took the rugged sea captain's arm and walked the gangway onto the ship. As the crew made ready to sail, *Grand-mère* waved good-bye from the rail, and Alex led Nicki away.

Sniffing against her handkerchief, she cried softly and tried not to think how lonely she would be without the woman who had been almost a mother during these past few weeks.

"You've still got me," Alex said gently, reading her sorrowful expression.

Clarissa has you, she thought, *I have no one*. But she didn't say the words. "I'm awfully tired, Alex. Couldn't we just go home?" Alex had planned for them to attend a small out-of-the-way theater production of *Lecompte*, but Nicki didn't think she could endure it. Not now. Not knowing what lay ahead.

"All right, if that's what you want," Alex conceded, surprising her. "Once you're living in town, we'll have time to do lots of things." His eyes, dark with hunger, said making love to her would top the list.

She forced a smile she didn't feel. "Of course."

The next two days dragged interminably. Since the harvest season was upon them, Alex had been extremely busy. Nicki was grateful for the time to complete her plans.

She would take only two muslin dresses and a horse. Not Napoleon or Maximillian—they were too valuable. Not Orange Blossom either, she was too old. Nicki planned to leave by the River Road, go straight to the docks in La Ronde, and catch the midnight steamboat upriver. But instead of going to Baton Rouge or Natchez, as Alex would guess, she would get off at one of the smaller towns along the way and head inland, for Jackson, Montgomery, or maybe even Atlanta.

Since she had no money, she would be forced to steal it from Alex. This was the part of her plan she hated. She knew where he kept an allotment for household expenses—she had seen it in the bottom drawer of his desk when he'd been working.

She would leave him a note, try to explain her reasons, assure him that somehow, some way she would pay him back. The horse he would find in La Ronde. Assuming no one stole it before he got there.

Only Danielle knew her plan. She trusted the plump little French girl, and she needed her help. Danielle could cover for her in the morning. Say she was sick, give her as much of a lead as possible before Alex found out and came after her—as she was certain he would.

If she was lucky, he would give up before he found her. Or realizing how much her freedom meant to her, maybe he would let her get away. Whatever happened, she was going through with it. He had given her no other choice.

Monday night at Belle Chêne finally arrived and Nicole fought to hide her nervousness. Alex had been watching her all evening—but it wasn't about her escape he'd been thinking. She knew by the hunger in his eyes that he desired her. Out of deference to her feelings, he had decided to wait until they reached the town house before he tried to make love to her.

But he wanted her—that much was clear.

Worst of all, she wanted him. Every time she felt his eyes on her, her heart began thudding unsteadily, and a slow warmth spread through her limbs. Thank God she was leaving.

"I'm awfully tired, Alex. If you don't mind, I think I'll go on up to . . . my room." She carefully avoided using the word *bed*.

Alex smiled indulgently, as if he knew what she had meant, even if she hadn't said it. "That's probably a good idea. We've a long day tomorrow. I want you settled in by tomorrow night." That he would be spending the night in her bed was written in the seductive curve of his mouth, the single groove that etched itself in one cheek. Rising from his chair, he came to her side. "I'll walk you up."

"I can manage," she said, but he didn't seem to hear her. Instead he took her arm and led her up the stairs to her bedchamber.

Turning her to face him, he tilted her chin with his hand. "Understand, *chérie*, tonight is the last time you will close a door between us."

When she didn't deny it, he leaned down and kissed her, a passionate kiss that left her weak in the knees and clinging to him. She didn't fight him; she wanted him to believe she had finally given in.

As soon as the door closed behind her, Nicki sagged against it, working to slow her pounding heart. Unconsciously her hand went to her stomach, where butterflies still fluttered. Damn him! It wasn't fair that a simple kiss could affect her so.

Danielle helped her remove her blue silk gown and put on her navy-blue riding habit, now the right length and properly fitted in the bust. She would wait an hour, give Alex time to fall asleep, but it really didn't matter. The rest of the household was quiet. If she went down the back stairs, he wouldn't be able to hear her.

"Tell him whatever you have to," Nicole told Danielle when the hour had finally arrived. "I'll need as much time as I can get." The two of them hugged briefly. Nicki grabbed her small ivory-handled carpetbag, took a deep breath for courage, and headed out the door.

The most dangerous part of her plan was stealing one of the horses. Patrick was her biggest threat, but even if he caught her, he probably wouldn't stand in her way. Earlier, while Alex worked in the fields, she had taken the money from his desk drawer, just the amount she needed for her escape. She had also taken his heavy cap-and-ball pistol.

Once at the stables, things went smoother than she had planned. The horses were used to her presence and didn't even stir. From the sound of his snoring, Patrick lay fast asleep. Maybe he had taken a wee nip o' the grog.

She smiled at that and thought of another friend she would miss.

Choosing Vespers, a sorrel gelding used mostly for errands, Nicki saddled him, led him to the mounting block, mounted, and quietly rode away. An hour later, she stood on the dock at La Ronde alongside three men, two in work clothes, one dressed as a gentleman; and a big-breasted woman who looked a little drunk.

At this late hour there weren't always passengers, so a lamp had been hung out, the signal for the boat to stop. Nicki took a cabin on the passenger deck, nothing fancy, just a place to get some sleep. The

Memphis Lady was old and a trifle rickety. Mostly she hauled cargo, and she never went much farther than Baton Rouge.

In the morning, Nicki planned to leave the old boat at the first promising stop, find transportation inland, and be on her way. She was giving herself a second chance, and she was determined to do it right this time. She would find work, she vowed. Make enough to take care of herself.

Without removing her clothes, Nicki lay down on the narrow berth. The walls, paneled in cypress, and a tiny bureau with a mirror above were all there was to the room. An inside cabin with no windows—it reminded her of a cell. You'll be out of here soon, she reminded herself sternly. No one will own you. No one will tell you what to do or how to feel. No one will demand you warm his bed!

No one will be there to hold you when you need it. No one will kiss you, tell you things will be all right.

Try as she might to stop them, salty tears rolled down her cheeks. She had loved Alexandre once. Loved him and trusted him. And Alex had destroyed that trust. On top of that, he had revealed the man he was inside by denying her one chance at happiness. In France she could have started over. In France she could have been Nicole St. Claire.

It was obvious Alex cared for her only as a possession, a willing consort to satisfy his lust, then be cast aside. He didn't know the meaning of the word love. He didn't believe in it.

After the way he had treated her, Nicki didn't either.

Closing her eyes against the sadness she suddenly felt, she concentrated on the sound of the paddle wheels churning up the water, the gentle roll of the boat. In time she would forget Alexandre. She wondered how soon he would forget her.

Alex awoke before dawn. He wanted to catch the first steamboat into New Orleans. Nicki had been packing for the past two days, so she should be ready. He damned well was.

It had been all he could do last night not to make love to her. The kiss they had shared had fired his loins; the taste of her had been heady. He had gone to bed hard and edgy, wanting her so badly he couldn't sleep. Twice he'd considered going to her, kissing her until she begged him to take her. He could do it, he was sure. She wasn't the kind of woman who could turn her feelings off and on.

To his surprise, he'd discovered neither could he.

Taking the stairs up to her room two at a time, Alex rapped on Nicole's chamber door. He pounded hard two more times before Danielle pulled it open.

"Is she up?" he asked.

"*Oui*, m'sieur. But it will be some time before she is ready."

"Tell her we've a boat to catch."

Danielle nodded and pulled the door closed. Alex headed downstairs to the dining room to get a cup of coffee. When Nicki didn't arrive and the morning meal was served, he went back upstairs. Another two raps on the door brought Danielle.

"She is not feeling well this morning, m'sieur. She begs your pardon. She says she will be down soon."

Alex watched the way Danielle kept looking at her feet. One hand played with the folds of her black cotton skirt, while the other twisted a single thick strand of her straight dark hair.

With an oath beneath his breath, he shoved open the chamber door, nearly knocking Danielle over. "Where is she?"

"She must have taken the back stairs down to the dining room."

Alex whirled on her, gripping her arms and dragging her up on her toes. "You're lying! I want to know where she is and I want to know now."

Danielle began to tremble. "She has left here. You may dismiss me, m'sieur, but she asked for my help and I gave it willingly."

"Where? Where has she gone?"

"I cannot tell you."

Alex's grip tightened and he shook her. Hard. "Where is she, dammit?"

Danielle's round gray eyes gleamed with fear, but still she would not speak. Alex growled low in his throat, and released his hold. "I was afraid she'd try something like this. I just thought she'd wait until she got into town."

"Nicki is very resourceful, m'sieur. She will be all right."

"All right? She's a runaway bond servant, for God's sake. Everyone knows about her. Someone will recognize her, remember her. If the authorities find out, they'll put her back in prison—or worse. It could take weeks before they let me know where she is."

"*Mon Dieu*, I never thought of that," Danielle said, beginning to look uncertain.

"I've got to find her, Danielle. Before someone else does."

Danielle wrung her thick-fingered hands. He could

read her indecision, the loyalty that warred with her fears. "What will you do to her?"

"Bring her back where she belongs."

Danielle released a sigh of resignation. "She took the midnight boat upriver. She was headed inland. That is all I know."

Alex swore softly. "I should have known," he said to no one in particular.

After stopping in his room for a change of clothes, his knife, and a pistol, since the one in his desk was gone—along with some of his money—he descended the stairs and strode to the barn. He had found her damnable note, telling him she would pay him back and asking him to let her go.

Let her go, he thought. If only it were that simple. He thought of her out there alone. Did she really want to leave him so badly? On the surface, maybe. But she was young and innocent. She didn't understand the ways of the world. As long as she remained with him, she would be safe and protected. She would have all the beautiful things she'd been denied for so long. Everything he was doing was in her best interests—why the hell couldn't she see that?

In the barn, he led Maximillian from his stall—the gelding's disposition far better suited to the task ahead than that of Napoleon. Alex had almost finished with the saddle when Patrick arrived and hurriedly completed the job for him.

"I hope the lass isn't in trouble again."

"If she isn't," Alex snapped, "she will be when I get hold of her." With that he mounted and rode out of the barn at a gallop.

13

In her tiny inside cabin, Nicole fell asleep just as the sky grayed with dawn.

Her mind conjured dreams of Alex. In the early morning mists, he followed her, trying to catch up to her but somehow unable. In a plaintive voice, he professed his love, repeating over and over how much he cared. Nicki just laughed, a harsh grating sound that called him a liar. He reached out to her, but she only drew farther away.

Eventually the disturbing dream faded, and Nicki slept a little more soundly. Since she had no window in the cabin, there was no morning sunlight to awaken her, and she woke a little later than she intended. But the rest, however fleeting, had been good for her. She felt ready to face what lay ahead, ready to get on with her life.

Pouring water from the blue china pitcher into the basin on the tiny bureau beside the berth, Nicki washed the sleep from her eyes and smoothed back her hair. She wore it braided and knotted into a chignon at the nape of her neck. With her small carpetbag in hand, she opened the door into the corridor and went out on deck. Once there, the wind brought some of the color back to her cheeks and she felt even better.

The boat made a stop to offload a bit of cargo, but there were few buildings and no sign of anyone who might be able to take her inland. There was just one more town before Baton Rouge, but Nicki decided it would be perfect, even if a bit disreputable. The city of Montagne was small, but not too small. She had been there once with her father. One road led out of town to the north on its way to Baton Rouge, while another road skirted the bigger city, but eventually connected with the road east to Hammond. She would take the Hammond road, then head north to Jackson or continue on to Atlanta.

"Goin' to Baton Rouge?"

The words, with their soft Southern accent, drew her attention to a lanky man who propped a boot on the rail beside her. He was shorter than Alex, but still tall. Fair-skinned and dark-haired with eyes that missed nothing.

"Montagne," she corrected, then regretted telling him the truth.

"Nice little town," the man said. He tipped his black, flat-brimmed hat. "Name's Preston, ma'am. Traver Preston. Pleased to meet you."

"The pleasure is mine, I'm sure," she said, instead of giving him her name. He didn't push her, just looked out over the rail, watching the passing shoreline, the trees and shanties that crouched at the water's edge. Near-naked dark-skinned children splashed and cavorted while their fathers stood some distance away quietly fishing for catfish.

Taking a slim cigar from the pocket of his waistcoat, Traver Preston struck a match against the rail and lit up. "Mind if I smoke?" he asked belatedly.

Nicki shook her head, inhaling the pungent scent of the tobacco. He had the look of a gambler in his black frock coat, ruffled shirt, and striped blue silk vest. More slick than polished. "I'd better be going," she said, "my husband will be wondering where I've gone. Nice to meet you, Mr. Preston."

"Pleasure, Miz . . . ?"

"Mrs.," she corrected. "Mrs. Donovan St. Michaels."

"Missus St. Michaels," he amended.

Though she turned her back to him, she could feel his eyes on her, assessing her with expertise. She wasn't much of a liar. In future, she reasoned, she had better learn to master the art.

At the Montagne docks, she departed among a small group of travelers, a fat man in a dirty blue frock coat, the big-breasted woman from the docks at La Ronde, a mother and father and their three small children. The town looked no different than she remembered; just a jumping-off point along the Mississippi, its main street lined with warehouses, taverns, and houses of ill fame. The more respectable shops were located on the narrow streets behind.

The day was bright by now; the sun felt warm, the air cool and not too sticky. Most of the businesses on Front Street had not yet opened; only a few served customers all night long.

Nicole watched the others depart, then headed up Front Street toward the freighting office, hoping to hire a wagon or carriage, someone who might be willing to take her inland.

"Lose your husband somewhere, ma'am?" Traver Preston's voice stopped her cold.

"He—he just went on ahead."

"Not much of a gentleman," he drawled, "leavin' a lady alone in this part a town." When he smiled like that, he wasn't bad-looking, yet there was something about him that made her uneasy.

"Is there something you want, Mr. Preston?"

"No, ma'am. Thought you might be needin' a little assistance."

"I don't need anything from you or any other man. I'm fine on my own." With that she squared her shoulders and started on down the street. Preston fell in step beside her, but she kept on walking, determined to ignore him. She was just about to insist he leave her alone when a tavern door swung wide and two brawling men nearly knocked her over. Preston's arm went around her waist, pulling her out of the way just in time, to keep her from falling.

"Easy to see a little slip of a thing like you doesn't need any help a'tall." He tipped his hat and started to walk away.

Hesitating only a moment, Nicki caught up with him before he'd gone ten feet.

"I—I'm sorry. That was rude of me. As a matter of fact, I could use some assistance. I'm traveling to Atlanta. I would very much appreciate it if you would help me secure some type of transportation."

He seemed incredulous. "Look, little lady, that's a damned long ways. You can't possibly make it that far on your own."

"I assure you I will, Mr. Preston." She wanted to add, *And I'm not your little lady—Alexandre's—or anybody else's.* "But it would be easier if you'd help me."

Preston hesitated only a moment, his eyes moving over her expensive clothes. "All right, ma'am, if you're that set on goin'. . . . Matter of fact, there's a gent I know'd be happy to take you. Hires his wagon out at least as far as Hammond."

"That would be perfect." She could catch a coach from there on east.

Preston excused himself and went into the tavern. He came out some time later with a squat little man about as wide as he was tall.

"This is Marcus. He'll take you into Hammond for ten dollars."

It seemed a fortune. "How about five?"

Marcus chuckled softly, his rotund belly jiggling with the motion. "Ten."

"Five," she haggled, knowing she hadn't much to spare.

"Seven," he pressed.

"Agreed." They shook hands and Marcus led the way down the street to the livery. Preston told her to wait where she was, and the two men went inside. They came out a few minutes later, Preston in front, Marcus driving a battered old wagon whose wheels looked as though they'd fall off at the first chuckhole. The horse Marcus had hitched up, sway-backed and bony, plodded along as if each step might be his last.

"Don't you ever feed him?" she couldn't resist asking.

"Old Zeke'll git ya there," Marcus assured her.

Traver Preston helped her aboard. "Thank you, Mr. Preston."

"My pleasure, ma'am." He tipped his hat and smiled as the wagon pulled away.

Nicki breathed a sigh of relief. She was off to a solid start. Once she reached Hammond and decided where to go from there, the odds of Alex finding her would be far less. She would probably never see him again. He would marry Clarissa, find a new mistress, and lead the kind of life he'd always wanted.

Uninvolved.

Unattached.

Unloved.

Why did it sadden her to think of him living without her? Why should his happiness matter at all? What was it about Alexandre that made people worry about him, want to take care of him? It came to her that Alex cared about *them*, so they cared in return. *He cares, all right. About everyone but me.*

"Whoa!" The sound of Marcus's raspy voice pulled her thoughts in another direction. He tugged on old Zeke's reins. They'd gone several miles out of town, past fields of sugarcane and black laborers hard at work. This stretch of road looked deserted. A swamp bordered one side, fallow fields the other. Several crows cawed mockingly from the overhanging cypress branches above them.

"What are we stopping for?"

"Gotta give old Zeke a rest," Marcus said.

"But we've only gone a few miles. Surely he can't be tired already."

Marcus just shrugged his beefy shoulders.

"Sorry, ma'am," came a voice from the edge of the swamp, "I hate like holy hell to do this, but here's as far as you're goin'." Traver Preston climbed up the embankment and started toward them.

"What are you doing here? What are you talking about?" Preston moved to the side of the wagon, wrapped an arm around her waist, and lifted her down.

"I've got to get to Hammond," she reminded him. "You said you'd help me."

"Way things go sometimes. Now if you'll be so kind as to hand me that little ol' carpetbag, me and Marcus'll be headin' on down the road." A glance behind him revealed two saddled horses. "I'll have to tie you up, but I won't tie you tight. Soon as you git loose, you can take that old wagon on back to town."

"You two are in this together?"

"Never saw the man before today," Preston told her, "but he looked like he could use the money, same as me."

"I—I don't have any money." She gripped her carpetbag tighter.

Preston's eyes roamed over her as they had before, taking in the fine cut and expensive fabric of her navy-blue riding habit. "Lady, they don't sell clothes like that down at the mercantile. Now gimme that bag."

He reached for it, but she jerked it back. "I'm telling you the truth. I don't have any money. At least not very much. What little I do have, I need to get away."

"Away?" He arched a fine dark brow. "Away from what?"

"I—I mean I need it to get to Hammond. I'm meeting my husband there."

"Donovan St. Michaels," he said sarcastically.

"That's right."

Preston chuckled softly. "Lady, I've seen some piss-poor liars in my time, but you're about the worst.

Tell you what I think. I think you're a runaway. I think Mr. Donovan St. Michaels, or whatever man calls you his, might pay pretty good money to get you back."

"She's sure enough a beauty, all right," Marcus said. "Take that perty red hair a' hers loose from all them pins."

"She's pretty, all right. Got style too. Not the kinda woman who'd be travelin' on her own."

"I'm not a runaway," she lied.

Preston ignored her. "If she doesn't have money, maybe we oughta take her back to Montagne. See if the constable's lookin' for her. She's probably some rich man's wife or daughter. Might be some kinda reward."

"No!" Nicki squeaked, edging away. "You take me back and I'll tell them you tried to rob me."

"If you are a runaway, and I'm bettin' you are, it'll be your word against ours."

"I'm not going," she said. Taking a quick step backward, she opened her carpetbag and drew out Alex's cap-and-ball pistol. "You take one step in my direction, I'm going to shoot you."

Preston only laughed. His hand went behind his back and he pulled his own gun from where he had shoved in into the waistband of his breeches. "See? I got one a' them too. Now, put that thing down before you get yourself hurt."

With a reassuring smile, he turned and lunged for her. Nicki pulled the trigger on the pistol, discharging a blast that knocked her backward and filled the air with the acrid smell of gun smoke. Traver Preston sprawled at her feet, moaning softly. She tossed Alex's single-shot weapon aside and dived for the one

Preston had pointed at her, now lying in the dirt beside him.

"Don't try it," she commanded Marcus, trying to keep her voice from shaking as he lumbered from the wagon, and pointed the gun at him with surprisingly steady hands. "I think it's fairly obvious I mean exactly what I say."

"Yes, ma'am," Marcus agreed.

"Get over here." He did as she told him. "Now turn around and put your hands behind your back."

Marcus crossed his beefy wrists behind him. Nicki took the handkerchief out of his back pocket and tied them together. The flimsy binding wouldn't hold for long, but then, she didn't need it to. Traver Preston had stopped moaning, and sat up hunched over the wound in his shoulder.

"I'm sorry, Mr. Preston," she said. "I certainly didn't intend to hurt anyone, but I'm sick and tired of being bullied. Stuff your shirttail into the wound to slow the bleeding. And get yourself to a doctor." With that she climbed aboard the wagon, picked up the reins, and urged the old horse on down the road. Surprisingly, he moved off at a trot and continued enthusiastically for some miles farther.

An hour later, she slowed him to a walk and they held that pace for the rest of the day. She wouldn't make Hammond, but there were bound to be a few small inns along the road. At the first one she came to she would stop for the night.

She tried not to think how close she had come to disaster. If Traver Preston had returned her to Montagne, sooner or later they would have discovered who she was—and to whom she belonged. Until Alex arrived to claim her—if he came at all—she would have been imprisoned. The thought sent a shiver down her spine.

Then her spirits lifted. Actually, now that the danger had passed, it occurred to her that she had handled the situation quite well, considering. She'd dealt with those men just as Alex would have, meted out justice, and defended herself. With a little luck and a doctor's care, Preston would be fine. She doubted he would report the incident, since she was already gone and with her any chance of reward.

Just as she had vowed, she had taken care of herself. She could do it again if she had to. She didn't need Alexandre or any other man. She'd made her first real step toward freedom.

Why did a voice inside keep saying that freedom from Alex was just another word for lonely?

Alex caught the *Belle Creole* out of La Ronde and headed upriver. He knew Captain Maddox, the graying man who had piloted the luxurious riverboat for the past five years. For a hefty sum of money to cover any lost time, the captain finally agreed to put into port at any additional stops the midnight boat, *Memphis Lady*, might have made.

Each time the steamboat docked, Alex briefly departed, asking questions of any who might possibly have seen a young woman traveling alone. At one stop a skinny blond man who worked at the terminal had traveled that same vessel the night before. He remembered the girl Alex described getting on in La Ronde, but hadn't seen her afterward, or noticed where she got off.

"She was one good-lookin' woman," the thin man said. "Hard to forget hair that color. Or those eyes—

sorta blue-green. She wasn't flashy, mind ya. Just pretty, and kinda wholesome-like.''

"That's her," Alex agreed, feeling a hard knot ball in his stomach. The man's too-apt description touched him someplace between anger and pain. Nicki was beautiful, naive—and alone. He didn't want men looking at her, wondering where her man was, why she was traveling by herself. He didn't want them near her.

Some distant part of his mind questioned his feelings. Why was she so important to him? Why didn't he just give back her indenture papers and let her go off on her own? Then he thought of her gentleness, the way she looked at the world through such fresh, innocent eyes, even after all she had suffered. She needed a man's protection—his protection. Setting aside her foolish pride seemed little enough price to pay.

Alex's jaw tightened. By God, Nicki was his. Right or wrong, he had taken her to his bed, she was his responsibility, and he wasn't about to let her go!

He would find her, he resolved, repeating the vow again and again, but by the end of the day, his worry had begun to mount. Only one more stop before Baton Rouge. What if she'd changed her mind and gone farther upriver? What if Danielle had lied to him? Both seemed unlikely. Danielle wouldn't dare, and once Nicki's mind was made up, she would be too damned stubborn to change it. If he found no trace of her in Montagne, he would check Baton Rouge, then start back downstream at the first opportunity. He'd go into each town and check more thoroughly.

"Damn!" Alex swore. Starting over would take time. Days he couldn't afford to lose.

He paced the deck and watched the passing shore-line. When he wasn't worrying himself sick over what might have happened to her, he was cursing her and planning the revenge he would extract when he finally got his hands on her.

"Next stop, Montagne," one of the stewards called out, passing Alex on the deck.

As he had at each stop, Alex left the boat along with those departing and made his way to the terminal.

"I recollect seein' her, all right," one of the baggage handlers told him. "She was real pretty. She sorta waited till the others left, then she headed down Front Street toward the freighting office."

"Thank you," Alex said, relieved. At least he knew where to start looking. "You've been very helpful."

After handing the man a coin for his trouble, he returned to the boat, picked his saddle bags up from the purser, hoisted them over his shoulder, and headed down to the main deck where Maximillian grazed beside several other horses.

Once ashore, Alex mounted the gelding and rode straight for the freight office. He found Nicki had never arrived. Fighting down his fear of what might have happened, he made his way to the livery stable.

"She come here with a coupla fellows," the owner, a balding man with a thick gray handlebar mustache, told him. "A short, stocky guy and a gambler. They hired an old, beat-up wagon, cheapest I had, and headed off on the road to Hammond. Leastwise the short fella and the gal did. Don't know what become of the gambler."

"How long ago did they leave?" Alex's worry increased with every passing minute.

"Just before noon."

"Thank you." They had a good head start, but if he pushed Max hard, he might be able to catch them. Or come upon some tavern where they'd stopped for the night. He prayed Nicole was all right. That she had hired someone who was only interested in her money.

His money, he corrected with another muttered oath. When he got his hands on the little minx he was going to make her pay.

Nicki felt bone-tired and now that the sun had begun to set, more than a little uneasy. It would be dark soon. If she didn't find an inn, she would be forced to sleep in the back of the wagon.

"Come on, baby," she cajoled the old horse she'd already grown fond of. "Just a little farther." She would get him some oats and a manger of hay, see that he had at least one decent meal before she left him and caught the stage. The horse nickered softly, as if he understood, and continued to plod down the road.

Darkness had fallen, the road lit only by a sliver of moon, and still she kept going. Rounding a bend that had seemed miles in coming, Nicki shivered against the early evening chill and wished she had a blanket. It was difficult to see where she was going, though old Zeke seemed to know.

They had traveled just a little ways farther when she spotted a tiny cluster of yellow dots in the distance. As the wagon grew closer, the dots became windows, and she recognized the two-story building in the distance as an inn.

"Thank God," she whispered, breathing a sigh of relief.

The hard wooden seat had bruised her bottom, the bone-jarring wagon had strained every muscle and joint. Drawing rein on old Zeke, she set the brake, climbed down from the seat, and tried to work the kinks from her back and shoulders.

Inside the tavern, she could hear men's voices and the sound of a piano being played just a little off-key.

"Need some help, missus?" A small black boy approached from around the corner of the building.

"Yes, if you please. My horse needs care. See that he gets some oats and a manger of hay."

"Yes'm," the boy said.

He led old Zeke toward the barn at the rear while Nicki headed up the brick steps and pulled open the heavy plank door. The tavern was low-ceilinged, with huge hand-carved beams overhead and ironwork covering the windows. It looked Spanish in design, though the interior had been bastardized by its owners and years of abuse.

"You are looking for someone?" the innkeeper asked, eyeing her from top to bottom. His accent was French, but much more pronounced than Alex's.

"I'm supposed to meet my husband. Donovan St. Michaels." It was as good a story as any.

"I am afraid 'e is not 'ere." The innkeeper was a big man, with thick black hair worn far too long, beefy shoulders and hands, and a heavy black beard.

"Well, he will be," she told him. "In the meantime, I'll need a room."

"You intend to stay 'ere alone?"

"I told you, my husband is due at any moment."

"*Oui*, that is what you said." He wiped his large hands on the front of the towel tucked into his heavy leather apron. "His name is *Donovan* St. Michaels, yes?"

"Yes."

"That is what I thought. When 'e arrives, I will send 'im up."

"I'd appreciate that."

"You must pay in advance."

"Of course," she agreed as if she had known that all along. Digging into her carpetbag, she pulled out a small leather pouch full of coins. "I'll need something to eat, as well. And the boy outside is feeding my horse."

He grunted an acknowledgment and told her the amount he would need, which again seemed far too high. Nicki felt too tired to argue. Besides, the tavern was full of men, most of whom had noticed her entry and now sat watching her. Several made whispered remarks, pointed in her direction, and laughed lewdly at their own private jokes. Two tavern wenches worked the room, busily filling tankards of ale or goblets of wine.

Following the Frenchman up the stairs, she heard the bell above the door jingle just as she reached the top. Below her, a red-haired man in a dusty dragoon uniform stepped into the room. Paying him little heed, Nicki waited for the tavern keeper to open the door.

"Back stairs lead to the privy," he told her.

"Thank you." At least she wouldn't have go out through the tavern.

Once inside the tiny room, she arched a brow, surprised to find it clean and neat, though Spartan. The bed was little more than a moss-filled mattress covering the slats beneath, but the blankets looked warm and clean. A scarred oak bureau rested against one wall beneath a tiny mirror. A pitcher and basin stood ready and waiting for her use. No fire warmed the hearth, but it wasn't really that cold.

Unable to undress until her food arrived, Nicki tossed her sachel onto the bed and began to unbraid her hair. Using the silver-handled brush she had taken from her room at Belle Chêne, the one luxury she'd allowed herself, she brushed the long, rippling strands until they gleamed in the light from the whale oil lamp beside the bed.

A knock at the door came just as she finished. A big-bosomed serving maid brought in a tray of food and set it on the bureau. "Thank you," Nicki said, giving her a smile for her trouble instead of money she couldn't afford. The aroma of crusty bread and thick beef stew made her mouth water.

She would eat first, then get out of her dusty clothes. As tired as she was, with a full stomach and a goblet of wine, she felt sure she'd be able to sleep.

The young red-haired dragoon pulled up a chair and banged on the oak plank table. "Fetch me some rum, wench, and be quick about it." The maid did as he asked, and he downed the drink in one long swallow. "Fill it again," he demanded, but his grin looked broad and he gave her a lusty slap on the rump. The broad-hipped maid giggled and danced away.

Any other night, Septimus K. Watkins would have thought her comely enough for a toss between the blankets, but not tonight. He had just been promoted. He intended to celebrate, drink himself blind, then buy himself the lustiest wench in the tavern.

"What be yer name, boy?" A balding, one-eyed

man with the look of a sailor sat down on the bench across from him.

"Sep Watkins." He extended one lean hand.

"A fine name for a fine fightin' man." The sailor accepted the handshake. "Sargeant, is it?"

"Corporal. As of today."

"Wheelock Upton's me name." The sailor slapped Sep on the back, then turned to the wench, who stood near his shoulder. "Buy the lad a drink," he said with a grin, "and bring another for me while you're about it."

An hour later, the sailor heeled over the table, well into his cups and singing a lusty sea song, Sep felt just fine. A little drunk, to be sure, but not so much he wouldn't enjoy his wench. Making his way toward the oak plank bar where the innkeeper worked tapping a keg, he drew the big man aside.

"I want the finest wench in the tavern."

"That would be Desiree," the Frenchman said, pointing to the broad-hipped maid who'd been serving him all evening.

Sep shook his head. "Not tonight. I've a pocket full of coins and a belly full of rum. It's something special I'm after." He jangled his purse on the bar.

The innkeeper stroked his beard. "I 'ave something special," he said with a glance toward the stairs. "But she is expensive."

"Tonight, I will pay."

"This one has hair the color of copper," he said, warming to his subject, "a waist sooo small"—he made a tiny circle with his hands—"and eyes like an aqua sea."

Sep smiled his approval, but the innkeeper shrugged it away.

"Then again, you might not want 'er. You see, she likes a man who is, 'ow do you say? Rough. A man who will take 'er against 'er most vehement protests. Show 'er 'e is really a man, *comprenez-vous*?"

The corporal puffed his chest out. "I'll give her a tumble she won't soon forget."

"You are sure?"

"She'll know a man's had her when I'm finished."

The innkeeper slapped him on the back. "Let me see the color of your money, m'sieur. It seems we will do business."

As the Frenchman promised, when Sep used the key to open the door, he sucked in a breath at the sleeping girl's beauty. For a moment he just stood in the doorway and watched her, holding his lamp high, enjoying the way her bright copper hair fanned out across her pillow.

Her eyes were closed, but a thick sweep of dark auburn lashes fanned over her cheeks, and her mouth was lush and a tantalizing shade of pink. She wore a simple white nightgown, but the thin material did little to disguise the rise and fall of her full, round breasts. Sep felt himself harden.

Stepping into the room, he closed the door and set the lamp on the dresser, where its soft light flickered across the sleeping figure. Silently and with great anticipation, he stripped off his sword, pulled off his heavy black boots, and unfastened the brass buttons on his uniform. Next went his long red underwear, leaving him naked, his body lean and toughened from his months in the service of his country.

Moving toward the bed, he eased himself down beside her, not certain what to expect. Still, she did not move.

With a shaky hand, Sep ran his fingers over her breasts, unbuttoned the front of her nightgown, and slipped his hand inside. At the contact with her smooth white skin, the nipple that pebbled beneath his palm, Sep's arousal hardened even more. He was aching to get inside her, dying to see what lay beneath the white cotton fabric.

Leaning down, he brushed her lips with a soft, sweet kiss and she sighed. Then her eye fluttered open, the most enchanting aqua hue he'd ever seen.

"Alex?" she whispered, and he wondered who the lucky man was.

With her lips parted as they were, the temptation to kiss her again became unbearable. Sep covered her mouth with his and forced his tongue inside. He heard her startled gasp just before her fingers gripped his bright red hair and her teeth sank into his tongue.

"Ouch!" he yelled, pulling away from her, his tongue beginning to bleed. Quickly he pinned her wrists while using his body to hold her in place beneath him.

"Get out of my room!" she yelled, trying to sit up but firmly held down by his hands and his body.

Sep only smiled. He was ready for this encounter. He was hard and aching—and he had been given fair warning. "I'll give you the ride of your life, sweet lady. You may struggle, or you may go easy. Either way, I shall have you."

"Nooo!" she shrieked, but he silenced her with his lips.

Nicki scratched and clawed, thrashed her arms and legs, twisted and pulled and tried to break free. She could feel the man's stiff member pressing against her thighs as he fought to settle himself between her legs. Though she valiantly struggled against him, her thrashing movements only managed to slide up her thin cotton nightgown and ensnare them both in the long copper strands of her hair. When she tried to bite him again, he used one hand to pin both her wrists, and covered her mouth with the other.

"I shall have you, lady. You shall know the touch of a virile man this night."

Clamping her legs together, Nicki forced herself to stay calm. Traver Preston's pistol was still in her carpetbag, lying just few feet away. If she could free herself, she could reach it.

If had never seemed a more uncertain word.

14

"May I be of 'elp, m'sieur?"

Alex answered the innkeeper in his native French. "I'm looking for a woman. Small. Hair the color of copper. Her eyes are aqua."

"You are her husband?" the Frenchman asked, obviously disconcerted. "You are Donovan St. Michaels?"

Alex smiled inwardly as he pieced together her ruse. "Then my wife is here?" he pressed, letting the man assume what he would.

"Yes, but . . ."

"But what? Which room is she in? I'll need a key."

The Frenchman looked worried. "I have some very bad news, m'sieur." His eyes flicked nervously back and forth, and he stroked his heavy black beard. "It seems your wife is upstairs with her lover. Apparently she did not expect you so soon."

"Her lover?" He had been holding his anger in check. Now it rolled over him like a wave. "You mean to tell me she's upstairs with a man?"

"*Oui*, m'sieur."

"Give me the key."

"I think it would be best if you went back home and waited for her there."

"Now."

The innkeeper handed him a key. "It is the room at the end of the hallway, but I am warning you, the man who is with her—he is a soldier."

Alex didn't bother to answer—just took the stairs two at a time, strode down the hall, and unlocked the door. When he pushed it open, he found Nicki lying beneath a naked red-haired man, her nightshirt open to the waist and her breasts exposed. The gown rode up her thighs, revealing her shapely legs. Alex's fury in that moment was so great it took a full five seconds for him to realize she was struggling, her fingers clutching her carpetbag, which she dragged toward her across the floor.

"I ought to leave you to him!" he roared, but instead reached for the back of the man's neck, clamped the nape in a grip of iron, and pulled him away as if he were only a boy.

"What the . . . ? The words died on the stunned man's lips.

Alex drove a fist into the dragoon's midsection, doubling him over, then punched him hard in the jaw. Nicki screamed when the man slammed into the bureau, shoving it into the middle of the room and nearly toppling the lamp. Two more bone-crashing blows had blood oozing from the soldier's broken nose and trickling from a swollen lip.

"If you want her that bad, you can have her," the dragoon choked out as Alex dragged him up by the hair. "She's already paid for."

Alex stopped his fist in mid-swing. "Paid for? What are you talking about?"

"I said you can have her."

"Who did you pay?"

"The Frenchman," he gasped out. "Twenty dollars. All the gold in my purse."

Alex swore soundly.

"Frenchman said she liked it rough. That she wanted her skirts tossed by a real man."

Alex let go of the man's hair, and he sagged to the floor. "Get out."

The corporal grabbed his uniform in one hand, his boots in the other, and staggered to his feet. Naked, he stumbled out the door.

Coming to her knees on the bed, her hair swirling wildly around her, Nicki held her tattered nightshirt together in an effort to cover her breasts.

Nom de Dieu—he had been right! Thank God he arrived when he did. Damn her stubborn little hide, she needed his protection. It infuriated him that she refused to listen. A muscle bunched in Alex's cheek. Somehow, some way, he had to make her see!

Nervously, she wet her lips. "Alex, I—"

"I'll deal with you when I get back." His hard look sent a shiver down Nicki's spine. With his jaw set and his mouth grim, he turned and headed out the door.

Nicki raced after him. She opened the door enough to look out, and peered through the crack. Hearing Alex's voice in the taproom below, she inched toward the rail until she could see him striding toward the Frenchman.

"*Merde*," the innkeeper swore just as Alex grabbed the front of his shirt. One-handed, he yanked the big, bearded man across the bar and punched him hard in the mouth, drawing a stream of blood. A second blow sent him stumbling backward, crashing into the rough wooden benches and knocking over tables. None of the men in the tavern made the slightest move to help him.

Growling low in his throat, the Frenchman charged. Alex sidestepped a skull-crushing blow, and punched him two more times. The man flew back against the wall, landing with a loud crack that snapped his head back. His eyes fluttered closed, and he slid down the wall.

When Alex turned toward the stairs, Nicki sucked in a breath. Never had she seen his eyes so dark, his features so angry. His mouth was a thin grim line, and a muscle bunched in his jaw. He spotted her and flames seemed to leap in his eyes. Nicki squealed and raced back into her room, locking the door behind her.

Alex turned the handle, found it locked, and, cursing, inserted the key he still carried in his pocket. He entered the room to find Nicki standing in the middle, her feet splayed, both hands gripping the pistol she pointed in his direction.

"I—I don't want to hurt you, Alex. I really appreciate your help, but I'm not going back with you."

He had never seen her this way, so wild, so pagan. Her hair gleamed like flames in the lamplight, her breasts heaved in the open front of her nightshirt, her nipples were rosy. Her eyes glistened with spirit and determination.

"Put that down," he commanded, moving nearer.

"I'm not going back."

"You have nowhere else to go."

"I'll find somewhere else."

One step closer, one deft movement, and Alex wrenched the pistol from her hand, accidently discharging the hammer. The gunshot echoed across the small room, knocking chips of wood from the ceiling above their heads. As Nicki backed away cursing, Alex examined the weapon more closely, the barrel still warm and smoking. One dark brow went up. He'd expected her to have a pistol—his pistol—but this gun wasn't his.

"Where did you get this?" he asked, fixing her with a gaze so hard she blanched.

"Well, I . . ."

"I'm waiting," he prodded.

"I—well—I . . ." She ran her tongue across her soft pink lips, reminding him that only moments before another man had been plundering their sweetness—reminding him of the danger she had been in.

"We both know what a very poor liar you are," he said coldly, his temper straining at the tight leash he held on it.

Nicki squared her shoulders and lifted her chin, meeting his hard look squarely. "I fired the pistol I borrowed from you. Since I needed another, I took it from the man I shot."

"The man you shot?" He couldn't quite believe his ears.

"Yes. He was trying to rob me. I needed every cent I had, so I shot him. In self-defense, of course. He was trying to attack me."

"*Sacrebleu*, that's it. That is all I can stand." Two long strides and he swept her up in his arms. Ignoring her flailing fists and salty protests, he carried her to the bed and sat down on the edge. Nicki found herself draped across his knees, his hard thighs pressing into her stomach.

"Let me go!" she shrieked, squirming against his efforts to pin her down.

"Twice I've let you off easy when I should have given you the thrashing you deserve." He hoisted her torn nightgown, exposing her smooth, round bottom.

"Stop it, Alexandre! Don't you dare!"

But he did dare. All her squirming and all her efforts to evade his stinging palm were to no avail. *Whack, whack, whack*, his big hand came down, searing her tender flesh.

"Damn you!" she swore.

"You run from me when I try to take care of you!" *Whack, whack, whack.* "You put yourself in danger, time and time again. I won't have it!"

"I won't be your whore!"

One last sound smack and he jerked her to her feet. Tears of anger stained her cheeks, but she didn't look away.

"Understand this, Nicki, and understand it now. You are a bond servant. My bond servant. Where I tell you to go, you go. What I tell you to do, you do." He tightened his grip on her arm. "From now on you will bow to my wishes. Do I make myself clear?"

Nicki set her jaw.

Alex shook her. "Do I make myself clear?"

"Quite clear, your grace," she said through clenched teeth. "But be forewarned. You may own my body, but you don't own my soul."

Eyes still dark with anger, he picked her up and tossed her onto the bed. Ignoring the vile expression she cast his way, he strode to the door and jerked it open, slamming it behind him so hard the window rattled.

Bastard, she swore. Dominating, infuriating—bastard! She rubbed her bottom through the folds of her nightgown. Though her flesh still burned like the fires of Hades, he hadn't given her the beating she'd half expected. She would never forget the blows he had rained on the man he'd found in her bed, or the swift, hard justice he'd delivered to the innkeeper, a man of powerful proportions himself.

Apparently he believed in restraint when dealing with a woman. Not like the others she had known. Not like Armand Laurent, or the guards at the prison. She wondered if in truth he hadn't acted partly out of worry for her. By nature, Alex was protective of the people in his care—and he definitely considered her his.

Listening to every passing sound, Nicki crawled between the blankets and fluffed her threadbare pillow. Where had Alex gone? she wondered, then prayed he wouldn't return until morning. It wasn't long before she heard his heavy footfalls, then the door opened and he stepped inside, his saddlebags slung over one wide, muscular shoulder.

Feigning sleep, she watched him from beneath her thick dark lashes as he tossed the bags carelessly onto the bureau. With only a brief glance her way, he sat down on the edge of the bed and pulled off his tall black boots, letting them fall to the floor with a heavy thud. He tugged his shirt free of his breeches and shrugged it off. When she heard the sound of fabric sliding down his muscular thighs, Nicki sat bolt upright.

"What do you think you're doing?"

"Getting ready for bed." He didn't bother to glance her way.

"Not this bed," she told him.

"Exactly this bed."

"Then I'll sleep on the floor." Grabbing one of the blankets, she started to rise, but Alex towered above her in an instant, his grip on her arm tight with warning.

"Get back in bed." The darkness in his eyes confirmed that his anger had little abated. One look at his muscular body, and the arousal she had already stirred, proclaimed his intentions.

"I won't let you touch me. I'll fight you every inch of the way."

His mouth curved into a mocking half smile. "You're mine, *chérie*. Tonight I intend to prove it."

"You're wrong, Alex." Nicki backed away.

His jaw tightened. "Your soldier said you wanted it rough. It appears he was right after all. You want it rough. Then that's the way you shall have it."

"He wasn't my soldier," she said with growing alarm. "I've never seen the man before."

"That, *chérie*, is most fortunate for both of you."

Watching the rise and fall of Alex's broad chest, the angry set to his features, the hands he clenched at his side, Nicki felt a coil of the old familiar fear. She had only experienced their one encounter, only known what it felt like to be taken with gentleness and compassion. Still, she was not a coward. Not anymore.

Jerking free, she scrambled from the bed and raced to the bureau. Grabbing the first object she saw—her silver-backed hairbrush—she hurled it at Alex, striking him viciously on the cheek. He growled low in his throat and dived for her. By inches, she darted away.

Her fingers curled around the handle of the pitcher, half full of water. She hurled it at him with all her might, but he ducked, and it smashed against the floor, spilling water everywhere. The basin flew past the side of his head to shatter against the wall behind him.

Alex was grinning now, enjoying the game, it seemed. "So, *chérie*, as I've long suspected, my sweet little minx is a fiery-tempered vixen after all."

"Get away from me!" She dodged him by climbing across the bed. "I hate you!"

"We shall see, *mon amoureuse*, we shall see." With a quick turn and step, Alex wrapped an arm around her waist and pinned her body solidly against his. Fists flying, trying to bite him, she fought until her muscles ached and her strength began to ebb. Still, he held her fast.

With his free hand, he caught the front of her nightgown and tore it away. A second rending tear, and she stood naked, forced along the muscular length of him, feeling his hardened shaft where it pressed against her flesh. In the eerie glow of the lamplight, his eyes seemed to glitter with anticipation, while his mouth looked hard and unyielding.

Nicki started to tremble, for the first time genuinely afraid. He would rape her now. Hurt her and make her forget the beauty of the night they had shared on their pallet before the fire.

Alex pulled her roughly down on the bed, and the image of the guards rose up before her. She could hear the sound of their fists pounding against flesh, hear the women screaming. One man laughed as he forced a woman's legs apart and thrust himself into her.

Nicki moved her head back and forth from side to side, trying to deny what was happening, trying to still her mounting fears. She felt warm hands on her breasts, but saw only the mocking face of the guard, expected any moment to feel his fingers plunging inside her, tearing her apart, then his member thrusting into her body while she cried out in pain.

Tears welled and trickled down her cheeks. "Please," she whispered. "Please don't hurt me."

Alex's movements stilled. His breath seemed frozen, caught somewhere in his chest. His hold on her gentled, became the merest touch of his hand. "Never," he said softly. "Never." He pulled her into his arms, one hand sinking into her hair while the other cradled her against him, holding her as if he'd never let her go.

"It's all right," he soothed. "I wouldn't hurt you. I would have loved you. But I would never have hurt you."

She looked up at him and saw that he was telling the truth. She clutched him tighter and didn't ask herself why.

"I was so worried," he said, smoothing back her tangled mass of hair. "So afraid you'd be hurt."

She drew back to look at him. "I could have made it, Alex, I could have. You must let me go."

He cupped her face between his palms, his eyes searching hers, willing her to understand. "I can't," he said softly. "I can't let you go."

Then he kissed her, a kiss so filled with yearning, so loving and tender that Nicki opened to it. She couldn't deny him, couldn't turn him away. Her tongue touched his, tangled with it, then slid inside his mouth. Her arms went around his thick neck.

With a soft groan, Alex pulled her closer, deepening the kiss, thrusting his tongue into her mouth while his hands smoothed over her body. He cupped a breast with one wide palm, then lowered his mouth and claimed it, his tongue laving, teasing white-hot flames that seared her from the inside out. He moved lower, his mouth trailing kisses along her body, his tongue delving into her navel. His hand skimmed along her flesh to cup her bottom and bring her closer.

She gasped as the heat of his hand touched the fire that still pained her there. Alex lifted his head, but didn't speak. Just bent over her and began to apply soft, sweet kisses across her stinging flesh. Each place his lips brushed felt soothed. He kissed her until he'd covered every inch he had pinkened with his hand. Then his fingers caressed where his mouth had been, slipped between her legs, and began to stroke the creaminess that his soothing touch had wrought.

Nicki moaned softly at each practiced stroke of his fingers. She rolled to face him, and he continued to caress her, his mouth returning to her lips, his kiss so deep and exciting she could think of nothing but the feel of him inside her, longed to know the length and breadth of him, wanted the surge of raw wonder and beauty only his passion could give.

Alex rose above her, as if he knew her thoughts. His shaft pressed against her, sought the wet warmth of her passage, and slid inside. He felt hot and hard and pulsing, so huge he filled her until she seemed a part of him. Surging up, he drove into her with a need she hadn't seen in him before.

She returned each thrust with equal abandon, lifting her hips to him, her muscles expanding and contracting, drawing him farther inside. She could feel it building then, that strange surge of pleasure she'd known before.

"Alex?" she whispered, clutching his neck.

"Let it come, *chérie.*"

And it did. A rising wave of passion that swelled and rippled with beauty and awe, then flooded her with a pleasure so intense she was certain to die of it.

Alex felt her contractions, felt her muscles bunching, sucking him inside her so deep he thought he might drown. His own body tensed as he pounded into her, riding her like some fiery, tempestuous force. He couldn't remember if he called her name out loud or only in his mind. He denied the words that followed, for surely they were just a man's passions speaking of the pleasure in his loins.

In moments they lay spent and entwined, but he didn't pull away. He couldn't bear the thought of being apart from her so soon. Not after all his worry. Not after his fears.

Eventually, they slept, until a sound in the night awoke him and he realized he wanted her again. He took her more leisurely this time, bringing her to climax gently, following in her wake, then both of them drifting back to sleep. When he awoke in the morning, sunlight streaming in across his naked chest, he found her already up and dressed. He did a poor job of hiding his disappointment—since it crested beneath his blanket.

Ignoring the tender ache, he pulled on his breeches and buttoned them up the front. "So eager to get back home, *ma chère?*"

"I don't see that I have much other choice."

None at all, he thought, but didn't say it. "Regrets?" he asked, and held his breath at her words.

"No, m'sieur. What I gave last night, I gave freely. You would have stopped had I but asked."

She waited for his confirmation. "Yes . . . I was bent on seduction, not rape."

Nicki looked relieved. "What we shared last night was given in affection for the care you have shown me, for the worry I may have caused."

"Gratitude?" he mocked, reminding her she had said those words before.

"No. I wanted you too. But understand this, Alexandre, from now on, what you want from me you will have to take. I am a St. Claire. I will never be your whore."

Alex cursed soundly. "No whore of mine has ever been shown the care I show you. Nor the worry. It is not as a whore that I treat you, but as my lady."

"Clarissa will soon be your lady. What will I be then?"

"Clarissa will soon be my wife. You will still be my lady."

"I think you may change your mind when you bring no willing mistress to your bed, but instead a woman who will fight you with her every breath."

Alex released a long, weary sigh. It wouldn't come to that, but she wouldn't believe him, and after all she had put him through, he didn't mind letting her think so. He raked a hand through his wavy dark-brown hair. "If that is the way you want it, so it shall be."

Alex tied Maximillian behind the rickety wagon, lifted Nicole aboard, then climbed up himself. Though the sun shone brightly, a brisk fall breeze ruffled his hair. It would soon be time for harvest.

"Thank you, m'sieur," Nicki said, interrupting his thoughts. "For old Zeke, I mean."

"I would rather you call me Alex. As for the horse,

one more animal in the pasture is hardly a burden, though the stablemaster will surely think me a fool."

Nicki smiled gently. "More a softheart, I imagine."

Upon arriving in Montagne, Alex paid the livery-man for the use of the wagon and a fair price for Zeke. The animal's ears perked up the minute they led him away from the stable.

"He must really hate that place," Nicki observed.

Alex smiled warmly. "I believe he'll appreciate the comforts of Belle Chêne."

"As I have not?" she said with an accusing look.

Alex's grin broadened until he dimpled. "I suppose you've shown your . . . gratitude . . . well enough at times."

Nicki cast him an outraged glance, but said nothing more.

After hiring a lad to care for Zeke and Maximillian until the boat arrived, they walked up Front Street toward the constable's office, a board and batten building set alongside the freighting office. By this time of day, the taverns along the street were in full swing, shrill laughter and bawdy songs coming from the open doorways, drunken river rats staggering arm in arm along the board walkways in front of the buildings.

"Are you certain this is necessary, Alex?" she asked as they walked along, wishing they could leave the matter alone. "The man I shot isn't likely to report it. After all, he was trying to rob me."

"That, *chérie*, is exactly the point."

They kept on walking, Nicki's small arm carefully looped through Alex's big muscular one. She was dressed in one of the two muslin dresses she had brought with her, this one a delicate pale pink. Alex wore a clean white shirt, fawn-colored breeches, and boots.

"He wasn't really a bad sort," Nicki finished. "I hope he's all right."

Alex muttered something beneath his breath. "Now you're worried about a man who tried to rob you."

"He would have let me go. He didn't want anything but my money."

"Then the man must surely be a fool as well as a thief," Alex said darkly, throwing her a heated glance.

At the constable's office, a no-nonsense establishment with two small oak desks, wanted posters on the walls, and a door at the rear that led to cells in the back, Constable Rhodes asked her for a description of the two men.

"What will happen to them if they're caught?" Nicki asked. Rhodes was a slender man with too little hair, a long neck, and tiny eyes.

"They'll spend the next few years in prison."

Nicki swallowed, her mouth suddenly dry. "I see."

"Tell them what the men looked like, *chérie*. We've a boat to catch."

"Well . . . it's kind of hard to remember." Alex's gaze swung to hers, but she ignored it. "One of them was blond and skinny. The other was shorter. With graying hair and a beard."

"A beard," Alex repeated, looking at her pointedly.

"Yes." It was hard not to glance away.

"Anything else you can remember?" the constable asked. "Somebody's name, maybe?"

"Well . . . I—I think one of them called the other Ben."

"Just Ben?" Rhodes pressed, scratching his sparsely haired head. "No last names?"

"Not that I recall."

"I think we'd better go," Alex said. After shaking the constable's hand, he tugged her firmly toward the door. "If you need anything else," he told Rhodes, "you can contact me at Belle Chêne."

"Sorry for the trouble, ma'am."

"Thank you, Constable Rhodes." Nicki turned and walked out the door.

Alex caught up with her in two long strides down the boardwalk. "I want to know why you lied in there."

"Who says I lied?"

"I do."

"Well, I didn't."

"Don't start with me, Nicki." His eyes bored into her.

"All right, I lied. I didn't want those men sent to prison. They seemed more desperate than mean. I wanted them to have a second chance."

"A second chance," he repeated, incredulous.

"Everyone should have a second chance."

He watched her for a moment. "Including you?"

She just looked at him.

Alex had trouble turning away. "We'd better get going. We're a long way from home."

"If you're speaking of the house on Toulouse Street, it's your home, Alex. It will never be mine."

15

<hr/>

At the dock, Nicki waited while Alex bought their tickets for the return trip downriver. The next boat in would be the *Hannibal*, a far more luxurious steamboat than the *Memphis Lady* she had traveled aboard to Montagne.

Around her, children laughed and pulled on their mothers' skirts. The ladies, mostly planters' wives, wore fashionable dresses of silk, lace, or dimity, and gaily trimmed bonnets and snowy white gloves. Parasols danced beneath the fading sunlight. Though Montagne catered to gamblers and other disreputables, for many it was the closest riverboat stop to their plantations.

Upstream the *hoot*, *hoot* of the whistle drew Nicki's attention to the gleaming white sidewheeler churning up a fountain of water, its smokestacks billowing thick black smoke.

"Steamboat's a-comin'!" came the cry, and it never failed to stir excitement.

Along with the rest, Nicki's heartbeat quickened just to look at such majesty. Gleaming red and white, rising four stories out of the water, the *Hannibal* paid tribute to man's determination to master speed and beauty. She could travel downstream at more than fifteen miles an hour carrying three hundred and fifty passengers and thousands of pounds of livestock and cargo.

"Ready?" Alex asked, walking up beside her.

She smiled at him. "I've never been aboard anything so luxurious."

"Then we'll make it an evening to remember."

She didn't remind him that neither of them was dressed for an elegant supper in the salon. Or that surely some of those present would know who he was, and of his upcoming marriage to Clarissa Endicott.

He was Alexandre du Villier, the Duke of Brisonne. He could dare anything—and usually did.

Alex guided her up to the Texas deck, where the first-class cabins were, but left her at the rail to enjoy the view.

"I'll put away our bags," he said, "then we'll take a look around."

She didn't notice which cabin he disappeared into, but it depressed her to think of the battle they would wage at the end of the evening when he tried to make love to her. She had made her position clear on that score. She wouldn't back down now.

"Ma foi, it cannot be!"

With a flash of remembrance, Nicki whirled toward the sound of the softly spoken French words.

"Michele!" she cried, spotting the slender French girl who had been her friend since childhood. The women threw themselves into each other's arms, laughing and hugging, wiping away happy tears.

"Ah non, I do not believe it," Michele said, pulling

back to survey Nicole from head to foot. "So often I have thought of you, wondered where you were. I heard stories. . . ." She shook her head and rolled her pretty green eyes as if what she had heard couldn't possibly be true. The ash-brown curls beside her cheeks bobbed their agreement.

Nicki's joy began to fade. "After you moved away, things got worse at Meadowood. Papa died. *Maman* not long after. There were debts, so many debts. . . ."

"I am sorry. I did not know. . . ."

Nicki forced a smile. "How could you? You were already gone."

Michele nodded. "We had our troubles too. But in France, my father found good fortune. He was able to rebuild. Last year we returned to Louisiana. Papa bought a new plantation just north of Baton Rouge."

"That's wonderful. Your father always worked so hard." She hugged Michele again.

"And you, Nicki, where are you living now?"

From over Michele's shoulder, Nicki saw Alex watching them as he approached. In seconds he would join them. Michele would know they were traveling together, would surmise their scandalous relationship.

She swallowed hard, not knowing what to say. "I— I've been at Belle Chêne. You recall, my father and Charles du Villier were friends."

"The lady has been kind enough to honor us with a visit," Alex put in smoothly, striding up beside Nicole.

"Michele Christophe, this is Alexandre du Villier."

Alex brought Michele's slender, gloved hand to his lips. "*Enchanté*, Mademoiselle Christophe."

Michele blushed prettily. "An honor, m'sieur." She turned back to Nicki, who kept her expression carefully blank. "You are returning to Belle Chêne?"

"Mademoiselle St. Claire has a town house in New Orleans," Alex answered for her. "And you, mademoiselle?"

"On my way to visit a friend in that same city. Oh, Nicki, is it not wonderful? We will be able to get reacquainted, spend some time together."

"Yes . . ." Nicole hesitantly agreed. "That would be lovely."

Michele pulled a black velvet ribbon from the pocket in the seam of her blue silk gingham gown. A small porcelain-faced watch dangled from the end. *"Je regrette,"* she said, "I have to go now. *Ma tante* Laverne is waiting for me. I am afraid she has the evening already planned."

"Where will you be staying in the city?" Alex asked. "I'm sure Nicole will want to visit."

"Eight twelve Royale Street. But maybe if the evening ends early, I could drop by your cabin, Nicki. Which number is it?"

Nicole's face paled.

"Room three hundred," Alex told her. "Just a few doors down from mine."

"If I do not see you later, I will see you in the city." Michele hugged Nicki and hurried toward the stairs.

Nicole stared up at Alex. "That was a very gallant lie, m'sieur, but one which will prove false should she arrive."

"Are you certain?"

Nicki almost smiled. "With you, Alexandre, one is never certain of anything."

He laughed at that, a deep rumbling in his chest. "Nor with you, *ma chère*."

True to his word after all, Alex had reserved separate cabins for them. Nicole had never been more grateful. She felt exhausted and edgy. And the thought of battling Alex for the remnants of her virtue seemed almost overwhelming.

Surprisingly, the evening was pleasant and not too taxing. They supped in a quiet corner of the elegant main salon beneath Gothic, carved wooden rafters painted white and trimmed with gold leaf. She had never seen finer appointments, from the intricate pattern in the plush floral carpets to the stained-glass skylights reflecting light overhead.

The tables were set with linen and crystal. A huge sterling silver water dispenser rested at one end of the three-hundred-foot-long room while a massive gilded mirror decorated the opposite end.

Afterward, she and Alex walked the deck in the moonlight. Sensing her fatigue, if not the battle she waged with herself every time she was near him, he made gentle conversation, carefully avoiding any unpleasant topics, then escorted her to her room. Nicki bristled as he leaned toward her, but he only brushed her mouth with the merest touch of his lips.

"Good night," he said, opening the door, then he closed it softly behind her.

Will I ever understand him? she wondered, but was too exhausted to worry about it. She was almost too tired to conquer the interminable buttons at the back of her dress, but eventually she succeeded and readied herself for bed.

By morning, after leaving Zeke and Maximillian in

La Ronde, they arrived at the docks in New Orleans. Ships from all over the globe were moored there, but the steamboats, dozens of them, took up one long line. Most of the more elegant "floating palaces," as they were known, would be sailing late in the afternoon, though smaller boats came and went all day long.

On Decatur Street, Alex hailed a hansom cab and they rounded the corner onto Toulouse Street, the gentle clip-clop of the horse's hooves pounding against the cobblestones. It wasn't far to his town house. Not nearly far enough to suit Nicki. When the driver reined up in front of the wrought iron enclosed courtyard, memories of her first time there swept over her and she felt her stomach roll.

She hadn't forgotten the wretched creature Alex had brought there from the prison that awful afternoon late last May. Or the beautiful raven-haired Creole woman who had lived there as his mistress. What had happened to Lisette? Was she somewhere pining away for Alex and the love they'd once shared? Was her fate the same one Nicole would suffer when Alex grew tired of her?

"Come, *chérie*," Alex said gently, his hands going around her waist to lift her down.

Nicki didn't look at him, just let him lead her through the garden courtyard up the front steps to the carved cypress door. The door swung wide even before he knocked. Frederick, tall and ramrod straight, stood in the foyer, very formal until he grinned at her and winked. Danielle flew down the stairs and stopped just short of embracing her.

"*Merci le bon Dieu*—you are all right." She crossed herself and looked at Nicole with round gray eyes that begged for understanding. *"M'sieur le duc* said you would be arrested. I did not know what to do. I— I was so worried for you." Her plump fingers twisted the folds of her skirt.

"It's all right, Danielle." Nicole reached out for the thick-fingered hand and gave it a gentle squeeze. "You did what you thought best." She didn't add that Alexandre's timely arrival had saved her from near disaster because she firmly believed she could have saved herself if she'd had to.

"Surely you aren't planning to stay here with me in New Orleans?" she asked, suddenly remembering Danielle's betrothed. "What about René?"

Danielle giggled. "It is said that absence makes the heart grow fonder. Maybe René will miss me and set a date for the wedding."

Nicki laughed softly. "Maybe he will." She turned her attention to Alex. "You've let Frederick come as well?"

"And Betsy." Betsy was Frederick's wife. "I trust she's feeling better . . ." he said to the tall black butler, his expression one of concern.

"Baby's settled down now." Frederick grinned, teeth gleaming white in his coal-colored face. "He's leaving mama alone till he gets born, then she'll really have her hands full." Betsy's first child would arrive in about six months.

"She's a strong girl," Alex said. "She'll do just fine."

Nicki looked at him as if to say, how do you know so much about babies? but didn't. The master of a place like Belle Chêne had to know a little bit about everything.

Alex smiled at her. "I thought you'd feel more comfortable with people you already knew."

"Yes. Thank you. That was very thoughtful."

"There's someone else I'd like you to meet." He guided her into the salon, where a thick-set man with huge arms and shoulders leaned against the gray marble mantel. He wore navy-blue duck pants and a homespun shirt. "Nicole, this is Bayram Sit, a friend of mine for many years. We met in Algeria."

The friend he had known in prison. "I believe you mentioned him." By the look that passed between them she felt certain she was right.

"I am sometimes called the Ram," the beefy man told her with an odd accent and a slight nod of his head that might have been meant as a greeting. "Ram will do."

Yes. The Ram. He looked like one. His head was completely shorn of hair, his eyelids smooth and slashed up in the way of the Mongols. A thick black mustache drooped below his jaw. She had never seen a man with arms so huge, or thighs as big as a small man's waist. "It's a pleasure to meet you."

"Ram will be staying for a while," Alex told her.

"At Belle Chêne?"

"Here," he said softly.

"Here?" Why would a man like that be staying in the town house?

"He'll see that no harm comes to you while I'm busy with the harvest."

"But surely I'm not in any—" Nicki stopped in mid-sentence as she realized why the man was really there. "He'll see that I don't escape, isn't that what you mean?"

"You just need time to adjust."

"This man is my jailer. I'm a captive here just as surely as I was at the Baronne Street prison."

"Ram is here to look after you," Alex said with growing tension. "It isn't as though you don't need it."

Nicki took a long, calming breath before she tried to speak. "I'm afraid I'm feeling a little tired," she said, sweeping past him. "I think I'll go on up to my room."

Alex didn't stop her, just let her race up the stairs, then quietly followed her up. He found her standing in the hallway, uncertain which room was hers.

"This one," he called from behind her, shoving open the door to the master suite.

Nicki's stomach knotted. Surely he wouldn't demand she sleep in Lisette's room—the woman's cloying scent alone would be enough to gag her.

"Is there no other I might use?" she asked softly, hoping he would understand.

Without answering, Alex drew her inside. Surprisingly, the room was empty except for a huge four-poster bed that dominated one wall.

"I'll leave it up to you. I want you to be happy here. This is a lovely room, the finest in the house. I had hoped that you would furnish it as you wish. Make it yours in every way. The bed was my father's. It means a great deal to me, but if it offends you, I will order it removed."

Nicki looked around, unable to believe the trouble he had gone to for her. "It would be costly to furnish the room. I know you have little money to spare."

"The amount it would take would be a pittance compared to what I need to repay Fortier. It won't matter one way or the other."

It *was* a lovely room. Freshly painted, with beautiful parquet floors and delicate shutters at each of the windows. And so sunny, with the garden below and the prettiest little wrought-iron balcony. "This room will be fine."

"Shall I have the bed removed?"

It, too, had been stripped and cleaned; every inch of the magnificent hand-carved mahogany glistened with polish. Only the slats of the bed remained, not even the feather mattress.

"It's a beautiful bed. I would be honored to sleep in it."

"My father would be pleased."

Nicki straightened her spine. "Your father would not be pleased to know you intend to share it with me."

Alex could not deny it. Charles du Villier would have had him horsewhipped if he had known the future Alex planned for the daughter of his lifelong friend. In truth, Alex didn't really understand the reasons himself. "I'm glad you have come to accept it. In time you'll see that it's for the best."

"Damn you! I haven't accepted anything. What I told you before still stands. I will not come to your bed as a willing *demimondaine*. I am not your whore and I never will be!"

Alex clamped his jaw and forced himself under control. "I'll be back in one weeks time. I trust by then you'll see reason. One way or another, we will both find comfort in that bed." With those hard words, he strode out the door, slamming it solidly behind him.

"Go to hell!" she shrieked after him.

But he'd only go as far as Belle Chêne. It was time

to begin the harvest. They would be working around the clock from now until Christmas, each man taking two of the three eight-hour shifts. Amazingly, the workers didn't complain about the long, arduous days. There was an air of festivity during harvest, as well as extra rations of food, whiskey, and tobacco, a bonus for each man at the end of the season, and of course, the lavish sugarhouse ball.

Nicki's mother had helped her father tremendously during the long days of the harvest season. Who would help Alex? No one. At least not this year. But next year he would be married to Clarissa. As efficient as Clarissa Endicott most surely was, she'd be a great help to her husband. She would fill the job of planter's wife as well as Nicole had been trained to—maybe even better.

Nicki sank down on the wooden window seat and looked out over the garden. Alex's marriage was scheduled for the tenth day of the new year. Right before Fortier's note came due. A little over two months from now. Before that time, Alex or no Alex, Ram or no Ram, Nicki had to leave. She would lay her plans more carefully this time. Wait until Alex relaxed his guard. Wait until she understood the man called Ram who was her jailer, and found his weakness. Until she had secured the money for her passage on a ship. Then she would make her escape.

In the meantime, she would occupy herself furnishing the chamber the way Alex wanted. As to his wish she join him in his father's big bed—on that he was in for a fight.

On Friday, François arrived. Having found her clothes already unpacked and hanging in an armoire in her temporary room, Nicki dressed in a stylish plum serge day dress. It was one of the two gowns she owned that were suitable for the cool fall weather.

"I'm here to take you shopping," François told her. "Alex says you need winter things and furniture for your bedchamber."

Grudgingly, she admitted Alexandre had been thoughtful, as usual. "That's kind of you, François." They shared some of the rich black coffee she loved and several delicate French pastries Betsy purchased each morning from the *pâtisserie*. A little while later, they had left the drawing room, readying themselves for their excursion, when Thomas Demming arrived.

"I came to pay my respects," he said, standing beside Frederick in the foyer, "and to be sure you were getting settled in."

"Why, thank you, Thomas." He looked handsome in his navy-blue tailcoat and light-gray trousers, his blue eyes sparkling with cheer.

"I'm afraid we were just about to leave," François said. "We've some shopping to do. You could join us if you like."

Thomas grinned. "I ought to. Just to set Alex on his ear. But I've work to do—"

A knock at the door interrupted their conversation. Frederick pulled it wide, and a well-dressed woman stood in the opening. For a moment the bright sunlight obscured her face. Then, stiff-backed and obviously angry, Michele Christophe marched in, passing François and Thomas as if they weren't there.

"We are supposed to be friends," she said, rushing

up to Nicki in a swirl of rose faille skirts. "You could have told me. I would have understood!"

Nicki couldn't help but smile. Michele had rarely raised her voice in all the years she'd known her. "I don't believe you've all met," she said, and Michele's cheeks turned as rosy as her dress. "Mademoiselle Christophe, this is M'sieur François du Villier, Alexandre's brother, and M'sieur Thomas Demming, one of his closest friends."

"It is a pleasure to meet you both." Michele glanced briefly at François, then at Thomas, whose eyes had taken on a warm, approving glow. Michele blushed again.

For the first time, Nicki realized how lovely her friend had grown in the years they'd been apart. Gone was the willowy, too-thin schoolgirl, replaced now by a young woman of stature and grace.

Though she still remained slender, her face had filled out and her neck arched gracefully. Her eyes, a gentle shade of green against her pale, peach-hued skin, were fringed with long, dark lashes. Her breasts were small but looked firm and tempting, as Thomas seemed to have noticed.

"We're going shopping," Nicki told her, hoping to put off their confrontation as long as possible. "You're welcome to come along."

Michele glanced from Thomas to Nicole and back to Thomas. "I am sorry for my outburst. It was unseemly. I hope you do not think I am always so outspoken."

"Actually, she's usually shy," Nicki said with some amusement.

"Friends should certainly be able to speak to each

other as they wish," Thomas said, adding, "We'd love to have you join us."

"I would not want to be an inconvenience."

"Oh, but you wouldn't be," Thomas assured her. "We'll go to Chartres Street first, then lunch at Le Petit Trianon down by the square."

"I thought you had work to do," François said with a barely suppressed grin.

"On the contrary. A little time off is just what I need."

They spent the day roaming the streets and shops. At François's insistence, Nicki ordered six new gowns of finest serge, merino, and cashmere, and a forest-green velvet riding habit, though she had far less use for it than she'd had at Belle Chêne.

François didn't press her to buy the ball gown the seamstress insisted upon. Alex wouldn't be taking his mistress to any of the coming extravagant affairs and they both knew it.

Though the subtle reminder dampened a bit of her day, she enjoyed their exquisite luncheon and afterward chose several handsome carved antique pieces for the bedchamber, including a rosewood armoire. She selected a soft pale-peach chintz—a reminder of Belle Chêne—for the curtains Betsy would sew, along with a matching chintz counterpane for the massive four-poster bed.

The room was sure to be lovely. She sighed, thinking how little time she would have to enjoy it.

Thomas and Michele got along famously. Nicki wondered how her friend had managed to escape the watchful eye of her aunt, but didn't ask. They were both grown women now. Except that Michele, unlike

Nicole, retained her innocence for the man she would marry.

"I believe I see a friend." François's soft voice interrupted her thoughts. "If you will excuse me . . . ?"

"Of course."

He left them a moment and stepped into a fashionable gentlemen's haberdashery. While Michele and Thomas lost themselves in conversation, Nicki wandered along the street to peek in the windows. When she came to the gentlemen's shop, she saw François engaged in an animated discussion with a handsome, pale-skinned young man who looked to be about his age.

The man was as tall as François, but much more slender, his cheekbones high and his lips well formed. He smiled at François almost seductively and moved so gracefully he appeared to float. When he flushed at something François said, François touched his cheek and the young man captured his hand, holding it in a manner that somehow seemed improper.

Nicki felt as if she were intruding on an intimate scene between two people who shared something deeper than mere friendship. Something more like love.

She blanched as if a blow had struck her. Eyes wide in disbelief, she started to look away just as François glanced up. For a moment they stared at each other, then Nicki turned away.

She returned to Michele and Thomas, feeling shaken and uncertain. She knew little about men whose affections belonged to other men, only whispered rumors of their existence. Certainly nothing of their forbidden passions.

Yet instinctively she knew François to be among them.

He returned looking as pale and shaken as she. "Jean Pierre is an old school friend," he said by way of explanation, but wouldn't meet her eyes.

At the town house, he hastily took his leave, still withdrawn and looking a trifle upset. Thomas departed grudgingly, and then only after receiving permission to call on Michele at her aunt's. Finally the two girls were left alone.

"You like him, don't you?" Nicki asked, when they were seated on the tapestry sofa.

"*Oui*, he is very charming. And so handsome." Michele rolled her pretty green eyes.

"I like him too."

Michele pulled off her gloves. "I am glad that I met him, but I came here to see you. What are these stories I hear? Surely they cannot be true."

"What—what have you heard?"

"*Ma tante* says you belong to Alexandre du Villier. That you are his bond servant. She says everyone in the *Vieux Carré* knows he bought you at the prison for an outrageous sum of money. Surely M'sieur du Villier was only trying to help you. After all, he and your father were friends."

Nicki came to her feet and began to pace in front of the fireplace. There was nothing left to hide, no more reason to lie. "Alex did help me. In most ways he's been good to me."

"Most ways?" Michele pressed.

"It's a long story, Michele, but suffice it to say it took a very long while for me to trust him. Eventually

I did. I believed he cared for me. I . . . allowed my feelings to get involved . . . did things I now regret. Since then, I've discovered that his intentions toward me were not what I believed." It was all she was willing to say. Let Michele deduce what she would.

"*Mon Dieu,*" she whispered.

"I thought I loved him," Nicki said softly, praying her friend would understand.

"And now?"

Nicki sighed and sat down on the sofa. "I don't know what I feel anymore."

"Surely, if you asked, he would release you from your contract."

"He will not."

"But why? It is what his father would have wanted, *n'est-ce pas?*"

Nicki sat forward, turning to face her more squarely. "I've asked myself that question a thousand times. I don't know why." *Because he wants me. Because he owns me and Alex keeps what he owns.* Still, Alex was not an unkind man, nor one given to putting his own happiness above that of others. That she belonged to him wasn't answer enough—yet what else could it be?

"Is there nothing I can do?" Michele asked.

"Only be my friend." Nicki smiled forlornly. "It won't be that easy, I assure you. I'm surprised your aunt allowed this visit."

Michele released a hesitant breath. "Actually, she forbade it. But I will tell you this. We were friends then. We are friends now." She squared her slender shoulders. "We will always be friends and nothing can change that."

Michele came to her feet and gave Nicole a hug. "You must let me know if you need anything."

"Alex sees to my needs," she said with a touch of bitterness. She didn't add she had no intention of seeing to his.

16

With little or nothing to do all day, the week dragged interminably. How she missed the wide-open spaces, the sense of freedom she had felt at Belle Chêne. Though the courtyard provided a place of solace, and the bustling city excited her, Nicki would always prefer the country.

Once she had made her escape, she vowed, she would return to that quieter existence.

Escape, however, without careful planning and with Ram underfoot, would not be easy.

The first step in her scheme involved finding the big Turk's weakness. Bent on that end, she spoke to him whenever she got the chance, asking him questions about Alex and their longtime friendship. He always answered politely, but with a watchful eye that seemed to be gauging whether or not she was worthy of Alexandre's attentions. It was obvious he thought a great deal of his friend.

For the first few days, Nicki watched him closely. He was a mysterious man, silent much of the time, and ever observant. Sometimes he seemed almost able to read her thoughts.

At night his wariness increased, as if he expected her to attempt to leave. Several times in the night, she thought she heard him in the hall outside her door. Twice she had seen him below her chamber windows, walking in the moonlit shadows of the garden.

Successfully escaping the Ram would be no easy task, but Nicki was sure that sooner or later she would find a way.

"Tell me about Algeria," she asked him one evening after supper. Ram sat at Alex's desk in the study, where he seemed to feel most comfortable.

Recalling long-ago events, Ram smiled and looked off into space. One beefy hand skimmed over his massive clean-shaven head, then his eyes returned to her face.

"We were young and foolish back then. Alexandre fighting for his French homeland, me fighting just for the fun of it—and of course, the bounty it would bring. The rebels captured several dozen mercenaries and some of the troops, and we were taken to a cave they were using as a prison. It was a terrible place, full of rats and the stench of dying men."

Nicki's stomach tightened as she recalled her own hellish experience. "But you and Alex didn't die," she prodded.

"No. In this place the strong survived. I was used to hardship. For me the prison was merely an inconvenience. Not like Alex, with his fine manners and fancy soldier's uniform. Alexandre was little more than a boy."

"Then you must have helped him."

"I helped him only to discover the man he was inside. It took just a little reassurance. A bit of knowledge. An ounce of skill. While the others withered away, Alexandre's strength grew. The men who challenged him learned the hard way that he was a man who gave no quarter. In time, he was feared and respected. To put it simply—he survived."

"As did your friendship," she said.

"Yes. When the French soldiers overran the prison, Alex fought two of his own people to keep me alive. I have not forgotten."

No one forgets Alexandre, she thought with quiet desperation.

She started for the door, but Ram's deep voice stopped her.

"I don't suppose you play chess?" he asked.

"Chess?" It seemed absurd coming from one so mighty.

"Yes. Alexandre taught me. We carved wooden pieces and played on a board drawn in the dirt on the floor of the cave. It helped to pass the time."

"As a matter of fact, I do." Nicki smiled. Needing a little distraction, she took a seat across from him. Ram smiled in return and reached for the beautiful inlaid chessboard.

As the week wore on, Nicki's worry turned from Alex's pending arrival to thoughts of François. She had hoped he would come to call, that maybe there was something he would say to her, or something she might say to him to bring back their once-close friendship.

"Danielle," she called to the ever-smiling French girl, who sat quietly sewing in her small upstairs room, "I was wondering if we might talk for a moment."

"But of course." She flashed Nicki a knowing

glance. "You are having trouble with *M'sieur le duc?*" Danielle seemed to get a secret thrill out of calling him that—though she never said it to his face.

"I'm always having trouble with Alex, but that's not the problem."

"What then?"

Nicki sat down on the edge of the bed across from Danielle, who set her embroidery aside. "I was wondering if you might have heard something about . . . well . . . men who are . . . different from other men. I know a little bit about them, but not enough."

"Different? In what way different?"

Nicki flushed just to think of it. "They're not interested in women. They're attracted to men."

"*Sacrebleu!*" Danielle's gray eyes went wide.

"Then you do know something. . . ."

Danielle smiled, flashing an expression of innocence that always made her look pretty. "I know only what I have heard when I should not have been listening."

"And?"

"They say it is a sin. The curse of the devil. A woman should pretend not to know, even if she does."

"Do you think they—"

"I do not know. And even I would not ask." Danielle's look turned impish. "But if you find out, you had better tell me."

Nicki almost smiled. The curse of the devil, she thought, picturing François's tortured face when he had spotted her standing at the window. Maybe it was.

Later that same day, after working up a second round of courage, she spoke to the Ram about it. He was, she was sure, the last possible person she should ask, but he did have a certain worldliness that most men lacked. And nothing seemed to bother him. She had never seen him embarrassed or judgmental.

"Good afternoon, Ram," she said, approaching him in Alexandre's study.

"For some maybe. I would prefer to be out-of-doors."

"And I would prefer you and Alexandre both take your leave, but apparently that is not to be."

The big Turk laughed, a heavy rumble that shook his massive chest. "I will only be here a short while longer. Just until after the harvest."

Nicki's temper fired. "Alexandre is certainly sure of himself. What makes him think I won't leave just as soon as you've gone?"

"You'll have to ask him that question." Ram glanced back down at the book he was reading, presuming she would leave.

She didn't, just watched his black eyes move carefully across the page. He was reading Richard Henry Dana's *Two Years Before the Mast*. At first she'd been surprised a man of his rough nature would be able to read, but he had explained that Alex had arranged for his instruction when he'd expressed a desire to learn.

"There is something I would know, Ram," she said, interrupting him again.

He swung his smooth-lidded gaze in her direction and smiled indulgently. "Yes?"

Nervous, she twirled a long copper strand of her hair. "It's a subject women aren't supposed to discuss."

"If you ask and I know, I will tell you."

Nicki wet her suddenly dry lips. "It's about men who are . . . attracted to other men."

"What is it you wish to know of them?" he asked, apparently nonplussed.

"Then you know of such men?"

"I have known a few. In the East it is more acceptable than here."

"What—what makes them that way?"

He shrugged his massive shoulders. "I do not know. Some say it is the work of Satan. I say it is only a whim of nature. Many seem to have the inclination from birth. Since I am not so afflicted"—he grinned wickedly, strong teeth white in his nut-brown face—"it is not for me to say."

"Is there nothing that can be done?"

"Not that I know of." He looked at her hard. "Why do you ask these things? I do not believe it is just curiosity."

"I think I know such a man."

"François," he said flatly.

Nicki sucked in a breath. "How did you know?"

"The signs are there. Alexandre refuses to see them."

"He loves his brother."

"That is so. But denying the truth cannot change it."

"I don't think most people suspect," Nicki said.

"That is also true, but Alexandre is not most people. And François is so afraid of causing his brother unhappiness, he ruins his own chance for happiness."

"I wish there was something I could do. I feel so sorry for him."

Ram watched her closely. "And what do you feel for Alexandre? Hate? Fear? Passion? Or love?"

Nicki lifted her chin but didn't look away. "Alexandre du Villier is my master. At one time or another I have felt all of those things and more."

"And now?"

"Now I only wish to be away from him."

The Ram said nothing else.

On Wednesday, the day of Alex's planned arrival, Nicki received a note from him. He had been detained at Belle Chêne, but would greatly appreciate the honor of her company on Friday evening at a performance of the Italian Singers at a place called the Verandah.

She scoffed at the formal invitation. It was a command, not a request, and they both knew it.

"Danielle!" she called out, marching determinedly up the stairs. "I need a servant's uniform. Something old and dismal and tattered. What can you find for me?"

"*Nom de Dieu*, what do you need with a uniform?"

"M'sieur du Villier has commanded my presence day after tomorrow night. We shall see how happy he will be to escort his bond servant."

"I do not think—"

"I know, and I agree, but I still want that uniform."

Shaking her head and tittering behind her hand, Danielle set out to find something Nicki could wear. Up in the attic, she found a dismal black uniform that belonged to the former housekeeper. It was old and frayed, but clean; the apron worn, but not yellowed. To make it fit her, they shortened the hem, took in the waist, and added a fichu of white piquet to increase the bustline.

"Perfect," Nicki said when they'd finished, glancing at her reflection in the antique mirror she had purchased on her shopping excursion last week. In just seven days, the room was almost furnished, the bed resplendent with a new feather mattress, soft cotton sheets, and a lovely yellow quilt until the peach chintz counterpane could be finished.

Pulling back her hair, Nicki fastened it at the nape of her neck in a simple but severe style and settled a mobcap atop her head.

"What about *M'sieur le* Ram? Will he not object?"

"I don't think Ram will interfere. He seems to find this whole affair amusing."

By six o'clock, Nicki had cleaned and straightened the entire upstairs. When Alex arrived, she was working in the dining room on her hands and knees, busily polishing the parquet floors.

His deep voice in the entry brought the hint of a grin, and Nicki moved just a little to watch him through the crack in the door. Seeing him standing there so tall and handsome, she almost wished she had accepted his invitation. She tried not to notice how imposing he was, how broad his shoulders, the warmth in his dark-brown eyes. But the attempt failed miserably. Against her will, her heartbeat quickened and butterflies swirled in her stomach.

As Frederick took Alex's black silk hat and satin-lined cape, his tailored black evening clothes glistened beneath the crystal chandelier.

"Tell Mademoiselle St. Claire I have come for her," he told Frederick, who had to be fighting a grin of his own.

"Yes, sir."

"Where's Ram?" he asked, and Frederick pointed to the sitting room. Though she couldn't quite see the big Turk, she knew he was in there. Probably so he wouldn't miss the show.

Alex started toward his friend, then noticed Frederick heading down the hallway to the dining room instead of going upstairs as he expected.

"M'sieur du Villier is here for you," the tall black butler said formally.

"Tell him I'm busy."

Alex heard her reply and strode past Frederick into the dining room. Spotting her on the floor, clutching a dirty oil-covered rag, he sucked in a breath.

"Nom de Dieu! What in God's name do you think you're doing?"

"Polishing your floors, m'sieur," she said sweetly, the oily rag gliding soundlessly across the already glistening wood.

Alex's expression turned murderous. "Go upstairs and get dressed."

"But I am dressed, m'sieur."

"Nicki, I'm warning you. Get up off that floor and get out of those dismal clothes."

"But I've so much work left to do—"

Alex crossed the room in three long strides. Sliding an arm around her waist, he jerked her to her feet. "Upstairs," he commanded. "Now."

"As you wish, m'sieur." Hiding a satisfied grin, Nicki went upstairs. But she didn't take off her clothes. Instead, she washed her hands, then removed her mobcap, and hung small diamond earbobs—a gift from *Grand-mère*—from each ear.

Grabbing her reticule and a black feathered fan, she headed back downstairs.

Alex stood in the salon, speaking to Ram.

"Enjoy yourself," Alex said, clapping his friend on the back. "You more than deserve a night's entertainment." Ram started to say something, spotted Nicki standing in the doorway with her dowdy clothes and feathered fan, and grinned.

"The evening's best entertainment appears to be here," Ram said, but wisely headed for the door.

Nicki smiled at Alex, whose dark expression had returned, more thunderous than ever.

"Just what exactly do you think you're doing?"

"If you wish to spend the evening in the company of your bond servant, I am ready, m'sieur."

Alex growled low in his throat. Stalking across the room, he grabbed her wrist, bent down, and hauled her over his shoulder. Grumbling something she couldn't quite catch, he carted her up the stairs like a sack of potatoes. Trying not to notice the heat of his hand on her thigh, Nicki just smiled and let him carry her up.

Unceremoniously, he dumped her onto the bed. "Get out of those rags."

Nicki set her jaw, but made no move to comply.

"Do it, Nicki, or I swear I'll do it for you."

She lifted her chin. "No" was all she said. With a sweep of his hand, Alex grabbed the front of her frayed black uniform and ripped it down the front, eliciting a scream of outrage.

"I'm not going!" she shouted.

Alex arched a brow and lifted one corner of his mouth in a smile that wasn't a smile at all. "You have no wish to spend an evening of entertainment at the Verandah?"

"It isn't as though I haven't warned you, Alex. You know how I feel about this."

"And you have received a similar warning from me, *ma chère*." Scowling, he bent over her, so close she could smell his spicy cologne. "Since you are so eager for my touch," he told her, his voice hard with determination, "we shall forgo the evening I had planned and get on to the task you have set for me."

Nicki swung her feet to the edge of the bed and tried to get up, but Alex pinned her easily, his hard arms pressing her down on the mattress. With several brisk but efficient movements, he stripped away the remnants of her shabby black uniform. Next went the petticoats, a fluffy white swirl on the floor at their feet. Nicki fought and cursed him to no avail. She found herself wishing she had agreed to the evening out after all. At least their confrontation would have been postponed.

Then again, an evening of waiting in dreaded anticipation might have been far worse.

Feeling his hand moving over her chemise, Nicki glanced up at him.

"What?" he despaired. "No corset? What kind of a servant would scrub her master's floors in a near state of undress?"

Nicki flushed at the mocking note in his voice. She should have worn the uncomfortable contraption. Alex would have had a deuce of a time getting it off!

"Next time I shall attempt to be more proper." She tried to wriggle out from beneath him, but instead felt his strong fingers slide inside her chemise, brushing against her breasts as he tore the fabric away. His eyes skimmed over her, taking in the rise and fall of her bosom, his pupils dark and hungry. He left her there, half-naked and trying in vain to cover herself.

Alex merely removed his cravat and stock, his jacket and waistcoat. She watched him pull something from his pocket just before returning to the bed. Sliding as far away from him as she could get, she drew her legs up under her and glowered at him, her back pressed hard against the cold wooden headboard.

Paying her little heed, Alex reached for her hand, jerked it toward him, and looped something silky around her wrist. She gasped as he drew the loop tight, then fastened a length of pale blue silk to the headboard.

"What do you think you're doing?" Her eyes went wide as he grabbed her other wrist and looped a second length of silk around it.

"Saving you from yourself," he replied. In minutes he had her arms stretched wide, the silken sashes carefully holding her in place in the middle of the massive bed. "I had hoped it wouldn't come to this," he added, "but knowing you as I do, I came prepared."

"Last time you said you wouldn't force me."

"Last time I wasn't certain your desire for me was as great as mine for you."

"And now you are?"

"Now I know it's only your stubborn St. Claire pride that keeps you from me."

She couldn't deny it. Just looking at his naked chest sent a thrill of desire through her body. She struggled against her silken bonds and felt an unwanted surge of anticipation.

"Damn you, Alex," she cursed, but Alex merely removed her embroidered white cotton drawers. "Oooh," she moaned as he captured first one flailing ankle and then the other, gently fixing each to a bedpost, spreading her legs and baring her most intimate parts to his view. She flushed crimson at the heated look that stole over him and the stiff arousal that pressed against the front of his breeches.

Aware of her embarrassment, Alex dimmed the lamp a little, but not so much he couldn't see exactly what he intended. In seconds he had stripped off the rest of his clothes and joined her naked on the bed.

"Tell me you don't want this." Alex leaned over to capture a breast. He suckled it gently. "Tell me to stop and I will."

Nicki's tongue wet the corner of her mouth. "Alex, please . . . I'm asking you not . . . to. . . ." But her words trailed off, her hips arched upward, and a soft sweet moan came from her throat.

"I hardly think so, *chérie.*" He bent his head and kissed her, just the gentlest brush of his lips before she turned away.

He kissed her cheek, though she tried to avoid him, the curve of her neck, then settled for a moment on the tender lobe of an ear. Tendrils of warmth flickered through her. Alex ran his tongue along the shell-like rim, slid it inside, then trailed soft wet kisses along her shoulder. A fire kindled inside her, a slow, langorous heat that hinted at flame.

Alex moved lower, his palms skimming over her flesh, his mouth caressing where his hands had been. In the glow of the lamplight, taut muscle rippled across his chest, and his curly brown chest hairs glistened as they teased her sensitive skin.

Alex cupped her breasts, sending shafts of heat searing through her, massaged and lifted each one, then took her nipple between his thumb and forefinger, kneading it until it hardened to a stiff, taut bud. His tongue circled the dark areola, raising goose bumps across her flesh, and Nicki moaned.

Trembling now, she pulled at her bonds, but they held fast, fanning her desire in some strange way. The soft blue silk didn't hurt her, just gave Alex the access to her body he intended.

"Your struggles are useless, *chérie*. Don't fight it. Just let me love you."

His tongue slid into her navel, circling the center, tasting her skin, rousing the sparks of fire into flame. Against her will, her body responded, her muscles tensing against the slow-burning warmth that crept over her. Alex's mouth moved lower, across her abdomen, nibbling and kissing, drawing with his tongue a hot line of wetness into the dark red hairs at the juncture of her legs.

Still he did not stop.

Kissing the smooth white skin on the inside of her thighs, he nipped her with his teeth then moved upward toward the core of her passion.

Nicki was moaning now, restless and thrashing. She couldn't stop herself, no matter how she tried. She didn't guess his intentions until he fastened his mouth over the throbbing bud of her womanhood, the feeling so hot and exciting that for a moment it conquered her embarrassment.

"Alex, please," she whispered breathlessly, torn between ecstasy and shame, "you—you can't do this."

Alex pulled back to look at her. "You have nothing to be ashamed of, *ma chère*. You are lovely in every way. What we enjoy together remains between us. I mean to give you pleasure this night, and in doing so, I will heighten my own."

His tongue traced fiery patterns on the flat spot below her navel. Again he moved lower, kissing his way up her thighs, caressing her with his hands. Then his mouth settled once more upon her most private place.

This time Alex was relentless. No amount of protest could sway him from his task. He was driving her to frenzy, sucking and tugging, using his mouth and his fingers until she felt the building, white-hot wave of her desire. Thrashing against the mattress, she moaned and begged him for more. When his tongue slid inside her, Nicki cried out his name. Her body tensed and her muscles grew rigid.

Like lightning in the eye of her mind, silver pinpricks of heat flashed over the horizon, lifting her up on the sweeping wave of pleasure that only Alex could bring.

Shuddering, she arched against him. "Please, Alex," she cried out, demanding even more. "I want you."

Alex kissed her then, thoroughly, passionately. She could taste her own musky scent on his breath as his tongue plunged into her mouth. She felt his manhood, hot and hard, then the length of him sliding inside, filling her and making them one.

Alex moved slowly at first, infusing her with sensation, forcing her to meet the rising tide of his passion. As her needs swelled with his, he moved faster, thrusting inside her, driving into her, pounding and pounding until her body seemed shaped by his will. Still it wasn't enough.

"Untie me," she begged, "I need to touch you."
She would surely die if she didn't.

Using every ounce of his control, Alex steadied
himself above her, his shaft still pulsing inside, and
slipped the silken ties off each of Nicki's wrists. With
a soft sob, she twined her fingers in his hair and
pulled his mouth down to hers. Using her tongue in
the most achingly sensuous manner Alex had ever
known, she drove it inside his mouth, darting it in
and out in rhythm to the thrusts he made into her
body.

The world as Alex knew it slipped away, replaced
by a high plateau where there were only the two of
them. He was loving her there just as he was here, his
muscular frame towering over her, his hard length
filling her, claiming her.

Crying out her name, he drove into her, desperate
to possess her, demanding she give back to him all
that he needed to give her.

Alex felt her body stiffen, felt her passage tighten
around him, and spent himself inside her just as she
reached her release. Her arms clutched his neck,
holding him to her, her small body pressed so tightly
against him that the two of them seemed one.

They spiraled down from that lofty plateau, and
still it seemed there was no one in the world but they.

"I've missed you," he said softly.

"God forgive me, but I've missed you too."

Sliding down her body, he unfastened the silken
bindings around her ankles, came up beside her, and
pulled her into his arms. It wasn't until he kissed her
cheek that he realized she was crying.

"Tell me what's wrong, *ma chère.*" He tightened
his hold on her waist.

She shook her head and glanced away.

"Please."

Nicki swallowed against the hard lump closing her throat. "It's just that now I know I fight not only you but myself as well."

Alex swore softly. Drawing shiny strands of copper hair away from her face, he brushed his lips across her cheek. "It's time this foolishness ended. You belong here with me. Surely you can see that. We desire each other, and this way I'll be able to take care of you."

Nicki turned on her side to face him. "I know you think what you're doing is best. For someone else, maybe it would be."

"But not for you," he finished dryly.

"No. Not for me." She laid her palm against his cheek. "That I desire you, you have proven without a doubt. That I care for you, I will freely admit. But I am a St. Claire. My family helped settle this country. You knew my father. You know how proud he was. He would never have acted dishonorably." Nicki's aqua eyes searched his face. "I'm his daughter, Alex. Just because I'm a woman doesn't mean I don't hold dear that same sense of right and wrong."

"Isn't your happiness—our happiness—worth more than some vague notion of honor?"

She looked at him as if she couldn't possibly have heard him correctly. "There is no such thing as happiness without honor."

Alex didn't answer, just pulled her back into the circle of his arms. "There must be some way," he said softly, kissing away her tears. But he knew in his heart there was none.

17

Alex rapped loudly on the door to 121 Royale Street. Around him well-dressed gentlemen, their ladies beside them, laughed and talked as they strolled the bustling street. Carriages and hansom cabs rolled past, carrying everyone from Irish laborers to aristocrats, beautiful octoroon women to sailors on leave.

Alex barely noticed them. At his second sharp rap, Thomas Demming's assistant, Jackson Turner, pulled open the heavy wooden door.

"Is Thomas in?" Alex asked.

"Yes, he is, Mr. du Villier." Jackson was a thickset man no more than thirty, but already losing his hair. "I'll tell him you're here." He disappeared down a narrow, dimly lit hallway lined with books and returned a few minutes later with Thomas.

"It's good to see you, Alex," Thomas said. The two men shook hands, and Thomas led the way back to his office, a wood-paneled room hung with framed diplomas and a painting of a full-rigged ship, her sails puffed out with storm. Thomas pointed toward one of the tufted leather seats in front of his wide oak desk, and Alex sank down heavily.

Thomas assessed his taut features, the eyes that looked hooded and dim. "I take it this isn't a social call."

"If only it were." Alex released a weary breath and raked a hand through his wavy dark-brown hair. "I've come today, Thomas, to speak to you as the friend you've always been to me, but also as one man to another."

Alex's voice held a note of formality Thomas didn't like. "Go on."

"It's about Nicole."

Thomas's head snapped up in alarm. "Has something happened to her?"

Alex waved away his concern. "No, no, it's nothing like that." Alex looked uncertain, as Thomas had rarely seen him. It seemed part of him wanted one thing, while another part wanted something altogether different.

"It's just that . . . Thomas, I need to know how you feel about her. You haven't had much chance to spend time with her, but still. . . ." He glanced away, his eyes coming to rest on the wind-tossed ship in the painting over Thomas's shoulder. He looked as if he were battling some inner storm of his own. "You know the two of us have been . . . together. There's no point in denying it. But I thought, if you cared enough, maybe that wouldn't make any difference."

Thomas felt stunned. "Are you trying to get rid of her?" *Good God, Alex had only just taken the girl to his bed!* "Are you asking me if I'm interested in taking Nicki as my mistress?"

"No!" Alex roared, coming to his feet. *"Nom de Dieu,* that's the last thing I want."

"Then what is it you're asking?"

"I watched you two at supper and then again at the soiree. I saw the way you looked at her. I'm asking if your interest in her includes marriage."

"Marriage?" Thomas's mouth gaped open.

Alex stiffened. "Is that so farfetched? I know her past is a bit uncertain, but I can assure you she came to me virgin. She's the most warm-hearted woman I've ever known. She's kind and caring. And honest to a fault. You'd never have a moment's regret."

"You misunderstand, my friend," Thomas said softly, beginning to understand the problem. Alex concern for Nicki showed in every line of his face, the way his shoulders seemed to sag under the weight of his distress.

Alex sat back down. His chest felt leaden, his mouth had gone dry, and his stomach was balled in a hard, tight knot. "Then your intentions toward her are honorable?"

"Alex, I have no intentions toward Nicole. Not since the first time I invited her out and you staunchly squelched the notion."

Alex glanced guiltily away.

"Nicki's a beautiful young woman, one of the loveliest I've seen. And I'm sure the things you've said about her are true, but—"

"But what?"

"First, I want to know why you're doing this," Thomas said. "If you're not tired of her—"

"Tired of her? I wonder if I could ever grow tired of her." Alex closed his eyes and sank back against the seat. "Nicki isn't like the other women I've known. Power, money, social position—those things mean nothing to her. What she values most is her honor. She'll do anything to keep it. Even if it means putting her life in danger. Last week she tried to run away from me. God in heaven, I was so worried. Anything might have happened."

"So rather than see her hurt, you're willing to let me have her."

"I trust you, Thomas. I know you'd be good to her. If I thought there was a chance for her to marry and be happy, I wouldn't stand in her way."

"How does Nicki feel?"

"I don't know. She just doesn't want to be my mistress."

Thomas rounded his desk. "At the party, I spent time with her because I thought she needed the distraction. You were there with Clarissa. From the looks you and Nicki were exchanging, it was obvious something was going on between you." Thomas sat down on the edge of his desk across from Alex. "I understand your situation, Alex. I know the problems you're facing with Fortier and Belle Chêne. I know you can't marry Nicki. I also know you've never been like this about any other woman."

"I'll admit she means a great deal to me—though as much trouble as she is, I often wonder why."

"The why is easy—you've discovered someone good and kind, someone you can talk to, someone who doesn't bow and scrape to your every command. In short, Alexandre, you've found a woman you can love."

Alex scoffed. "I don't believe in love. You of all people should know that by now."

"Well, I do. And I won't be happy until I've found it."

Alex chuckled softly. "You're a sentimental fool, my friend."

"And you, Alexandre, are a cynic."

Alex laughed. He felt relaxed again, back in control now that he knew his friend had no interest in Nicole. Yet wasn't that exactly why he had come here—hoping his friend would marry her and see her safe? "Do you think I should pursue the idea?" he forced himself to ask. "As lovely as she is, it should be easy to find a decent man who would marry her."

"Do you think you could give her up?" Thomas asked pointedly, and Alex glanced away.

"I don't want to, Thomas, I can tell you. When I'm with Nicki, I feel like I've reached a haven from the problems of the world."

He loves her, Thomas thought. *And Nicki loves him.* He had been certain of that for some time. "Nicki cares for you, Alex, just as much as you care for her. On top of that, she's safe with you, as she hasn't been in years. Look what happened to her when she went off on her own before."

"So you think I should keep her with me—even without her approval?"

"She belongs to you, doesn't she?"

"What if she tries to run from me again?"

"Surely you can keep an eye on her until she gets resigned to the situation." Thomas's voice turned gentle. "You realize she may already be with child."

"Actually, that was exactly what I'd been hoping. I felt certain that once she carried my babe, she would accept the course of her future."

"Exactly," Thomas agreed.

Alex stood up and Thomas walked him down the hall to the front door. "At least now your conscience is clear. You tried to find her a husband, but none was available—at least none of whom you'd approve.''

Alex grinned so broadly, he dimpled. Feeling as though a weight had been lifted from his shoulders, he clapped his friend on the back. "Thank you, *mon ami*. You always seem to have the answers."

"Maybe not always—" A knock at the door interrupted the balance of Thomas's response. Opening it, he found Michele Christophe and her aunt Laverne standing on the banquette, the walkway out front.

"My twelve o'clock luncheon appointment is here," Thomas said to Alex with a grin. "Ladies, won't you please come in?" Wearing a walking dress of rich coffee-brown, Michelle stepped inside, followed by her aunt. "Mademoiselle Christophe, I believe you've met Alexandre du Villier."

"Good afternoon, m'sieur."

"And this is Madame Trepagnier, her aunt."

"*Enchanté*, madame," Alex said gallantly.

"*Bonjour*, m'sieur." The robust woman forced a tight-lipped smile. She was dressed in a dark-green day dress with a too-high collar and carried a hand-painted fan. It was obvious she had heard stories of Alex's newest mistress—Etienne St. Claire's daughter, the Christophes' old family friend. But Alex was too relieved to care.

"Well, I'd better be going." He extended a hand to Thomas. "I'll stop by the next time I'm in town."

After a formal good-bye to the ladies, Alex headed into the street. The sun seemed brighter somehow, the air a little cleaner. It felt good to know he'd been right all along—seeing to Nicki's welfare the best he knew how—considering their current set of circumstances. That his own chance for happiness had just soared dramatically he didn't bother to deny.

And he planned to make her equally content. Sooner or later, Nicki would see that her foolish pride meant little in comparison to their happiness. Once she was round with child, she would settle in, accept the special place he meant for her to hold. Until then, he would do whatever it took to keep her with him.

Sometimes it seemed it was he who had no other choice.

All the way down the street, Michele on one arm, Madame Trepagnier on the other, Thomas wondered at his advice. He had known Alexandre for years, but never seen him so distraught. Maybe Alex was too blind to see, but Thomas wasn't.

Alex was in love with Nicole.

He would marry Clarissa—in that he had no choice. But with Nicki as his mistress there was still a chance he could find happiness.

But what about Nicole?

Again Thomas felt his advice had been correct. It was just as obvious that Nicki was in love with Alex. On top of that, she had no one else to look after her, no family, no money, no possible way to take care of herself. The last time she had tried she had wound up in prison. Besides, just as he had said, Nicki might already be carrying Alex's babe.

No, he had done the right thing, he decided. At least they'd be together, and though Nicki's damnable pride might suffer, Alex would eventually make her happy.

He glanced over at Michele and his heart swelled

with warmth. Every man should have someone to love. Someone who would love him in return.

"It's a beautiful day," he said to her.

Michele smiled back at him, her pretty green eyes alight with a sweetness he had found in few other women. "It is now," she said. And Thomas felt again that he had done the right thing.

Nicki waited impatiently throughout the morning for Alex's return. She had no idea where he had gone or why. Then again, that was probably the way a man treated his mistress.

In her soft teal day dress of velvet-trimmed merino, Nicki sat on the ice-blue brocade sofa in the salon, trying to occupy her mind with a book of Shakespeare's sonnets when Alex opened the door. Handing Frederick his narrow-brimmed gray high hat, he strode in whistling and smiling—a far happier man than the one who had left her that morning. In fact, he looked downright cheerful.

Too cheerful.

Nicki didn't like it one little bit.

"I've the carriage waiting outside," he said, "why don't we go for a ride?" Bending over, he brushed her lips with a kiss. "Soon we'll be forced to stay indoors, but today it's far too nice for that."

Though his words were spoken with a casual air, his eyes swept over her, taking in the swell of her breast, the narrow circle of her waist. After the hard arousal she had left him with this morning, she was surprised he hadn't demanded they spend the day upstairs in his big feather bed.

"That would be lovely," she replied, anxious to put off that confrontation for as long as possible.

No matter what had happened last night, she didn't intend to make things easy for him. Holding him off would be difficult if not impossible, but sooner or later he was bound to grow weary of the effort it took to bed her. Maybe then his attentions would focus on someone less difficult, and he would let her go.

Nicki swallowed hard. Just the thought of him making love to somebody else turned the blood in her veins to ice.

"Where shall we go?" she asked, pretending equal nonchalance.

"I need to spend a moment with my factor—my estate manager—Louis Mouton. Afterward, we'll just see what catches our fancy."

Alex gave Ram the rest of the day and evening off, and he and Nicki went out front, where the carriage he kept in the city, a shiny black calèche pulled by a pair of sleek bay horses, stood waiting. The factor's office was down on Decatur Street, across from the wharf.

Threading a path through the bustling city traffic, the carriage arrived at their destination a short time later. Certain Alex would want few people to know he kept a mistress, Nicki's eyes widened in surprise when he rounded the calèche to help her down, then led her to the door, apparently unconcerned about the impropriety. From the street, the brick building looked old and in need of paint. Inside, Louis Mouton's office, the enclosed front portion of a ware-house, was a showplace.

The receiving area, where his assistant worked, had the subdued yet elegant look of a finely furnished inn. In his private office, original oil paintings, many by artists of renown, lined the walls, and the floors were covered by plush Oriental carpets. Mouton's desk was Louis Quatorze and exquisite beyond compare.

"Alexandre," Louis Mouton said, smiling warmly and shaking Alex's hand. "What an unexpected pleasure."

"Louis, this is Mademoiselle St. Claire."

"*Enchanté.*" Mouton kissed her white-gloved hand. He was a man of medium build, attractive in a slightly arrogant way, with a straight, aristocratic nose, fine teeth, and light-brown hair just beginning to recede from his forehead.

"A pleasure, I'm sure," Nicki said. The men discussed the coming harvest, how many hogshead of sugar would go to each of several shipping destinations, and how much each shipment should bring.

Mouton glanced pointedly at Nicki. "There is another subject we need to discuss, Alexandre. May I speak freely, or would you prefer we talk later?"

"Whatever you have to say you may say."

Nicki felt a rush of warmth at the trust Alex's words implied.

"After a careful examination of your accounts," Mouton told him, "I don't believe you will have the amount necessary to repay your debt in full to M'sieur Fortier."

"I'm very well aware of that, Louis. In fact, that's the reason I've come here today. I wanted to assure you the money will be made available for payment well before the mortgage is due."

Mouton seemed surprised. "You were able to borrow such a sum?"

"It's more a matter of acquiring additional collateral. Elmtree will soon become a part of Belle Chêne."

Nicki's stomach tightened.

"I see." Mouton smiled. The tension seemed to drain from his body. "I must say, I am relieved to hear it."

Alex smiled too. "You've nothing to fear, Louis. As long as I'm master of Belle Chêne, you've a job for the next fifty years."

Fifty years, Nicki thought. Where will I be then? Certainly not growing old with Alex, as Clarissa would be.

The three of them walked to the door.

"By the way, Alexandre, did you bring your personal set of ledgers? The year is coming to a close. It's time we set things in order."

"I've been so damned busy—" Alex pulled open the door. "I'll see that you get them by the end of the month if I have to tie myself to the desk to get them done."

"Fine," Mouton said.

Alex and Nicki stepped out into the street.

"He seems quite efficient," Nicki said as they climbed into the carriage.

"He's been with our family for years."

"My father worked with a man named Arcenenaux. It's amazing how much we came to rely on him. He took care of all our finances, even advanced money to us if the crops fell short or something else went wrong."

"Yes, Louis has been a tremendous help."

The carriage rolled along the crowded streets of the *Vieux Carré* and turned up Esplanade, one of the most beautiful streets in the Quarter. Uniformed soldiers marched in precision on the grassy parade ground, to the delight of both children and adults who watched from beneath nearby magnolia trees.

They rolled past the United States Mint, a big brick building stuccoed and trimmed with granite that was built in the Greek Revival style.

"In my father's day," Alex said, "Fort St. Charles stood on that spot."

"I remember my father talking about it too. He said Andrew Jackson personally reviewed the troops there before the Battle of New Orleans."

At the corner of Rampart Street, the carriage turned again, traveling a ways, then passed Congo Square, where black people, both slave and free, gathered on Sunday afternoons to dance and play music, much of it with a wild African beat.

"My father brought me here once," Nicki said a bit wistfully. "We watched the Negroes dancing to the *Bamboula* and the *Danse Calinda*. It was wild and primitive and pagan. And so beautiful I never forgot it."

Alex chuckled softly. "I believe some of their inspiration may have rubbed off on you—at least in bed."

Nicki flushed crimson and glanced away, wishing she hadn't spoken such intimate thoughts. Alex turned her heated face with his hand.

"That was a compliment, *chérie*. A passionate woman is a treasure."

Nicki felt the warmth of his fingers and desire curled softly in the pit of her stomach. *Then I must be worth a king's ransom*, she thought, but forced the notion away.

A few blocks later, at the end of St. Peter Street, Alex instructed the driver to stop. He climbed to the ground and helped Nicki alight. The Place d'Armes was crowded with elegantly dressed men and women who strolled the grassy square just as Alex intended they should.

Seeing the elite of New Orlean's society, Nicki hesitantly accepted his arm. "Are you sure about this, Alex? What happens if someone sees us? What will people say?"

Alex covered her suddenly cold fingers with his strong hand. "I've told you before, many men marry for reasons other than their personal happiness. It's not uncommon for them to spend time with someone else who fulfills that need."

"In other words," Nicki said, lifting her chin, "nobody gives a damn."

Alex chuckled again. "I give a damn, *ma chère.* That's all that matters."

"That's all that matters to you," Nicki corrected. Alex blanched, looked as if he wanted to deny it, but said nothing more.

They strolled along the square and stopped to watch a young French artist who sat in front of his easel painting the beautiful St. Louis Cathedral on Chartres Street. Nicki stood there, engrossed in the young man's skill with palette and brush, until she felt Alex's hand at her waist grow taut. Up ahead, she saw the reason. Valcour Fortier walked toward them. Nicki sucked in a breath as she recognized the woman on his arm.

Lisette!

Fortier grinned with satisfaction. "Good afternoon, Mademoiselle . . . St. Claire, wasn't it? And Alexandre—I believe you know Lisette."

Alex pinned the small French woman with his eyes.

"Excuse us a moment, won't you?" he said to Valcour, taking a firm hold on Lisette's arm and tugging her a few feet away. He turned her to face him, his eyes ablaze with anger. "What the hell is the matter with you? Surely you know his reputation? You know the way he treats his women."

"I do not believe a word of it!" She tossed her pretty head, and with it her mane of thick black hair. "Besides, it is no longer your concern."

"I don't want to see you get hurt."

"Valcour will take care of me. 'E knows a good woman when 'e finds one—not like you. You toss me over for that . . . that English bit of baggage."

"She's half French, and I didn't toss you over. You have a perfectly lovely little house at the edge of the city, just as you wanted."

"Yes, well, soon I will not need it. I will be mistress of Feliciana."

Alex cursed low in his throat. "You little fool. Valcour will never marry you."

Lisette drew herself up in an angry pout. "'e is not like you. Valcour loves me. It has been years since his wife disappeared. 'E will take me as his bride, you will see."

Turning away from him in a swirl of royal-blue silk faille skirts, Lisette left him swearing on the boardwalk behind her. Lisette and Valcour swept off down the banquette and around the corner before he reached Nicki's side.

"I hope you're not angry," he said. "I had to speak to her, try to make her understand."

Nicki didn't answer. Watching Alex with Lisette had left her feeling sick inside and even more uncertain. It had been all she could do to concentrate on

Valcour's words, which held their usual taunting in-
nuendos.

"You were jealous," she finally said, glancing up
though she feared what she would see. "She must
still mean a great deal to you."

"Jealous? *Mon Dieu*, no." Alex slid an arm around
her waist. Heedless of the ladies and gentlemen who
strolled by, he drew her into his arms. "I was worried. Lisette was once my responsibility. I don't want
to see her get hurt. Concern for her welfare is all I
felt, just as I would for anyone else."

"Then you aren't sorry she's gone?"

"No, *ma chère*. I'm only sorry I didn't find you
sooner."

Nicki tried to ignore the overwhelming relief she
felt at his words. "Tell me about Valcour. Why do you
hate him so much?"

"I don't really hate him. Mostly, I feel sorry for
him." Alex looped her arm through his and they
strolled along the square. "Valcour's my age. We've
known each other since childhood. His father and
mine were rivals, both men competing to build their
empires. Though each achieved success, it was never
enough for Gibert, Valcour's father. He drove himself
and his son like a madman."

"What of his mother?"

"His mother was the daughter of a Spanish don, a
lovely, genteel woman, according to my father."

"So you knew Valcour as a boy?"

"Off and on, since I spent much of my time in
France. Unfortunately for Valcour, his youth was far
different than mine. Gibert Fortier was a strict disci-
plinarian. He believed in 'Spare the rod and spoil the

child.' Valcour was his only son, and Gibert expected perfection."

"But surely his mother protected him."

"Valcour's mother died when he was seven. After that his father's demands grew worse, his punishments even more severe. I'm sure the beatings Valcour suffered had much to do with the way he is today."

Nicki said nothing. Her insides had turned to ice. She knew what it felt like to be treated with the kind of cruelty Valcour had suffered. "And I suppose Gibert expected his son to compete with you, just as he competed with your father."

"Exactly. Valcour always held his own, but"—Alex grinned—"if I may be immodest, he rarely bested me."

Fighting a grin of her own, Nicki nudged him in the ribs. "Just stick to the story."

Alex drew her beneath a huge magnolia, its scattered leaves crunching beneath their feet. "When Fortier was twenty-four, he met a Spanish girl named Feliciana and fell in love with her. She was beautiful. Dark, like Valcour, but soft and gentle like his mother. Valcour worshipped her."

"What happened to her?" Nicki asked.

"No one really knows for sure. By the end of their first year of marriage, Valcour had become obsessed with her. At parties, he refused to let her dance with other men. He fought several duels because someone had insulted her—or so he believed. Feliciana withdrew. She stopped going out at all, which suited her husband just fine. Then one night, she disappeared. Valcour swears she had the fever and wandered into the bayous in delirium. . . ."

"But you don't believe it."

"It's possible. But the whispered story, the one told by the servants, is that Valcour caught her talking to a peddler who had stopped by to ask directions. Apparently, the man was handsome and charming, and Feliciana was so lonely she invited him in. Nothing happened, but that night, Valcour tied her up and beat her. Afterward, he forced her to make love to him. The next night, Feliciana ran away."

Nicki looked up at Alex. "He hurt the very thing he loved most."

"Yes . . ." Alex agreed, his sudden change in tone hinting at thoughts she couldn't discern. "The Fortier estate used to be named Terre Sauvage—the wild earth. After his wife left him, Valcour changed the name to Feliciana. I think he still believes she'll return."

Nicki shuddered involuntarily and Alex's hold tightened. "You're cold," he said. "We'd better be getting back."

Nicki nodded her agreement. But the chill she felt came from inside, not out.

18

By the time they had returned to the town house, Alex's thoughts had turned in the direction she had feared.

Seated beside her on the sofa, he watched her with warm, dark eyes while his finger traced circles in the palm of her hand. Nicki's stomach fluttered and her heart beat a little too fast. Damn him, she thought, struggling to ignore her building desire.

"I've been thinking, Alex—about what the factor said." She smiled, intent on postponing their confrontation as long as possible. "Since you're determined to keep me here, why don't you let me be of some use?"

Alex grinned. "You've been a good deal of use already. Though I assure you, we've only just begun."

Nicki cast him an exasperated glance. "That's not what I mean and you know it. I want to help you with the ledgers. I did much of the accounting at Meadowood, and the Ramseys taught me even more. I could save you hours of work, and it would keep me from getting bored."

Alex leaned down and kissed her, his tongue urging

her lips apart, then sliding inside to tease and coax. "I certainly wouldn't want that to happen," he said against her mouth, then he flashed her a second outrageous grin, this one bringing those sensuous grooves to his cheeks.

"I mean it, Alex." Nicki fought to calm her racing heart. "Don't you think I can do it?"

Alex sighed. "If you say you can, then I believe you. You never cease to amaze me." He brushed back a stray lock of her hair. "I'll have them brought to you as soon as I return to Belle Chêne."

"Thank you," she said.

"Thank *you*. There's nothing I hate more than accounting. I thank God every day for Louis Mouton."

They ate an early supper of oysters, shrimp jambalaya, and *pistolettes*, little rolls of warm, hard-crusted bread. Though Betsy's home-style cooking tasted far different from that of the French chef at Belle Chêne, Nicki finished every bite on her plate.

"I see you enjoyed the meal." One corner of Alex's mouth tilted upward.

"It's more like what we used to eat back home."

Alex seemed pleased.

After pralines and café au lait, they retired to the drawing room for sherry and brandy. They had finished only half a glass when a loud knock sounded at the door. In minutes Frederick strode in.

"There's a message for you," he told Alex. "A problem's come up at Belle Chêne."

Alex set his brandy snifter down and unfolded the note Frederick handed him. "It seems you've a reprieve, *ma chère*."

"What's happened?"

"Problems with the cane crusher. Unfortunately the overseer has been hurt."

"Badly?"

"Let's hope not. But there's no one there who knows how to get things running again." It went unsaid that once the harvesting and refining process started, it continued around the clock. "I've got to go."

Nicki walked Alex to the door, hating to see him go, yet thankful he was leaving.

"Frederick," Alex said pointedly to the tall, well-built Negro, who spoke better English than most of the servants. Though the Nat Turner laws forbade it, Alex had secretly helped him educate himself. "Since I thought I'd be staying, I gave Ram the night out. That means you are in charge. I'll expect to find Mademoiselle St. Claire here when I return. If for any reason she is not, you are the one I will hold responsible. Do I make myself clear?"

One look in Alex's hard, dark eyes was all Frederick needed. "Don't worry," he said. "She'll be here."

"Now I have two jailers!" Nicki cried, no longer sorry to see him go.

"Ram will be back in the morning," Alex told Frederick, who nodded. He hauled Nicki into his arms and kissed her so soundly her knees went weak.

Once the door closed behind him, she sagged against it. The man was impossible! Alexandre du Villier was dominating, infuriating—and she fell a little more in love with him every day. He was wearing her down, constantly draining her will, and bringing her closer to his control.

With a glare of betrayal at Frederick, who merely shrugged, Nicki headed up to her room. At least Alex would be busy for a while. She would have time to think things through and get on with her plans.

"Danielle!" she called down the stairs, and the plump, dark-haired girl poked her head out the dining-room door. "I need you a moment."

When Danielle arrived at her bedchamber door, Nicki surprised her by pointing to the table and chairs she had arranged before the window. "How would you like to learn to play chess?"

Ever since Nicki's first game of chess with the Ram, an idea had been forming in her mind. When Ram played chess, the rest of the world went by unnoticed. It seemed the roof could fall in and he wouldn't care.

Once he had discovered Nicki enjoyed the game, too, they had played almost every night. Nicki smiled as she pulled out her chair. After Danielle learned to play, Ram would have another opponent. Someone else who could elicit his deepest concentration and keep his mind off Nicole. When their games became routine, Nicki would strike.

The roof might not fall in, but Ram would probably think so. A good hard hit on the head would knock him unconscious. It was just about the only thing she could think of to insure her chance at escape. Of course there was still money to obtain, and Frederick, too, was now a problem. . . .

One step at a time, she told herself.

Meanwhile, she would teach Danielle all she could about chess, and she would go and see François.

After sending him a message and receiving his reply, Nicki set off with Ram late one morning to François's suite at the St. Charles Hotel.

"He may not appreciate your interference," Ram warned as the carriage rolled up in front of the impressive brick building and a liveried doorman helped her alight.

"I know."

Marching through the extravagant hotel lobby with its beautiful molded ceilings and crystal chandeliers, Nicki climbed the wide carved staircase to François's third-floor room. It was a bit unseemly, but what did it matter? What little reputation she had left hung in tatters.

"I'll wait out here," Ram told her, seating himself on a plush velvet bench in the hallway. Brass-and-crystal sconces lit the corridor, and deep Aubusson carpets covered inlaid mahogany-and-cypress floors.

After Nicki's light rap on the door, François pulled it open. He stood just inside, dressed in light-gray breeches, a burgundy brocade waistcoat, and a dark-gray tailcoat. Her own cashmere day dress, done in a rusty shade, matched the turn of the leaves outside and the crisp fall weather.

"It's good to see you," François said, his voice a little strained. He bent to plant a chaste kiss on her cheek.

"I've missed you," Nicki said, meaning it.

They took a seat on a cream silk sofa that nestled in front of the fireplace, though no fire burned in the hearth. The room was exquisitely done in cream and beige, the carpets thick and luxurious. Colorful floral paintings in gilded frames lined the walls, along with pastoral scenes from nearby farms, paintings of birds winging over the bayous, and ships lined up on the bustling docks of New Orleans.

It dawned on Nicki that each had been done by the same artist, whose abundant talent was obvious.

She glanced around the room. "Are these yours?"

"Yes. Do you like them?"

"I love them!"

Just as before, François's rigid posture fled, along with his brooding expression. "You really like them? You wouldn't just say that?" As his eyes searched hers for the truth, he seemed almost childlike in his need for reassurance.

"I wouldn't say it if I didn't mean it. They're wonderful, François. Some of the nicest work I've ever seen." Nicki walked around the room, François beside her, surveying each piece, asking questions about his technique, and commenting on the beauty of the work.

"I want to study in France," he told her, and Nicki turned in surprise.

"Does Alex know?" she asked. "But then, how could he? He doesn't even know you paint."

François sighed. "I'm afraid he will think I'm being foolish. I couldn't stand it if he laughed at me."

Nicki led him over to the sofa. "I can't imagine Alex laughing at anyone. And certainly not his brother. Do you really think he would?"

"He was furious with me for the way I mismanaged Belle Chêne. He ridiculed me for making such a mess of things. Called me an incompetent fool. Later he apologized, but it was not that easy to forget."

"Everyone makes mistakes. You made mistakes with Belle Chêne. Alex made a mistake in the way he treated you. Belle Chêne means a great deal to him."

"Everything," François corrected. "But there is more to it than that. He is worried about *Grand-mère* and me. And the people who live and work there. He is terrified of what will happen to them if Fortier becomes master."

"I've heard of his cruelty."

"In truth, Val is not overly harsh with his workers —at least not compared to some. Slaves are chattel to him, you see. Possessions. A man does not destroy what belongs to him." François raked a hand through his wavy dark-brown hair in a gesture that reminded her of his brother.

"But to Alex," he was saying, "they are more than that. He knows most of them by name, urges them to marry and baptize their children, treats them more like trusted servants than slaves. Up until the Nat Turner laws, they were even given schooling. Alex feels responsible for them. Even his own happiness comes second."

"Why are you telling me this?" Nicki asked, but in her heart she knew.

"So you will understand why he must marry Clarissa."

Nicki glanced away, a hard lump swelling her throat.

"The future of Belle Chêne depends on it," François said softly. "And that future includes all those Alex feels responsible for."

Nicki raised her eyes to his face. "It seems, in one way or another, Alex and I will both have to pay. But you, François, you still have a chance. Tell your brother about your painting. Ask him to send you to France."

François's expression grew bleak. "As much as I want to go, I cannot."

"But why?"

François shook his head. "I wish I could tell you, but some things are best left unsaid." His dark eyes looked hooded, his boyish features taut.

Nicki laid a hand on his arm. "It's because of Jean Pierre, isn't it? You don't want to leave him."

François closed his eyes. She could see the battle he waged for control. "I was afraid you had noticed. I had hoped you wouldn't find out."

"I know little about such things, but I have come to know you. I believe you are good and kind. That you mean no harm to anyone. If it makes you happy, take Jean Pierre with you."

François shook his head, his expression even bleaker. "I haven't the money, and Alex would never understand."

"He might," Nicki said, but even she didn't believe it. In every way, Alexandre du Villier was a completely masculine man.

"I can't take that chance," François finished.

They sat quietly for a time, each comforted by the other, though no words were spoken.

"Thank you for explaining about Alex," Nicki finally said.

"Thank you for coming," François told her.

He walked her to the door, and she stood on tiptoes to kiss his cheek. "Take care of yourself. And please come to see me."

François smiled. "I shall come on Thursday, if it is all right. We will lunch, then watch the artists painting in the square."

"That sounds wonderful." For a fleeting instant, she thought of asking François to help with her escape. But he probably wouldn't, and even if he

•

agreed, it wouldn't be fair to drive yet another wedge between him and his brother.

With a last brief hug, Nicki left him. She found Ram waiting patiently in the hall, just where he'd been before.

"Feeling better?" he asked, coming to his feet.

"Much." Together, they headed down the stairs. "But I'd feel better yet if I could find some way to convince Alexandre that his brother should study in France—along with his friend, of course. Then everything would be perfect."

Ram laughed aloud, such a husky roar that people turned in their direction. "Alex bought himself a hundred pounds of trouble, my girl, when he bought you."

Though it sounded like an insult, Ram's look said just the opposite. She wished she knew for sure.

Nicki slept fitfully that night. She kept dreaming of Alex, imagining him making love to her. Twice she woke up bathed in perspiration, her nipples hard and aching.

"Damn him," she swore, but couldn't help wondering where he was and what he was doing. At least he no longer visited Lisette. Then it occurred to her that in a very short time, he would be sleeping with Clarissa.

"I have to get away," she resolved aloud. "Before it's too late."

Though she received several warm notes from Alex, he remained at Belle Chêne, immersed in the sugar harvest. She spent the following Thursday with François, and Thursday night and much of Friday playing chess with Danielle.

"If I can get some money," Nicki told Danielle as they sat before the fire in her chamber, "and you can keep Ram busy—I'm leaving sometime next week." She flashed her friend a pointed glance. "This time, I'll make it."

Danielle rolled her round gray eyes. "He can cut out my heart. This time, I will not tell."

Nicki grinned.

When the chess game was over, she shoved the board away and came to her feet. "You're getting better," she said, though she had beaten Danielle with ease.

"It is fun. Besides, I do not have to play well. I shall use my feminine wiles on the big Turk. 'Please, *M'sieur le* Ram,'" she mimicked, batting her thick, dark-brown lashes, "'I know you are far more intelligent than I, but surely a man such as you could teach a lowly woman . . . ?'" Danielle giggled and Nicki laughed out loud.

They headed downstairs, bent on a *pot de crème* before bed, but voices in the hallway stopped them midway there.

"*M'sieur le duc,*" Danielle whispered.

"Yes." Against her will, Nicki's heart started thumping and her fingers trembled on the rail.

When Alex glanced up and saw her, his smile went so wide he dimpled. It was all Nicki could do to keep from racing into his arms.

"Good evening, m'sieur," she said instead, working to keep the tremor in her hands from reaching her voice.

As Nicki descended the last few stairs, Alex strode toward her, his long, muscular stride carrying him swiftly. He scooped her into his arms and kissed her, his mouth so hot and demanding that Nicki found herself clutching his neck.

"What are you doing here?" she asked breathlessly, when he finally pulled away. "What about your overseer and the problems with the harvest?"

"The overseer is going to be fine, just a gash on the arm and a minor concussion. The problems are resolved for the present—and I missed you so damned much I couldn't stay away."

Nicki's heart felt near to bursting.

"Ask Betsy to get me some supper," he told Frederick, taking Nicki's hand, "and bring a goblet of wine for each of us."

Alex led Nicki into the salon, his eyes fastened on the gentle rise and fall of her bosom. He felt a tightening in his groin just to look at her. Even in her simple blue serge dress, she looked beautiful—and far more tempting than he could have imagined. Her cheeks were flushed from his kiss and her pretty aqua eyes tenderly searched his face. *She's glad to see me, too, the little minx. Even if she won't admit it.*

And Nicki wasn't about to. Now that she had recovered from her surprise, she realized exactly why he had come. Three times each week, he had gone to see Lisette. If it weren't for the harvest, Nicki was certain he would be pounding on her door with equal regularity.

The more she thought about it, the more disgruntled she became. By the time Alex had finished his meal of cold roast chicken, bread, and cheese, and downed his goblet of wine, her temper felt close to bursting.

Alex seemed not to notice. "You look tired," he

said, a teasing light in his eyes. "I think it's time we went upstairs."

"I'm not tired at all," Nicki told him, and Alex's soft look faded. "In fact, I think I'd enjoy a walk in the garden."

"I've come some ways, *chérie*. I've worked hard all week, and I'm too damned tired to play your childish games."

"You may think they're childish. I do not. I'm not your mistress, Alex, as you seem set on thinking. I'm not now, nor will I ever be your willing bedmate. Excuse me," she said, standing up. "I'll be out in the garden." Squaring her shoulders and lifting her chin, Nicki started for the door.

"Maybe you're right," Alex agreed, catching up to her in two powerful, angry strides. "A little exercise might be just the thing." But instead of heading outdoors, he drew her firmly against him, slid an arm around her waist, and against her protests, led her up to their room at the top of the stairs.

"Come here," Alex ordered once the door was closed, his eyes dark and hungry. "I've waited far too long already."

"No," Nicki said firmly, backing away from him.

Alex clamped his jaw. Forcing a calm he obviously didn't feel, he shrugged out of his coat, pulled off his boots and dropped them onto the floor, then removed his shirt.

Drawn to the sight of his wide bare chest, the soft thatch of curly brown hair that beckoned in the warm yellow glow of the lamp, Nicki wet her suddenly dry lips. Alex unbuttoned the front of his trousers and slid them down his long, muscular legs, the sound a slow *whoosh* that sent gooseflesh dancing across her skin.

"Damn it, Nicki, I know you've missed me just as much as I've missed you."

"It doesn't matter."

"It does matter!" He sighed. "Shall I tie you up again?" he asked. "I can, you know, though I'd rather feel your arms around me."

"How can you enjoy this when you know it's not what I want?"

"It's exactly what you want," Alex replied, his eyes roaming over her. He hadn't missed her suddenly shallow breathing, or the taut pink nipples that strained against her bodice just from watching him undress. "It's exactly what we both want."

Naked and aroused, he strode toward her. Nicki glanced from right to left, but before she could think to move, Alex had her by the waist, turning her back to him. With practiced ease, his fingers worked the tiny covered buttons on her dress, then he pulled open the bodice, and slid it off her shoulders. Next he unfastened the tab on her petticoats and drew her from the fluffy folds in only her corset and chemise.

Now, her mind said. *Run from him now.* But she really didn't want to, and there was no place for her to go. She stood there half-naked, thinking how easy it would be to let him love her, how easy to succumb to his charm. She wanted him, had from the moment he'd stepped into the foyer. Only her pride kept her from him. Only her pride—and her honor.

Alex tugged on the laces of her corset and it fell away. Deftly, he pulled the pins from her hair, and the silky copper mass tumbled loose around her shoulders.

You made a vow, she told herself firmly. If she fought him, at least the servants would know for certain she wasn't there by choice. As Alex fumbled with the sash to her white cotton drawers, Nicki mustered her courage and jerked away from him.

"If you intend to take me, you'll have to do it by force."

Alex swore softly, but seemed unsurprised. "When was your last monthly?" he asked, the question so far from what she expected that Nicki's eyes went wide.

"What?"

"Your last monthly?" he repeated, as if she weren't quite bright. "When was it?"

"Last week," she said, "but what has that got to do with—"

Alex cursed again, this time more soundly. "I shall bed you every chance I get, until you carry my child."

"What?" Nicki drew farther away. "But what difference . . . ?" She broke off in mid-sentence as the light of understanding dawned. "That's why Ram is planning to leave after the harvest. Your damned masculine pride is so great, you're sure I'll be with child!" Nicki's bosom heaved, and she clenched her hands into fists. "You think that will change things— that I'll be forced to stay here with you."

"What else could you possibly do?"

"The same thing I would have done from the start. Take care of the babe myself."

"Don't be absurd," Alex snapped, coming closer. "The last time you tried to take care of yourself you wound up in prison."

"I'm older now and a whole lot wiser."

Alex scoffed. "That remains to be seen."

Nicki picked up the apricot-colored vase she had purchased just that afternoon. "This is going to get expensive," she warned, holding the vase above her.

Alex grinned, dimpling his cheeks. "One way or another, a man must pay for his passions."

"Damn you!" Nicki hurled the vase at his head and raced toward the door. Alex ducked and it shattered against the wall. He slammed the door closed just as she pulled it open.

Grabbing her arm, he carried her, cursing and struggling, toward the bed.

"I hate you!" she raged, breaking free and trying once more to escape.

"Only for the moment," he said with a mocking grin. Using his body to hold her in place, Alex pressed her down on the mattress. Nicki freed her arms and twisted away from him onto her stomach, her hips sliding over the edge. It was definitely a mistake.

Alex captured her arms and drew them above her head. "We've had so little time, *ma chère*. You've only begun to know the pleasures of a man and woman." His hold turned gentle. Warm lips touched her shoulders while his hand swept the fall of copper hair from her cheek.

"They'll be bastards, Alex," Nicki whispered.

"It doesn't matter." He nuzzled her ear and nipped the back of her neck. "They'll still be ours to love."

Nicki tried to ignore the warmth of his breath on her skin, the touch of his lips as they trailed hot kisses across her shoulders. Bands of muscle rubbed against her back, and his hard shaft pressed against her bottom.

Alex slipped a wide palm inside her chemise to cup her breast, his fingers warm and strong. With practiced skill, they teased her taut nipple, making it even harder and sending a surge of moisture to the place between her legs. He lifted and molded the soft round flesh, and his mouth and tongue worked their magic until she trembled.

"Oh, God," Nicki whispered when his hand moved lower, across the flat plane above her navel to stroke and tease. He untied the cord of her white cotton drawers and slid them over her hips. Then he carefully lifted the hem of her chemise.

When Alex settled himself against the soft white globes of her bottom, Nicki moaned. Parting the folds of her sex, he found her wet and ready, and eased himself inside. She could feel the powerful length of him, filling her, stirring a host of new sensations. His shaft, hard and throbbing, pulsed with a need that matched her own.

Alex let go of her wrists, circled her waist with his hands, and raised her hips to meet him as he came to his feet still deep inside her. Nicki arched her back and went up on her knees, wanting to feel every hard inch of him. Grinding her hips against him, she forced him even deeper.

Alex groaned and whispered her name, speaking soft French love words. Caught up in a world of heat and passion, Nicki barely heard them. Alex drove deeper, his strokes more powerful. Flesh pounded flesh until nothing mattered but the feel of him. Nothing mattered but the penetrating thrusts of his shaft.

Alex plunged into her, driving himself like a man gone mad. Nicki moaned and writhed beneath him as he pulled back and entered her again and again. The enormity of her response amazed him, stirring his passion higher and higher and sending him over the edge.

They reached their peak together, surging as one to that high plateau. Alex shuddered and his hold tightened around her hips. Again and again he impaled her, until both were spent and covered with a shine of perspiration. Then he pulled her down on the bed beside him, smoothing the hair from her face, kissing the side of her neck.

"You're mine," he whispered beside her ear. "You belong to me and nothing can change that."

For a moment she didn't answer. "You won't own me forever. One day I'll again be free."

Alex smiled into the darkness. "I speak not of your contract, *mon amoureuse*, but of what lies in your heart."

Nicki drew away from him, refusing to acknowledge the feelings she fought so hard to hide. "Were you sure of Lisette, as well?"

Alex's gentle look hardened. "You're nothing like Lisette."

"No? I'm your mistress, aren't I? Just as she was."

"It isn't the same."

"Why not?"

"Lisette meant nothing to me."

"And what do I mean to you, Alex? What exactly do you feel for me?"

Why couldn't he tell her? Why couldn't he say that having her there meant everything to him? That he needed her as he had never needed a woman. That when Nicki smiled at him, the problems he faced fell into shadow, replaced by sunshine and warmth?

He couldn't tell her because a man wasn't supposed to feel that way about a woman. His father would have laughed at him—*mon Dieu*, he laughed at himself.

"Go to sleep, *chérie*," he said instead, and snuggled her into his arms.

* * *

By the time Nicki awoke, Alex was gone. Twice in the night he had made love to her again, and she hadn't protested. There was something in his manner that made his need of her apparent as it never had been before.

Still, this morning, when she'd felt his hard arousal, she pretended to be sleeping. Alex hadn't pushed her, just held her in his arms a little longer, then quietly climbed from the bed.

She had wanted him again, too, but his words the night before had stilled the notion. She had been lucky so far. Unless she'd conceived last night, she was not pregnant. Escape would be easier. Better one to care for than two.

Though she'd known the risks from the start, she had pushed them to the back of her mind. Now that he had forced her to face them, and uncertain how many more times he would come to her before she could get away, she decided to speak to Danielle.

Danielle would soon be wife to René. It would not be untoward for her to speak to her married friends, discover the ways of prevention, though it was all too clear how seldom they worked.

Not that Nicki didn't want children. If things were different, there could be no finer gift than that of Alex's child. That he would allow his own flesh and blood to be called bastard seemed harsh, but men thought differently about such things. From the way Alex had spoken of his father, she felt sure Charles du Villier had sired such children either here or in France.

She shuddered at thoughts of the same sort of fate for her own children.

Maybe with the problems of the sugar harvest, she could be gone before Alex returned. Would he come after her? She wasn't afraid of him now—and yet there was a side of him she wasn't quite sure of. Alexandre du Villier kept what was his. At any cost.

She would have to succeed this time, or God alone knew what he might do. A second shudder rumbled through her at the image of Alex's powerful frame towering over her, his hard eyes black with rage. It was almost enough to end her scheming.

Almost—but not quite.

19

~~~·~~~

Working to set events in motion, Nicole sent a note of invitation, and a few days later Michele came to call.

Though Nicki dreaded the favor she must ask, she was excited to see her friend. Seated on the ice-blue brocade sofa in front of a slow-burning fire, they talked and laughed just as they had when they were children. Michele spoke often of Thomas, confiding that he had been calling on her almost every day.

"Alex thinks a great deal of him," Nicki told her.

"Yes, he is a very honorable man. But more than that, he is gentle and kind." She fluttered her cream lace fan, her smooth cheeks turning a faint shade of pink. "I think I am falling in love with him."

"I'm happy for you," Nicki said, though the words brought thoughts of her own unfortunate circumstances.

"He hasn't spoken of marriage, but I think he will soon."

Nicki glanced away. Even though she needed Michele's help dearly, she hadn't been certain she could ask for it. Now, at her friend's talk of marriage, she felt she had no choice.

"Today has been fun," Nicki said, "just like old times."

"*Oui*, it has been."

The last of Nicki's soft smile faded. "In truth, Michele, as much as I've enjoyed our time together, I asked you here for more than conversation."

Michele seemed unsurprised. "I feared it was so."

"I've got to get away, Michele. I can't stay here after Alex is married. Will you help me?"

Michele's slender fingers covered Nicki's hand and gave it a gentle squeeze. "You know I will. What can I do?"

"I need some money. Not too much. Just enough to give me a fresh start someplace else."

"But Alexandre owns your contract. Will he not come after you?"

"Not if I plan well enough. I intend to book passage on a ship headed north. I'll leave in the middle of the night and sail with the tide. If I'm careful and no one sees me, I'm certain it will work."

Michele looked hesitant. "I do not know, Nicki. M'sieur du Villier does not seem a man who gives up easily. He will do his best to bring you back."

"I have to try. Could you be with Thomas if he were married to someone else?"

Michele sucked in a breath. "*Mon Dieu*, no! I love him. I could not share him with another woman."

"Then you know why I must go."

Michele squared her slender shoulders, her pretty green eyes determined. "I will ask Thomas for the money. I am certain he will give it to me."

"But surely Thomas will want to know what it's for?"

"I will tell him it is for my sister. I do not think he

will ask many questions. Thomas is very careful of my feelings." She smiled tenderly at thoughts of the man she loved.

"It's a great deal to ask of you," Nicki said. "Are you sure?"

"Of course I am sure. If Thomas and I marry, his money will be mine, too, so it is the same as borrowing from me. If we do not, then I shall pay him back."

"I will pay him back," Nicki said with quiet determination. "It may take a while, but I will, I promise you."

Michele leaned over and hugged her. "The money will be yours before the end of the week."

Nicki blinked back a well of tears. "Thank you."

From that day forward, Nicki's hours were filled with making the final preparations. Alex sent several messages, explaining how busy he was and asking her to be patient. Though she missed him terribly, thought of him even when she tried not to, and still fought passionate dreams, Nicki thanked God for every moment he stayed away.

As promised, Michele brought the money three days later, and Danielle secured passage for Nicole on a ship bound for Charleston, South Carolina, on the Wednesday morning tide. From there she would take a ship farther north.

Tuesday night, if all went well, she would be free.

On Monday, while Danielle played chess with the Ram, as was their now established routine, Nicki had a visitor.

It might not have happened if she hadn't been standing in the foyer speaking to Frederick when the soft knock came at the door.

Frederick excused himself and pulled it open to reveal a small, dark-silhouetted figure hidden in the folds of her cloak. Trembling on the stone steps out front, the woman fought to keep the breeze from blowing the satin-lined hood from her head.

"I am sorry to bother you," came the woman's heavily accented soft French voice, "but I must speak to Alexandre. Is 'e at 'ome?"

"I'm sorry," Frederick said, "but he's in residence at Belle Chêne."

The woman sagged against the door frame, her composure giving way to sobs. "I am sorry to 'ave bothered you." She turned to leave, but Nicole stepped forward and stopped her with a gentle hand on her arm.

"Come in, Lisette. Alex isn't here, but I am. Please tell me what's wrong."

Lisette raised her tear-stained face and shook her head. "I could not."

"Alex would want me to help you."

"If I 'ad listened to Alexandre, none of this would 'ave 'appened." But she let Nicki lead her inside, each step measured and so stiff that Nicole's uncertainty changed to alarm.

"Are you injured?" she asked with a sideways glance at Ram and Danielle, who had just stepped into the foyer.

Lisette wet her lips, which looked brittle and pale. "I . . . I . . ." Ram caught her up in his powerful arms just as she sagged unconscious to the floor. Her cloak fell away, freeing the mass of glistening black hair that tumbled loose around her shoulders, and exposing a dark purple bruise beside her eye. Effortlessly, Ram carried her upstairs to the guest room.

Danielle turned down the sheets while Nicki removed Lisette's heavy black cloak.

"Gently," Nicki instructed Ram, though she needn't have bothered. "I'll take care of things from here."

As soon as the big Turk had settled his small burden and left the room, Nicki went to work removing Lisette's blue serge dress. She gasped at the angry marks on the woman's smooth, dark skin. There were teethmarks along Lisette's shoulder, angry purple bruises on her ribs, back, hips, and legs.

"Valcour," Nicki whispered. "How could he do such a thing?"

Danielle made the sign of the cross. "Such a wicked, evil man. All the stories about him must be true."

"Yes," Nicki said, the word no more than a breath of air.

"I hate the thought of René working for such a man," Danielle said staunchly. "Once we are married, I will beg *M'sieur le duc* to give him a position at Belle Chêne."

Nicole didn't remind Danielle that *she* might well not have a position, once Alex discovered the part she had played in her mistress's escape.

A movement on the bed caught her eye. Lisette moaned softly, and her wide, dark eyes fluttered open.

"Do you feel like talking?" Nicki asked as Danielle applied a thick gray salve to the wounds on the Frenchwoman's shoulder, then carefully secured a bandage.

Lisette smiled feebly, her long black hair spilling in

soft, dark waves around her face. "You are very kind to 'elp me. I can see why Alexandre loves you."

"He doesn't love me. Alex doesn't believe in love. You of all people should know that."

"Maybe 'e does not know it yet, but love is not something 'e can control."

"No," Nicki softly agreed, "it isn't."

"Even after what 'e has done to me, I still love Valcour."

"But he beat you!"

" 'E did not mean to." Lisette gazed off in the distance. "It started as a game of seduction—Valcour is a man of great passion." She smiled weakly. "When 'e came to me tonight, 'e was angry. Something 'ad 'appened at Feliciana, some problem with the 'arvest. . . . It was nothing unusual, but 'e was upset. We made love fiercely, violently. Still, it was not enough."

Nicki kept silent, urging Lisette to continue by a look that held no rebuke.

" 'Let me show you the pleasure there can be in pain,' 'e said. By then I wanted 'im so badly, I would 'ave agreed to anything." Lisette shuddered with the memory. "Val knew exactly what to do with the leather. Not 'urting me, just teasing, and warming me in a way I 'ad not known."

Nicki drew a strand of thick black hair from Lisette's tear-stained cheek.

"At first it was exciting," she continued. "Val looked fierce, and 'e was wild with desire for me. Then something 'appened. It was as if 'e lost track of time. 'E started 'itting me—'arder and 'arder. I begged 'im to stop, but 'e wouldn't. 'E is so strong. . . ."

Lisette's tears began anew, her soft sobs touching Nicki's heart. "Over and over, 'e called me Feliciana. Called me whore and a dozen other vile names. Then 'e took me. Roughly, cruelly. By the time it was over, Val was crying. Begging me to forgive 'im. 'E is such a tortured man."

"I'm sorry," Nicki said. "For both of you."

Lisette's sobs quieted. Nicki sat beside her, smoothing her wind-tossed hair until she fell into an exhausted sleep, and Nicki was able to get a few hours rest as well.

The following morning, Lisette sought her out in the dining room.

"You're sure you feel well enough to go home?" Nicki asked, sliding back her heavy carved wooden chair and coming to her feet.

"I am fine now, thanks to you."

"I'm glad I could help."

"And I am glad Alexandre was not 'ere," she told Nicki, who looked at her in surprise. " 'E would 'ave gone after Valcour and I do not want that. Alexandre is still a friend, and I love Valcour. I do not want either of them 'urt." She turned dark, pleading eyes on Nicki. "Promise me you will not tell 'im."

"Aren't you afraid Valcour will hurt you again? Surely something should be done."

"Promise me," Lisette pressed.

"All right. I won't tell him."

Lisette smiled. "Thank you again for 'elping me. I 'ope you will find 'appiness. Alexandre deserves it. I 'ave come to believe you do too." With a sweep of her blue serge skirts, she was gone.

Another problem laid on Alex's doorstep. Nicki

prayed this one would not reappear—for Lisette's sake as well as Alexandre's.

In a way she was glad she wouldn't be there to find out.

"So far everything is going smoothly," Danielle told Nicki, who stood in front of the oval mirror in her chamber. It was Tuesday night and all was in readiness.

"Good. I'm just about ready." With her hair pulled back and hidden beneath a wide-brimmed bonnet, and dressed in a simple brown wool dress, Nicki felt sure she could pass through the streets unnoticed.

"You had better keep your head down. If someone should notice your eyes, they will not soon forget you."

Nicki nodded. "Where's Ram?"

"He is setting up the chess board. He says I am a rapid learner. I told him he was being far too modest, that my game was improving because he was such a good teacher."

Nicki grinned. "Use that kind of approach with Alex and maybe you'll be able to appease his temper."

"I shall weep and wail and throw myself at his mercy."

"That should do it."

"Do not worry for me. I will be fine."

Nicki hoped so. "I'm going to miss you."

"I will miss you too." The two women hugged. "Give me at least half an hour," Danielle said. "By then the sleeping potion will have had time to take effect."

They had amended the plan from a blow on Ram's

head to a draft of sleeping potion obtained from
Marie Gabardet, an infamous voodoo queen who
lived in the Quarter. Everyone knew of her special
elixirs—from love potions to curses to death charms.
A simple powder added to Ram's nightly goblet of
wine was no problem at all.

"He is supposed to sleep from sunset to sunset,"
Danielle told her.

Twenty-four hours. She would need every second.
"You'd better get downstairs."

Danielle nodded but made no move to leave. "I
have saved this news till last," she said with a grin.
"René and I have set a date for our wedding. We will
be married in just two months."

Nicki squealed with delight and hugged her.
"That's wonderful, Danielle."

"We talked about it on Sunday." Danielle's day off.
"He says he has missed me every day since I have
been gone."

"I guess it worked out just the way you planned."

"*Oui,*" Danielle said. "Now it is time we finished
what *we* have planned." With a last brief embrace,
Danielle headed downstairs.

Since Frederick's mother had fallen ill just that
morning and he had returned to Belle Chêne, their
plan was progressing even better than they'd hoped.
Now all Nicki had to do was make her way to the
docks and board the ship. Even if her arrival at this
hour seemed odd, it was unlikely the captain would
investigate, and they would be gone by morning.

A little over half an hour later, Nicki headed downstairs. Danielle stood over the Ram who was slumped
on his face in the middle of the chess board, snoring

loudly, the pieces scattered beneath his massive arms.

Wordlessly, they headed toward the rear of the house and Danielle pulled open the door. *"Bonne chance,"* she whispered. Nicole waved and slipped silently away.

Clutching her heavy woolen cloak around her, she glanced up at the cloud-covered sky. Not even a moon lit the way. Tiny drops of rain had begun to fall, and the wind whipped her cloak and sent a chill through her veins.

Across the rear yard of the town house, past a small vegetable garden, she hurried out through the heavy wooden gate. Silently, she crept down the alley toward the street, intent on hailing a hansom cab.

She had only gone a short way before she noticed it —the heavy padding footfalls of a man. Picking up her pace, Nicki hurried along the alley, her dark cloak billowing out behind her. A second set of footsteps, crunching against the earth, joined the first, and Nicki's alarm began to grow. She was running now, racing toward the street. Since it was a little after midnight, the tall gas lamps had been snuffed out, so the darkness didn't lessen.

And neither did the footfalls, which seemed to pound in Nicki's ears.

Who are you? her mind screamed as she raced faster. Surely Alex hadn't hired more men to watch her.

They were almost upon her now. Nicki dodged to the left in an effort to avoid one of them, but her cloak got caught in the brambles of a bush and the other man cut her off.

"Let me go!" she cried, feeling his hard arm

tighten like a band around her waist. She struggled and tried to break free, but his grip only grew tighter. There was no gentleness in his touch, no regret for the pain he inflicted on her ribs and her arms.

These aren't Alex's men! she realized with a flash of certainty and a surge of terror. It was her last coherent thought before the white cotton cloth they held over her nose and mouth sent her spinning into darkness.

Nicki felt something warm on her cheeks and her eyes snapped open. Blinking against the bright yellow sunlight and the pounding in her temples, she followed the brilliant rays to a window covered by a heavy black wrought-iron grille designed in lacy scrolls.

A glance at her surroundings revealed a white-plastered room furnished sparsely with heavy carved wooden pieces in the Spanish mode. A carved wooden chair with a thick leather seat sat in one corner, while a terra-cotta jug filled with dried willow branches rested in another. The bed she lay in was wide, with a square-cut canopy above her head.

Ignoring the dull ache in her temple, Nicki swung her feet to the cold, wide-planked floor, and realized for the first time that she was wearing a white cotton nightshirt instead of the brown wool dress she'd had on the night before. She shuddered to think who had undressed her.

Where in God's name was she? And what did they want with her?

Fighting down the urge to panic, Nicki walked to the window. Through the lacy black scrolls that served to bar her escape, she looked down on a court-

yard walled by a high stucco fence. Red-tile walkways formed paths between the shrubbery, and a
terra-cotta fountain spewed a cool stream of water in
the middle.

The scene looked inviting, in contrast to the memories of her struggle the night before—which had returned with vivid clarity.

Where am I? she wondered again. But no answer
came. Moving around the room, Nicki spotted an
expensively cut, navy-blue day dress with velvet-
trimmed collar and cuffs hanging from a massive antique armoire. One quick look said the dress would fit
her, and Nicki's heartbeat quickened to match the
pounding in her head.

Someone had gone to a great deal of trouble. But
how had they known her plans? Had they been
watching her ever since she arrived at the town
house? Or was this some scheme of Alex's to punish
her for trying to run away?

Finding fresh underthings in a neat little pile beside the gown, Nicki hurriedly dressed and opened
the door, surprised to find it wasn't locked.

The halls were also of heavy white plaster, and decorated in the same Spanish motif.

"The massa awaits you downstairs."

Whirling at the sound of the woman's words, Nicki
found a tall, cocoa-skinned Negro standing in front of
a second bedchamber door.

"Who?" she asked. "Who is waiting for me?"

"Fortier," the woman said flatly, and Nicki's stomach turned to ice.   ·

"Feliciana," she whispered more to herself than
the servant who stood nearby.

Without answering, the tall Negro led her down the

stairs to the receiving salon, her long red African *batakarik* billowing out behind her. The house smelled vaguely of incense. "Wait here."

In minutes that seemed hours, Fortier joined her. He wore tailored black riding breeches and a white linen shirt, clothes not unlike those Alex dressed in when he was working. But where Alex's chest was wide and muscular, Valcour's was lean and hard. High cheekbones rose above the sharp planes of his face. Long brown fingers reached out for her hand, and unconsciously Nicki backed away.

"Come," Valcour said, ignoring her obvious unease, "you must be hungry. I've already eaten, but you should have something."

He spoke as if there was nothing the least unusual in her being there. She was a guest, nothing more.

"Why have you brought me here?"

"I have brought you home."

She almost said Belle Chêne was her home, but caught herself. The beautiful plantation she had come to love would never be her home again. "I belong to M'sieur du Villier—or have you forgotten the price he paid?"

"I have not forgotten. I shall see that his money is returned."

"You don't think he'll object?" she asked, incredulous.

"It really doesn't matter. You should have belonged to me from the start. Alexandre had no business getting involved."

Nicki didn't answer. She wasn't in a position to argue.

Fortier led her into the dining room, where a meal of grillades of beef, grits, and fresh-baked bread had

been set out. Her stomach rumbled at the aroma of
the hot food.

"When you've finished, I'll show you around your
new home." He left her there, but she was sure he
hadn't gone far.

And even if he had, it wouldn't matter. Nicki
glanced toward the tall, hard-muscled Negro who
stood in the doorway. Everywhere she went someone
watched her. Someone Valcour owned. Someone
who feared him enough to do exactly as he commanded.

Nicki's eyes filled with tears. Her ship had sailed,
her clothes and her money were gone, no one knew
where she was, and Valcour Fortier had plans for her
she refused even to imagine. Good Lord, why
couldn't things go her way just once?

Nicki took a long, ragged breath. Straightening her
shoulders, she drew herself up. She wasn't defeated
yet. She wouldn't give up till her last shred of hope
had died. In the meantime, she would do what Fortier told her. What other choice did she have?

Knowing she'd need every bit of her strength, Nicki
ate the meal set in front of her. Valcour returned just
as she finished.

"Shall we go?" It wasn't a question.

Playing the perfect host, Valcour showed her Feliciana. Ten thousand acres—nearly as large as Belle
Chêne. They rode the dirt lanes in a small black phaeton pulled by a glistening black horse, Valcour
charming and handsome in his own hard way, and
obviously proud of his accomplishments. It was difficult to believe he was capable of the cruelty he had
shown Lisette.

"It's taken my family forty years to build Feliciana

into what it is today." Valcour pointed toward the cane fields, which stretched across the horizon. Workers used long billhook machetes to cut wide swaths through the stalks, while others driving two-wheeled carts rolled along behind, loading the cane and hauling it off toward the mill.

"You've obviously worked very hard. Your father would have been proud."

Valcour swung his dark-eyed gaze to her face. "What do you know of my father?"

"Not much. I know he expected a great deal of you. If he were alive, I'm sure he would not have been disappointed."

A flicker of some emotion she couldn't discern lit his eyes and was gone. "He was always disappointed."

After a tour of the mill, which took much of the afternoon, they turned back toward the house. The outside was also Spanish in style, with a red-tile roof two stories above the ground, and balconies that ran the length of the second floor. It was painted a soft shade of yellow.

"I added the wing you're staying in some years ago."

"When you married?" Nicki asked, and Fortier's look turned hard.

"Yes," he said. "You are sleeping in the room I prepared for Feliciana. No one has slept there since she left."

Nicki felt a wave of unease. "Why me?"

"Why not?" he said coldly, putting an end to the conversation.

When they went back inside, Valcour led her to the

room she had occupied upstairs. A little uncertain, Nicki paused outside the door.

"Supper's at seven," Fortier said, ignoring her reluctance. "You'll find proper clothing set out for you." He smiled. Not the pleasant, charming smile she had seen before, but a hard, cold smile that left no doubt about his thoughts. "I suggest you get some rest," he said. "I've an interesting evening planned—one that will require a certain degree of . . . participation."

Nicki's stomach knotted.

"I'll see you at supper." With that he opened the door, held it as she walked into the room, then closed it softly behind her.

Watching the soft yellow lights go on in the window of the main house, René Bouteiller waited until just after dark before making his way toward one of the horses. As head groomsman, it wasn't unusual for him to be riding, but Valcour Fortier was a man of uncanny insight. And René was afraid of him. Just the thought of being caught turned his insides to water.

Still, Danielle's mistress was in danger. There would be no marriage, he was sure, if he stood by and did nothing. Besides, this was all his fault.

Picking a docile bay gelding he hoped would go quietly, René saddled and bridled him, mounted, and headed off toward Belle Chêne. The consequences of his involvement in her abduction would be dire—of that he had no doubt. But he was not an evil man. He would rectify his wrong. Maybe M'sieur du Villier would understand his motives, believe he had really meant no harm.

Unwillingly, René remembered a time when he had seen the big Frenchman angry. A time someone had purposely injured one of his beautiful horses. One blow had sent the man spinning into the dust with a broken jaw—not that he didn't deserve it. René could well imagine what he would do to the man who harmed his mistress.

René shuddered. In that moment he wasn't certain who he feared most—Valcour Fortier or le Duc de Brisonne.

20

"Was the meal to your satisfaction?" Fortier arched a sleek black brow. Nicki sat beside him in the dining room, beneath a heavy wood-and-wrought-iron chandelier. Thick hand-carved beams supported the ceiling above their heads.

"Yes," she answered nervously, "it was lovely."

"Not nearly so lovely as you." His dark eyes moved to the curve of her breast above the low-cut bodice of her gown.

The dress of aqua silk and intricate black Belgian lace fit her perfectly. She had examined it earlier and discovered the hem had been shortened, the bust let out just a little. She was sure the dress had belonged to Feliciana, and her worry increased with the thought.

"Thank you." So far the evening had gone smoothly, Valcour's charm almost making her forget her perilous circumstances. No wonder Lisette had been duped into loving him.

"A gentleman finds it difficult to accept a woman's gratitude for merely speaking the truth," he said.

Nicki glanced away, not wanting to encourage

him. All afternoon, she had searched for some means of escape. But the bedchamber had been secure and a servant always posted in the hallway. She'd tried to get a message to René Bouteiller, Danielle's fiancé, by begging the tall black woman she'd seen that morning to help her. The woman merely turned away.

Even now she could see the servants' guarded expressions, their uneasy stance as they watched Fortier for his slightest instruction. They're all afraid of him, she thought. Well, she was afraid too. Deathly afraid. But this was not the old fear. This man wasn't some haunting memory from her past. He was flesh and blood and she could fight him.

Fortier twirled the heavy sapphire ring he wore on the third finger of his left hand. "Did Alexandre find you virgin?" he asked, as casually as if they discussed the weather.

Nicki's head came up in surprise, followed by embarrassment, and then a surge of anger. "I hardly see where that's any of your concern."

The dark skin over Fortier's cheekbones grew taut. "Answer me," he demanded in a soft, low voice that did nothing to allay her growing fear.

"Yes." *You've got to get out of here!* All evening she'd been looking for an opening, some slight edge that would give her a chance at escape. Each time she'd entertained the thought, Valcour seemed to know. It only appeared to heighten his anticipation.

His smile fell back into place. "We'll take brandy and sherry in my study." With a nod of instruction toward the elderly graying slave who stood beside the dining room door, Valcour shoved back his chair and came to his feet. Rounding the table, he pulled out

Nicki's chair, helped her up, and guided her out of the room.

When he turned toward the staircase, Nicki drew back on the arm that urged her in that direction. "Where are we going?"

"To my study," he repeated, and started walking again.

"But—"

"It's upstairs."

Nicki glanced around. Two black men stood beside the huge front door. Another servant stood just a few feet to her left. There was nowhere to run, no place to go.

"Shall we?" Valcour pressed, his hold tightening on her arm.

Nicki nervously wet her lips.

"They will *assist* you . . ." he pressed, "if that is what you wish."

Squaring her shoulders, Nicki lifted her chin. "I don't need their help—or yours." When she tried to jerk free, Valcour's grip increased until she winced.

"A glass of sherry should help ease your nerves."

Only being some good distance away would ease her nerves, Nicki thought.

At the top of the stairs, Fortier lifted the latch on a heavy wooden door and guided her inside a masculine room that indeed was his study. For a moment she felt relieved. But when he closed the door and slid the bolt, Nicki's heart started thumping against her ribs.

"I believe you will find the balance of the evening . . . amusing," he told her, picking up the stemmed crystal glass of sherry that waited on his desk beside a snifter of brandy. He handed her the glass and Nicki took a nerve-calming sip.

Valcour took a drink of his brandy, smiling at her above the rim of his glass. He set the snifter aside and surprised her by walking to the bookcase on the far wall and reaching between several leather-covered volumes. With the grinding sound of metal against metal, he pulled a lever and the whole wooden case swung wide. A second room, obviously his bedchamber, was revealed behind the wall.

"Feliciana's room adjoins mine on the other side. I liked to be near her, so I had my study built up here. Very convenient, wouldn't you say?"

Heart thundering, Nicki backed against the door, but her eyes were drawn to the room softly lit by the glow of candles. On the far end wall, wearing the same aqua and black lace gown that Nicki had on, a portrait of Feliciana watched them with a soft ruby-lipped smile and gentle, dark-brown eyes.

"Come," Valcour instructed, extending a fine-boned hand. Nicki didn't move. Eyes still fixed on the painting, she vaguely noticed the huge, carved four-poster bed against one wall, the thick Aubusson carpets.

"Come," Valcour repeated, his voice growing impatient and drawing her from her trance.

"No," she whispered.

"Yes," Valcour said coldly, striding toward her. He caught her just as she turned to flee.

Weary from another long day of the sugar harvest, Alex sat before the fire in his study, booted feet propped up on his desk, sipping a snifter of brandy.

Warming the amber liquid in his palms, he stared into the flames, thinking about Nicole.

Mon Dieu, he had missed her. She was all he thought of during the long hours of the day, all he dreamed of at night. Once he had been foolish enough to believe that after she warmed his bed, he would be able to forget her—or at least relegate her to a less important place in his life.

In truth, the opposite had happened—he couldn't get enough of her no matter how he tried.

Alex took a warming sip of his brandy, feeling the fiery liquid burn a path into his stomach. A memory of Nicki smiling with excitement as they rolled through the streets of the *Vieux Carré* rose up before him. She never grew bored with the people and places around her, seeming to find an endless amount of goodness in anyone she met. He loved the sound of her laughter and found himself wishing he could make her laugh more often.

He would, he vowed. He would make her happy, he was certain he could.

The thought of her naked and responsive, her full breasts heaving against his chest, caused a tightening in his loins. He groaned softly. Only once, in front of the fire in his lodge, when she believed he intended marriage, had she come to him willingly—though what he now took from her, he had no doubt she enjoyed.

Still, the gift of her love, freely given, was something he prized above all else. And one day, he vowed, he would win it.

"Excuse me, Master Alex." Mrs. Leandre stood in the doorway, a worried look on her aging face. "René Bouteiller is here to see you."

Alex swung his long, booted legs to the floor. "Bouteiller?" The name conjured a vague note of familiarity.

"Danielle's fiancé. He looks awfully upset."

Alex felt a chord of unease. "Send him in."

Dressed in sweat-stained canvas breeches and a homespun shirt, and clutching his brown floppy-brimmed hat in hand, René Bouteiller stepped into the study.

"I am sorry to bother you, m'sieur. But I have some very bad news." He was a slender man, just a year or two younger than Alex, with coffee-brown hair and hazel eyes that were already lined at the corners. Obviously distraught, René twisted his hat with hands that trembled, and Alex's worry began to build.

"Go on, man, out with it."

René swallowed so hard his Adam's apple bobbed. "It is Mademoiselle St. Claire. Fortier has taken her."

"That's impossible. She's nowhere near here." But even as he denied the words, the slender man's tortured expression said it was the truth.

"He has taken her to Feliciana."

Alex felt a moment of rage so great he could scarcely see through the bright red haze. "Wait here." Striding into the hallway, he headed for the foyer. "Go to the stables," he told his tall black butler. "Tell Patrick to saddle Napoleon. Tell him to hurry." Without waiting for a reply, he turned and stalked back into the study.

"How?" Alex asked, opening his bottom drawer and removing a pistol. "How could he have taken her?"

"I am sorry, m'sieur, but I am to blame." The slender man looked as if he might faint. "I beg you to forgive me."

"Get on with it," Alex commanded in a tone that did little to hide his ire.

"M'sieur Fortier has been paying me for bits of news about Belle Chêne. Things I might hear from Danielle. I did not see the harm. I planned to use the extra money for Danielle's wedding gift. I never dreamed it would come to this."

"So you've been spying on me."

René dropped to his knees in front of the place where Alex stood. "I beg of you, m'sieur—"

"Tell me the rest," Alex said coldly.

"Mademoiselle St. Claire was planning to . . . she had made arrangements for a ship to take her to Charleston and then farther north. I mentioned this to Fortier. His men must have been waiting for her. I didn't know what he planned; I didn't know she was even there until I saw her in his carriage this afternoon."

Alex fixed his hard, dark gaze on the slender young man, who paled even further. "I'll deal with you when I get back." Grabbing his jacket, Alex moved to the door. "I warn you, do not think of running. If you're not here when I return, I'll find you, and the consequences will be far worse than they are now."

With that he strode down the wide marble hallway, jerked open the heavy front door, and headed off toward the stables.

"You're a dead man, Fortier," he swore beneath his breath. But all he could see was Nicole—running away again, trying so desperately to leave him that she had fallen into the deadly embrace of another vicious master.

"Finish your sherry," Fortier warned, forcing the glass Nicki held against her trembling bottom lip. "You need to relax."

Seated beside him in front of the slow-burning fire in the chamber where he had dragged her, Nicki looked at him beseechingly. "Why? Why are you doing this?"

Above the hearth, Feliciana looked down from her portrait reproachfully, her dark eyes watching them in the eerie, flickering firelight. Nicki forced her mind away from the ominous warning she felt every time she glanced up.

Fortier, too, studied the portrait, but did not answer.

"Women find you attractive," Nicki went on. "Lisette is in love with you. What do you want with me?"

Valcour set his brandy aside. "She told you that? That she was in love with me?"

"Yes." Nicki didn't mention the beating he had given the poor girl, though it took all her will not to.

"Lisette is a fool. How could a woman love a man who has treated her as I have?"

"Love is never easy to understand."

Fortier scoffed aloud. "Feliciana is the only woman I will ever love."

Though he spoke with conviction, Nicki sensed an underlying doubt. Maybe Lisette meant more to him than he believed. "You didn't answer my question. What do you want with me?"

One corner of his hard mouth curved in what might have passed for a smile. "You are his—Alexandre's—just as Lisette once was. But you he values even more." He ran a lean brown finger along her cheek, and Nicki shivered. "For that reason alone I shall have you this night."

"Lisette wanted you. I do not."

Valcour merely shrugged his shoulders.

"Does hurting Alex mean so much to you?"

He laughed, a harsh sound that sent a second shiver down her spine. "We have always been rivals, Alex and I. . . . Did he tell you Feliciana was in love with him?"

Nicki's head came up. "No."

"Well, it's true. That was before she met me, of course."

"Of course," she agreed with a hint of sarcasm Valcour didn't seem to notice. "So you're doing all this because of Alex."

A flicker of some dark emotion passed over his face. "Yes."

"But that isn't the only reason," Nicki pressed.

Arching a sleek black brow, he smiled. "Perhaps I look to you for salvation—maybe my very last chance." His expression less guarded, he stared up at the painting. His eyes grew distant as his mind drifted off in the past. "She tortures me still," he said softly, "the same as the night I found her with the peddler—naked and curled in his arms."

A tendril of ice moved over Nicki's heart.

"She was lying there weeping, looking at me with her soft brown eyes and begging me, over and over, not to hurt him. I had always wanted to please her, always done anything she asked. . . . That night I did the same, and the cowardly dog slipped away and never looked back."

"But I thought nothing happened. Surely there would have been gossip among the servants."

Valcour closed his eyes against a wave of remembered pain. "Those few slaves who knew the truth have long since been sold."

"What did you do to her?" Nicki fought an image of Lisette's battered face and bruised body.

"I wanted to forgive her. I tried to. . . . That next night, I went to her. Even then I desired her as I had no other woman. At first she pretended passion, but I wasn't fooled. It was the peddler she wanted, the peddler she desired above the master of Terre Sauvage."

"Dear God."

"I don't remember hitting her, only her begging me to stop. But I remember taking her—never have I known such triumph, such ecstasy." His fingers tightened on the stem of the glass. "At the very moment I lost her forever—I glimpsed both heaven and hell."

Valcour turned to face her, the tears that shimmered in his hard black eyes matched those in Nicki's own.

"I'm sorry," she said, "so sorry." He had loved her so much he had destroyed her. Now he was destroying himself.

Nicki watched his face in the eerie glow of the lamp. As quickly as the emotion had come, it was gone, replaced by a look so cold he seemed a different man. "We've talked enough." Setting his brandy aside, he drew her to her feet.

"Please let me go," she said softly. "You don't really want to hurt me."

"No. I hope this time things will be different."

"And if they aren't?"

"That, my dear, is exactly what I mean to find out."
Whatever regret she had glimpsed in him was gone.
There would be no reprieve.

With a quick flick of her wrist, Nicki tossed the last
of her sherry into his face and bolted for the door.
Cursing, Fortier stumbled after her. Nicki's trembling fingers worked the lock, slid the bolt back, then
his arm closed around her, dragging her back inside.

"I shall have you, little flower," he said against her
ear as he carried her scratching and clawing back
into his chamber. In seconds he had her pinned
against him, her wrists bound in front of her, then
her hands secured above her head, tied firmly to the
bedpost. She stood beside the massive bed, fighting to
hold back tears.

"Why?" she repeated. "At least tell me why."

Fortier grabbed the front of her aqua silk gown and
the thin chemise that was all she wore beneath. With
a vicious twist, he ripped them away. "Because
you're nothing like her. Because you are fair and she
was dark, because your hair is fiery and hers was the
color of midnight. Because even wearing her gown
you are not her."

He laced his hands through her shiny copper hair
and painfully jerked her head back. "Tonight I mean
to cleanse myself of these hellish demons that tor-
ment me—once and for all!"

With that he kissed her, his cruel mouth punishing,
bruising her tender lips until she tasted her own
blood. As his tongue thrust savagely between her
teeth, one hand slid inside her bodice, his long brown
fingers clutching the soft flesh of her breast until she
cried out in pain.

Trembling all over, Nicki fought to break free, but

his hard body pinned her against the bedpost. "You do this," she warned, "and I swear to you, I'll kill you."

Valcour laughed. "You may try, little flower. In fact, I shall be disappointed in you if you do not. But in the end, I will break you—or you will set me free."

He pulled open her bodice, affording himself a better view of her breasts, white and smooth in the firelight. "I promise you, I will go slowly. Give you all the time you need. Tonight you will learn the pleasure there can be in pain."

"Dear God." Nicki felt the bile rise up in her throat. Twisting toward him, she jerked her knee up hard, catching him unaware, and eliciting a yelp of pain. Considering the frothy barrier of her petticoats, the blow did far more damage than she had expected.

As he doubled over and fought for breath, Nicki struggled with her bonds, trying in vain to loosen them.

"Bitch!" he accused, regaining his strength, his black eyes glittering with rage. "You're nothing like she was. You're a thief, the scum of the earth. Not fit to wear her clothes. Not fit to walk in Feliciana's footsteps!"

"That's where you are wrong, Fortier," came a menacing, deep voice from the doorway. "She's a lady. My lady. And you have made the fatal mistake of trying to do her harm."

Stifling the cry in her throat, Nicki blinked at a haze of tears. Alex stood in the doorway, his tall muscular frame silhouetted in the lamplight, his broad shoulders nearly filling the entrance. He had come for her! Again he was there when she needed him. How had he known?

Fortier backed off. "Always you interfere, du Villier. Always you win. Not this time." Moving toward the carved walnut nightstand beside the bed, Valcour slid open the top drawer. The flash of silver in the firelight betrayed the gleaming blade he clutched in his hand as he whirled in Alex's direction. "Before this night is through, you will watch me take her—again and again—and be powerless to stop me."

"Be careful, Alex!" Nicki called to him, but Alex ignored her. His concentration centered on the man he intended to destroy.

Pulling his pistol from the waistband of his breeches, Alex tossed it onto the bed. "I ought to shoot you, Fortier, but that would be too easy."

While Valcour circled him warily, brandishing the knife, Alex removed his jacket and wrapped it around his forearm. "I'm going to break you," Alex said with soft menace. "This is the last woman who will suffer your cruelty."

Fortier slashed with his knife, missing Alex's chest by only the breadth of the blade. Though Alex stood several inches taller and was far more solidly built, Valcour was lean and hard. His knife more than evened the odds.

"Come and get me," the Spaniard taunted. "I want this done so I can take my pleasure with your woman."

Alex fought down the rage Fortier worked to build. Anger meant loss of control, something Alex could ill afford. Nor could he chance a look at Nicki. From the moment he'd seen Fortier's eyes on her breasts, her soft pink lips bruised and tender from the cruelty of his mouth, Alex knew he would kill the man this night.

Fortier slashed and Alex dodged away. Again they circled, Alex keeping his coat-wrapped arm in front of him, waiting for the opening that would leave Fortier at his mercy. Then Valcour feigned left but lunged right, and the blade struck home, slicing through the layers of cloth as if they were barely there, sinking into Alex's flesh until it struck bone.

Nicki cried out at the sight of his blood on the blade, and Fortier glanced in her direction. Diving forward, Alex grabbed Fortier's knife-hand and squeezed the man's wrist until the blade dropped to the floor with a clatter. Alex's fist connected with Valcour's jaw, sending him crashing against a chair and onto the floor. Head lowered, Fortier gained his feet and charged, driving both men to the ground. Fortier struck a blow to Alex's cheek, his heavy gold ring drawing blood. Alex punched him hard in the nose, sending a spray of red across his clean white shirt.

Back and forth they battled, Fortier holding his own though Alex rained blow after murderous blow to his body. Blood drenched Alex's shirt from the wound in his arm, but still he would not stop. Fortier hit him hard in the jaw; Alex drove a fist into the Spaniard's stomach, then threw a steel-hard clout to his chin. Another heavy blow sent Fortier sliding unconscious to the wood plank floor. Bending over, Alex grabbed the front of his shirt, lifted him up and punched him again and again.

"Alex!" Nicki shrieked, "You're going to kill him!"

Alex ignored her, his fist falling with a dull thud that forced a groan from Fortier's bloody lips.

"Stop it, Alex," Nicki pleaded. "You aren't like he is. Please don't do this." For the first time that night,

Nicki's tears fell unchecked. "Please, Alex, please don't kill him."

At last her words and the sound of her soft pleas began to reach him. Releasing his hold on Fortier's shirt, Alex moved unsteadily across the room, picked up Valcour's knife, and cut Nicki's bonds. The minute her arms were free, she threw them around his neck, clutching him, sobbing against his chest.

Alex closed his eyes and gripped her tighter, burying his face in the silky copper hair that swirled around her shoulders. So close she had come to being hurt or maybe even killed. A hard lump swelled in his throat, and he blinked against the moisture in his eyes.

"It's all right, *ma petite*," he said, his voice husky, "we're going home." But she wouldn't let him go. Just clung to him as if she couldn't bear to leave him.

Alex stiffened. It was a lie and he knew it. Leaving him was exactly what Nicki wanted. She had tried to tell him, tried to make him understand and yet he had refused to listen. Instead, he'd convinced himself that she needed him, that keeping her with him was only for the best, that with him she would be safe.

He had even believed he could make her happy.

Alex scoffed at his foolishness. He should have kept his emotions in check as he always had. Should have found the kind of woman who was impressed with his title and his lands. The kind who would fall at his feet at the mere thought of warming his bed.

A woman who could satisfy his passions without ever touching his heart.

Alex cursed himself for a fool. The last thing he wanted was a woman who didn't want him. Nicki wanted only to be rid of him—and from this moment forward she would be.

He pulled away from her, and Nicki saw the blood that drenched his shirt.

"Your arm!" she cried, cradling it against her to examine it more closely. "We need something to bind it with."

"Tear a strip from the sheet," Alex instructed. Nicki did as he asked, then wrapped the white cloth around his arm and tied the ends securely.

Holding the front of the aqua silk gown together as best she could, Nicki leaned against Alex, who leaned against her for support. Together, bruised and battered, they made their way toward the door.

Valcour's voice, coming from behind them, stopped them cold. "Just remember, du Villier, the girl is Belle Chêne property. You fail—she comes to me!" Alex turned to find Fortier, breathing hard and bleeding, leaning against the wall.

"Alex?" Ignoring a tendril of fear, Nicki glanced up at him. His jaw was clamped, his body tensed again, ready to return and finish what they had started.

"No!" Nicki pleaded. "Please, Alex, please take me home." Where exactly home was, or just exactly what Fortier had meant by his ominous words, she didn't know. But all of that could wait.

At the bottom of the staircase, the tall Negro woman with the cocoa-colored skin silently draped a shawl around Nicki's shoulders. The other servants were nowhere to be seen.

"Thank you," Nicki said softly. She glanced back up the stairs. "Will you care for him?"

"I will heal his wounds, but I cannot heal his soul."

Nicki touched the woman's arm, then let Alex lead

her out the door. Napoleon nickered and blew at their approach. Alex helped her up, then swung himself up behind her. Leaning against him, she was surprised to discover the tension that remained in the bands of muscle across his chest. Though his hard arms surrounded her, he was careful not to touch her, and even the muscles in his thighs felt taut.

"Are you all right?" she asked.

"I'm fine."

She didn't miss the anger seething just beneath the surface. She had seen him enraged a dozen times, had expected no less if she failed when she had set her plan in motion. But this time he seemed different, guarded, as if the fury he still carried was directed more at himself than at her—or was there to protect him.

But from what?

"The bleeding seems to have slowed," she said with a worried look at his arm. "Are you sure you'll be all right till we get back?"

"I told you before, I'm fine." He threw her a glance so cold, she shivered. "And you, Nicki? Are you fine, as well? Are you going to tell me you didn't need my help? That you could have managed without me?"

"No, of course not. God only knows what would have happened to me if you hadn't come."

Alex did not reply.

They rode in silence, covering the distance to Belle Chêne at an easy gallop.

"How did you know where I was?" she finally asked.

"René Bouteiller has been spying on you. He told Fortier about your . . . voyage . . . to the north. Apparently his conscience got the best of him. He didn't want to see you get hurt." He waited for her reply, but she said nothing. "What did you do to Ram?"

"I—I didn't hurt him. I just put a sleeping potion into his wine."

Alex cursed roundly. "And of course you accomplished all this with no assistance from my loyal staff."

"I forced Danielle to help me."

Alex scoffed. "She helped you, all right. She dished you up to Fortier like a prime fillet."

"You mustn't blame her, Alex. She trusted René. She's in love with him."

"So at last you can see there is no such thing as love." Words he had spoken to her that day in the dining room so many months ago.

Nicole fell silent once more, her heart aching unbearably. If Alex had ever been close to loving her, he certainly wasn't now.

When they reached Belle Chêne, Alex helped her down and handed the reins to a waiting groom.

"Maybe we should ride on into La Ronde," she suggested, thinking of the gossip her arrival was sure to bring. Alex ignored her, guiding her firmly up the front steps and into the foyer. "What about the servants?" Nicki whispered. "What about Clarissa?"

"Mrs. Leander!" Alex called out, and the graying woman appeared in a heartbeat. She flashed an uncertain smile at Nicole, then her face went pale at the sight of Alex's blood.

"Take Mademoiselle St. Claire up to the guest room. Have a bath sent up and something for her to eat."

"I'm not hungry," Nicki said softly.

"And a goblet of wine," he added, as if she hadn't spoken. "Send one of the servants to fetch Mrs. James. Tell her my arm needs stitching." The overseer's wife did most of the doctoring on Belle Chêne —which was a full-time job in itself. "And tell Bouteiller he can spend the night in the stables. I'll speak to him in the morning."

The housekeeper nodded and left to do as he asked.

"Please, Alex," Nicki said to him once she was out of sight. "Can't we talk about this?"

Alex pinned her with a hard, dark glance. "What is there to say? I was a fool for believing I could make you care enough to stay. A fool to believe I could make you happy. It was a mistake I shall not make again. Good night."

With that he headed up the stairs, leaving Nicole and Mrs. Leander, who had just returned to the foyer, to trail along behind.

Nicki felt sick inside. Alex was angry, all right. Furious, in fact. She had seen him enraged a dozen times, but she had never seen him so cold and remote —and so far from her that she feared she would never reach him again.

21

〰️🙰🙰〰️

Nicki finished her bath and toweled her hair dry in front of the fire. In the corner, the empty bed beckoned, offering the sleep she so desperately needed.

She should be grateful for Alex's consideration. He was letting her sleep in the guest room, leaving her alone, insuring there would be no gossip among the servants that might reach Clarissa. Some might say he was only protecting his own reputation, but Nicki knew better.

Alex wouldn't give a damn what his future wife thought—or anybody else!

Pulling on a soft white cotton nightgown that Mrs. Leander had brought her, Nicki climbed up in bed, settled herself between the cool clean sheets, drew the blankets beneath her chin, and closed her eyes.

She had tried to get Alex to let her help him with his arm, but he had refused. Only Mrs. Leander's heavy footfalls on the staircase, alongside the lighter steps of Nora James, insured that they had finished their grisly task. Stoic as always, Alex made no sound at the painful stitches that pierced his flesh.

Nicki rolled to her side and fluffed the deep feather

pillow. Exhausted as she was, sleep seemed nowhere near. Instead, her mind replayed Alex's dark expression as he'd stood in Fortier's entry, calling himself a fool.

A hard lump swelled in Nicki's throat. She hadn't meant to hurt him, never dreamed he would believe she had left him because she didn't care enough to stay. But they never spoke their feelings. Alex seemed unable to tell her how he felt, and she would only make matters worse if he knew how much she cared.

Tears welled, and she tried in vain to blink them away. She thought of the way he had held her at Fortier's, so close she could hear his heartbeat as he whispered soothing French words. He was always there for her, always protective. Tonight he had risked his life for her.

She thought of his big hard body sprawled in restless slumber on the wide four-poster bed.

She should be grateful for Alex's consideration. Grateful he hadn't demanded she join him. Instead she imagined him making love to her, kissing her and caressing her and soothing away her fears.

She wanted Alexandre. Wanted him as she always did. Even more so this night, when she had come so close to a violation of her body far different from the loving they had shared.

She wanted Alex as always, desired him with a desperation that bordered on madness. And so she dared not go to him. Dared not tell him the truth that welled in her heart.

I love you. So much, I die a little each time you touch me and then have to leave. Each time your hands work their magic, and I know those same hands will soon caress Clarissa. So much, I would give the sun and the moon to bear your children, to be near you each day of our lives.

But not so much that I can give up my honor. Not so much I will disgrace my family name.

Nicki rolled onto her stomach and cried into the pillow. How could she tell him she loved him, when knowing the truth would insure his hold on her forever?

Then again, how could she remain silent, allow him to believe she had merely responded to him in passion? To be convinced through the years there was no such thing as love.

Nicki's body shook with her sobs, and the pillow grew wet with her tears. It was all she could do not to go to him, to seek his comfort and give him hers in return.

But she did not go. Instead she whispered his name into the darkness and clutched the pillow instead of his powerful chest. Once in the night, she got as far as the heavy wooden door and even lifted the latch. Then her thoughts turned to Clarissa and the bastard children Alex's marriage would force Nicole to bear.

I love you, she said again, and wished she had admitted the truth to Alex before it was too late.

A pounding at the door in the middle of the night awoke him. Alex slipped from the bed, pulled on his burgundy velvet robe, and opened the door to find Ram standing in the hallway, his eyes red-rimmed with worry, his mouth grim and lined by fatigue.

"It's all right, Ram. Nicki's here and she's unharmed."

"May Allah be praised," the big Turk said, though

he was not of that faith. He slumped against the door in relief.

"I sent word. You were probably already gone."

"Whatever those women gave me took hours to wear off. When I finally woke up, I looked everywhere. I threatened to slit Danielle's throat, but still she would tell me nothing." He smiled at that. "Nicole is lucky to have such a friend."

"If Danielle had been as closemouthed with her fiancé, Fortier wouldn't have taken Nicki in the first place."

"Fortier?"

Alex nodded and motioned him inside. "How about a brandy?"

"Yes, thank you. I could use it." The men moved into the bedchamber, and Ram sank down heavily in one of the tapestry chairs in front of a fire that had burned to coals. Alex handed him a glass of brandy, poured one for himself from the crystal decanter on the marble-topped dresser, and took the opposite chair.

Ram tossed a log into the fire and stoked the coals into flames. "I feel as if I've failed you."

Alex waved away his words. "Nonsense. If anyone's to blame, it's me. I should have told her the truth about Fortier. I should have told her she would have to stay with me until after the marriage—and I should have stayed out of her bed."

The big Turk grunted. "You know what they say about hindsight. . . ."

Alex nodded wearily.

"What will you do about Bouteiller?" Ram asked.

"You know him?"

"He came several times to visit Danielle."

Alex shook his head. "I don't think he meant any harm. Besides, if he hadn't come to Belle Chêne, I wouldn't have known Valcour had taken Nicole. René risked a great deal, and I sure as hell can't send him back—God knows what Fortier would do to him."

"Sometimes those who are shown forgiveness become one's most loyal subjects."

Alex agreed. "Nicki believes everyone deserves a second chance. Tomorrow I'll give René his."

"And Danielle?"

"If she's as loyal to Nicole as you say, there is no one I would rather have near her." For the first time that night, Alex smiled. "I should like to be a fly on the wall when Danielle discovers her fiancé has been carrying tales to Fortier."

The big Turk laughed aloud. "Yes. I believe it is only fair his punishment be left to her."

After finishing their brandies, Ram headed for a room down the hall and Alex returned to his bed. His loss of blood had helped him sleep earlier; now it wouldn't be so easy.

He was too close to Nicole, too near the door that led to her chamber, to the bed where she lay sleeping. He loved to watch her, had done so often, though she never knew. She looked so sweet and innocent without her defenses. What would it have been like to have taken her to wife? To have her beside him, working to build a future together? With her desire to help others and love of Belle Chêne, how much might they have accomplished?

Alex clenched his fist, his chest suddenly taut. It did no good to ponder such things. The path ahead had been laid out—and it did not include Nicole.

He thought of her in her room down the hall. Just the memory of her soft, sweet body molded against him sent a rush of blood to his loins.

Alex stared up at the canopy above his head. As much as he wanted her, he wouldn't take her. It was a vow he had made before he ever reached Feliciana. If God would protect her until he could get there, he would leave her be.

Besides, by running away from him again, she had made her feelings clear in a way her words could not. What she felt for him was little more than passion. Not enough to bind her to him. Not enough to keep her by his side.

Alex closed his eyes and tried to conjure sleep. He needed his rest, needed all the strength he could garner to return Nicki to his town house and leave her without so much as a farewell kiss.

He could do it—of that Alexandre had no doubt. He was a man who did what he set out to do. Still, saying good-bye to Nicole St. Claire would be the hardest thing he had ever done.

Alex leaned against the rail of the *Memphis Lady*, watching the passing shoreline. Beside him, Nicole clutched the folds of her borrowed cloak over one of the servants' dark wool dresses. Her face looked pale and there were smudges beneath her eyes. The wind whipped strands of her shiny copper hair.

"Alex?" At the sound of her voice, soft and a little uncertain, Alex turned to face her. "I know how angry you are."

"Why should I be angry?" Try as he might, he couldn't keep the sarcasm from his voice. He had played the fool for her too long—he would not do it again. "You are a woman alone, being forced to stay with a man you obviously care little about. Were I in your position, I would do exactly as you have. I would do everything in my power to leave."

She reached toward him, but he moved away. He didn't want her nearness, didn't want the temptation her gentle touch would bring.

The distant shoreline passed by, tiny wooden shanties lining the bank where Negro children played beside their mothers. Dark-skinned men swung cane knives into towering, dark-green thickets as the sugar harvest progressed.

"Fortier said Feliciana was in love with you," Nicki said softly. "Is that true?"

Alex swung his glance in her direction. "No. We rarely saw each other before she and Valcour were married." Recalling Valcour's state of mind, he shook his head. "Our so-called love affair grew from his jealous fantasies."

Nicki didn't seem surprised. "What did he mean about my coming to him if you fail?"

It was the question Alex had been dreading. "I had hoped you wouldn't find out. I didn't want you to worry." Her eyes searched his face, bright aqua pools that made him want to hold her and soothe away her fears.

"Please tell me."

Alex released a weary breath and raked a hand through his wavy, dark-brown hair. "When I bought your contract, you became a part of Belle Chêne. Fortier holds a note against the land and all of the personal property."

"Chattel," she whispered, and Alex's heart lurched against his chest.

"Yes."

"And that includes me."

"Yes."

"If you don't marry Clarissa, you can't pay the mortgage, and Fortier gets Belle Chêne along with its chattel—including me."

Alex nodded. "It isn't going to happen, so you've no need to worry. As far as what's occurred between us, at least now you understand that I couldn't have let you go even if I'd wanted to. If you leave before the note is paid in full, Fortier has every right to go after you himself. Which, as you've so clearly proven, he would most surely do."

"You should have told me."

"I didn't believe it would keep you from leaving. And as I said before, I was fool enough to believe I could make you care enough to stay. I wanted you with me because you wanted to be, not because you were afraid of Fortier."

"Alex—"

"From now on, the town house will be yours. I'll stop by on occasion to be certain you're all right, but I will not expect you to . . . entertain me . . . in anything other than polite conversation."

"Alex, please—"

"Since we've still got quite some distance to go, if you'll excuse me, I believe I'll go inside and join Ram in a game of chance." With that he strode away from her, his long legs carrying him away.

Watching his tall, retreating figure, Nicki's heart beat painfully against her chest. He was such a proud man, so strong and caring. Yet deep inside he was lonely. He had needed her far more than she'd guessed—and she had hurt him deeply.

Nicki's fingers trembled, and she tightened her hold on the rail. At least now she would be free. Once the note was paid, Alex would let her go. Since he believed she didn't want him, he had no reason to keep her.

It's what you've wanted from the start, she told herself firmly. *You'll be your own person again. Free to live whatever life you choose.*

Why did it suddenly seem so unimportant?

Nicki fought the ache that closed her throat and the lie she tried to hold on to. How could she have let this happen? How could she have come to care for him so deeply that her own happiness seemed unimportant? That even the pain their bastard children would suffer seemed to pale beside her need to give him the comfort and shelter he needed?

Please, Papa. Tell me what I'm doing is right. Tell me once more that honor and righteousness are worth this terrible price. But her father's comforting words would not come. No image of his gentle face looked down on her. No warm memory blossomed to guide her way.

She glanced down at the frothy black water that rushed beneath them. "Protect him, dear Lord," she whispered. "Make him happy—and one day let him understand."

They reached the town house and a worried Danielle saw Nicki and burst into tears.

"*Mon Dieu,* what has happened? You should be gone from here. How did he find you—I swear I did not tell." She glanced fearfully at Alex, who scowled back at her.

"I appreciate your loyalty to your mistress," he

said, surprising her. "But I believe she may have some disconcerting news about your fiancé. You may discuss it with her in my absence."

"René has not been injured?"

"No, Danielle," Nicki said, "René is fine."

At the sweep of Alex's hand, the servants filed quietly away, and Alex turned to Nicki. "I trust you will take care of yourself these next few weeks. Once the note has been paid, I'll see you're made comfortable anywhere you choose." His hard look softened, his dark eyes almost a caress.

"Until, then, *ma chère*, know that I shall miss you as I never have another."

Nicki's throat constricted. "Have no doubt that I shall miss you as well," she whispered.

Alex nodded solemnly and turned to leave.

"Alex?"

His hand froze on the knob, but he didn't look back. Instead, he pulled open the door and stepped out into the courtyard. With measured care, he closed the door behind him.

Three weeks passed, with no sign of Alex. Danielle had railed at René until he had begged her forgiveness, promising her his undying love if she would still have him. He sang Alex's praise until Nicki had to leave the room, her eyes glistening with tears.

François came to call, looking nearly as despondent as Nicki. "Alexandre is in misery. I have never seen him like this. He's working eighteen hours a day, trying to bury himself in his duties. Clarissa is furious. She thinks he's ignoring her—which he is." François shook his head. "For a while he seemed so happy. I just don't understand it." He looked imploringly at Nicki. "I know how much he cares for you, surely you can speak to him, find out what is wrong."

"Alex doesn't come here anymore."

"What? But why not? I thought—"

"As soon as Alex and Clarissa are married, he's giving me back my contract. I'll be leaving. Going to Savannah, I think, or maybe Charleston."

"But I thought you loved him. You didn't say so, but I thought for certain—"

"I can't be his wife, François, and I won't be his mistress. Even if my beliefs weren't involved, I couldn't share him. Surely you of all people can understand."

François sank down on the sofa. "Yes," he said, "I believe I do."

They didn't speak of Alex again.

November passed with little fanfare, but the hustle in the city increased, a reminder that the Christmas holidays were fast approaching.

Twice she met Michele for luncheon. Though Nicki found it hard to concentrate, and the gaiety of the patrons seemed somehow out of place, she was glad, as always, to see her friend.

"Tell me about Thomas," Nicki prodded, wanting to hear happy news for a change.

"He has asked me to marry him and I have said yes."

"Oh, Michele, that's wonderful!" Reaching across the table, Nicki squeezed her friend's hand. "Have you set a date?"

"Four months from this Saturday. It seems like forever, but Thomas will return with me to Baton Rouge to ask my father's permission." She smiled. "I am not worried. Papa will love him."

"I'm sure he will, and your mother too."

"Even my aunt sings his praises."

"Thomas could charm a beggar out of his shoes."
Michele laughed at that. "And what about you,"
she asked, her green eyes searching. "Alexandre has
not returned?"

"No." Nicki glanced away. "I've missed him more
than I ever would have guessed."

"Oh, Nicki. I am so sorry."

"I've been working on his ledgers. I wanted to do
something for him before I left. Besides, it helps pass
the time. . . . I've gone back through the last ten
years, but unfortunately, I need Louis Mouton's set of
books so I can compare the two."

"Why don't you send a note to Alexandre? Maybe
he would bring them himself."

"I've thought of it. But if I see him again, it'll only
make things harder."

"Yes, I suppose so. Still, if it were Thomas, I would
want to share what time we had left."

All afternoon, Michele's words echoed in her ears.
So little time was left to them. And yet she dared not
seek him out. She wasn't sure she would ever have
the strength to leave him again.

"Alex, it's good to see you." Thomas extended a
hand. "You remember Michele?"

"Mademoiselle Christophe." Alex raised her gloved
hand to his lips. "It's nice to see you again."

"You're getting thin, Alexandre," Thomas chided.
"You must be working too hard."

"We're a little behind with the harvest, but I think
we'll be back on schedule soon. The new equipment's
doing an even better job than we had hoped. Which is

one of the reasons I came by. I thought we should go over those new shipping contracts Mouton sent over."

"Speaking of M'sieur Mouton," Michele put in, surprising them. "I luncheoned with Nicole yesterday. She's been working on your sugar ledgers. She says she's almost done, but she needs your factor's set so she can compare the two."

Alex worked to keep his expression carefully blank. "I'll see that she gets them. Thank you for telling me." He forced a smile that felt a little stiff. "I hear congratulations will soon be in order for the two of you."

"That's right, my friend," Thomas said. "And I owe it all to you. If it hadn't been for you and Nicole, Michele and I would never have met."

"Yes. . . . It seems there are many things for which Nicole is responsible."

After finishing his business with Thomas, Alex headed straight for Louis Mouton's office. He tried to deny the voice that told him the ledgers were just an excuse to see Nicki again, but in truth he didn't care. He just felt grateful for the chance.

When he reached Mouton's office, Louis wasn't in, but at Alex's unbending insistence, the young man who worked for him finally turned over the ledgers. Before he could take them to Nicki, Alex had two more business appointments, which seemed unending, and an early supper engagement with a friend, who remarked on his preoccupation and half-hearted attempts at conversation.

"You're working too hard, Alexandre," Jonathan Whitmore said. "This isn't urgent. Why don't we discuss it when you've got a little more time."

"Maybe you're right," Alex agreed with a sigh of relief. "There are a few things on my mind this evening." *Like my meeting with Nicole St. Claire.* Of course, he wouldn't be able to make love to her. Wouldn't even be able to touch her. Just seeing her again would have to be enough.

By eight o'clock he was headed down Toulouse Street toward his town house. Through the garden, he noticed only a few lamps lit the windows, one in the study where Ram would most likely be, and one in Nicki's upstairs bedchamber. His heartbeat quickened just to think of her.

Carrying an armload of heavy leather-bound volumes, Alex knocked on the carved cypress door. Frederick opened it, his smile warm with welcome.

"Good evening, sir."

"Good evening, Frederick." His eyes strayed toward the staircase leading up to the bedchamber he had once shared with Nicole.

"She took supper upstairs," Frederick explained. "She's been doing that quite often lately."

Alex frowned. "She isn't sick, is she?"

"No. It's nothing like that." Frederick seemed about to say more, but didn't.

Alex didn't press him.

"Shall I tell her you're here," Frederick asked, "or would you prefer to do it yourself?"

He knew he should stay downstairs, keep things less personal, himself less vulnerable. "I'll let her know," he said instead. Still carrying the ledgers, his hands growing damp on the dusty leather, he climbed the staircase and knocked on her door.

22

A moment passed and then another. Alex's grip tightened on the ledgers. Then Nicki pulled open the door and the breath he'd been holding rushed from his lungs.

Standing in the lamplight in her simple cotton nightshirt, her copper hair brushed out and hanging to her waist, Nicki looked more beautiful than he had remembered.

"I was at Thomas's this morning," he told her, his voice a little husky. "Michele was there, and she told me you'd been working on the ledgers, that you needed Mouton's set in order to finish."

"Yes," she said, the word just a whisper.

"Louis wasn't there, but his assistant rummaged around until he found them." Careful to avoid her, Alex walked past her into the room and set the books on a desk Nicki had installed in one corner. His hand shook as he slid them away from the edge and turned to face her.

"You're going to bed awfully early, aren't you?" Just saying the word caused a tightening in his loins.

He wanted to go to her, sweep her into his arms,

carry her over to the deep feather mattress and strip away her clothes. He wanted to kiss her until she could barely breathe, wanted to feel her breasts in his hands. He wanted to sink into her, make her respond to him, make her feel what he felt for her.

"I've been working up here in the evenings," she said, her hand toying self-consciously with the pink satin bow that closed the front of her nightgown. Her hands looked delicate in the pale-yellow lamplight. Alex remembered the way they felt against his skin. When she ran her tongue nervously across her lush bottom lip, it was all he could do not to stride across the floor and haul her into his arms. She would be his again, at least for a while.

"I hope everything's working out for you," he said. "I mean, I hope you're happy."

I haven't been happy a single moment since the day you left. "I'm doing fine, thank you. And you? The harvest is progressing smoothly?"

"Yes. With Rillieux's steam vacuum system, the quality and quantity are even better than we expected."

"And everyone's fine at Belle Chêne?"

Everyone but me. "Just the usual problems. Nothing to worry about."

"Will you be staying the night?"

Nom de Dieu, I want to. I want to stay this night and every night. But only if I can share your bed. "I can still make the late boat. I'd probably better be getting back."

"I suppose that would be wisest." But when Alex nodded with such bitter resignation, Nicki's heart did a queer little twist. "When will you be returning?"

"I'm not sure. I'll send someone to pick up the ledgers just as soon as you're through with them."

What if he didn't come back until she was gone? What if this was her very last chance to tell him the truth?

"I appreciate all your hard work," he told her.

"It was nothing. The least I could do to repay your kindness."

"Kindness?" Alex's expression turned grim. "It was kind of me to take your maidenhood? It was kind of me to keep you in my house against your will? It was kind of me to betray your father's friendship by forcing his daughter to become my mistress?"

"Don't say that, Alex. None of that matters now."

"It matters to me," he said. "It always mattered. I just couldn't seem to help myself." His eyes searched her face. "I wish there was a way I could make it up to you."

Nicki's throat felt so tight, she could barely speak. He looked so tall and handsome. So masculine and proud.

And so very lonely.

"You can," she whispered.

"Tell me," he said, "tell me and it will be done."

"Stay with me tonight."

Alex just stared at her.

"Don't you know I love you? That every day without you has been an agony. That if things were different, I would stay with you forever."

Long, powerful strides carried him across the room. Alex reached for her, swept her into his arms, and buried his face in her hair. "I love you," he whispered beside her ear. "I love you more than life. I've tried to deny it, but I can't."

Nicki clutched him tighter. "Oh, Alex." Her fingers slid into his hair as she held him close. "I wanted to believe you cared, but I wasn't sure. I never thought to hear you say it."

"I need you, Nicki. Now that I've found you, I don't know if I can make it without you."

Nicki kissed his eyes, his nose, his mouth. "Make love to me, Alex. Make me forget everything but you."

"I love you," he whispered, kissing her until she was as breathless as he. He could feel her heartbeat against his chest, hear her shallow breathing. She smelled of violets and faintly of the feminine scent that always inflamed him. He wanted her so badly, his hands shook and he fought an urge to take her roughly, drive into her and demand she tell him over and over that she was his.

Instead he kissed her tenderly, passionately, then pulled the ribbon that closed up her nightgown and settled his mouth on her breast. Nicki moaned and swayed against him. Her fingers worked the buttons on the front of his shirt, then her hands slipped inside to tease a flat copper nipple.

Alex groaned. Stopping only for a moment, he tugged his shirt free from his breeches and pulled off his boots. Nicki helped him ease his shirtsleeve over the bandages that still covered his injured arm. Leaning down, she pressed her mouth against the flesh above the wound.

"I love you," she whispered, and Alex cradled her face between his palms and kissed her, a deep, tender, loving kiss that answered the words she had spoken.

Sliding the nightgown off her smooth white shoulders and down her hips, he lifted her up, carried her across the room, and settled her on the bed. Naked and aroused, he trailed warm kisses along her flesh, then gasped when he felt her fingers close over his manhood.

With a gentle touch, Nicki urged him onto his back. Using her lips and tongue, she teased a heated path across his chest and down the hard planes of his abdomen. Alex tensed when she didn't stop. Just kept on nipping and kissing him and moving lower, until her soft full lips closed over his pulsing shaft.

Since their night in the cottage, this was the first time she had given herself to him freely. Wanting to show him how much she loved him, Nicki used her mouth and her tongue, tentatively at first, but sensing his powerful response and the thickening of his already rigid manhood, with more and more confidence. Alex groaned, but she didn't stop until his wide hands circled her waist and he lifted her astride him.

"I have dreamed of this, *ma chère*. Dreamed of the day you would welcome me inside you without being forced."

"You have never really forced me," she told him truthfully. "I've loved you from the start."

To prove it, Nicki slid along his body, felt his hardened arousal at the entrance to her passage, widened to him, and eased him inside. With a groan of pleasure, Alex thrust home, burying himself deeply and sending ripples of heat the length of her.

She felt hot and cold all over. Shivery and pulsing with need. Tightening the muscles of her thighs, Nicki worked to set up a rhythm of passion that Alex matched stroke for stroke. In minutes she gave in to the swirling sensations, no longer in control. She barely noticed when his palms cupped her bottom, just felt an intense surge of pleasure when he drove himself farther inside.

Then with one deft movement, he lifted her up and turned her onto her back. Looming above her, he drove into her with long, powerful strokes.

Nicki's fingers dug into his muscular shoulders and she cried out his name, but Alex made no effort to slow, just kept pounding against her, driving relentlessly, until both of them reached the edge of the precipice, and tumbled over.

"Alex," Nicki whispered, then heard him call her name just as a tremor of passion washed over her. Alex's muscles tensed and he spilled his seed with a force that proved his possession.

For moments he remained above her, his body damp with the sheen of his efforts. Then he settled himself beside her, pulling her into the circle of his arms.

"I never thought to hold you like this again," he whispered.

In a way she wished he hadn't. Because the awful truth at last was clear. "I won't leave you, Alex. Not for as long as you want me to stay."

"Then you'll stay with me forever," he told her, and kissed the side of her neck.

They slept for a while, made love again, this time more slowly, then again with the first light of dawn.

"There's something I want you to know," Nicki told him as they lay sated, she cuddling peacefully against his wide chest.

Alex grinned and cocked a brow. "You missed your last monthly."

Nicki smiled and poked him playfully in the ribs.

"No. It's about what you said last night. About the things you believe you've done to me."

Alex's expression turned serious. Tension seeped into the solid arms around her.

Nicki touched his cheek. "Maybe you should have handled things differently," she told him. "If you could do it over, maybe you would. At the time, you did what you thought was best. And whatever you took from me, you gave threefold in return."

"I've given you nothing but grief," he said.

"You're wrong, Alex. You saved me from a fate I can only image. You cared for me, took me into your home, gave me food, shelter, and your friendship. You believed in me when no one else would have. But even more important, you gave me back my courage. You gave me back myself." Alex brought her hand to his lips and gently kissed the palm.

"Before you came," Nicki said, "I had forgotten who I was. Now I know and I won't forget again. No matter what happens, Alex, it's the greatest gift I'll ever receive."

Alex kissed her tenderly. "And I shall never forget the precious gift of your love that you have given to me."

Regretfully, Alex left for Belle Chêne that day, promising to return as soon as he could and no later than three or four days.

Even under the circumstances, Nicki felt light-hearted. Alex loved her. Until now she had both yearned for and feared the words, knowing how strongly they could bind her to him. They did so now, but with her own feelings out in the open, his love for her brought only joy.

Nicki refused to think much further than the few days ahead when Alex would return. Thoughts of his marriage, just a few weeks away, she pushed to the back of her mind.

Along with another fact she refused to consider. In truth, Alex's guess had been right about the monthly she had missed. Part of her wanted to smile, knowing how self-satisfied he would feel. Alex's arrogance at his coming fatherhood would know no bounds.

And yet he would never be able to acknowledge the child as his own.

She just wouldn't think about it, she told herself firmly. Burying her problems was an achievement she had learned during her long days of indenture. She had become well versed.

Instead she worked on the Belle Chêne ledgers, busying herself with tasks that made her feel close to Alex and to the place she still thought of as home. It wasn't until the morning of the third day that she began to notice something was wrong.

"Ram," she called down to him. "Could you come up here for a moment?"

The big Turk sauntered up the stairs, unconcerned that he was being summoned to a woman's bedchamber.

"I know you like to read," she said as he stood across the desk staring down at the big leather volumes. "Are you any good at ciphering?"

"I'm afraid not. Why?"

"There's a discrepancy in these two sets of books. The ones Alex keeps show a substantial profit over those kept by Louis Mouton. Of course, I'm not certain yet, but I soon will be."

"How substantial?" Ram asked.

"Ten years' worth. It's a great deal of money, Ram."

"We must tell Alexandre right away."

"Not until I'm certain. Alex has worked with Louis Mouton for years. He trusts him implicitly. It wouldn't be right to accuse the man of wrongdoing until we know for sure."

"All right. We won't tell him yet."

"We'll know soon enough." Nicki smiled. "That is, if I stop talking and get back to work."

Alex arrived early that evening. The worry lines had left his face and his body had already begun to lose its gauntness. His shoulders seemed broader, his back a little straighter. For the first time, Nicki felt as if she had done the right thing.

"*Mon Dieu*, it's good to see you." With one powerful arm, he swept her against him. "Three days seemed like thirty."

"I've missed you too."

They enjoyed a quiet supper alone. René had called for Danielle and the couple had gone out for the evening. Ram left with a sly look and a wink at Alex that said he had plans of his own.

After supper they sat by the fire in the parlor, Alex content, it seemed, just to look at her. But by the time he had finished his brandy, he once more seemed tense.

"There's something I want to say to you," he told her, his expression serious.

Nicki's heart set up an uncomfortable rhythm in her chest. "What is it, Alex?"

"I want you to know that if I thought there was a chance, no matter how small, that Clarissa might loan me that money without the wedding, I'd ask her."

Nicki laid a hand on his arm. "I know you would, Alex."

"I haven't because I know how she thinks. To Clarissa this marriage is strictly business. She isn't about to do me any favors unless I give something in return."

"And that something is Belle Chêne."

"Yes. I could give up the plantation, but that wouldn't stop Fortier from taking over your contract. Even if I'd killed the bastard, you'd belong to his heirs, wherever they might be. It could take years before his estate was settled. God only knows what might happen to you in the meantime."

"I understand, Alex. I know you have no choice."

"Yesterday I went to see her," he continued, and Nicki's stomach tightened. "I asked her if she had any reservations, any concerns about going through with the marriage."

"And?"

"She told me that as far as she was concerned our wedding—and our business arrangements—went hand in hand. She was looking forward to becoming mistress of Belle Chêne, and she hoped I felt the same about Elmtree."

It was the first time Nicki had thought about the advantages, other than repaying his note, Alex would gain from marrying one of the richest women in Louisiana. Elmtree was nearly as large as Belle Chêne—to say nothing of the Endicott family's engraving business and myriad other financial concerns.

"I know you did your best." She swallowed and

glanced away. "I'd appreciate it if we didn't talk about it anymore."

Alex just nodded. That night they made love as passionately as ever, Nicki careful to blot Alex's grim conversation from her thoughts.

François arrived just as Alex was about to leave the following morning. They were standing in the foyer, Alex kissing her good-bye, when the soft knock sounded at the door.

"Hello, Alexandre," François said with surprise as Frederick ushered him in. "I wasn't expecting to find you here."

"From now on, you will find me here at every opportunity." Alex grinned so wide that his cheeks dimpled. He winked at Nicole.

"I'm happy for you," François said a bit forlornly. Today it was he who looked wan and pale.

"And you, *mon frère?* You're looking a little under the weather. Is something wrong?"

François glanced at Nicole, who nodded her encouragement. "It's just that I feel so useless. There are things I wish to do . . . things I feel I must do, and yet I cannot."

"What things?" Alex pressed, beginning to look disgruntled.

François twirled the narrow-brimmed high hat he held in his hands. "I had been hoping to speak to you. I suppose now is as good a time as any." He took a steadying breath. "I want to return to France, Alexandre. I want to paint."

Alex just stared at him. "Paint?" he snapped. "If you want to paint something, return to Belle Chêne and I shall arm you with brush and pail."

"Alex!" Nicki broke in. "What in God's name is the

matter with you? François is telling you his wishes, opening himself up to you, and you are . . . are acting like an overbearing ass!"

Alex pinned her with a single hard glance. "Excuse me, Mademoiselle St. Claire. But I believe this conversation was between my brother and myself. Should you wish to speak in my stead, I shall leave you to it. Good day."

"Don't you dare walk out that door!"

But as usual he did dare, slamming it loudly behind him.

Nicki sighed in frustration. "I love him dearly," she told François, "as stubborn and arrogant as I know he can be."

"I told you this would happen."

"So you did." She laid a comforting hand on François's arm. "But you mustn't give up yet. Why don't we have some coffee? Have you eaten?"

"I had that in mind when I came here, but I am afraid I've lost my appetite."

Nicki just nodded. "No one knows better than I how frustrating Alex can sometimes be."

François pulled open the door.

"Let me talk to him," Nicki said. "After he's had time to think things over, maybe he'll listen."

"I doubt it, but I would appreciate it if you would try."

Alex wouldn't be returning for at least a few more days. In the meantime, Nicki went over and over the Belle Chêne ledgers. By Friday she was sure—Louis Mouton was stealing from the du Villiers and had been for years.

"We'll tell Alex as soon as he arrives," Ram said.

"No, Ram. I've a better idea. If Alex discovers what Mouton's been doing, he's very likely to kill him—or beat him senseless at the very least. Mouton might never return the money. I think we should go to him. Threaten to expose him unless he returns what he has stolen—with interest. We'd have leverage—bargaining power. Mouton's reputation means everything to him. To say nothing of the years he would spend in prison."

Ram grinned, his olive skin growing taut above his smooth-lidded eyes. "With the money, Alex could repay Fortier. He wouldn't have to marry Clarissa."

Nicki's smile was so bright it lit the room. "Exactly."

23

"Why, that is absurd! Utterly preposterous!"

"Is it, M'sieur Mouton?" Nicki challenged. "I hardly think so." She and Ram stood in Mouton's elegant inner office, in front of his expensive Louis Quatorze desk.

"And who are you to question me?" Mouton demanded. "Alexandre's latest mistress—nothing but a whore."

Ram stepped forward, his powerful biceps bulging as he glared at Fortier. "I warn you—do not insult the lady. Before Alexandre discovers your mistreatment and beats you senseless, you will deal with me."

Mouton sank down in his chair. He ran a fine-boned finger between his stiff white collar and his anger-reddened neck, then straightened the front of his snowy linen stock. "Who has come to you with such tales?"

"Your assistant gave Alexandre your set of ledgers," Nicki said. "I am the one who has discovered your thievery."

"You! But you're a woman. Surely you know nothing of accounting."

"My father was Etienne St. Claire of Meadowood Plantation. I learned from him."

Mouton's blue eyes looked glazed and slightly desperate. "In the first place, the ledgers my assistant gave Alexandre are . . . are not the current set. There are expenses not accounted for in them. The books he should have been given show the expenditures—legitimate expenses that used up the profits you speak of."

"Is that so?" Nicki arched a brow. Brushing an imaginary speck of lint from the front of her fur-trimmed navy-blue silk faille day dress, she lifted her chin and fixed her gaze on Mouton. "And why was it necessary for you to keep two sets of records?"

"It . . . it was just a precaution—in case something happened to the other set. You do not understand the intricacies of this business."

Nicki flashed an unpleasant smile. "If that is so, then I suggest we call a watchman. I'm sure the constable of police will be able to set the matter aright—with Alex's assistance, of course."

Mouton swallowed hard. "There is really no need for such extreme measures. . . ."

"No? There wouldn't be—not if you paid Alex back."

"But I tell you, I've stolen nothing!"

"Ram? A watchman, if you please."

"With pleasure." Ram turned to leave, but Mouton's high-pitched voice, close to hysteria, stopped him at the door.

"No! If you are determined to cause trouble, then . . . then you leave me no choice. I shall see that Alexandre is repaid the money in full.

"With interest," Nicki added.

Mouton groaned. "You will break me."

"I doubt it. I'm sure the money—with your astute stewardship—has grown tenfold."

"How shall I give it to him without his knowing about our . . . arrangement?"

"That's up to you. Tell him a long-lost relative has died and left him an inheritance. Tell him whatever you wish. I'm sure you'll think of something."

Mouton nodded stiffly.

"After that, I'll expect you to leave New Orleans."

"Leave? I've spent years building up this business. How can you expect me to leave?"

"You've spent years cheating people out of their money. I doubt you'd have much business left—once they discovered the truth."

Mouton's shoulders sagged, his face pale and haggard.

"I'm afraid I'll have to keep your ledgers," Nicki added. "Just to be sure you abide by our agreement."

"But how do I know you will not turn me in?"

"You don't. You'll have to accept my word. But I assure you, I value it far more highly than you do your own."

"I'll need a little time to raise the money."

"A week," Nicki told him. "Then I go to the authorities."

"Do not try to leave," Ram warned. "The law will find you—if they do not, I will."

"Have a pleasant day, m'sieur," Nicki said sweetly and turned to leave. Ram pulled open the door and they walked out through the outer office and onto the street.

Ram chuckled softly. "How does it feel to know you will soon be a duchess?"

Nicki grinned and hugged herself, twirling in pleasure beneath the bright December sunlight. "In truth, I hadn't thought of it. I just want to marry Alex and go home."

With Alex's wedding only a few weeks away, Nicki waited impatiently for his return. She couldn't tell him about her meeting with Mouton, but she could settle another matter that had been bothering her since his annoying departure last week.

He arrived on Wednesday evening, looking tired but glad to see her, and considering the temper he had left in, maybe a little contrite.

They talked of the weather, supped on *étouffé*, a heavy crawfish stew served over rice, then took brandy and sherry in the salon. Outside, the weather had turned colder as winter approached, but the evening skies were bright and clear.

Nicki took a sip of her sherry. "Have you seen François lately?" she asked with feigned nonchalance.

Alex's relaxed expression faded. "He hasn't been to Belle Chêne, if that's what you're asking."

"I'm asking if you've seen him, Alex. Your brother loves you. He misses being able to talk to you."

"All he has to do is come home."

Nicki set her glass down on the marble-topped table. "Belle Chêne is your home, Alex, not François's. He isn't interested in being a planter. François has his own life now, his own goals and needs."

"François has no goals. Surely that is plain, even to someone as determined to see his good side as you are. François refuses to grow up, to accept responsibility. He refuses to see life as it really is."

Nicki gently touched his arm. "This time it is you, Alexandre, who refuse to see life as it is."

Alex jerked his arm away. "And what is that supposed to mean?"

"It means François is . . . different. He is gentler than some men, a little more . . . sensitive. His needs are different from yours."

Alex's expression turned bleak. "His needs are different, all right. As different from mine as night and day."

"Does that make him bad?"

Alex didn't answer. His eyes locked with hers and his breath seemed lodged in his throat. "You know about him, don't you?"

Nicki's heart went out to him. She should have known Alex had guessed the truth about his brother —or at least suspected. "I know very little of . . . matters such as these, but I know François is kind and caring. I know he loves you and he needs your love in return—whether he is . . . different . . . or not."

Alex released a long, weary breath, his worried expression making him look years older. "I hoped that sooner or later he would be as he was before. That this was only a phase. I felt sure once he came back to Belle Chêne and started working, his . . . preferences . . . would return to normal."

"He is as he is, Alex." Nicki smiled softly. "He's a wonderful artist, incredibly talented. He wants to study in France. I think he could be happy there."

"With his friend," Alex added darkly.

"Yes."

"And you believe I should help him?"

"He loves you as you are. You must show him you feel the same."

Alex cleared his throat, his voice a little husky. "I only wanted what was best for him."

"I know."

Alex watched her a moment, then slid an arm around her waist and pulled her onto his lap. "You never cease to amaze me," he said and nuzzled the side of her neck. "How did I ever manage without you?"

Nicki grinned. "I'm sure I can't imagine."

Dipping his head, he kissed her, a slow, tender, loving kiss that thanked her for understanding him so well. "I'll do as you ask," he told her when he finally pulled away. "Tell him I want him to be happy."

Nicki's eyes filled with tears. "He will know."

In the morning, Alex woke early, dressed for his business meeting in dark-brown breeches and a crisp white linen shirt, and set out a gold brocade waistcoat and dark-green frock coat.

"I've a meeting with Louis Mouton," he whispered in Nicki's ear as she lay curled against the pillow.

Nicki bolted upright. "You do?"

Alex kissed the tip of her nose. "This morning at seven." He returned to the rosewood mirror above the bureau, and tied his white stock neatly around his neck. "He sent a messenger to Belle Chêne yesterday, saying it was urgent. I hope to God nothing's gone wrong with the shipping contracts."

"I—I'm sure it's nothing like that." Nicki just prayed Mouton would do exactly as he promised and give Alex back his money.

"I hope you're right," he said. After buttoning his

waistcoat, Alex grabbed his jacket and strode to the
bed. "Why don't you get a little more sleep?" Brushing tangled hair away from her face, he kissed her
cheek.

"When will you be back?"

"Not for a few days, I'm afraid. I've got to get back
to Belle Chêne, but I promise I'll return as soon as I
can."

Nicki stretched and yawned, her back braced
against the cold mahogany headboard. Lifting her
copper hair away from her neck, she gathered it together and pulled it over one shoulder. When she
glanced up, she found Alex's dark eyes fixed on a naked breast, exposed where the sheet had fallen away.

"I assure you, mademoiselle, Louis Mouton can
wait, if that is what you wish." His hand found the
heavy swell and cupped it gently.

Nicki felt the heat of it all the way to her toes.
"No," she whispered, her voice a little strained. "You
had better see what he wants."

Alex sighed resignedly, bent down and kissed her.
"I'll be back as soon as I can."

The minute he had gone, Nicki flew out of bed. She
called for Danielle, ordered a bath sent up, then hurriedly bathed and dressed. She was certain Alex
would return just as soon as he heard the news.

She wanted to look beautiful when he asked her to
marry him.

Nicki waited all afternoon, but Alex didn't arrive.

Maybe Mouton hadn't given him the money. Maybe
Alex had gone to Feliciana to see Fortier and pay off
the note. Maybe he had gone to see Clarissa, get
things settled once and for all.

Surely tomorrow he would come.

Again, she waited, but Alex never arrived.

On Friday, Nicki sent Ram to Mouton's office. The big Turk found the factor packing his things, readying himself for his trip from the city.

Ram returned with the news. "Mouton has done as you asked. He showed me papers, signed by Alexandre, accepting the sum in full—an inheritance from some unknown relative in France."

"And you believe him?" Nicki asked.

"He was too frightened to lie. He has repaid the money."

"Then why hasn't Alex come?"

"There is still the note to pay—and matters to settle with Clarissa."

But Nicki's apprehension only grew stronger. "Maybe that is so . . . then again, maybe I have once more misread his intentions. Alex and I have spoken of many things, but marrying me has not been one of them."

"Alexandre loves you," Ram said. "He will offer marriage."

Nicki didn't answer. A few hours later, a messenger came from Belle Chêne with a note of Alex's arrival. Tonight she would know the truth.

"You must not worry," Danielle assured her as Nicki fought to calm her jangled nerves. "Everything is going to be fine."

"I pray you're right, Danielle." At the sound of Alex's voice downstairs, Nicki dabbed a spot of perfume behind each ear with trembling fingers. The gown she had chosen was a simple dark-green silk, since Alex had made no mention of any special plans, but it was flattering, and one of his favorites.

She found him standing in the foyer dressed in black evening clothes, his eyes warm and filled with love. Unmindful of the servants, he kissed her soundly, lifting her clear off her feet.

"We're going out," he said when he finally set her down. "Someplace elegant and expensive." He walked to the gilded table in the entry and picked up a big box tied with a bright pink ribbon that he had set there. "For you, *mon amoureuse.*"

"What's this?" With a smile of excitement, Nicki accepted the box and hastily pulled the bow.

"Just something I thought you might like."

She lifted the lid to find a beautiful gold silk gown trimmed with tulle and decorated with clusters of delicate pearls. Raising on tiptoes, she kissed his cheek. "It's lovely, Alex."

"François gave me the name of your seamstress, so it's sure to fit."

"You spoke to him?"

"Yes. We talked as we should have long ago—thanks to you." Alex pulled her into his arms. "I love you, Mademoiselle St. Claire."

Nicki's heart pounded. *He's going to ask me! He's going to ask me tonight!*

"We'd better change and get out of here," Alex whispered against her ear, gently nibbling the lobe, "or we're likely not to leave at all."

Nicki didn't really care. She just wanted Alex to speak the words she had been waiting to hear for so long. Instead, she nodded and they went upstairs to change.

"Where are we going?" Nicki asked a little later as

they swept out through the courtyard toward a gleaming black brougham Alex had hired, its enclosed interior being warmer for winter. Secretly, she hoped they might be dining at the St. Charles, the most fashionable spot in New Orleans. If he took her there, it would mean he had spoken to Clarissa, that their wedding had been cancelled. That he was free to marry Nicole.

"I know a charming little place at the edge of the city. It's small, but lovely. I think you'll like it."

And no one will see us. Some of Nicki's enthusiasm began to wane. Then again, maybe Alex was just being romantic, wanting her all to himself. "That sounds wonderful."

And it was. The restaurant was built in an old abandoned Spanish rampart, thick-walled and cozy, with dim yellow lamps near the timber-studded doorways, soft music, and lovely potted palmettos to lend intimacy to each candle-lit table.

"You look beautiful," Alex told her, stripping her elbow-length gloves from her hands, then kissing the tips of her fingers. He spoke to her in French, as he seldom did, telling her he loved her and devouring her with his eyes. The dress he had bought was daringly low-cut, displaying her breasts in a manner that brought warm color to her cheeks.

"It's all I can do not to take you right here," Alex whispered, and Nicki's face grew warmer still. Her pulse pounded, and her skin tingled just thinking of Alex's touch.

They dined on *soupe de poissons*, a delicate fish soup; *noix de St. Jacques au courtbouillon*, poached scallops; and *noisettes d'agneau poêlées*, medallions of lamb with spinach and mushroom stuffing; along

with a variety of wines. For dessert they shared a
pear soufflé and drank champagne.

Alex spoke of François, and later, of a letter he had
received from *Grand-mère*. But the words Nicole
longed to hear did not come.

"How is the harvest progressing?" Nicki asked,
hoping he might warm to the subject of Fortier and
the note he most surely had paid.

"For the most part, we're finished. But I'm afraid
I'll be needing the services of a new factor. Louis
Mouton is leaving the city."

Nicki's stomach tightened. "After all these years?"

Alex sighed. "Who could have guessed?"

"Did he say why?"

"Just that he needed the challenge of someplace
new." Alex squeezed her hand. "Let's leave business
aside, shall we? Tonight we speak of more important
things."

Nicki smiled, and her heartbeat quickened. "Such
as?"

"Such as making love." His eyes swept down her
throat, across her shoulders, and fixed on her bosom.
"I think it is time we went home."

Alex rose and pulled out her chair. Nicki flashed an
uncertain smile and stood up. *The carriage*, she
thought with growing desperation. *He'll ask in the
privacy of the carriage.*

But he didn't. Just kissed her with such force she
found herself responding. His wide hand slipped inside her gown, cupped her breast and teased the nipple into a hard, dark peak.

Nicki moaned and leaned into his hand. By the
time they reached the town house, she felt breathless
and dizzy, and aching with desire for him. Then the

driver pulled open the door, letting in a burst of cold air and with it a return of her senses.

He isn't going to ask me, she realized with a sickening sureness that washed over her like a cold, dark wave. He's going to marry Clarissa, just as he planned.

She started toward the house, feeling shaken and disoriented. When she missed a step and stumbled, Alex swept her up in his arms.

"I think you've had a little too much champagne."

"Yes. I—I am feeling a bit light-headed." *And sick all the way to my soul.*

Alex carried her up the stairs. Nicki wrapped her arms around his neck to steady herself. Using his foot to shove open the door, he carried her over to the bed. One look at her pale face, and Alex's dark brows drew together.

"You don't look good. Maybe I should send for a doctor."

"No. It's just the champagne. I'll be fine in a minute."

Alex undressed her with a hand that shook when he accidentally touched her breasts. Nicki forced herself to ignore the warm sensations he stirred.

"Alex?"

He kissed her forehead. "What is it, *mon amour?*"

"I need to know if anything has . . . changed between us? I need you to tell me exactly what you feel."

Alex gripped her cold hands between his warm ones. "I love you more every moment. I intend to take care of you and make you happy. Nothing has changed."

Nicki swallowed hard and fought to hold back her

tears. "I know you want to make love, Alex, but I'm really not . . . feeling very well. Will you mind terribly if we wait?"

"Of course I'll mind." He grinned, the cheek-dimpling smile she loved so well. "Especially since I must leave again at first light." He brushed her lips with a kiss. "But I'll be content to hold you, if that is what you wish."

"Thank you." They finished undressing, Alex's movements brusque and businesslike, but his hard arousal was evidence of the passion he fought to subdue. Her own body stirred with those same urgent feelings, but she refused to give in to them.

That Alex wanted her she had no doubt. She could even believe that in his own way he loved her. But he also loved Belle Chêne. Alex loved the dynasty the du Villier family had built, and he intended to keep right on building. Now Nicki knew, with a certainty that chilled her to the core, that Alex had never considered marriage. From the moment he had discovered his desire for her, he had planned to make her his mistress—and he had succeeded far better than she would have believed.

Alex's marriage to Clarissa Endicott would stand. The du Villier power and fortune would more than double by the single act of his wedding. How could she have been naive enough to believe he would willingly give all that up?

And for what? To marry a penniless bond servant?

Nicki's throat ached with the unshed tears she fought to keep from spilling down her cheeks. Through the long hours of the night, she felt Alex's arms protectively around her, his hard body pressing against her. Though she pretended, sleep remained elusive. At dawn, when Alex awoke, she looked more wan and pale than she had before.

"If you're not feeling better by tonight," he said, "I want Ram to go for the doctor."

"I'm fine," she said softly. "Really I am."

"I'll be back tomorrow night to see for myself. Sooner, if you need me."

"I told you, I'm fine."

Alex kissed her tenderly. "I love you, *ma chère*. Trust me. Everything is going to be all right."

Trust you. How many times had she done just that? "I trust you, Alex. You would never do anything to hurt me."

He looked at her oddly, seemed as though he wanted to say something more, but didn't.

"I'll see you tomorrow."

"Yes." He kissed her one last time, and Nicki found herself clutching his shirtfront, kissing him back with all the love she felt but now must deny. "Take care of yourself, Alexandre," she called to him at the door.

"Tomorrow," he repeated. And then he was gone.

"Now do you believe me?" Nicki asked Ram, who joined her and Danielle in the study later that day.

"It is as you've said. The wedding is to take place as planned, though the note to Fortier has been paid in full."

Nicki sank down on the leather sofa in front of the fireplace. "Then you'll do as I've asked? You'll help me to leave?"

"You will not confront him—try to make him see reason?"

"I've done that before."

Ram nodded, realizing the truth of her words. "I will help you."

Nicki handed him the morning edition of the *Daily Picayune*. "Turn to page three." Ram did as she asked. "About halfway down the page. The article on the Republic of Texas."

Ram folded the paper in half and scanned the article. "You cannot be serious." He glanced up at her with astonishment.

"I'm perfectly serious."

"You want to travel to Texas? Marry a man you have never even seen?"

"Texas is a land of opportunity. They need families to settle there. I'd be traveling with a man who wants me for his wife. My past wouldn't matter, and the republic is so vast I wouldn't have to worry about being discovered."

"Alexandre wouldn't let you go before. Why should he do so now?"

"Because you will tell him I know of his 'inheritance.' That I know he could have paid Fortier and married me if he had wanted. I could never forgive his deception and Alex will know it. This time he won't come after me."

Danielle sniffed back tears. "I still cannot believe it. I was so certain that he loved you."

"Love and money," Nicki said softly, "desire and power. Each is a far different thing."

"You must hurry," Ram said, "if you are to be gone before his return."

"My bags are packed. If Frederick will load them into the carriage, I can be off. There's a steamboat leaving for Texas at one o'clock. It arrives in Galveston sometime next week—just before the Peters col-

ony is planning to depart. After I'm . . . married
. . . my husband and I will travel inland by steamboat and wagon. According to the article, the group
is planning to settle somewhere along the Brazos."

"I'm going with you," Ram said, "at least as far as
Galveston."

"No, Ram. You've given me your money, that's
more than enough."

"I go or you stay. Make your choice."

There was no arguing. The set of Ram's beefy
shoulders, the uncompromising look in his slitted
black eyes told her that much.

"What about Alex? You need to be here. You need
to make him understand so he won't follow."

"Leave him a note. Tell him the truth. If he follows,
I will stop him."

Nicki's head snapped up. "You mustn't go against
him, Ram. No matter what happens. You and Alex
have been friends for years."

"The Alexandre du Villier who was my friend is no
longer. He would never have behaved as he has."

Nicki hesitated only a moment. "I'll get my
things." She would write a note Alex could not ignore. She would tell him that she knew the truth
about Fortier and his marriage to Clarissa, then appeal to his sense of honor—however faint it might be
—and beg him to let her live in peace.

In her heart of hearts, she believed this time he
would.

24

~~~~~

"Nicki!" Alex tossed his hat to Frederick and headed into the salon. He had been planning this moment for days, now he found he was as nervous as a schoolboy. It was insane and he knew it—Nicki loved him and he loved her.

Then again, Nicole St. Claire was a woman with a mind and will of her own. He was never completely sure of her, which only made him love her more.

"Ram!" he called out, wondering why the house seemed so cold and empty. When no one answered, he tried the dining room, then his study, but neither yielded the object of his search.

"You might save me all this trouble and tell me where she is," he said to Frederick in a tone he hoped rang with authority but was sure sounded joyous instead.

Frederick merely shrugged his shoulders. Normally, Alex might have noticed the stiff set to the tall black butler's spine, the way his mouth clamped together in a disapproving line. Instead, Alex took the stairs up to Nicki's room two at a time and found it, too, was empty.

"Danielle!" he called toward the servants' quarters in the rear, but the plump little French girl didn't come running, merely poked her head out the door, then sauntered down the hall in his direction. "Where has your mistress gone?"

"She has left with Ram."

"With Ram? But she knew I was coming. Where did they go?"

Danielle glanced away. "She left this for you." She handed him a plain white envelope with his name on it, written in Nicki's delicate hand and very carefully sealed with wax.

Alex broke open the seal and began to read the finely scripted words:

My darling Alex—for you will always be that to me, no matter how far life carries me away from you. . . .

Alex's hand began to shake, and the chill in the hall seemed suddenly colder. In the body of the letter Nicki told him she knew of the money he had inherited, knew that the debt he owed Fortier had been paid, but that he still intended marriage to Clarissa. She didn't fault him. Instead, she told him she understood how much Belle Chêne meant to him, understood the advantages of uniting his family with that of the Endicotts.

No, Nicki didn't fault him, just ended the letter with a plea that he grant her that same understanding:

We have spoken many times of honor. Of my feelings about children and family. I respect your wishes for the future. Now I beg you to respect mine. Let me go, Alexandre. Show me your words of love were not just hollow phrases. Let me go on with my life as you will go on with yours.

It was signed simply, *Love, Nicole.*

Alex leaned against the fine mahogany banister, his hand shaking so badly the stiff paper crackled with a harshness that seemed to echo in the silence of the hall.

"Where is she?" he asked, forcing his words past the ache that closed his throat.

"I do not know, m'sieur."

"You know," Alex said, his dark eyes pleading. "And I beg you in the name of God to tell me."

"There is nothing, *M'sieur le duc*, you can do or say that will make me tell you."

Alex blinked against the moisture that suddenly blurred his vision. "I think there is, Danielle. If only you will listen."

It took six days to reach the port of Galveston. Six of the hardest days of Nicki's life.

Because the days she had spent with Alex, giving herself to him freely, had increased her love for him a hundred times over. She missed him more than she would have dreamed possible. No matter how she tried to occupy her mind, she thought about him, wondered where he was and if he might be missing her too.

She told herself it didn't matter. Alexandre had proven beyond a doubt that Belle Chêne was all important. Belle Chêne and the du Villier fortune.

What happened between them was past—one more moment in a life fraught with hardship.

Even the voyage had been rough, the seas wind-tossed and heavy. For the first few days, Nicki had battled severe rounds of nausea, unable to hold anything on her stomach and confined to the narrow berth in her small cabin.

It seemed God had been benevolent in sending Ram along after all. A sailor himself, Ram suffered none of the malaise of the passengers. Instead, he helped care for those of them who fell ill, and even pitched in to help the crew.

Nicki was always his chief concern, and with his constant attention, by the fourth day she felt better. They arrived at Galveston Island under a cloudy sky that forecast rain, and a chilling wind that matched Nicki's desolate mood.

Aside from her fears of marriage to a man she had never met, of a country that was sparsely settled and overrun with tribes of wild Indians, her menses had started the day she'd left home.

She should have felt grateful she didn't carry Alex's child. That the baby wouldn't be a burden to the man she would marry—but she wasn't. She had come to think of the babe as a small part of Alex that would stay with her always. Alex's son or daughter would have been the fruit of her love for him. A flesh-and-blood memory that would keep him alive for her wherever she went.

Most of the passengers had departed by the time Nicole and Ram left the boat, Nicki grateful for the feel of something solid beneath her feet. Around them, the wharf bustled with activity, mostly centered on the cotton trade, but the harbor was nowhere near as chaotic as the docks in New Orleans. Making their way among sailors and settlers, pigs, dogs, chickens, and cows, they walked toward the dusty street that faced the water. Nicki stared in wonder at a place so different from the cosmopolitan city she had left behind.

"It is not nearly so pretty as the *Vieux Carré*," Ram said, parroting her thoughts.

"It's not nearly so congested, either," she answered with a determined tilt to her chin. Ignoring his rumble of laughter, she pulled the article she had clipped from the *Daily Picayune* out of her reticule and reread the words, though she knew them almost by heart.

"We're to contact a Captain Mercer, the head of the expedition, at the Galveston Hotel near the square. I wonder which way it is?"

As Ram glanced toward the wood-frame buildings and small wooden houses, his satchel in one hand, her steamer trunk propped on one wide shoulder, Nicki strode toward a tall man in military dress just a few feet away.

"Excuse me, sir. Could you tell me the way to the square?"

The tall man smiled, his teeth gleaming white in a face tanned dark by the sun. The stiff breeze ruffled his thick brown hair. "Lieutenant Brendan Trask, Republic of Texas Marines, at your service, ma'am."

Trask. The name had a familiar ring. Glancing at his well-defined, masculine features, an image of the equally tall sea captain, Morgan Trask, who commanded the vessel, *Sea Gypsy*, that *Grand-mère* had sailed aboard to France, came to mind. Except for the color of their hair and eyes, the two men looked a great deal alike. She wondered if they could be brothers, but didn't ask. The fewer people who knew of her past the better.

"Hello, Lieutenant," she replied instead. "As I said before, I'm looking for the square."

"Yes, ma'am. It's right up Main Street. Just keep on goin' till you come to the church. Galveston Hotel's there. Such as it is."

"Thank you, Lieutenant."

"My pleasure, ma'am." He tipped his uniform hat.

As Nicki walked away, Ram flashed the lieutenant a warning glance. The tall, lean soldier only grinned and kept on watching. She could feel his light-blue eyes on her back—more probably a little lower—and smiled in spite of herself.

They reached the square, only a few blocks away, at a little after two o'clock. Though Galveston was a tiny town with none of the elegance of the city she had left behind, it was obvious the people planned to celebrate the Christmas holidays, which were less than two weeks away. Wreaths hung on store windows, decorated with berries and popcorn, and paper ornaments draped across door frames.

Nicki tried not to notice them. For the past three years her Christmases had all been dismal. Why should this one be any different?

Picking up their pace, they eventually located the hotel, a two-story wood-frame structure with only the most meager amenities, and checked in.

"Cap'n Mercer'll sure be glad to see you, ma'am," the desk clerk said. "He's got hisse'f a batch a randy . . . er . . . pardon me, ma'am, a group a homesteaders just itchin' to find theirselves a bride."

Nicki forced a smile. "Where will I find him?"

"He'll be back about suppertime. Meanwhile, why don't you git yerself some rest, or maybe take a look-see 'round town?"

"Thank you. I could use a little rest." What she really needed was some time alone. "Why don't you go on, Ram? I'm sure you'd enjoy seeing the city." Such as it was.

"I'll just put this trunk in your room first."

Nicki nodded and followed him up the stairs.

Sometime later, she returned to the lobby and eventually located the man she had been seeking.

"It's a pleasure to meet you, ma'am." Raymond Mercer, a middle-aged man with thick mutton-chop whiskers, sized her up with a single sweeping glance.

"Thank you, Captain." Nicki extended a small hand and the barrel-chested man shook it briefly.

"Why don't we sit down?" he suggested. They took a seat on a small walnut settee that rested back to back with another one just like it.

"Will your wife be traveling with us?" Nicki asked, noticing the thin gold band on his third left finger.

"My wife is staying with her sister here in Galveston. She's expecting a child in a few months. Had a little trouble with the last one, so we're playing it safe this time."

"I see." Nicki fiddled nervously with the sash of her brown wool dress. Standing not far away, Ram leaned a beefy shoulder against the wall beside a huge brick fireplace draped with holly. At Nicki's insistence, they had supped together on a meal of beefsteak, corn, mashed potatoes and gravy in the tiny little hotel dining room, where Ram's thick frame and Oriental features had caused quite a stir.

"What about the others?" Nicki asked. "Surely there are women besides myself who have come?"

"There are six of you in all," the captain said. "You'll be meeting them tomorrow in front of the hotel, when you choose the man you will marry."

"How . . . how will it be done?"

"We plan to draw names from a hat. Whichever woman's name comes up first will get first choice and so on down the line."

"That . . . seems fair."

Captain Mercer flashed her a sympathetic glance. "With your looks, you could probably go out tonight and find yourself a husband—if that's what you want to do."

Nicki's stomach rolled over. "No," she said softly. "I'll take my chances along with the rest of the women. At least these men are set on building a home and raising a family."

"They're all hard workers, I can vouch for that. Maybe not the best looking or the most educated, but whoever you wind up with will be good to you. Too few women in these parts for a man to risk losing the one he's got."

Nicki smiled half-heartedly, and Raymond Mercer stood up. "Well, I'd best be going. Lots to do before we leave tomorrow."

"Thank you for explaining, Captain. I appreciate your kindness."

"My pleasure, ma'am." Captain Mercer settled his flat-crowned hat on his head, touched the brim in farewell, and turned to leave.

Ram walked up as he left. "Are you sure this is what you want?"

"I'm sure of very little these days, Ram. But I've made my decision. I'm going through with it."

Nicki lay awake for most of the night. Tomorrow everything she had ever known in life would change. Even Ram would be left behind as she headed into the Texas wilderness with a man she had only just met. A man who would expect her to cleave to him from the moment she spoke the marriage vows.

Nicki swallowed hard. She'd known only one man's touch. Alex could stir her just by a look, a softly spoken word, the brush of a finger across her cheek. What would it be like to lie with a stranger? Would he be gentle or cruel? Would she find him repulsive or be able to submit without having to steel herself against her own emotions?

Nicki's eyes filled with tears. Tonight she would allow them to fall for the very last time. Her husband would not see them. The pain was for her alone to bear. Whatever it took, she would make him happy, and she prayed one day he might make her happy too.

Nicki hugged the thin feather pillow, pretending it was Alex, remembering the way he had held her, his softly spoken words of love. Tomorrow, she vowed, her regrets would end, along with her tormenting thoughts of the man she had left behind. She would blot him from her mind just as surely as she had the screams she'd heard in the darkness of the prison.

Nicki swallowed the ache that closed her throat, and hugged the pillow tighter. Why couldn't things have been different? Why hadn't he loved her enough?

The tears came in force then. For the man she had

loved and lost. For Alexandre's child, who was as lost to her as he. She indulged in them, allowing them to fall until they soaked through the thin cotton sheet, using them as a final means of release.

Tomorrow she would begin a new life, she vowed. Somewhere in the night she would find the courage to face it.

"Good mornin', ma'am."

"Good morning, Captain Mercer." The barrel-chested man studied her face, noting, she was sure, the blue-gray smudges beneath her eyes, the sallow look to her cheeks that her wan smile could not disguise.

The streets of Galveston seemed quieter today, the blustery cold having finally driven most of the residents indoors. Flat gray clouds blotted the sun and a biting wind whipped the folds of the thick woolen cloak Nicki wore. Though several heavy wagons laden with freight and building supplies rolled past, most of the activity remained at the docks with the constant arrival of ships.

Nicki let Captain Mercer lead her along the boardwalk past an Indian woman with her small child in tow, toward a group of women gathered not far from the front door of the hotel.

"Ladies," the captain said by way of introduction, "I'd like you to meet Nicole St. Claire. Miss St. Claire, this is Isabelle Jarvis, Maria Gonzales, Eleanor Hoskins, and Priscilla Fontaine."

"Hello," Nicki replied. Apparently as nervous as she, each woman merely nodded or smiled, or repeated Nicki's softly spoken greeting.

"I thought there was going to be six of us," she said to the captain.

Mercer shrugged his shoulders. "So we had hoped. There's a chance the last woman may still arrive, but we can't afford to wait."

Standing next to the women, a far larger group of men had gathered. A rough-looking band, some were dressed in buckskins while others wore homespun shirts and canvas breeches. Some were clean-shaven, some bearded, their long hair mussed by the wind. Others had made a gallant effort to look presentable, slicking down their locks with macassar oil and wearing starched white collars and clean white shirts. As the captain urged her nearer, the scent of lilac water seemed nearly overwhelming.

"You men gather round," the captain said, and Nicki took several nerve-calming breaths. "Silas"— He pointed to a man in the crowd who grinned with anticipation—"you can draw out the names."

Captain Mercer drew six slips of paper from the pocket of his shirt, stuffed the missing woman's name back in, and dropped the other five in the crown of his upturned hat.

The man named Silas, a dark-haired, skinny little man with a tooth missing in front, drew them out one at a time and handed them to Raymond Mercer.

"Miss Jarvis, Miss Gonzalez, Miss St. Claire, Miss Fontaine, then Miss Hoskins. I'll give you ladies a minute or two to look these fellas over, then I'll expect an answer. The preacher will be here any minute, and we've got a long way to go before sundown."

Nicki nervously wet her lips. The men shuffled their feet and looked expectantly across at the women. Isabelle Jarvis, a beefy woman who looked to be about thirty, wasted no time.

"This'n'll do," she said, stepping up to a bulky man a few years her senior with a square jaw and a warm smile. When he doffed his sweat-stained hat and grinned, a hoot of approval rose up from the crowd.

"Matthew Springer," the big man said to her, looking pleased. "I'd be honored, Miss Jarvis." Another chorus of shouts arose from the men, and Isabelle Jarvis smiled. Nicki thought the woman had chosen well.

"Miss Gonzales?" the captain said.

"*Sí, Señor* Mercer. I am ready." Maria was a pretty, slender girl, young and dark with flashing black eyes. The men's anticipation was obvious— though it was also obvious the girl was with child and quite some months along. "If he will have me, I choose the man on the end." A short dark-skinned man of Maria's same Mexican heritage stepped forward.

"I will make a good papa *por su niño*," the small man said, and Maria's brown-hued cheeks turned crimson. The Mexican proudly draped an arm around her shoulder and led her away.

All eyes swung to Nicole, who opened her mouth to speak, but couldn't seem to find the words.

"Miss St. Claire?" the captain urged.

"I—I . . . the gentleman in the plaid flannel shirt." With a hand that shook, she pointed to a man several years older than she who watched from behind two others. Tall and a bit too thin, but with a kind face and gentle blue eyes, he glanced at the man on each side of him, then down at his plaid flannel shirt. "Me?" he said, his eyes wide in disbelief.

Nicki just nodded. She had chosen the man who seemed the least threatening. Someone she hoped would treat her with kindness.

"Damned," he said, "fancy that!" For a moment she wasn't sure he was going to accept. Then he grinned and stepped forward. "I'm one lucky man, I can tell you gents that." They all laughed, and several whispered teasing remarks behind their hands.

"Name's Simon Stillwater, late of Tennessee. Pleased to meet you, ma'am." Simon doffed his floppy-brimmed hat and extended a thin, raw-boned hand. It felt warm to the touch but a little bit damp. A hard knot formed in Nicki's stomach.

While the captain finished his matchmaking for the other two women, Nicki let Simon lead her to a bench in front of Harbison's General Store, just a little ways down the walk.

She sank down on the wooden seat gratefully, desperate for the chance to compose herself.

"I'll take real good care a' you, ma'am," Simon was saying, his thin face serious.

It was all Nicki could do to concentrate on his words. "I'm sure you will, Simon."

"Since we're about to be hitched and all, would it be all right if I called you somethin' besides ma'am?"

"Of course," she said, but didn't think to supply her name. Across the way, the bell above the church began to toll. Nicki slowly stood up, drawn to the sound that reminded her of the beautiful church bells in New Orleans.

"Are you all right, ma'am?" Simon asked, watching her drawn features, the glazed look in her eyes.

"I—I'm fine. I just need a minute or two alone." Without waiting for his reply, Nicki started across the dirt street, her skirts whipping around her legs in the biting winter wind. As she pulled open the heavy wooden church door, she glanced back to see Ram speaking with Simon, who was nodding his agreement to what were most likely Ram's words of warning.

With a sad smile, Nicki realized she had come to depend on the big Turk's gentle support almost as much as she had Alexandre's strength and passion. She would miss him sorely.

Nicki felt a dry lump swell in her throat. *I will not cry*, she swore. I will not weep again.

Those days were behind her. She had come to the church to gather the strength and courage to go forward. Genuflecting, she settled herself on a hard wooden pew, then knelt and steepled her hands in prayer. Focusing her attention on the soft yellow glow of the candles burning beneath the altar at the front of the church, and the crucifix that gave comfort from above, she began to pray.

Nicki wasn't sure how long she had been kneeling, she only knew her knees were beginning to ache and that Simon Stillwater should have come looking for her by now.

But it wasn't Simon's thin, reedy voice that broke the silence in the near-empty church. The words that drew her attention were spoken with depth and resonance and such warmth that her heart lurched at the beloved sound.

"You would rather marry a man you have never met than be mistress to the man you love. . . ."

Turning at the sound of Alex's voice, she found him standing in the aisle beside her, more handsome than she remembered, even with the worry that creased his brow and the weariness that haunted his masculine features.

"I prayed you would not come," she whispered. "I believed this time you would understand and let me go." Alex reached a hand toward her cheek, but she moved away.

"I could never let you go," he said, his voice husky.

Coming to her feet, Nicki lifted her chin to look at him. It took every last ounce of will to say the words her heart begged her not to. "It is a matter of honor," she said softly. "Without honor, there is nothing."

"Yes . . ." he said. "So you have taught me."

"Please, Alexandre . . . please don't do this." But Alex seemed not to hear. Instead he lowered his tall frame to one knee, unmindful of the dirt floor that soiled his trousers, or the distant God who watched them from above. Lifting her icy hand, he clasped it between his warm ones.

"Mademoiselle St. Claire, I love you desperately. The thought of living without you is unbearable. Would you do me the greatest of honors and become my wife?"

Nicki swayed against the hard wooden pew. When Alex raised her trembling fingers to his lips and kissed them, the tears in her eyes slipped down her cheeks.

"I would have asked you sooner," he said when still she did not answer, "but I wanted to give Clarissa a chance to save face, and I was waiting for this." From the pocket of his waistcoat, he withdrew a tiny velvet box and carefully flipped open the lid.

On a bed of gleaming white satin, a diamond ring glittered in the soft yellow glow of the candles. In the center of the shimmering stones nestled a square-cut perfect aquamarine, exactly the color of Nicki's eyes.

"Oh, Alex," Nicki whispered, reaching out to him.

Alex pulled her into his arms. Holding her against his chest, he kissed the top of her head, grateful to God he had found her in time. "Marry me," he said beside her ear, his fingers splayed in the soft copper hair at the nape of her neck. "Right here. Right now."

Nicki clutched him tighter. He could hear her gentle weeping, hear her whispering his name over and over, as if the sound of it insured he was there.

"I love you, Alex," she said, her pretty aqua eyes bright with tears. "So much, I thought I would die of it." She planted small, soft kisses over his cheeks, down his throat, then kissed him full on the mouth. Alex groaned with the feel of it, knowing there had never been a touch so sweet, a breath so heady.

"Thank God I found you. I shouldn't have waited to ask you. I caused us both such grief. . . . Can you ever forgive me?"

"I shouldn't have doubted you. I should have had more faith in you."

"I'll always love you, *ma chère*. Never doubt me again." He captured her lips in a warm, sweet kiss and Nicki clung to him, kissing him back with equal passion.

Finally he pulled away. "You haven't given me an answer."

Nicki smiled and kissed him again. "It seems I'm already betrothed," she teased. "What am I to do with my fiancé?"

"Simon Stillwater has been gracious enough to decline his suit—once he understood you were already spoken for."

Nicki grinned. "Then, M'sieur du Villier, since you have asked so nicely, I would be proud to marry you."

Alex bent his head and kissed her, a long, sensuous kiss that stirred thoughts better dealt with someplace else. "I promise you'll never be sorry."

Nicki smiled softly. "I have never regretted a single moment I've spent with you."

Looping her arm through his, Nicki let him guide her down the aisle toward the altar. From the depths of a doorway, a small black-haired priest stepped forward, his long robes billowing out behind him.

"May I be of assistance?" he asked.

"Father, I know this is a bit unusual," Alex said, "but we need to be married as soon as possible." He flashed Nicki a grin that dimpled his cheeks. "I intend to have this lady installed in my bed within the hour—and I wouldn't want to soil her honor."

"Alex!"

Alex's grin only deepened. "Well, Father?"

The little priest seemed nonplussed. "There are times, my son, when the rules must be bent just a little. This, it seems, is one of them."

Alex turned to Nicole. "We'll do it in grand style when we get home, but I'm not taking any more chances of losing you."

"Nor I you," she agreed. "I promise I've made my last escape."

25

Alex and Nicole were married by an indulgent priest in a tearful, joyous ceremony quite unlike the uncertain ones performed in the dusty Galveston street outside the church.

Ram gave away the bride and acted as Alex's best man while an elderly Mexican woman, weeping sentimentally beneath her black lace mantilla, stood beside Nicki. After the final vows were spoken and Alex kissed his bride, he slid an arm beneath her knees, lifted her up, and carried her off down the aisle.

"A honeymoon in the Galveston Hotel is not exactly what I had in mind, *chérie*, but for now it will have to do."

"I don't care where we go as long as we're together," Nicki told him, hugging his muscular neck.

"We'll rest here a few days, then we're going home."

"To Belle Chêne?"

"Yes, *ma chère*, Belle Chêne. Where you should have been all along." Alex gave her another resounding kiss. "We'll be back in time for Christmas—and afterward, the sugarhouse ball."

"Christmas at Belle Chêne," she said wistfully. "It must be beautiful."

"Mrs. Leander has been working on the decorations for weeks."

Nicki smiled softly. "I can hardly wait to get there."

Once they were outside the church, Alex set Nicki on her feet. From the corner of his eye, he noticed Ram, whose face looked more somber than the joyous occasion called for.

"What is it, my friend?" Alex asked.

"Friend?" Ram repeated with a sarcastic twist. "If I had truly been your friend, I would not have doubted you. After all these years, I should have known you would do what was right."

"You acted just as I would have wanted you to— you protected the woman I love. That's exactly why I entrusted her to you in the first place."

Looking vastly relieved, Ram broke into a grin. "I hadn't thought of it quite that way, but I suppose you are right." Ram clapped Alex on the back. "Now that my job is finished—and you've someone else to look after you—I'll be leaving."

Alex was not surprised. "Where will you go?"

"There is a ship of the Texas Republic heading to Mexico, looking to arm a group of rebels fighting the Mexican government on the Yucatán. Since the overthrow would help their cause, the Texans are looking for mercenaries. I have never been to Mexico. I mean to sign aboard."

"I know of the expedition," Alex said. "Morgan Trask's brother is among the soldiers who are going. I spoke to him briefly when I arrived."

Nicki's attention swung to Alex. "I believe we met him when we docked."

"He looks much like his older brother. Brendan's a bit impetuous, not nearly so sensible as Morgan, but a good man, I believe."

Nicki turned to Ram, sorry to see him go, but knowing the adventure would make him happy. "We're going to miss you." As the sun broke through the clouds, Nicki rose on tiptoes to kiss his smooth-skinned cheek.

"There will always be a place for you at Belle Chêne," Alex told him, clasping Ram's beefy hand.

Across the way, most of the men and women of the Peters Colony had retreated to their wagons to make final preparations for their journey, but the white-collared preacher who had performed the marriages still remained. He was about to complete the last couple's ceremony when Nicki noticed the man speaking his vows was Simon. The woman beside him was short, dark-haired and buxom, with brown eyes and a sturdy chin that stirred a faint chord of memory. The sixth woman had finally arrived.

And Lorna Mackintosh had chosen Simon Stillwater to be her husband.

With a cry of joy, Nicki grabbed Alex's hand and raced toward her friend. Lorna turned at the sound of running feet, and her eyes went wide in recognition.

"Nicki, lass! Can it really be you?"

"I can't believe it," Nicki said, hugging her tightly. "How did you get here?"

"Man who bought me died last month. While the vultures were fightin' o'er his possessions, I made off. They willna come this far to bring me back."

"Knowing you're free at last is the best wedding present I could have been given." The women hugged again and wiped happy tears from their eyes.

"Seems there's a present ye've given me, as well," Lorna told her, with a warm glance at her new husband.

Simon grinned, obviously pleased with his bride.

"This is my new husband," Nicki said, smiling up at Alex. "Alexandre du Villier, meet my dear friend, Lorna Mackintosh."

Lorna flashed him a winning smile and extended her hand, which Alex warmly accepted.

"I've much to thank you for," he said, recalling now the dark-haired woman who had tried to help Nicki at the prison.

"Dinna be thankin' me. It was yerself who saved her. Ye married a woman ye kin be proud of." She laughed, a hearty, robust sound Nicki had seldom heard in the confines of their dismal cell. "Ye thought ye'd bought yerself a pig in a poke, but look what a treasure ye got instead."

Alex heartily agreed. "Nicole has spoken of you with great affection. She has never forgotten the way you helped her."

"I tried to warn her against that blackguard, Fortier, but I fair believed he was bound to have her. When I saw ye had bought her instead, I knew she'd be all right."

"Fortier has done his last evil deed." Alex turned Nicki's face with his fingers. "A few days after I repaid the note, Valcour died by his own hand."

"Dear God," Nicki whispered, tightening her hold on Alex's arm.

"Good riddance, I say," Lorna put in.

"As much as I should have hated him," Nicki said, "I felt only pity. I believe he wanted to change, but his scars were just too deep."

"You may be right," Alex agreed. "He left a great deal of money to Lisette. I think he may have loved her after all."

Nicki blinked back a sudden mist of tears. "I hope she'll be all right."

"Lisette's young, and still unsure of what she really wants. This will give her some time to find out."

From a few feet away, Simon Stillwater pointedly cleared his throat and all heads swung in his direction. "I don't mean to break up this happy reunion, but the cap'n's gettin' anxious to leave, and I ain't kissed my bride."

Everyone laughed, and Lorna flashed Nicki a grin. "We kinna have that, kin we, husband?" In two determined steps, Lorna reached the lanky farmer, slipped her arms around his neck and pulled his head down for a long, thorough kiss. When she broke away, both of them seemed a little shaken.

"I believe I've made m'self a bargain after all," Lorna told them with a smile of pleasure.

Simon grinned. "I may be a little shy to start with, wife, but I expect you'll find that bargain even better once I git you between the blankets."

Lorna blushed—and so did Simon, who looked as if he couldn't believe he'd said the words. With final farewells and warm wishes, the travelers departed, and Ram headed off toward the docks.

"Well, *wife*," Alex said, mimicking Simon, "why don't I get you between the blankets so you can see what kind of a bargain you made?" His eyes turned dark and drifted to the curve of her breast.

"As I recall," Nicki teased, "I've yet to earn the two thousand dollars you paid for my contract. Maybe now's a good time to start."

Alex chuckled softly. Pulling a document from the inside pocket of his coat, he unfolded it and handed it to Nicole. "Even if you had said no, this would have been yours."

Nicki read the words that had caused her so much grief. With a determined rip, she tore the contract in half and then in half again.

She smiled and pointed to the beautiful aquamarine-and-diamond wedding ring she wore on her third left finger. "This contract is far more binding. Now I belong to you forever."

"You're wrong, *ma chère*. It is I who belong to you. What you didn't know was that I have been yours from the start."

Nicki kissed him then, unmindful of the passersby who watched them with envy, feeling only the warming rays of the sun on her back, and her husband's strong arms around her. She was Nicole St. Claire du Villier. Alexandre's wife and partner. She would love him, give herself more freely than ever before.

Then they would return to Belle Chêne. To the life she was meant for. At last she was going home.

And look for *Savannah Heat,*

the next historical romance from Kat Martin. Join the adventures of Major Morgan Trask as he sails for the Yucatán in search of his brother—only to come up against the indomitable, fiery-tempered vixen Silver Jones. The following is an excerpt from the first chapter of Kat's exciting next book.

Savannah Heat

"Take care, Major," Ferdinand Pinkard warned, turning to leave. "She'll do anything to keep from going back to that island. I'd watch my back if I were you."

"I'll keep that in mind," Morgan Trask replied.

Silver's brown eyes swung to the tall, dark-blond man with the scar on his cheek who stood in the middle of his cabin aboard the *Savannah*. The major's look said Pinkard's warning concerned him not in the least.

Good, she thought. The man who underestimates his opponent is the easiest to defeat.

"You know where to find me," Major Trask finished as Pinkard stepped out into the passageway. "I'll have your blood-money ready and waiting when I get back."

"You do that, Major. Both William and I are more than grateful for your assistance—even if it has been given with some reluctance." With a last glance at Silver, Pinkard walked away.

Morgan turned his attention to Lady Salena Hardwick-Jones. Though she held her head high, there were smudges beneath her eyes that betrayed her fatigue, and her wrists were chafed and raw from the too-tight bindings. His brows drew together as he assessed the red mark across her cheek left by Pinkard's hand. The bastard hadn't the conscience God gave a snake.

He leaned into the passageway. "I'll need a bath brought in and something dry for her to wear," Morgan told Hamilton Riley, one of his men. "Jordy's about her size. Get something from him." Jordan Little was his cabin boy, a youth of just thirteen.

Morgan stepped back inside and closed the door. "We need to talk, Salena."

"My name is Silver."

Even tired and bedraggled, and wet clear to her bones,

there was an air about her. He scoffed at the notion of aristocratic bloodlines, which William held so dear, and yet . . .

"If that's the name you prefer—"

"It's the only name I'll answer to."

Morgan ignored a tiny pinprick of anger. If he just took it slowly, made her understand that her father only had her best interests in mind, the girl would soon settle down and accept the inevitable.

"If you'll promise to behave, I'll cut your bindings."

Silver nodded. Morgan slid a small stag-handled knife from the sheath at his hip and slit the leather thongs that bound her wrists. She glanced toward the door.

"Don't even think about it," he warned.

"I was just hoping the bath would hurry." It was a lie, and they both knew it.

"Your father was a friend of mine," he told her, hoping to ease the moment. "We knew each other in London." But at his words, she only grew more tense. She glanced away for an instant, then her brown eyes fixed on a point on the wall above his head.

"What are you planning to do with me?"

"I'm going to take you home."

You're going to try, Silver thought. "I don't suppose there's anything I can say to change your mind."

"I owe your father. Seeing his daughter returned to him safely is the least I can do."

A shiver raced up Silver's spine.

"You're cold." Morgan stepped toward her, but Silver instinctively stepped away. "I was only going to get you a blanket."

"The bath will warm me enough." She turned as a light knock sounded at the door. When Trask pulled it open, two young seamen walked in, one with a heavy copper tub, the other carrying dry clothes tucked beneath his arm and two steaming tin pails.

"I'll be just outside if you need anything," Trask told her when the men had left, then he stepped out into the passageway.

"Thank you, Major." It was all she could do not to laugh.

The man underestimated her sorely. She would be bathed, dressed, and away before he knew what had hit him.

And hit him she would. One solid blow to the top of his handsome blond head, and he would be out for the night.

In the meantime, determined to take advantage of the tub and clean garments, she bathed quickly and dressed in the cabin boy's clothes. A search of the room turned up a pistol, which she shoved into the waistband of her breeches, and a heavy wooden belaying pin that would make the perfect weapon. Securing her pale-blond hair at the nape of her neck with the leather thong the major had cut from her wrists, Silver dragged a chair behind the door, then pulled it open.

"Excuse me, Major," she said sweetly, "could I see you for a moment?"

Trask stood up, his tall frame nearly touching the low ceiling in the elegantly furnished salon. He was definitely a handsome man, she thought, in a tough, no-nonsense sort of way. He had the greenest eyes she had ever seen, and his skin, dark from the sun, looked smooth except for the jagged scar that marked his cheek.

She wondered fleetingly what kind of man he was, then, remembering his friendship with her father, figured she already knew.

Silver picked up the heavy wooden belaying pin, climbed up on the chair, and waited. When the major walked in, she swung her heavy blow.

"Damn," Silver swore as Trask turned to avoid it and the weapon glanced off his head and onto his shoulder, sending him crashing to the floor. She wished the blow had been more effective, but she couldn't bear to hit him again. Instead, she raced past where he sat groaning, trying to recover, and dashed into the empty salon.

Heart hammering hard against her ribs, Silver checked to be sure no one had seen them, then climbed the ladder to the deck. Running to the rail, she climbed over and jumped down onto the dock.

Duck soup, she thought with a smile of satisfaction and a last glance over her shoulder. Silver sucked in a breath at the sight of Morgan Trask racing toward her, his face a dark mask of rage.

Damn her conscience! It was always getting her in trouble. She should have made sure she knocked him out cold.

Silver ran faster, dodging sailors who strolled the dock, flea-bitten mutts who sniffed through rotting garbage, and a doxy or two who busily plied their wares. When she accidentally bowled into one, the whore cursed her soundly, but Silver just kept running. She had to find someplace to hide, some dark alley where the major couldn't find her.

Rounding a corner, Silver fought the stitch in her side, the pounding of her heart, and every burning breath she had to take. Her legs were beginning to ache with the powerful effort and still she drove on, knowing she dared not slow.

And she didn't. Not until an arm snaked out of nowhere, circled her waist, and slammed her up against a rough brick wall.

Morgan Trask towered above her, his hard body pinning her, his green eyes glinting with rage. Silver struggled against the corded muscles of his chest, tried to duck beneath his arm, tried to pull her pistol, fought to kick and bite him—all to no avail.

"Enjoy your bath, milady?" his deep voice mocked, but there wasn't a trace of amusement in the unforgiving lines of his face.

Silver lifted her chin. "I found it quite delightful."

"Good," he said, jerking the pistol from her waist and stuffing it into the back of his breeches, "because you're just about to have another." With one quick movement, he scooped her into his arms, carried her the few feet to the edge of the dock, and dumped her in.

"Damn you!" Silver broke the surface sputtering, cursing, and fighting the hair that had come loose from its bonds and threatened to drown her. "Damn you to hell!"

Morgan watched with satisfaction as she came up twice more, thrashing loudly and fighting to catch her breath. He would let her get good and tired, then throw her a line. He'd been a fool not to heed Pinkard's warning. But she'd looked

so damned pitiful—and far too exhausted to cause him a[ny]
trouble.

Now he had a pounding head and a bruise on his should[er]
to remind him not to make the same mistake again.

Morgan glanced at the water. Only a few tiny bubb[les]
arose where Silver had gone under the last time. She shou[ld]
have come up by now, he realized, cursing himself again.

Bloody hell! Calling her every vile name he could think [of]
Morgan pulled off his boots, shed his heavy blue unifor[m]
jacket and the pistol she had stolen, and dove into the wat[er.]
When he found no trace of her, he began to worry in earne[st.]
Just his luck, the wench couldn't stay afloat long enough [to]
learn her lesson. Then a niggling suspicion crept into h[is]
mind. Morgan broke the surface just in time to see Silv[er]
grinning in his direction and climbing up on the pier som[e]
distance away.

Bloody hell! Hauling himself up a rickety wooden ladd[er]
he raced after her, catching up to her a block away, barreli[ng]
into her, and knocking them both to the ground.

"Lady, you are really pushing your luck," he said throu[gh]
clenched teeth. He pressed her facedown against the rou[gh]
wooden boards of the dock, making her gasp for breath, b[ut]
Morgan didn't care. He dragged her to her feet and forc[ed]
one of her arms behind her, brushing his palm across a ta[ut,]
wet nipple in the process. Her slender derriere pressed s[e-]
ductively against his lower body. Morgan felt a tightening [in]
his loins and cursed the bitter fortune that had placed her [in]
his care.

"You're going back to the ship one way or another," [he]
said, determined not to spend the next few weeks putting [up]
with the hateful little wench. She'd learn to do as she w[as]
told or damn well regret it. "You might as well resign you[r-]
self."

He smiled grimly. Whatever man she had run after owe[d]
him a debt of gratitude. The poor son of a bitch would nev[er]
know how close he had come to a lifetime of hell with Silv[er]
Jones.